## PRAISE FOR ALISON TAYLOR

# *SIMEON'S BRIDE*

"Watch out, P. D. James and Ruth Rendell. Alison G. Taylor throws down a gauntlet with the brilliantly executed *Simeon's Bride*."
—*The Evening Telegraph* (London)

"Impressive . . . a disturbingly good debut."
—*The Times* (London)

"Hers is a new and distinctive voice, and that is all too rare in crime fiction."
—*Ham & High*

"This book is destined to be a classic of the genre—magnificent."
—Icarus, *Mensa Journal*

*By the same author*

Simeon's Bride

# IN GUILTY

# ·NIGHT·

## Alison G. Taylor

**BANTAM BOOKS**
New York   Toronto   London   Sydney   Auckland

This edition contains the complete text
of the original hardcover edition.
NOT ONE WORD HAS BEEN OMITTED.

IN GUILTY NIGHT
A Bantam Book/Published by arrangement with Robert Hale Ltd.

PUBLISHING HISTORY
Robert Hale hardcover edition published 1996
Bantam Crime Line paperback edition/June 1998

CRIME LINE and the portrayal of a boxed "cl" are trademarks of Bantam
Books, a division of Bantam Doubleday Dell Publishing Group, Inc.

ISBN-0-553-57582-1
*Published simultaneously in the United States and Canada*

Bantam Books are published by Bantam Books, a division of Bantam Doubleday Dell Publishing Group, Inc. Its trademark, consisting of the words
"Bantam Books" and the portrayal of a rooster, is Registered in U.S. Patent
and Trademark Office and in other countries. Marca Registrada. Bantam
Books, 1540 Broadway, New York, New York 10036.

PRINTED IN THE UNITED STATES OF AMERICA

WCD   10   9   8   7   6   5   4   3   2

*Er cof*
Gladys Edwards
(1906–1974)

The author wishes to acknowledge the award of a Disabled
Writers Bursary from the Arts Council for Wales

Acknowledgement is due to Aaron Taylor, without whose
technical support and expertise this novel
would not be possible

"I am not wicked—fiery blood
is all my malice, and my crime is youth.
Wicked I am not, truly I am not wicked;
though wild upsurgings oft may plead against my heart,
my heart is good."

*Johann Christoph Friedrich von Schiller (1759–1805)*
*[Don Carlos, Act II, Scene 2]*

# •Chapter•
# 1

Impatience tugging at the corners of his mouth, Jack Tuttle frowned at the figure in the wheelchair. A red honeycombed blanket, stamped on one hem with the logo of the hospital trust, slipped off the knees of the man in the chair, and to the floor, exposing torn britches and scuffed boots.

"I could do with a cigarette," McKenna said.

"You can't have one, sir. The hospital's all non-smoking." Jack retrieved the blanket, looking again at McKenna's haggard features. Impatience surged, bettering tact and respect for rank. "You really should have more sense! Especially at your age!"

"Sense about what?" McKenna asked. "Smoking?"

Jack sighed. "And careering round on horses." Elbows on knees, the plastic-covered chair squeaking under his weight, he leaned forwards. "What on earth possessed you?"

"One would think I'd done something completely outrageous," McKenna said testily. "I was on a horse. I fell off. Is that a problem for you?"

"It's extra work while you're laid up."

McKenna swore under his breath.

"Hurts, does it?" Jack asked.

"What d'you bloody think it does?"

"I don't know. I've never dislocated my shoulder."

McKenna shuddered, the sickening thud as he hit the

ground and the crunch of rending sinew still awesomely loud in his head.

"You're lucky it's not worse," Jack said. "You could've broken your neck."

McKenna smiled weakly. "Be a pal and wheel me outside for a smoke. It'll be ages before they strap me up."

"No, I won't. You've got to have an anaesthetic."

"Power's already gone to your head, hasn't it?" McKenna snarled. The fingers of his good arm eased a crumpled pack of cigarettes from his pocket. Jack snatched it away, and put it in his own.


Beyond the window of Jack's office, frosty November night shrouded the city. A few cars and a lone bus droned down the road, exhaust fumes silting the air.

"How long will Mr. McKenna be off, sir?" Dewi Prys asked.

"Not long, according to him," Jack replied.

"He can't drive, can he? Has he got his arm in a sling?"

"No he can't, and yes he has."

"Did you take him home?"

"Yes."

"Can he manage on his own? Shouldn't we see if he wants anything?"

"Oh, for God's sake!" Jack seethed. "You do nothing but ask bloody questions!"

"Occupational conditioning, sir. Shall I look in on him anyway?"

"Mrs. McKenna's probably still there."

"That's nice for everybody."

"That's no way to speak about your chief inspector."

"I wasn't talking about Mr. McKenna."

"And it's no way to talk about a senior officer's wife!"

"Ex-wife, near enough."

"I haven't heard about any divorce."

"They've been apart over six months, and I can't see them

getting together again, for all Mrs. McKenna acting like Florence Nightingale when it suits."

"Gossip like this is spiteful and unnecessary!"

"It's nothing to the gossip round Port Dinorwic where she's got that posh flat on the marina."

"I don't think I want to know," Jack said wearily. "There was enough backlash when they split up."

"All North Wales'll know soon enough, never mind them in Port Dinorwic and us in Bangor," Dewi said. "It's bad for Mr. McKenna if she's flaunting herself, and she's spending money faster than water comes over Aber Falls."

"She gets maintenance. She's got a part-time job. And she had half the profit from the sale of the house."

"Mr. McKenna had less than five thousand in his pocket when the mortgage was paid off." Dewi picked up a file from the desk. "She's managed to buy a posh new car, and she's got more clothes than royalty. Mind you, she's got to keep up with the Jones-Jones, hasn't she?" He pulled on his jacket. "But I'll leave it at that, 'cos I daresay you'll hear the rest soon enough."

"And where are you going?"

"To read the Riot Act at Blodwel. They're still not telling us when kids do a runner."

"They found the last bunch of absconders."

"One's still missing."

"Then they can find him, can't they?" Jack snapped. "We're not employed to chase bloody delinquents all over the country! Your tax and my tax pays for cosy places like Blodwel, and those kids go missing in droves almost every week. They should be locked up!"

"Folk say Blodwel's far from cosy," Dewi commented. "And Mr. McKenna says absconders are at risk."

"Not half as much as the rest of us, with thieves and muggers and arsonists on the loose."

"They're not all like that, sir."

"Enough of them are for the few that aren't to make no difference."

• • •

Stifling a yawn, the engine driver applied his brakes, slowing the late express from London for the last but one stop on the long haul to Holyhead. Frost on the rails glittered before the engine's powerful headlights, a billion tiny points of silver swallowed up in the black maw of Talybont tunnel. The wheels screamed as the brakes bit, a gentle shudder ran through the carriages snaking behind the engine, and the driver searched for debris on the line, ever mindful for mischief on this isolated stretch of track. In perfect perspective, the twin rails ran clear and bright to the tunnel mouth, then darkness engulfed the lights of the train. Or perhaps light ate up the dark, the driver thought, imagining himself carried in a moving vault of light, knowing without looking that his shadow travelled alongside on the tunnel wall, and that his reflection gleamed before him and at each side, suspended like his own disembodiment between light and dark. He lost the thought, but the dread lingered, as the engine nosed out of the tunnel, and he glimpsed the sprawled shape beside the track, its frosty hair stiff in the draught of the great engine wheels.

# •Chapter•
# 2

Emma Tuttle yawned. "It's nearly two in the morning."

"I know." Jack pulled on a sweater, watching her reflection in the bedroom mirror. "Believe me, I'd far rather stay home."

"It's your job. Keeps us fed and housed, if nothing else."

"Denise wasn't so understanding," Jack commented, turning from the mirror.

Emma smiled. "Isn't Dewi Prys a gossipy old woman? He probably gets a lot of tittle-tattle from his mother."

"Is it just gossip and tittle-tattle?"

Emma yawned again, and burrowed under the quilt. "I don't know. I haven't seen Denise for weeks."

"He must've been brought down the embankment from the track over the tunnel," Eifion Roberts said. "Your crime scene's not up to much, is it? All you'll find in that undergrowth is a ton of litter."

Sooty fungoid smells fouled Jack's throat as he and the pathologist huddled against blackened brickwork tarnished with long cataracts of greenish salts and webbed with soot. "Can we move the body?" he asked. Police and forensic officers moved slowly down the tunnel, their shadows huge in the floodlights. Water dripped relentlessly in the darkness beyond the lights, the brittle rail shuddered under his feet, whining as someone out of sight tripped, and sent a great clanging noise crashing from wall to roof and back again along the length of the vault. "You sure he wasn't killed here?"

"He wasn't hit by a train," Dr. Roberts said. "And I don't imagine he was strolling through the tunnel and happened to keel over from natural causes, dressed as he was in his birthday suit. Or his deathday suit, as the case may be."

"Don't be flippant." Jack watched other lights dancing through the thickets and trees along the embankment and sparkling on the rails which ran towards the other tunnel, where the signal light hung like a dark sun, dripping bloody brilliance on frost-white ground. The moving lights disturbed the trees and tangled in their branches, the rails held the two tunnel mouths in tensile balance, and he fancied himself suspended in a mathematical environment of light and dark, perspective and absolute. He flinched as an owl swooped over the treetops, its wings beating the air.

"Why isn't your boss here?" Eifion Roberts asked. "Tucked up in bed with his cat, is he? Better company than his wife, I daresay."

"Can't you all shut up about Denise McKenna?" Jack rounded on the pathologist. "Dewi Prys at work, Emma at home, you here. I'm sick of the bloody woman! I have to work with her husband!"

"Really? What's the latest, then?"

"I don't know!" Jack snarled. "I don't care! And you should be doing your job instead of gossiping about a woman not worth the time of day!"

"This is one of those times when I hate the bloody job." Eifion Roberts surveyed the small shape zipped inside a black mortuary bag. "He's no older than your lasses." Chewing his bottom lip, he added, "Might he be the lad still missing from Blodwel? It's no further than a mile as the crow flies, is it?"

"He doesn't look like one of theirs," Jack said. "In my experience, thugs look like thugs."

·   ·   ·

Icy mist off the distant mountains slithered against the windows of Jack's office, breathing on the glass and turning day into white night.

"He's someone's child, Dewi. Or was," he said. "Did Blodwel staff give you a photo of their absconder?"

"No, sir, and they wouldn't fill out a missing persons form either. They'd rather we minded our own business, them being social workers who know about children, and us being ignorant hostile coppers."

"I'd better see what they've got to say now."

"Will Mr. McKenna be coming in?"

"I don't know. I haven't asked him." Jack stood up, leaden with fatigue. "And he's signed off sick for at least a week."

"I'm sure he'll want to when he knows."

Dragging his coat from the peg, Jack said, "And I'm sure you'll tell him as soon as my back's turned, so you can find out for yourself, can't you?"


Beyond the prefabricated buildings of the industrial estate, the lane meandered to a dead end at the gateway of a tall gabled house built as an orphanage at the turn of the century, and still home to children threatening to befoul the mainstream of society. As he parked his car, Jack thought the orphans favoured with brighter horizons than the delinquents, for behind high stone walls topped with jagged uprights of local slate, what was once a fine formal garden and shrubbery was now on one side of the drive a tangled mass of rotting vegetation and winter-brown grass, and on the other, an expanse of concrete car-park.

Curtain nets hung limp at the windows, and the building seemed filled with the mist that wreathed around its walls and obscured the rising hillside. Dim lights shone here and there inside the dark shell, but not a sound disturbed the morning, even his footfalls muffled as he trod the narrow concrete path towards the glazed front door. He rang the bell, and stamped his feet and slapped his gloved hands together. No one answered his summons. He rang again, then knocked, hammering on the glass until it shook, and a pale face loomed towards him, mouthing grotesquely.

Jack shook his head in bewilderment. A scowl creased the face, and a pale hand reached out, clutching a bunch of keys. Unlocked, the door edged open a fraction.

"What d'you want?" the woman asked.

Feeling like a tinker offering laces and pegs, Jack said, "Who's in charge?"

"I am."

"Then I suggest you let me in. I'm a police officer."

"Are you?" The scowl returned. "Show me your identification." She scrutinized the warrant, the photograph, his face, then opened the door wide enough for him to edge through, before locking it once more.

"Wait here."

She shuffled away down a corridor, leaving him in a hall barely warmer than outside, eddying with stale institutional smells, and a sour odour which made his scalp prickle. The walls were disfigured by finger marks and neglect, and the ornate hearth, boarded in with painted plyboard, was scarred with knife wounds and hot spilt liquid.

She returned with a cardigan around her shoulders. "Mr. Hogg's off duty 'til nine. You'll have to come back."

"You said you were in charge."

"Mr. Hogg's in charge of Blodwel." She fidgeted with the keys.

"What's your name?"

"Dilys Roberts. Why?"

"Have you found that missing boy yet?"

"No. He'll be dossing with some mate. You should do something about it. Mr. Hogg says harbouring a runaway's a criminal offence." She frowned. "Anyway, I've already said you'll have to talk to him."

"And where is he?"

"In his flat."

"And where's his flat?"

"At the back of the building. But you can't disturb him at this time of the morning!" Scowling ferociously, she took him to a shoe-box of an office, its walls pocked with drawing-pin holes, its space cluttered with old metal desks, filing cabinets, an assortment of cast-off chairs. Seated in one of them, Jack wondered when the heating came on. Dilys Roberts sat opposite, her bare legs crossed, kneecaps gleaming white.

"I've been up most of the night," Jack said. "And I don't feel like getting the runaround. What took you so long to answer the door?"

"There's only me here 'til the domestics start. I'm doing a twenty-four hour shift from two yesterday. We all do them, except Mr. Hogg, of course." The zeal of something like martyrdom briefly animated her eyes. "He doesn't do shift work because he's in charge."

"Does he not? Senior police officers work shifts. Why can't your boss?"

"That's quite different. Mr. Hogg's a senior social worker."

"So tell me about the missing boy." He shivered violently. "And find a photo, will you? You must have one somewhere."


"D'you know him?" Jack asked.

Dewi looked at the photograph. "Doesn't look familiar, sir. You wouldn't forget that face, would you?"

"You claim to know most of the villains this side of the English border."

"Doesn't look much like a villain, does he? Why was he in Blodwel?"

"Something about 'avoidably impaired development,' according to that Dilys Roberts. Whatever that might mean."

"I know her." Dewi grinned. "Not a fire you'd fancy poking, is she?"

"Wipe that smirk off your face! You're as crass as that butcher Roberts sometimes. And ring that damned children's home and say we want someone at the mortuary." He glanced at the wall clock, rubbing eyes already gritty with tiredness. "Our Mr. Hogg should be out of his snug little bed by now. He'll do."

"These kids never learn, do they? Won't listen to anybody, do their own thing and damn the consequences! They're an ungodly lot! Rotten to the core with original sin, if you want a personal opinion I wouldn't dare voice in the current climate, except to someone like yourself. Your job's bad enough, but thankless isn't the word for ours. But who cares? We can't afford to train staff, we can't even afford to employ what we need, and in any case, most of them don't know the meaning of words like "commitment" and "vocation." All they worry about is time off and holidays and pay rises."

Jack stopped at the pedestrian crossing by the hospital carpark. "Mr. Hogg, have you quite finished?"

"You wanted to know," Hogg countered.

"I'm only interested in how Arwel Thomas managed to disappear from Blodwel, and end up dead on the railway line."

"I've told you. They think absconding's a game."

"Arwel won't be playing again, will he? You're sure it's him?"

"Such a pretty-looking boy, wasn't he? You wouldn't believe there was an ounce of badness in him. Now look where it's got him."

"Where what's got him?" Jack asked, unlocking his car.

Easing into the front passenger seat, Hogg clipped on the seat belt, and a trace of Blodwel's sour smell drifted under Jack's nose. "Stupidity's the best word for it. He spent no more than seventeen days in school in the year before he was admitted to care."

"What was he doing with his time?"

Hogg shrugged. "Same thing they all do."

Jack accelerated down the hill towards the main road.

"Perhaps you'd make sure the staff are available for questioning later. I intend to question the children, too."

"Oh, I think your senior officers will need to clarify areas of responsibility with the director of social services first. That boy went missing almost a week ago, and you heard what the pathologist said as well as I did."

"Dewi says the locals reckon Hogg's a pompous, loud-mouthed arsehole," McKenna said, "And a bully."

"You're off sick," Jack said. "Why don't you go home?"

"Why don't you? You're exhausted." Lighting a cigarette, McKenna asked, "When's Eifion doing the post-mortem?"

"He was about to start when I turned up with Hogg." Jack yawned, and yawned again, jaw cracking. "Hogg reckons Arwel was a bad lot, for all he was so 'pretty-looking.'"

" 'Pretty' isn't an adjective usually applied to teenage boys, is it?"

"Depends on how you see them, I suppose." He yawned again. "Hogg sees teenage boys as a general pain in the neck. Girls too, I imagine."

"Where's Jack Tuttle?" Eifion Roberts asked.

"At Blodwel," Dewi said. "Mr. McKenna's gone to see Arwel's parents. Janet Evans is driving him."

"I'm surprised he's not laid up. Dislocating your shoulder's no pleasant thing. Must be tougher than he looks, eh? Still, he's more use to himself at work instead of brooding and fretting about the house." He fell silent, then said, "The autopsy'll take longer than I expected."

"Why's that?"

Roberts sighed. "Anal injury, Dewi. Old healed lesions, and every indication the lad was savagely raped not long before he died, so I have to proceed on the assumption HIV may be present, and that's quite a rigmarole."

•   •   •

"The director of social services issued instructions, Inspector," Ronald Hogg announced. "I'm in no position to disobey him." His office was well furnished and stiflingly hot.

"And where else do we start if we can't interview staff and children?" Jack demanded.

"The boy was a runaway." Hogg tapped a thin sheaf of papers on his desk. "I've already had to disrupt important routines and treatment plans on his account, and been left with a bunch of kids more het up and disturbed than ever. Whatever you need to know is written down here, although nobody knows anything to speak of."

"Did Arwel have any money?"

"Pocket money's locked up in the other office."

"What was he wearing?"

"I don't know."

"Who does?"

"Nobody. The children had other things on their mind, and Dilys Roberts was in bed."

"Why does she do so many sleeping-in duties?"

"I've already told you we're chronically short-staffed."

"Surely you keep clothing lists?" Jack persisted. "You must be able to tell what's missing from Arwel's things."

"You can't know from one day to the next what belongs to anybody." Hogg smiled disarmingly. "And you know exactly what I mean because you've got teenagers of your own."

"Did your boss tell you to be obstructive?"

Hogg sighed. "I've got to shield everyone from thoughtless interference, and we often encounter prejudice, so you'll have to forgive me if I seem defensive. I'm only human, after all. Too many police officers think locking up youngsters is the answer to everything." He smiled again. "If only they realized social workers just shovel shit another way!" Pushing the sheaf of reports across the desk, he added, "Don't think I'm being impertinent, but isn't it more important to find out where the boy spent the last week? He wasn't with the others. Talk to that man they call Dai Skunk. I'm sure you're acquainted with him."

• • •

Crackling over the car radio, Dewi's voice eddied like the mist from Menai Strait rolling over the cars and trucks and the roadworks traffic signal, and on towards the mountainous hinterland. The car heater blasted fuggy air in McKenna's face, a mix of exhaust fumes and that foul stench coming off the sea at low tide.

Janet switched off the radio. "The phone won't work either, sir, there's too much static." She shivered. "My father'd call mist like this a cloud of human wickedness. He's surprised God doesn't use the cover to destroy all the points of reference on the human landscape, and start again." The traffic light changed to amber, and she put the car in gear.

"Eifion Roberts says God wouldn't have a choice about starting again if He knew what sort of Christians inhabit North Wales."

"My father actually believes Dr. Roberts is a heretic. His name's forbidden at the manse." She followed the long tailback of traffic, accelerating in the wake of a sleek silver car. "I expect his work made him like that, don't you?"

An extension of its eastwards counterpart, this new road between Bangor and Caernarfon obliterated all sense of place, the landmarks of centuries obscured behind mounds of clay and man-made bulwarks. Dubbed by politicians as the Road of Opportunity, it was better named the Road to Hell, McKenna thought, opportune only for criminals bringing further ills to a poor society already beset.

"HQ say to expect the ram-raiders in Caernarfon and further west now the road's finished," Janet commented. "Crime's our only growth industry, isn't it? Still, I suppose that's not surprising in a place people call the fag end of Creation."

Like the new road, the council estate beyond Caernarfon was stripped of individuality and character, a model of cultural conformity reduced to the lowest common denominator. Housed in a terraced block at the centre of the estate, the

Thomas family lacked even a glimpse of the Snowdon range to the south or the sea to the north, their horizons limited by the narrow-mindedness of others. Waiting for Janet to lock his car and set the alarm, McKenna was slapped in the face by freezing air, and around the ankles by litter cavorting on a rising breeze. Light-headed, a little hungover from too many analgesics, he pushed open the decrepit wooden gate, and led the way up a scabrous concrete path. As she knocked on the door, he massaged the hand drooping from its sling, the fingers bluey tipped.

"You should wear gloves, sir," his companion offered. "It's cold enough to give you frostbite." She smiled. "What Inspector Tuttle would call a 'worst case scenario'." She let the smile die as the front door opened.

"Yes?" the woman asked, looking from McKenna to the girl. "I'm not buying, so if you're selling, you can sod off! And we don't owe nothing to nobody except the council and Manweb, and they can sod off as well."

"Mrs. Thomas?" the girl asked.

"Who wants to know?"

"We're police officers," Mckenna said. "My name is McKenna, and this is Detective Constable Janet Evans."

Thin of face, scrawny of body, she stood on the doorstep and chewed the inside of her mouth, looking somewhere beyond McKenna's shoulder, while he looked in vain for a shadow of the beauty which had emblazoned the face of her son. "He's not here," she said. "He's not been here either. I told that copper come the other day. If he's legged it from that Blodwel it's their fault. Nothing to do with me or his father. He's gone on the run before. They should keep him under control. He's worse now than when he went there."

"Might we come in?" Janet asked. "We need to talk to you, and it's bitter cold out here."

"I suppose so." She turned to walk inside. "Shut the door behind you."

She led them to the back parlour, a cramped and shabby room overlooking a cramped and shabby patch of garden. As poorly proportioned as her dwelling, she sat in an armchair covered in dull brown vinyl, and chewed the inside of her mouth again. "What d'you want?"

"Is your husband at home?" McKenna asked, easing himself into another armchair. Janet sat at the table, crimping the cloth between her fingers.

"No, he's not."

"At work?" Janet asked.

"Gone to town."

"Why's that?"

"Gone to sign on, hasn't he? What's it to you anyway?"

"When d'you expect him back?" McKenna asked.

She shrugged. "When he comes."

McKenna wondered how old she was, this care-ridden creature. "Mrs. Thomas," he said, "is there anyone who could come in for a while?"

"Why?"


Jack began to munch his third sandwich. "I'm starving."

"You'll put on weight," McKenna observed.

"Probably. I'm not blessed with a supercharged metabolism like you." He wiped his fingers on a napkin. "You can light up now I've finished eating." Gesturing to the Blodwel reports, he added, "They're not worth the paper they're written on, and Hogg won't let anyone talk to us. How did you fare with Mrs. Thomas?"

"Little better." McKenna fidgeted with an unlit cigarette. "She didn't cry, or do anything very much except chew her mouth and say Arwel would never be told."

Jack sighed. "They're heaping all the blame on the lad. He's reaped whatever he sowed."

"It's a very bitter harvest for a fourteen year old. Any news from Eifion?"

"He won't've finished." Jack yawned. "Did Mrs. Thomas have any idea why Arwel ran away, or where he went?"

"Nothing, or so she said." McKenna lit the cigarette.

"Hogg said kids often abscond when they're due in court, only Arwel wasn't, so there wasn't much point saying it. There's nothing on Hogg in the computer. Pity, really."

"That would be too easy," McKenna said. "Brace yourself for a trawl of the sex offenders and deviants feeding on the underbelly of our little society. We'd better take Hogg's advice and start with David Fellows, even though he rigorously confines his activities to those over the age of consent as far as I know. I expect you'll persuade him to part with the names of those who don't share his refined sensibilities."

"Has he harboured kids on the run before?"

"If he has, no one told us," McKenna said. "I'm going to see Mrs. Thomas again. We left her with a neighbor 'til her husband came home."

"Arwel's social worker from Area Office should be able to tell us more about his admission to care. Dodging school doesn't seem much of a reason, and he's got no criminal record."

"Make an appointment for this afternoon." McKenna stood up, embattled by the pain which consorted with every movement. "Which school did he go to?"

"He didn't. Blodwel's got a schoolroom and one full-time teacher. The local schools don't want kids from care on their patch," Jack said. "Folk probably don't think they're worth educating. Written off right from the start."


The last dying leaves, bronzy-green and edged with black, withered on the branches of the ash tree outside McKenna's office window, and shivered in a wind rising off the Strait. Ragged ends of mist lingered between the tall narrow buildings behind High Street, drifting around their footings.

As he pulled his arm from its sling and stretched carefully, Eifion Roberts walked in without knocking and sat down.

"You're a very depressing sort of person to have around."

"Why's that?" McKenna asked.

"Never functioning on all cylinders, dying by visible degrees, *ergo* a very uncomfortable reminder of my own mortality. Hurts, does it?"

"The rest of me's in agony. This is numb."

"I daresay it'll be hurting soon for you."

"And is that good or bad?"

"Depends."

"I won't ask on what, because I've an appointment with Arwel's social worker at half two." McKenna lit a cigarette. "Finished the post-mortem?"

Dr. Roberts nodded. "Done the cutting up, and the stitching up, and sent samples off for analysis, and I've never seen such a mess on a boy that age. What's his background?"

"Taken into care for non-school attendance. No convictions. The commonplace story of an aimless juvenile at the edge of delinquency."

"Any rumors about Grandad or Uncle or Mam's boyfriend?"

"Not a whisper. His social worker might know."

"You're an optimist, aren't you? Social Services'll deliver a load of garbage about professional ethics, and hope the problems'll resolve themselves without intervention. Some hope, especially if the HIV tests come positive. That'll put the fear of God into whoever's been buggering the lad."

"They'd have to know," McKenna pointed out. "We're not advertising the fact. Is there any risk to people who handled the body?"

"The railwaymen wore gauntlets, else they'd've had ice burns off the track, and the rest of us are too canny." The pathologist fell silent, age and disillusion shadowy on his face.

"You don't look too good yourself," McKenna said.

"When I have to cut up a child, I feel like the child under my own knife." He rubbed his forehead with the back of his hand. "I contacted the GP practice which looks after Blodwel children. Arwel had a routine medical on admission, and they saw him once after, when he had summer 'flu. Glandular-fever tests were negative, and he wasn't tested for anything more sinister."

"And what killed him?"

"A huge depressed fracture on the left side of the skull and a broken neck. He fell, or was thrown, very hard against some smooth solid object. There's no external wound, and no visible debris."

McKenna fidgeted with his lighter. "Can't you be more precise about the time of death? Some time between Friday night and Sunday morning isn't really much use."

"It's been so cold, and I don't know how long he'd been exposed naked, so it's the best I can do for now," Dr. Roberts said. "There's substantial subcutaneous bruising, variously healed, around the lower torso and thighs, so he's probably taken more than his share of beatings. You should be taking Blodwel apart, whereas I hear you can't get your foot through the door. Can't your boss lean on the director of social services? There must be some old favour due in between blood brothers of the Taffia, unless it's already being repaid."


Arwel's social worker was perfectly adjusted to her role, McKenna thought, irritated by the dribble of platitude and evasion. "One of the children in your care is dead," he snapped.

"He wasn't in my care, and he was on the run, anyway. Runaways come to grief, but they won't be told."

"Having a client murdered doesn't sound like a new experience for you," Janet said. "Are many of them persistently beaten up, as well? And persistently sodomized?"

"Blodwel's placements are Mr. Hogg's responsibility, and he reports to the director. I'm not involved with those children on a daily basis."

"So when did you last see Arwel?" McKenna intervened.

"Six weeks ago. Seven, perhaps."

"Why not check your records?" Janet suggested. "Where did you see him?"

"I had a word with him when I took another child to Blodwel."

"Mrs. Thomas tells us Arwel wasn't allowed home leave," McKenna said. "Why was that?"

"I can't discuss casework decisions with you."

"Can't you discuss them with the parents, either?" Janet asked. "How was he when you saw him?"

"The same as usual."

"And how was that?" McKenna asked.

"Uncommunicative at first, then quite insolent when he eventually condescended to open his mouth. Mr. Hogg said he was involved in a lot of trouble with the others, so that's probably where he got the bruises you're talking about."

"And where'd'you think he might've got the anal injuries?" Janet asked.

"He was obviously up to something nobody knew about." Staring at Janet, she added testily, "We can't help people who don't want help, and he rejected all the treatment plans we drew up."

"You didn't like him, did you?" McKenna asked.

"Personal feelings aren't an issue. We give every client the best possible service."

"Then I'd hate to see your worst," Janet said.

"I haven't noticed the police doing much good with juveniles! We've had some notable success with Blodwel placements, probably because Mr. Hogg's seen as an ideal father-figure. His wife puts many of the children's own mothers to shame."

"What good is that for the parent-child relationship?" Janet asked.

"The children learn to overcome their parents' failings."

"Which children on your books would know Arwel?" McKenna asked.

"I can't tell you. Our client files are confidential, children's included. You wouldn't open your records to us, would you?"

• • •

Janet hunched over the wheel of McKenna's car. "I toyed with the idea of social work for a while. Did you ever hear such claptrap?"

"Social-work speak." McKenna lit a cigarette. "And she's in thrall to Mr. Hogg, like the rest of the world."

"I do wish you wouldn't smoke so much, sir."

"Not you as well!"

"I'm trying to stop, but it's awfully hard, and the fag-fascists give you the evil eye if you dare smoke in the canteen."

"You can have one if you want," McKenna said, "though it's a bit like offering the needle to a heroin addict."

"You'll get done for sexual harassment if the senior lady officers with the short sharp haircuts and jolly voices hear about you." She ran her fingers through her own luxuriant dark hair. "I'd love a cigarette, and I don't think Mr. Hogg holds people in thrall. He's just persuaded everyone he's Mr. Clever Dick with the answer to all their problems, so there's a huge vested interest in keeping him sweet." Taking the cigarette, she added, "Arwel's social worker's such a stereotype, isn't she? She read the label round the lad's neck, and that was the end of it. Sociology calls it the process of dehumanization: first the label, then abuse, then extermination. I suppose it's one way to rid the world of its problems."


"Why are you sulking, Prys?" Jack demanded.

"I'm not sulking."

"Are you not?" Jack regarded the sullen face. "What are you doing, then? Dealing with a severe case of constipation?"

"It's not fair!" Dewi burst out. "Why couldn't I drive Mr. McKenna instead of slogging over the computer all afternoon? And I've got to sit in while you talk to that stinky git in the interview room."

"Had your nose pushed out of joint by our little lady detective, have you? Afraid of being elbowed out of the chief inspector's favour?" Jack grinned. "For all people reckon you're quite the most handsome young copper Bangor's ever been lucky enough to have patrolling its mean streets, I'm sure WDC Evans is much more congenial company, because she has attributes, Dewi Prys, you'll never have and wouldn't want. And apart from that, some jobs need a woman officer, as you well know."

"That's very snide, Mr. Tuttle. You're implying Mr. McKenna might be fancying her. Janet Evans is younger than me."

"She's pretty enough, she's over twenty-one, and she's single. Could do him a world of good."

Christened David Fellows, reared in a frilly suburban villa along the coast, and well on the road to perdition before he was out of school, the man known in his middle years as Dai Skunk sat tidily on an upright chair in the interview room, sipping from a mug of tea.

"I had a bath this morning," he announced to Jack and Dewi. "So you can both stop breathing through your mouths."

Dewi snickered, then winced as Jack's heavy shoe caught his ankle bone.

"Do you know why you're here?" Jack asked.

Fellows shrugged. "Some little queen squealing to a big butch copper, I suppose. Gives you an excuse to persecute me. Not that you need one, even though I never do anything illegal. Our kindly government changed the law quite a long time ago."

"And a sorry day that was," Jack observed, dreading the onslaught of the sickly odour. Once told by McKenna that a rare and obscure medical condition might be its cause, he labelled rampant homosexuality neither obscure nor a medical condition, but simply a vile perversion. Fellows, short and painfully thin, swallowed the last of his tea, and wiped his lips on a grubby handkerchief.

"Do I need a solicitor?"

"You're not under caution. You can have a brief if you want."

"I'll save myself some money, then. Aren't I too trusting?"

"We're interested in an exchange of information," Jack said. "We have some information about you. You can tell us whether it's true or not."

"Mr. McKenna said we had to lean on people," Dewi pointed out.

"Did he?" Fellows leaned forward, sending his smell ahead like an advance scout. "That should be exciting!"

"Pack it in!" Jack warned.

"The bigger the aversion, the harder you're leaning on the closet door." Fellows smiled as rage turned Jack's face thunderous. "Too bad you're not my type, isn't it? I prefer them a bit younger, like your pretty friend. Look at those lovely blue eyes and that gorgeous black hair!"

"Just how young d'you like your playmates?" Jack asked quietly.

The smile died in Fellows' red-rimmed eyes, and he began to rub the side of his neck. "You snidey git! You've got me here because of that boy you found on the railway line."

"He was on the run from Blodwel, and we're told you might've let him rest his weary head at your place."

"I don't know any kids from there." Fellows rubbed his skin viciously. "Who told you I do?"

Jack took Arwel's photograph from the file, and placed it on the table and, as Fellows looked, his restless hand stayed itself. "Oh, God! Wasn't he beautiful?" His hand came to rest beside the picture, fingers smearing blood on the table. "What a bloody terrible waste!"

"You've made your neck bleed," Dewi said, watching a crimson globule well from the dark lesion below Fellows's ear. "What's wrong with you?"

The other man looked at his hand, then wiped the blood from his neck with the grubby handkerchief. "Only my badness coming out." He smiled wryly, all flirtatiousness gone. "Don't you know I've got AIDS? My name's been changed to Dai Death." Looking once more on Arwel Thomas, he added, "I wouldn't even breathe on a beautiful boy like him."


Janet sat again at the table in the back parlour of the Thomas home, McKenna beside her on a chair which sagged painfully under his buttocks. Peggy Thomas hunched in her armchair, and the thin pot-bellied man she had wed leaned against the mantel, cutting off heat from the meagre fire. In the other armchair, hands clasped so tight colour bled from the knuckles, was a girl who looked little older than Arwel. Unable to take his eyes from her, McKenna wondered how the parents, lacking even the distinction of true ugliness to mark them from the herd, produced the beautiful boy eviscerated on the autopsy table, and this girl. Perfectly proportioned, slender and fine-boned, hair and skin pale and luminous, her loveliness was that rarity demanding awe. She looked up suddenly, dark saddened eyes gazing into his, and he imagined her body brittle under the weight of sweating urgent lust. Janet's voice broke into the nightmare.

"We're terribly sorry to bother you again."

Tom Thomas grunted. "What's done is done." He gestured to the figure of his daughter. "She's Carol."

"There's just Carol and Arwel, is there?"

Peggy nodded. "Just these two." She favoured Carol with a look full of emotion, pity, or its spiteful twin, there in abundance.

"When did you last see Arwel?" McKenna said.

Staring at her daughter, Peggy said, "Three months ago. We went to a case conference or something."

"And how often had you seen him before then?"

"Twice since he went to Blodwel." She chewed the inside of her mouth. "Eight months back, just before Easter."

"After the first time," Tom intervened. "Mr. Hogg told us

not to come again 'til he said, because Arwel went off his head when we left."

"He said the kids had to settle in, and family visits upset things," Peggy added.

"Didn't you mind?" Janet asked. "Didn't you think you had the right to see your own son?"

She shrugged. "They know what they're doing, don't they? That social worker in town said Mr. Hogg's very clever with kids like Arwel, so it's not for us to go against him, is it?"

"And Arwel had no home leave?" McKenna asked.

"Mr. Hogg said he hadn't earned enough points."

"Enough points?"

"Blodwel's got a points system. When kids behave themselves, they earn points towards home leave and outings."

"Behaviour modification," Janet said.

"Something like that." Tom moved away from the fire, releasing thin tendrils of warmth into the rest of the room. Rubbing his hands down his buttocks, he leaned against the windowledge.

"But didn't you want to see Arwel?" Janet persisted. "Was he happy at Blodwel? Was he miserable? He might've gone up the wall because he was upset and homesick."

Tom rounded on her. "He got what was coming to him!"

"People keep telling us that," McKenna said quietly. "Why, do you think?" He turned to Carol. "Why should Arwel deserve to die?"

She stared at him mutely, violet eyes dark with pain, their colour mirrored in the shadows beneath the sockets.

"He was a bad lot, wasn't he?" Rancour soured the man's voice. "Don't know where he got it from. We've always done our duty by them." He too stared at his daughter. "And she's going the same way. Two rotten apples!"

Carol scrambled to her feet, looked at her father, lounging against the windowledge, then at McKenna, before walking out of the room. He heard the pad of feet on the staircase, then the thud of an upstairs door.

"Little madam!"

"Has Carol been in trouble as well?" Janet asked.

"Depends what you call trouble," Peggy said. "Can't keep her hands off the men." She chewed her mouth. "No better than the tarts down town. She's got the same look in her eyes. Makes me ashamed to be called her mother!"

"Perhaps the men can't keep their hands off her," McKenna said. "They couldn't keep their hands off Arwel, either."

"Little bastard!" Tom spat. "Flaunting himself!" He turned accusingly to his wife. "And she must've known. Little bitch probably put him up to it!"

Janet jumped up. "You don't mind if I look through Arwel's things, do you? You don't need to bother getting up. I'm sure Carol can show me."

"When is it, then?" Peggy asked McKenna as the door shut behind Janet.

"When is what, Mrs. Thomas?"

"The funeral. Want to get it over and done with, don't we?"


"Miserable, bloody bitch!" Janet plunged a spoon through the froth on her coffee, as if it were a knife through the cold heart of Peggy Thomas. "Miserable, mean, black-hearted bitch!"

McKenna gazed through the café window, at empty pavements and the new bus station erected over the funeral pyre of a small department store.

"She's too bloody mean even to cry for him!" Janet snatched another cigarette from McKenna's packet. "If Carol goes with men, d'you blame her? Can you blame Arwel? There's no human comfort in that godforsaken hole!" She gulped the coffee, cringing as hot liquid scorched her throat. "And not an ounce of love!"

"Did you talk to Carol?"

"No." Janet drained her cup. "She didn't say a word. Shuffled in front of me like a zombie, showed me Arwel's room, and disappeared. One of the neighbours said Carol works at the hardware shop on High Street, so I thought I'd try to get her on her own."

"She's a High Street star," McKenna said. "Like the thousands of pretty girls standing behind counters day in and day out, inspiring fantasy and romance like the silent film stars. That pert little minx from the supermarket who walked out with Dewi for a while is another one. I expect people dream about them, wonder what they do, who they do it with."

"Carol's definitely a star." Janet smiled. "Ethereal and untouchable."

"Not according to her mother."

"I don't understand that woman. My mother'd be down on me like a ton of bricks if she thought I was putting it about. That miserable bitch just slags off her daughter to the whole world. God knows what goes on when Carol's alone with her."

"More of what we saw today, I imagine." McKenna lit his own cigarette, then placed it carefully in the ashtray while he picked up his cup. Numbness seeped from his arm, chased by the promise of real pain. "How d'you rate Tom Thomas as a child abuser?"

"You can't tell by looking, can you? He didn't seem worried. Surely he would be?"

"So what was he feeling?"

"Nothing very much, because he's a miserable sod, like his wife's a miserable bitch. They'll grieve more about not winning the lottery, because nothing touches them. They're almost sub-human."

"Don't adopt the same judgmental attitudes you condemn in others, Janet. The Thomases and millions like them live in the dark shitty world others make for them." He dragged on the cigarette. "Tom and Peggy Thomas are as human as you. Hitler carried his own brand of political correctness to its logical conclusion, and look what happened to the rest of us for letting him."

•     •     •

Jack yawned massively.

"Don't you think you should go home?" McKenna asked. "In case you fall asleep while you're driving."

"I'll go soon," Jack said.

"What's going on downstairs?"

"We've got a bit of a problem," Jack said evasively.

"We've got a bloody big problem," Dewi said. "Dai Skunk's got AIDS, and he bled all over the interview room."

"Don't exaggerate! He was rubbing a mole on his neck, and it bled a bit. There's a smear on the table."

"Sir, you panicked like hell, and rang Dr. Roberts screaming for help. Then you got hold of that lot who charge us a small fortune for cleaning up when some poor sod spreads his brains all over the place. You've even had the furniture taken away for incineration."

"Did you call HQ?" McKenna asked.

"Of course I did!" Jack snapped. "Who d'you think gave the go-ahead?"

"Sounds as if everything's taken care of," McKenna said.

"And what about us?" Jack demanded.

"Oh, you're safe enough. Dai only breathed on you."

"He fancied Prys."

"He would, wouldn't he?" Dewi said. "He'd already said you're too old for him."

"He's running true to form," McKenna said. "AIDS or not. What about Arwel?"

"Never set eyes on him, he says," Jack said. "And not inclined to grass up anyone in particular, although he did say most of the men in North Wales are at it like jack-rabbits with each other and any bit of fresh meat coming on the market."

"He says we should be chasing the reverends, because all that reformist guilt gives them a taste for the innocence of childhood," Dewi added. "And he said tourists've never come here just for the scenery, because we're famous for our butches and queens."

"Maybe it's something in the water." McKenna massaged

his chest, trying to ease the pain tightening muscle and tendon as it passed through his body, his lungs unable to expand in their rigid case of rib and sternum and clavicle. He drew a deep panicky breath.

"You OK, sir?" Dewi stood up. "I'll get some aspirin, shall I?"

"Dai Skunk scared me half to death," Jack said, as the door closed. He shivered. "He's changed his name to Dai Death."

"He won't be bothering us much longer. You could look into your heart for some compassion."

"He's brought it on himself."

"Like Arwel?" McKenna asked. "We all bring things on each other."

"He's corrupt. He's corrupted others. He may well kill others."

"Someone corrupted him when he was as young as Arwel. He once told me of the pain and blood and terror."

"So why did he keep on doing it?"

"He also told me of the lust and joy, of having a nerve touched at the very heart of his being, as if someone touched his soul. That was the sickness he caught. AIDS is only a secondary infection."


"How come all these social workers, as well as his parents, didn't have a clue what Arwel was doing?" Dewi asked.

"Teenagers have secret lives," Jack said.

"Establishing a separate identity is a normal part of growing up," McKenna added.

"I remember." Dewi smiled. "I'll bet Arwel's mates knew."

"We need to find them. Janet's going to talk to Carol tomorrow," McKenna said. "Dewi can come to Blodwel with me this evening."

"I doubt they'll let you through the door," Jack commented.

"We'll see. Anything else from Eifion Roberts?"

"Not much. He says Arwel was carried rather than dragged to the tunnel, so we're probably looking for two people, because it's quite a haul from the track overhead and down the embankment." Jack perused a sheet of notes. "He's noted unusual muscular development in the thighs, buttocks, lower back, shoulders and belly. He's thinking about that."

"What sort of unusual?"

"Out of proportion." Jack yawned again. "Overdevelopment in comparison with the general musculature."

"Go home, before we have to put you on a hurdle."

"Soon." Jack rummaged again through the notes. "Transport police've questioned all the drivers, conductors and railwaymen working from early morning on, but either they weren't looking, or it was too foggy and dark. The engine driver's neurotic about slowing to a dead crawl in the tunnel since he nearly ran his express into a concrete sleeper some comedian left on the track."

"Newspapers, radio and TV are asking passengers to contact us if they saw anything," Dewi added. "And notices are up in all the stations between Holyhead and London Euston, and in Liverpool and Manchester."

"Is the crime scene search finished?"

"Enough litter to fill the old quarry pit in Bethesda. Forensics wanted to know what they're supposed to be looking for," Jack said. "I said we'd tell them when we knew."

McKenna went home to feed his cat, and to swallow two of the analgesics provided by the hospital, Dewi's aspirins fallen within minutes to the mighty force of pain invading his body. Denise had visited, filling his refrigerator with expensive food, and his house with her presence, and he already regretted giving her a key. Caught at a weakened moment, guard relaxed, he let her encroach once again.

The cat whined and grizzled around his ankles, complaining of loneliness and neglect and weather unfit for adventure.

Her claws had shredded more of the tattered cover on the armchair.

"Why don't you go out, little one?" He stroked her ears and back. "You're getting stir-crazy." She jumped on his lap, burrowing under his good arm, and fell asleep, twitching only once when the telephone rang.

"I hear you plan to breach the Blodwel fortress," Eifion Roberts said. "D'you want some extra artillery to help undermine the foundations?"

"We've fired warning shots across their bows already. Didn't do much good."

"Don't mix metaphors."

"Why don't you go and annoy somebody else?"

"In pain, are you? Well, I did warn you. Did Jack Tuttle say I called? I've been thinking about that unusual muscular development, and searching the anatomical tomes . . ."

"And?"

". . . but it was thinking about your arm gave me the clue. Horses and so forth. I'd wager young Arwel did a deal of horse-riding."

"Funny no one said." McKenna tried to light a cigarette without dropping the telephone. "It's the sort of thing people comment about."

"Do they? I suppose you'd know."

"Is that the extent of your ordnance?"

"You've a nasty tongue, McKenna, even when you're not in pain," Dr. Roberts commented. "I've had a call from the locum who treated Arwel when he was poorly. He complained about the bellyache, about pain when he went to the loo, about this and that and the other, but there was nothing specific except a bit of tenderness in the gut and symptoms of summer 'flu.' "

"So what use is that?"

"This guy's worked with abused kids in a Liverpool hospital, and he thought Arwel showed all the signs. He said it's to do with general responses and these unspecific physical factors, so he contacted Blodwel with his suspicions, and recommended a full paediatric examination."

"Who did he tell?"

"Doris Hogg. And before you go off half-cocked, you weren't told because this kind of thing is a bloody great minefield for the medical profession since the Cleveland fiasco. Arwel was Social Services' responsibility anyway, and the world and his wife assume a child in care is safe as houses. If the state decides the parents aren't good enough then by definition, the state must be better than good."

Blodwel at night, studded with dim lights, resembled a tall ship run aground in the lee of the hill. Admitted by a young woman clad in pale green overalls, Dewi and McKenna, like thieves come under cover of darkness, were shunted to a long narrow room at the side of the building. She disappeared, offering neither information nor a hot drink to take the chill from their bones.

Dewi inched back the net curtain and stared at frost-rimed grass and bright sharp stars in an indigo sky. "You wouldn't credit the fog earlier, would you, sir? Gone like it'd never been." He scratched the glass with his fingernail. "Jack Frost's out with the graffiti, and it's so bloody cold in here we'll be able to see the lies coming out of people's mouths." Letting the curtain fall into place, he wandered around the room, reading newspaper clippings tacked to a large cork wallboard. "Mr. Hogg receiving the gift of a snooker table from a grateful community," he intoned. "Mr. Hogg similarly receiving the gift of a colour telly. Mr. Hogg behind his desk, looking like a smug bastard. Mr. Hogg with a bunch of kids, still looking like a smug bastard. I thought children in care weren't supposed to be identified in the press?" He moved a little further along. "Mr. and Mrs. Hogg standing by a minibus with 'Blodwel' daubed on its side. Mr. Hogg outside the front door in a bloody big chair, looking even more like a smug bastard. D'you think he fancies himself King of Wales, like poor Charlie Pierce who keeps getting shut up in Denbigh? I'm surprised there isn't a picture of Mr. Hogg with the sun shining out of his arse."

"Stop being so bloody negative, and shut up! Someone's coming."

The door opened, and a tiny Yorkshire terrier trotted into the room, shadowed by a stout woman, her body grimly corseted beneath a long pleated skirt and a jumper gaudy with metallic threads, her mouth gaudier still with bright red lipstick. "How can I help you?" She stared at the men, then picked up the dog, fiddling with the red ribbon tied between its ears.

"This is Mrs. Hogg, sir," Dewi said.

McKenna coughed, throat rough with cold and thirst. "I'd like to see Mr. Hogg."

"He's not on duty 'til tomorrow."

"Where is he?"

"Off duty."

"You've already told us that," McKenna said testily. "Perhaps you'd care to tell him we're here?"

"He's not well."

"He was all right this morning," Dewi said.

"He's not now." She sounded wearied. "He's had a terrible shock over that stupid boy getting himself killed."

McKenna sat on one of the hard upright chairs, tired of waiting to be asked, tired of standing out of politeness. "And what's your job here, Mrs. Hogg?"

"Senior care officer."

"Is there a deputy?"

"No."

"Then in Mr. Hogg's absence, you must be in charge."

"I can't talk to you." Her face and body tensed. "I can't tell you anything."

"We'll see, shall we?" McKenna countered. "Why don't you sit down? I've no intention of leaving for quite a while."

•   •   •

Ignoring a muttered comment from the girl who escorted him to the children's sleeping-quarters, Dewi shut the door of the room which had been Arwel's billet. Created by partitioning a much larger room, of which the ornate ceiling cornice still showed on three sides, this room, Dewi thought, was like a cell, but one mocked-up for a film set to let cameras be mounted in the ceiling. Perspectives wrong, the floor area too small for the height, he began to feel as if the walls were closing in.

Arwel's bed, narrow and short, draped with a thin quilt, lay against one wall, a decrepit chipboard cabinet at its side. On the opposite wall, with barely room to move between the two, stood a wardrobe and drawer unit in the same chipboard, and a dirty washbasin below a small mirror. The window looked out to scrubby grass, the bulk of the hill rising oppressively close, and Dewi thought of meanness of spirit, of spite, or misery and wilful neglect. He lifted the quilt, exposing a crumpled greying sheet, then hefted the mattress, exposing only thin wooden slats and the little balls of dusty fluff his mother called "slut's wool," drifting about the linoleum tiles. Replacing the bedding, absently smoothing sheet and quilt as his mother had taught him, he opened the door of the bedside cabinet, to find dog-eared comics, a school exercise book, a Mars Bar wrapper, and a ball of dirty socks. He pushed the exercise book in his pocket, and turned to the wardrobe unit, then moved back to the bed, dragging it away from the wall, searching for secrets taped to the back of the headboard, wincing at the screech of bed-legs on lino, staring ruefully at black greasy tracks on the floor. He found nothing save the legend "Llewellyn ap Kilroy woz 'ere," scored and inked on the cheap wood, nothing on the bedside cabinet, nothing secreted behind the wardrobe or underneath drawers. Putting the contents of drawers and wardrobe on the bed, he thought it a pitiful collection, of shrunken shapeless T-shirts, unpressed trousers, grubby underclothes, cheap socks with holes in toe and heel, a tattered plastic sponge-bag holding a worn toothbrush and a noxious flannel; only the meanest and barest of necessities. On hangers in the wardrobe, he found a bright red shirt, colour run to orange in places, and a bright red jumper, both bearing the name "Blodwel" in large yellow letters and, like the bus in the photograph, a stigma to mark out the children from their peers. He was struck by the absence of graffiti, except for the hidden legend, and decided Ronald Hogg made his own marks upon the place and its accoutrements too powerfully for the children to dare their own.

Pushing aside the heap of clothes, he sat on the bed. The mattress sank, and the metal bedframe bit deep into his thighs. Distant voices were suddenly raised in anger, words unintelligible, and he realized that until now, he had heard only the creaking of frost-brittle branches outside and the muffled blare of a television somewhere in the building. He wondered how almost a dozen children could be kept so quiet, or why anyone should feel the need to do so, and, gazing round the miserable cell, its walls bare of posters or pictures, where he, had he been incarcerated like Arwel, would hide his precious secrets. Screwed to the wall beside the wardrobe was a rail, draped with a raggy white handtowel. Pulling the towel aside, he lifted the thick plastic rail from its cups, and held it end on to the light. An object fell out, hitting his cheek before hitting the floor with a sharp crack.

Sitting again on the bed to look at his trophies, Dewi eased out the tight roll of paper from the guts of the rail. Unfurled, the paper tube became two glossy enlarged photographs. In one, eyes screwed up against the sun, Arwel sat astride a slender bay horse, looking down to the camera, a smile to his angelic face. He wore long black boots, fawn breeches, a quartered jersey and silk cap. Dewi turned the print over, to find the verso blank. In the other photograph, a man sat astride a silvery-grey horse, against a backdrop of cloud-swagged silvery-grey sky. He too wore long black boots and fawn breeches, a checked hacking jacket, and a black velvet hat, its peak shadowing his features. Dewi stared at the man and whistled to himself, before putting both photographs in his pocket. The other trophy, a black leather key-fob depicting a Harrier aeroplane, he too put in his pocket, before switching off the light, and opening the door to find the girl waiting for him, leaning against the far wall with her arms folded.

"Find anything?" she asked.

"A keyring with a Harrier jumpjet on it."

"Oh, that. He got it from RAF Valley Airshow." She nudged Dewi towards the end of the corridor, anxious to be rid of him and the disturbance to routine he represented. "Surprised he didn't take it with him," she added. "He was always bragging about it. Made the other kids jealous, though I can't think why."

"He didn't have much you might call personal. What about his sportsbag?"

"Didn't go to school, did he?" She sounded bored, Arwel already consigned to the past, his means of passage an irritant to be tolerated with ill-grace.

"Surely he went out? He can't have stayed in all the time."

"Well, he was allowed out sometimes."

"On his own?"

"Are you kidding?"

"Was he or wasn't he?"

"The kids aren't supposed to go out without staff." She held open the door to the administration corridor. "And you've no idea the trouble that causes."

Dewi laid two plates of fish and chips on McKenna's kitchentable, the cat squirming around his ankles. "Shall I cut up yours, sir?"

"No thanks, Dewi. Take the end off my fish for the cat, please."

"She's got a good thick coat for the winter." Putting the plate of fish on the floor, he watched her eat. "I like cats. They're good company."

"They can," McKenna said, chopping his food into mouthfuls, "be very trying. Seen that chair in the parlour?"

"You should've seen Arwel's bedroom." Dewi poured the

tea. "Furniture in there the gipsies'd throw on a council skip."

"Social Services are broke. Massive budget overspend." McKenna forked chips into his mouth, his right shoulder and elbow locking with each movement.

"From what I've heard, Hogg reckons kids like that aren't worth spending on," Dewi said, "partly 'cos they've no respect for anything, and partly 'cos most of 'em come from slummy council houses and wouldn't know the difference anyway. And," he added, spearing a chip, "Mr. Hogg thinks he shouldn't give the kids ideas above their station by letting them have a nice place to live in."

McKenna put down his fork and picked up a mug of tea. "I'm not sure if what you say is decent hearsay, or your own interpretation of odds and ends of gossip."

"Same difference. There's plenty of gossip around about Hogg and his missis and Blodwel, and none of it good."

"You said."

"But nobody wants to listen, do they?" Dewi ate the last piece of fish, crunching the tail of batter. "What did Doris have to say about the doctor who thought Arwel was at risk?"

"She said: 'Stupid man!,' and tutted. Social workers apparently spend half their time fending off over-reactive doctors. Everything's gone to blazes since Cleveland."

Dishes washed and dried, a fresh pot of tea warming on the hearth, Dewi and McKenna sat at the parlour table. Dewi smoothed out the two photographs, and placed the exercise book and keyring neatly to the side.

"Not much to go on, sir. Fancy Arwel being able to ride a horse like that, eh? Maybe he was just allowed to sit on it."

"They're both splattered with mud. Been for a good gallop by the looks of it."

Dewi grinned. "More than you'll be wanting to do for a while, isn't it?"

McKenna picked up the other photograph. "And how

come he knew Elias ab Elis well enough to ride his horse and have a photo of the man?"

"Dunno, sir. We'll have to ask." Dewi opened the exercise book. "There was nothing else personal in Arwel's room. According to the wardress, he didn't have a bag either."

"Mr. Hogg obviously likes to keep to the Christian ethic of coming into the world with nothing and going out the same way."

"Most kids have all sorts of junk. What about his room at home?"

"Janet says it's stripped bare, as if he never existed."

"Will she be driving you again tomorrow, sir?"

"Why?"

"Just wondering."

"Anything in the exercise book?" McKenna asked.

"A few crosswords and doodles. The extent of his Blodwel education, probably."

"You'd better go home. Come for me about half-eight, will you?"


The first crossword, a simple grid of unevenly drawn squares quickly resolved itself. "Green," "vehicles," "bard," McKenna wrote, filling in the blanks and learning from the last that Hogg was a bastard. The second, its clues more complex, defeated him. Yawning, he put the book aside, and went for a bath, lying sleepily neck deep in warm water. The upper half of his trunk, left shoulder and upper arm were daubed with livid reddish-blue and purple bruises. Drying himself with difficulty and not a little extra pain, he went downstairs to make a drink and swallow more analgesics. Waiting for the kettle to boil, he debated with himself if he was as lacking in sense as Jack believed. But, he thought, mixing hot chocolate in a beaker, Jack would never know the thrill of clinging to half a ton of horse-flesh plunging over tussocks and hills at thirty miles an hour, with only his own skill and God's fresh air between himself and disaster. Arwel had known, but not the skill to avert disaster.

The telephone rang as he searched the bookshelves for a government report on the management of children's homes, a volume generated by a deluge of nationwide scandals. He waited for the answering machine to take the call, standing with the thin blue book in his good hand. Denise wanted to know if he was well, if he wanted for anything, if he would like her to cook dinner tomorrow, if he minded that she called so late. He watched the red light blink on and off as the call registered, then took hot drink and book up to bed.

*Certain individuals,* he read, *seem to work out their personal pathology in the brutal subjugation and terrorizing of powerless and defenceless children, through sexual abuse, and humiliation. There is no fail-safe system to prevent such people from obtaining posts in children's homes. Random violence and emotional abuse may also be an occasional feature of management and control models adopted by some less experienced staff, particularly in response to challenging or disruptive behaviour by older children. In some children's homes, where staff are unaware of modern requirements for child management, archaic practices which are in themselves abusive may also be found.*

He scanned the next few pages, then dropped the book to the floor, knowing no nuggets of gold nestled amid the dross of the patently obvious. Drifting into sleep, the cat heavy against his legs, he thought again of the photographs and keyring, and wondered if Arwel had so carelessly abandoned his treasures because they ceased to be such.

# • C h a p t e r •
## 3

Turning the corner into McKenna's street, at 8:25 on a freezing November morning, Janet Evans, dressed in brown suede boots, olive cord trousers, a waxed jacket and high-necked olive sweater, almost bumped into Dewi Prys, making his way to McKenna's door.

"Mr. McKenna expecting you, is he?" Dewi asked, his mouth as cold as the wind.

"No."

"He's expecting me."

"Lucky Mr. McKenna." Janet turned on her heel. "I'll see him in work."

Waiting for McKenna to answer the door, Dewi stared at the retreating figure, shapely even under her thick garments, and thought it sad that a sharp mind and an acid tongue should sour the charms of the sweetest-looking woman.

"Normally," Jack Tuttle observed, "the whole world's up in arms if a boy of fourteen gets murdered."

"This isn't normally," McKenna said. "This is a boy on the run from a children's home, and in the eyes of the world, a bad lot." He put the photographs and exercise book on the desk. "I want these crosswords copied and handed out, and solved as quickly as possible."

"There's not much point Mr. Tuttle having them," Dewi said. "He can't speak Welsh."

"He can speak English a lot better than you can," Janet observed.

In a lengthening silence, McKenna watched the three officers, assessing the mischief set in motion by bringing Janet into the already fraught relationship between Dewi and Jack. "We have a nasty, thankless and very important job to do. Should any of you let personal feelings interfere, in any way, the consequences will be serious. I trust I make myself clear?"


"Nobody's repaired the wall yet where those two coaches crashed in the summer," Dewi said, changing down to first gear to take the car up the precipitous hill past St. Mary's. "Mr. ab Elis'll never make Lord Lieutenant of the county if he's dodgy with the kids, will he?" A magpie fluttered suddenly in front of the windscreen, eyes bright and hungry. "One for sorrow, two for joy, three for a girl, and four for a boy." He tapped out the metre of the old rhyme on the steering-wheel. "Can you see its mate, sir? I can't help but wonder why a posh bloke like Elis should be wanting to associate with a bad boy like Arwel was supposed to be."

"People like him do a lot of charity work," McKenna said. "He might have been the only oasis in the desert of Arwel's life."

"Most folk never do owt for nowt. Why should he be any different?"

McKenna shuddered as pain, dormant since he woke, suddenly ground its teeth around his bones.

"The weather won't help," Dewi observed. "The milk bottles'd frozen to the doorstep this morning. Mam had to pour warm water over them. There's a full moon in a few days, so we'll probably have some snow." Turning left on to a narrow unmade lane, he slowed to a crawl, car wheels crunching through drifts of brittle golden leaves. "Our posh bloke lives at the end of the lane, and I just hope he's not blinding along in his big posh Range Rover, because I can't see a bloody thing over these hedges, and neither can he."

"How d'you know he's got a Range Rover?"

"Traffic copped him doing a ton on Port Dinorwic bypass a while back. He got off with a warning, which isn't surprising with the connections he must have. He's also got a big posh horsebox, tractors and whatnot, and a great big, shiny, super-posh, custom-built, Italian sports car his wife drives most of the time. You know who she is, don't you?"

"A county councillor," McKenna said, weary already of the intricate nexus of relationships which formed the local power group, and which he must carefully and tactfully unravel in search of sickness and depravity rotting the tight-woven fabric.

"Madame Rhiannon Haf ab Elis is chairperson of the social services committee no less, most likely best mates with Ron and his missis, too."

"And probably the obvious connection between Elis and Arwel."

"That's as may be, but who's to say that's where it begins and ends?" He let the car coast down the lane. "That's Bedd y Cor, sir. Weird calling your house a 'dwarf's grave,' isn't it?"

Slated roof misty with dew, the house stood on a natural terrace, fronted by lawns and shrubbery, and the glimpse of a formal garden. A grove of winter-bare oak and ash, and the rising hillside, shielded its back from mountain storms. Acres of pasture and heath swept towards the foothills, grazed by horses swaddled in crested rugs.

"Mam says it was long house in the old days, and a near ruin when the Elises bought it," Dewi added. "I looked them up in *Who's Who* this morning. Her family's riddled with the sort of money that breeds like maggots on a corpse. He's director of this, that and the other, and probably got shares in half the world, but I don't expect he's ever done a day's proper graft in his life. I wonder if the money's what the Yanks call old or new?"

"You read too much pulp fiction, Dewi Prys. Money is money, and old or new, it buys the same. Mr. ab Elis's money has bought some very fine horse-flesh."

"It might've bought some very fine human flesh as well, sir, but I daresay that came a lot cheaper."

Leaving Dewi by a huge five-barred gate of weather-bleached wood, McKenna walked down the drive towards the house, feet crunching on finely raked gravel. Moss-grown boulders and rocky outcrops strewed the undulating landscape around what was once a yeoman's dwelling, the character of which the Elises' restoration had destroyed nothing. Set on an east–west axis, like so many older houses, only north and south-facing walls bore windows. The east wall faced the hillside, where a silvery tumble of water seemed to disappear beneath the foundations. An enormous oak tree, its trunk arched by centuries of prevailing winds, touched the other, and spread its branches over the roof. White paint gleamed on cob walls and squat chimneys, flashed with shale to throw off the rain. Riotous with autumn colours, the north wall was garbed from roof to footings with Virginia creeper, and McKenna imagined the house in summer, canopied by the oak tree, like the house built of leaves in an ancient Welsh poem. Old barns in the adjoining field had been converted to stables and feedstore and garage, their yards laid with smooth cobbles, their roofs yellowy-green with lichen.

A girl who spoke with the harsh accent of Arwel's home town opened the door, and took him through a hall floored with worn stone slabs, down a passageway where the slabs were covered in coarse druggeting, and to a room which looked out over the gardens and down the hillside.

Russet leaves draped the window like a frame around a tranquil winter landscape, blazing logs in a huge stone fireplace filled the air with heat and sweet woody scents, lit pale-leather furniture and pearly-grey carpet, and walls and ceiling of a colour so subtle McKenna felt adrift in room without angles or demarcation. Seated on the edge of an armchair, good arm cradling the bad, he examined the painting above the mantel, where a dark-robed figure drifted in desolate twilight between sea and strand, and surveyed the shelves of fine limed oak built in the chimney alcoves, where old buckram- and leather-bound books were stacked beside a brass-bound casket of burnished wood. Against the far wall, away from the heat, matching shelves housed racks of records and compact discs, and the most expensive hi-fi console he had ever seen.

Fidgety, wanting to smoke, he stood up and walked to the shelves, leaving tracks in the lush carpet pile, and tilted his head to read the book titles. Many were biographies of Beethoven, in German and English, the others devoted to Mozart and Salieri, Dittersdorf and Gassmann, Handel, Spohr and Benda. He leafed through the yellowed pages of an arcane text on counterpoint, and wondered what delayed Elis. Perhaps he played with time, McKenna thought, hoping to subvert its momentum as these composers had done, and thus recreate the time-space in which Arwel Thomas still lived and no questions need be asked.

He looked again at the painting, troubled by the feelings it evoked, then made new tracks towards the other picture, a chalk portrait hung to catch the best light, sepia-toned like the pages of the text. He felt a draught as the door behind him opened.

"Beethoven, at the age of fifty-one." The voice was cultured and soft. "A marvellous face, don't you think? Of course, the original is still in Bonn." Elis smiled wryly. "All the money in the world can't buy some things. Do sit down. Mari's bringing coffee." Tall and muscular, he wore a heavy woollen jumper, riding breeches splashed with mud, long wool socks, and his wealth without ostentation.

The girl followed him into the room, and put coffee and a silver ashtray on a delicate painted table, offering no deference to Elis, but simply a beguiling smile as he thanked her.

"I do apologize for keeping you waiting. I was grooming

my horse." Pouring coffee into fine china cups, pushing McKenna's within hands' reach, he asked, "What have you done to yourself?"

"Dislocated my shoulder."

"That must be painful. What happened?"

"A tumble."

"We don't bounce so well as we get older, do we?" He stood by the fireplace, fumbling with cigarette and lighter.

"That's a fine painting," McKenna observed. "Who's the artist?"

"Caspar David Friedrich, who died a near madman. An excess of vision, I suppose, like his contemporary. They make you suffer with them, don't they? Friedrich with his solitudes, Beethoven with his music."

"Perhaps we should accept suffering as one of the great structural lines of human life," McKenna commented. Elis sat opposite, frowning. "Perhaps," McKenna added, "we should find it sufficient to rejoice in their vision." He gazed at Elis, at the trembling hand holding the coffee cup. "And much as I would like to discuss music and art, Mr. Elis, I didn't come here to seek your opinions on either."

"I know." The cup clattered on the saucer, slopping liquid. Dabbing at the spill with a napkin, Elis said, "Arwel didn't turn up as usual, so I called Blodwel. They said he'd absconded."

"And how often would he come here?"

"Every weekend. Sometimes, he'd arrive without warning on a schoolday. I always let them know, and no one ever told me to send him back."

"We've been told the children aren't allowed out unaccompanied."

"Have you?" Elis said wearily. "You'll no doubt hear other half-truths, as well as blatant untruths."

"How did you know him?"

"I try to use my own good fortune for the benefit of others." Elis smiled bitterly. "Look what I managed to do for Arwel."

"Please keep to the point, Mr. Elis."

"I take children out of care, as my predecessors hired from the workhouse. Mari came a couple of years ago, after spending childhood in so many foster homes everyone lost count. She was thrown out of care the day after her sixteenth birthday. Not what I call good parenting, but who am I to cast the first stone?"

"Arwel, Mr. Elis."

"Early in the summer, I asked Social Services if any of the Blodwel children might like to help with the horses. Doris brought Arwel."

"And you let him look after valuable bloodstock?"

"Mari's from Caernarfon. She said he was a decent boy. And I," Elis added fiercely, "never found anything to prove her wrong. He was that rare person without fear of horses. They seemed to liberate him. He loved and respected them, and they responded in kind."

"You taught him to ride?"

"And to groom and feed and muck out, to recognize injury and sickness." Elis tossed his cigarette in the hearth. "He was gifted with horses, Mr. McKenna. Almost fey."

"Did you take him out?"

"We went to Chester Races in early July, to Newmarket later that month, to Valley Air Show in August, to the first National Hunt meeting at Bangor on Dee last month, then to Aintree for the day, because he wanted to see the Grand National course." Elis smiled, pain forgotten. "I think he decided to be a jump jockey the first time he galloped a horse." Pain returned to rampage through his composure. "That was the last time I saw him."

"Did you pay him?"

"Children in care aren't allowed to earn. I sent Hogg a cheque for a hundred pounds each month, to be put in Arwel's savings account. He deserved much more, but Hogg said he was spoilt already, the others would be jealous, and boys like him didn't deserve privileges in any case. I gave him cash every so often, and told him to keep quiet."

"Did he ever discuss his family? Or Blodwel? His friends? His hopes and dreams and fears?" McKenna sipped his coffee.

"He was quite reserved, even shy, except with the horses, but I never expected his confidence in any case, because I'm forty-one, and to Arwel's generation, that's almost inconceivably old. Like most youngsters, he was a little secretive, but never devious, and he liked quietness, and privacy. He read quite a lot, too." Elis looked at the bookshelves, frowning. "I'm sure he left one of his books here. Mari should know where it is. He talked to her a lot and I often heard them giggling in the kitchen. I think she took a fancy to him."

"Hardly surprising. He was a very beautiful boy. His sister is equally beautiful."

"Yes, I know." The voice was quiet, the eyes downcast, the hands trembling violently as if in the throes of delirium.

"You know the family?"

"In his greater wisdom, Hogg banned family contact. Arwel was desperate to see them, so I took him one Sunday afternoon. I don't think I'd recognize the parents if I fell over them." Elis paused, to light another cigarette. "Carol was in that horrible back parlour, standing in front of the window. The sun was behind her, and I thought she must be made of light."

"According to her parents, she's wholly of the flesh."

Elis stared at the painting over the mantel. "To see them all together was like witnessing a law of nature; Carol and Arwel the light to their parents' darkness, each necessary to the other, neither able to vanquish the other. At least, I thought so. How else could I believe there may be justice and reason in the world?"

"Nature is prone to accidents of beauty as much as to those of genius and idiocy." McKenna stood up, pain cavorting from neck to knee. "Would it be possible to see Mari now?"

Elis glanced at his watch. "She'll have gone shopping, but I'll give you her number. Don't look so astounded! She has a self-contained flat in the house, because this is her home for as long as she wishes. The only relative is an aged grand-mother in Caernarfon, whom Mari visits from time to time."

Dewi leaned on the wall by the gate, watching the grazing horses. "That ginger one looks like she'll drop her foal any minute."

"Chestnut, not ginger."

"Whatever you say, sir. Who's the girl? She drove out about ten minutes ago."

"What was she driving?"

"A grey Peugeot 305."

McKenna climbed into the car, fumbling for the seat belt. "She must have a car as well as her own flat and telephone number."

"Who must?"

"Mari from Caernarfon. Elis's maid, or whatever, who spent her life in foster homes until he rescued her from a life of drudgery."

Dewi leaned over to fasten McKenna's seat belt. "You sound like you've taken against the man, sir. Did you see his wife?"

"No."

"Is the house posher inside than out?"

"It's very discreetly the home of very rich people who don't need to bother about any of the things which trouble us ordinary mortals," McKenna said. "And they have open fires everywhere. Maybe Mari doubles as Cinderella for them."

Bumping up the lane, Dewi remarked cheerfully, "Mam always says even the pope and royalty have to go to the lavvy." He laughed. "Did you know Henry the Eighth employed a 'Gentleman of the Stools' to wipe his backside for him? I saw it on TV. When Henry took a laxative, the man wrote: 'The King had a veritable siege of the bowels.' I'd call Hogg a veri-table siege of the bowels." He slipped the engine to first gear to take the brutal hill past St. Mary's. "D'you reckon Elis is another? Did he know where Arwel might've been for nearly a week before he turned up dead?"

"That girl is absolutely stunned with grief, sir," Janet told McKenna. "She's like a zombie."

Easing himself into the chair behind the desk, McKenna searched for his cigarettes. "Did she not have much to say?"

"She didn't even answer my questions. She was off somewhere else altogether." As the smoke from McKenna's cigarette rose pungent in the air, Janet sniffed.

"D'you want one?"

"It's not the smoke. I took Carol to a poxy café for some lunch and my clothes stink of frying. She hardly ate anything, just picked at a few chips. She's painfully thin. D'you think she's anorexic?"

"Elis says she seems to be made from light."

"Fancy him knowing her. Hardly the same social circle."

"Arwel took him to meet the family. It seems he thought a great deal of Mr. Elis."

"And what did Mr. Elis think of Arwel?"

"He's as much stunned in his own way as Carol."

"I'm not surprised. His reputation could be on the line."

"He's no fool," McKenna pointed out. "His live-in maid was in care, and I want her interviewed as soon as possible." He scribbled Mari's telephone number on a sheet of paper and pushed it across the desk. "Be nice to her. She knows the Thomases, and Elis thinks she was sweet on Arwel."

"No word from HQ yet about interviewing Blodwel kids," Owen Griffiths told McKenna. "I'll chivvy them along in a while. Social Services might be trying to hide something, but then again, they might just be following the rules about questioning minors, and confidentiality and what-have-you." The superintendent sighed. "Pain in the arse, like most rules."

"You'll be retired and away from it all soon." McKenna smiled. "Honourably retired."

"Don't be snide. Policing's a dirty job at times, and some folk get their hands in the muck a bit too deep." Griffiths pushed his coffee mug round and round on the blotter. "My wife's got the next five years organized to the minute. She's afraid I'll get bored."

"You're more likely to wonder how you ever found time to work."

"You think so?" Griffiths asked, his eyes bleak. "My job's so much a part of my life I can't imagine being without it, but there's hellish pressure to take early retirement. HQ want to make room for others, and the family say I should get out before I'm too old to do anything but sit in a rocking-chair going gaga. You thought any more about applying for the vacancy? I have it on good authority it'd be nothing more than a formality."

"I'm not sure I want to return to uniform, promotion or not."

"You've been sure about nothing since you split with Denise. You've spent the last six months in limbo, waiting for God knows what."

McKenna fidgeted, snapping his lighter off and on. "It's hard making plans for yourself. Collapsing marriages cause a huge convulsion in the personality, I'm told."

"Denise isn't having problems, from what I hear."

"She'll sort herself out in her own way. Women usually cope much better."

"I hear she's found someone to take the edge off her misery."

"I know. It's nothing to do with me. She's a free agent."

"Not everyone will be so magnanimous. She's still Mrs. McKenna to most folk, and her cavorting around with a boyfriend isn't good for you. Either tell her to be a bit more circumspect, or give her a divorce. She's dead wood you're carting around, and unless you hope to have her back, you should finish things properly, before you fall in the shit-pile she's busy making. She's holding you back."

"From what?"

"From going forward. Life's all about moving on, isn't it?"

"Mr. Tuttle's gone tilting at windmills, Detective Constable Miss Janet Evans buggered off without condescending to say where, and nobody can make head or tail of the crosswords," Dewi said. "Dr. Roberts telephoned. The local paper and BBC and HTV've been pestering us, so I referred them to HQ, which went down like a lead balloon. BBC want to know if it's true Arwel got hit by a train, HTV want to know the same, and the local paper wants to know how often Blodwel kids go on the run without anybody telling us."

"Stop sniping about Janet Evans," McKenna snapped. "I've warned all of you. She's interviewing Elis's maid. What did Eifion Roberts want?"

"He said there's no chance of releasing Arwel's body. Apart from waiting for tissue and sample results to come back, somebody else might be asked to PM the boy to make sure he didn't dream up the sexual abuse. And there's been no inquest yet."

"Nobody's asked him to release the body."

"Apparently, sir, Councillor Mrs. Rhiannon Haf ab Elis talked to the hospital management on behalf of the Thomases and those caring souls in Social Services. People want Arwel six feet under as soon as possible, so they can get on with the business of grieving and recovery. Personally, I reckon folk hope out of sight'll put the boy out of mind. Should one of us tell the lady councillor to mind her own sodding business, sir?"

"She'll keep. Why can't anyone solve the crossword clues?"

"They're like codes." Dewi riffled through sheets of photocopies, and pointed to the word. "Elijah." "I remember Elijah from Sunday School, but *proffwyd* doesn't fit, because it's eight letters, not five."

"Try the Welsh form, Dewi. I'm sure you'll find 'Elias' will fit perfectly."

"Dewi Prys says you've been tilting at windmills," McKenna said.

"I might as well've been." Jack shivered. "God! It's cold!" He glanced through the window of McKenna's office. "And bloody night-time again already. Will we ever see the sun again?"

"Arwel won't."

"Why don't you stop laying it on with a bloody trowel? We know he won't! That's one of death's tragedies, whatever age you are."

"The inquest is fixed for next Tuesday. Will we have anything to say?"

" 'Arwel Thomas is dead, enquiries are proceeding.' "

"People want him buried." McKenna lit a cigarette. "Do we need to delay the funeral?"

Jack shrugged. "Leave it to the coroner. We might've witnessed a revelation by then, but I doubt it." He shivered again, and moved his chair nearer to the radiator. "I swear it's colder than last night."

"Anything to report apart from the state of the weather?"

"Nothing much. We can probably write off the parents, even though you think they're capable of violence towards either of their kids."

"I said Peggy Thomas is overly concerned with what the neighbours think. She punishes Carol enough."

"Her sort never do anything though, because they'd have nothing to carp about after. Anyway, there isn't even a hint Arwel got as far as Caernarfon, and if the Thomases killed him, we'd've found the body in a local skip, or down an alleyway."

"What's the word on David Fellows?"

Jack shivered violently. Under the harsh fluorescent light, his face was ashen. "Gone to earth, people say. Since he was diagnosed with AIDS, he's kept himself to himself. Pity he didn't do that before, isn't it?"

"So no spurned lover is claiming he's got an interest in the kids?"

"We've shown pictures of Arwel to all his neighbours, and no one's ever seen the boy. They'd remember him, wouldn't they?"

Janet sat in an antique Victorian armchair upholstered in rose-pink velvet, surveying the pretty sitting-room of Mari Williamson's flat, and pondering the chance that placed one homeless and unwanted girl in this luxury when many of her peers scavenged the streets, prostituting bodies and hope for the bare necessities. She felt resentment, an unwholesome enjoyment in the distress she brought to the girl, who sobbed bitterly, rubbing her eyes with her fists.

"I can't talk to you while you're crying. When did Mr. Elis know Arwel was dead?"

"I don't know!" Mari flushed. "Why don't you ask him? Somebody from that dump probably phoned Mrs. Elis."

"Who d'you know at Blodwel?"

"A few of the kids from Caernarfon."

Janet picked up her file from the rose-pink carpet, and read out a list of names. "Any of these? They went on the run with Arwel."

"No."

"D'you know where he stayed when he absconded?"

"No."

"Did he ever say why he ran away?"

"Are you stupid?" Mari demanded. "That place is worse than a bloody prison!"

"How is it worse?"

"It is."

"How would you know? You've never lived there."

"Why d'you think they ran off all the time?"

"Teenagers do that kind of thing," Janet said. "I expect I would at that age. Like bunking school, isn't it?"

"You dodged school?" Mari asked, the ghost of a smile to her lips. "Dear me. I thought coppers had to be squeaky clean."

"I suppose I was lucky. I was never found out."

"Arwel was," Mari offered. "That's why he was put in care."

"I know."

"Not," Mari went on, standing to stare through a window giving on to a side garden grey with mountain mist, "that you could call it 'care.' More like neglect."

"What happened to you?"

"Me?" Mari turned, leaning against the window-sill, staring at Janet. Dressed in black from head to foot, her clothes sat well on the small neat body. Brown shiny hair, cut in a modish bob, shadowed her pale face. "Nothing special. Mam had me when she was sixteen, then ran off with some bloke. My Nain took me in, but she couldn't manage with her rheumatism, so I went to a foster home."

"Then what?"

"Then I went to another foster home, then another and another. I lost count years ago. Social Services might know."

"Why so many?"

"That's how things go." Smoothing the skirt over her thighs, Mari sat down again, twisting her hands until the knuckles showed angry red. "I got blamed for anything going wrong with their marriage or their kids. I was always on sufferance, always waiting to get chucked out on the streets." She paused. "Some of them cared, in their own way, I suppose, but not very much. One family was trying to foster as many kids as they could to get an OBE off the queen and their names in the paper, and another couple took me because they couldn't have children of their own, and they were too old to adopt."

"Why didn't you stay?"

"I started growing up. They wanted something quiet and pretty to dress up and play with." She smiled at Janet, a wise smile too old for her pretty young face. "You begin to understand people, even if they don't understand themselves. You don't get too fond of them, because it won't last, but they feel rejected so you're out on your ear even faster." The smile vanished, leaving her eyes hard. "Their own kids bully you, and lie to cause strife with the parents, and tell everybody in school what you are, and it's even worse when people say you're their 'special' child."

"You survived," Janet said quietly.

"I even landed on my feet. I didn't need to saddle myself with a baby to get a roof over my head. I've only got to be nice to Mr. Elis and his wife."

"And is that hard?"

"He treats me like anyone else, but she can act like I'm a charity case." Mari smiled. "You might've noticed I don't speak too badly. That's her doing."

"You sound like a Cofi to me."

"So? I'm from Caernarfon. You talk chapel Bangor."

"My father's a minister."

"My father was a drunk, according to my Nain."

"Who was he?"

Mari shrugged. "Who knows? God knows who I'm related to. I'd never go with a local lad. For all I know, he could be my half-brother."

"D'you ever see your mother?"

"Not a word in all these years. She might be shacked up with some man. I might have half-sisters and half-brothers I'll never know. She might be flogging her assets on the streets." She fell silent, looking inward. "I'm eighteen. She's only thirty-four, if she's not dead."

"You could try to find her. The Sally Army finds lots of missing people."

"Why should I want to? I don't expect she's got anything I might want after all this time."

"You make life sound terribly bleak."

"I learned how bleak it is before I could think properly. It'll take you a lot longer to find out the same."

"You're depressing me."

"You should grow up a bit, then!" Mari snapped. "Is there anything else you want to know?" She looked at her watch, a thin gold disc on a gold bracelet. "My eighteenth birthday present from my kind employers, in case your little copper's mind is thinking otherwise. And it'll be their teatime soon."

"There's a lot I want to ask you, actually, such as how Mr. and Mrs. Elis get on together."

"Same as most married people, I suppose. Good days and bad days."

"What causes the bad days?"

"I don't know."

Janet sighed. "You don't want to gossip. That's understandable."

"There's nothing to gossip about, is there? Pillars of the community, aren't they?"

"Has Mr. Elis ever made a pass at you?"

"No, he hasn't." Mari stared at Janet, bitter humour twitching the corners of her mouth, while her cheeks flushed.

"What's the joke?"

"You wouldn't understand."

"Try me."

Mari fidgeted. "I'm not gossiping, OK? Only I heard them having a row once. She was complaining about being lonely in bed, if you get my drift."

"And?"

"And he was hedging and not answering, so she lost her temper. She's got a real bitch of a temper at times."

"And?"

"She was shrieking about diseases people catch in posh public schools. Took me a while to work out what she meant."

"I see." Janet leaned back in her chair, feeling the soft upholstery cradle her shoulders, staring at Mari.

"No, you don't," Mari told her. "Not if you're thinking he was after Arwel." Her face twisted with sorrow. "He really loved Arwel, like his own son. Arwel didn't understand either, until I told him. Then he realized how important he was to Mr. Elis, learning to ride and going places with him."

"Told Arwel?" Janet frowned. "What did you tell Arwel?"

"About the boy."

"For God's sake stop talking in riddles! What boy?"

"Their son. That boy. He's fifteen, and he's an idiot, a vegetable. He's locked up in a posh private home in Meirionydd, and he should've died years ago, only he's too well looked after by all that money." She looked scathingly at Janet. "Didn't you know they had a son? Don't you coppers know anything?"


Seated at his old dining-table, prey to the creeping sense of inadequacy wrought by Elis's riches and erudition, McKenna surveyed the faded paper upon the walls of his little parlour, the chesterfield clad in threadbare green velvet, the carpet threatening baldness where thousands of footsteps had worn pathways among leaves and scrolls and old-fashioned roses. In the small collection of CDs and albums, the chain-store hi-fi system, the books denoting no particular interest or learning, the old prints of which he had been so proud, what had he to show for his forty-four years? Lack of money had company in the heart of poverty, he realized. A dearth of spirit, a pernicious wasting of imagination, which condemned the children of Blodwel to repeating life-patterns already marked out by parents and grandparents, their existence a ricochet from crisis to crisis to disaster.

The cat lay on her back before the fire, paws draped over her fat little belly. She looked at him upside down, and he wondered idly if she saw him inverted, or if those sleepy slitted eyes saw anything at all. She yawned, turned over, and tucked her paws under her shoulders, staring at the flames. When the doorbell pealed, her ears twitched.

"Don't mind me calling late, do you?" Eifion Roberts stood on the step, Michelin Man inside a padded jacket. He waved a bottle wrapped in off-licence tissue paper. "Brought something to warm the innards. It's bloody freezing again. Your lot are out on the A55 by Aber."

"Why's that?"

"A whopping great truck jack-knifed over the central barrier. Lucky the road was clear, else I'd have a few to cut up in the morning."

"What d'you do when there's no body to autopsy, Eifion? How d'you fill your days?"

"Well, I might tour the hospital wards turning off intravenous drips here and there, but it's a lot more fun putting carbon monoxide in the odd oxygen cylinder." The pathologist bared his teeth. "What the hell d'you think I do?" He dropped the jacket on the floor and sat on the chesterfield, bringing a sigh from the springs.

"How much do you weigh?" McKenna asked.

"Don't know and don't care. You're beginning to look anorexic. D'you run to glasses in this place, or must we swig from the bottle like common folk?" He bent down to stroke the cat, running his fingers over her haunches. "She's coming on a treat, isn't she? Must be all that affection you lavish on her."

McKenna put two tumblers on the floor, and uncapped the bottle of whiskey. "Owen Griffiths reckons Denise is making a scandal out of her affections, and it'll rub off on me."

"Why?" Roberts gulped his drink. "You're not her keeper."

"I'm still her husband. Tarnished reputations and all that." He sighed. "She's taken up with some bloke."

"You know, do you? Folk think you don't, which is why they're not knowing what to say and what not to say. Who told you?"

"Denise." McKenna smiled wryly. "She couldn't wait. He's a well-heeled type from Cheshire with a boat at the marina."

"Let's hope he's giving her whatever you wouldn't, then," Roberts observed caustically. "Married is he?"

"I don't know."

"And I hope you don't care. Take no notice of Griffiths and his chapel mentality. Nobody gives a toss if Denise hops in and out of every bed between here and Manchester. How's the shoulder?"

"Very painful, like the rest of me."

"What else d'you expect? Coming off that horse, you hit the deck fast. Folk only get mangled in car crashes because when the car stops, they're still going as fast as the car when it hit whatever it hit." Dr. Roberts drained his glass, and poured more whiskey. "You wouldn't credit some of the messes I've had on the table before seat belts came in."

"Are you planning to drive yourself home?"

"Only if I can't sprout wings and fly like a big fat bat. Stop being an old woman! What's new with the boy?"

"Not much." McKenna lit a cigarette, and stared at the fire. "We can't get near the Blodwel kids or staff. Hogg insists there's nothing more to tell us, and Social Services insist the boy was nothing to do with them because he was on the run."

"Pontius Pilate spawned more offspring than he ever knew." Roberts chewed his lip. "What's the word with the local perverts?"

"We should credit them with more sense, because no one would risk spending ten years on Rule 43 for a bite of fresh meat." McKenna shivered, the drink running fiery in his belly. "I hoped for something from that quarter. Somebody taking the opportunity to settle a score, perhaps."

"They're shit-scared, 'cos this is too close to home, and they're sitting ducks. Any of the staff at Blodwel got form?"

"Clean as the driven snow, according to our records. There have been complaints about Hogg in the past."

"What sort of complaints?"

McKenna shrugged. "Dewi Prys reckons he's a brutal sod. Griffiths was told the complaints are vicious fabrications, fabricated by disgruntled ex-residents or their families."

"And who told him that?"

"Guess." McKenna stubbed out his cigarette. "Our own hierarchy is as jumpy as everyone else."

"You could have fifty ex-kids-in-care telling you Hogg is a psychopath, but it's no help to Arwel. Can't you get at the staff?"

"They don't seem to breathe without Hogg's permission."

"Ex-staff, then. Some bod with an axe to grind."

"And who'll tell us where to find them?" McKenna lit another cigarette.

"You could get that pretty girl you've taken under your wing to waylay Blodwel kids on their way back from school."

"They don't go out to school, and they don't go out without staff."

"Arwel did, unless he got buggered with an audience." Draining his glass for the second time, Dr. Roberts stared at the sputtering flames.

McKenna broke the lengthening silence. "Elis's wife has been overheard to comment about diseases caught in public school."

"What's he like?"

"Very rich, very cultured, very charming. He has a son slightly older than Arwel was. Mari said the boy's a vegetable."

"Poor sod! Enough to ruin any marriage."

"People say a handicapped child can bring a couple closer together."

"People say a lot of things which aren't true. Religion and philosophy depend on two opposing elements creating a unifying third. Elis and his wife created an idiot, so what hope have they got?" Settling deep in the sofa cushions, the pathologist added, "Denise might know the low-down on Elis's non-public persona. She's running with the rich crowd, and they're as cliquy in their own way as the queer boys and faggots."

"Elis rather outclasses someone with a tatty boat in Port Dinorwic marina."

"How d'you know it's tatty? It could be an ocean-going

yacht for all you know." Dr. Roberts stared at McKenna. "Elis and his ilk aren't averse to trawling gutters for their kicks, as his goodly wife might well know."

"I hear she tried to get Arwel's body released."

"So maybe she knows something she doesn't want you to find out."

"Like what?"

"How should I know? It's a bastard of a case, and you won't get far without tapping into the gossip networks, picking up the innuendo, scrutinizing anyone with access to young boys." Dr. Roberts sighed. "Nothing's changed in the history of man, and some things never will. You can't bypass Elis, or that Hogg. How d'you rate him as a paedophile?"

"He doesn't look like a child abuser." McKenna raked his fingers through his hair. "Listen to me! It's the drink talking. You can't tell from looking."

"Can't you? I'll lend you my rare copy of Cesare Lombroso's *Criminal Man*. He reckoned the bad guys have distinguishable physical differences, but no one believes him these days, even though any artist could tell you the same. We prefer Freud and his excuse theories."

McKenna smiled. "Despite appearances, you'll become a criminal if you get in your car with all that whiskey sloshing round in your belly."

"Who's to know except you and me?"

"What if you hit something?"

"And what if I don't? I'm not the bizarre collection of subconscious impulses Freud described as a person. I'm aware of my limitations."

"Not all psychiatry is problematic, Eifion."

"I've yet to be convinced. If Elis was buggered in public school, and abused Arwel, the shrinks'll argue he can't help repeating a learned behaviour pattern, so he's not wilfully hurting anyone."

"Lombroso's theory has the same inevitability."

"He never overlooked choice. Child abuse is a choice, an

aspect of recreational sex, as Dai Skunk could tell you. It's certainly not a biological imperative." Dr. Roberts drained his glass. "By the way, that bleeding lesion is Kaposi's Sarcoma, and Jack's convinced the HIV virus is airborne. He's too terrified to listen to sense."

# •Chapter•
# 4

Morning brought simply another absence of night, and a dense obscuring fog off the sea. Looking from his window at blankness, unrelieved by even the ghost of a shape to confirm the continued existence of his world, McKenna thought of the fog as an entity, pressing against his windows for ingress to his house and his throat and his lungs, suffocating and life stealing. Great beads of icy dew hung from the lintel above the window and dribbled like grease down the glass. He lit the gas fire, hunched on the edge of the sofa, nursing a body riotous with pain. The cat leapt up beside him, and made a ball of herself in one corner.

Doris Hogg sat on the hard bench fixed to the wall of Blodwel's cloakroom, hunched inside her dressing-gown, feet bare and blue with cold inside the grubby carpet slippers. She shivered, watching the boy who sat on an identical bench fixed to the opposite wall, tearing his nails until blood seeped from the quick, gnawing his knuckles until the crude blue letters tattooed on the flesh turned purple. He stared at the cheap dirty trainers on his feet, waiting and listening, and heard the dog scratching at the locked door to be allowed in from the fog.

"I'm hungry," he said.

"You had breakfast." She shuffled to the door to let in the whining dog, clothing creased around her rump, a crude embroidery of varicose veins behind her knees.

"I only had cornflakes."

"You'll get something later."

The dog sidled in with wisps of fog about its body and dew beading its hair, snuffled at her feet, then at his, and because it was Hogg's cur, the boy wanted to kick it back out and over the hill, to repay the animal for the cruelties of the master.

She sat again, the dog slumped by her feet, their breathing noisy, adding to the strata of smells in this room and the building, which would haunt the rest of his days, he thought, like the memorable lessons so painfully learned. Hunger groped at his innards, nausea wormed in his gut, wriggling amid undigested cornflakes and weak tea, like the vein in the woman's foot, wriggling like a sandworm whenever she changed the locus of pressure.

"I feel sick."

She yawned. He heard the wrench of jaw muscles and the clicking of teeth. "Be sick, then. And you needn't think they won't come because of the fog. It's clearing already."

He swallowed the bile, and stared through the window. Wisps of fog wriggled in and out of the thin trees behind Blodwel, torn by a little wind. The dog yawned too, tongue curled up inside its mouth, then snatched at the end of her dressing-gown belt, pulling open the garment to reveal snagged pink nylon clinging to her navel and the rolls of flesh around belly and waist. "What was that you said?" she snapped, as he muttered under his breath. She sneered. "You'll get your comeuppance! You won't be running away again in a hurry."

"Maybe I won't want to."

Her eyes glittered. "You're an evil monster! It's your fault Arwel Thomas got killed!"

"I said I'm hungry."

"You can't be hungry if you feel sick."

"I've got my rights. I want a proper breakfast."

"You've got no rights! Mr. Hogg said tea and cereal, and that's all you're getting." She stared at him. "Count yourself lucky you got that. You don't deserve anything!"

He raised his head. "I'm not evil or a monster. You are, because you do everything he says, even when you know it's wrong."

"Don't you speak to me like that!"

"Why not? Truth hurts, does it?"

"You deserve to be locked up!"

"You just said I don't deserve anything. Why don't you make up your fucking mind?" He watched her face. "What'll your mates do with me gone and Arwel dead?"

Fear raked its claws down the pasty morning skin of her face, leaving reddish weals at the side of her mouth and down her neck. "Shut up!" She stood up again, and leaned over him, her sour smell dribbling into his nostrils. "Shut up, or you'll be sorry!" She backed away, and sat down, never taking her eyes from his face. The dog stared too, tongue lolling from its ratty mouth.

Above his head, he heard bed springs scrape. He would be long gone before staff roused the other children, and as quickly forgotten here as at home, his place filled in like a grave. The sounds and smells of Blodwel were as familiar as those which once marked the passage of his days and the boundaries of his territory elsewhere, and he wondered how he might fare cast into the wilderness beyond, his choices whittled to nothing.

"You'll be sorry if I chuck myself out of the car on the way."

She yawned again. "Will I?"

Blurry shapes passed the window, like thunderclouds rolled from the mountains. The door-handle dropped, then rose when the door failed to give. She rose again, keys swinging and clanking. Two men stood on the threshold, huge inside thick jackets. They nodded to the woman, then to the boy, and walked away. He picked up his bag and followed, hearing the door thud in its frame and the muffled falling of tumblers. As he trailed behind the men, foggy dew moistened his hair, like the tears his mother shed over him, he thought, when the social worker and policeman wrenched him from her arms to bring him to Blodwel.

Drawn from the warmth of the breakfast-room by the sound of horse's hooves in the stable yard, Rhiannon pulled a sheep-skin jacket from the rack by the back door and went outside, tucking up her hands inside the sleeves. Mari's piquant face swam in the gloom behind the kitchen window.

"Surely you're not going out. The roads'll be like glass."

The great grey horse fidgeted at the bit, breath mingling with streamers of mist, flanks twitching. Elis buckled up the girth, soothing the animal.

"And it's still foggy." Blanketing the coast, lying dense in hollows and little valleys, the mist swirled upwards, drawing smoky shapes across a watery sun low in the eastern sky. "It won't clear," Rhiannon added.

She watched her husband, and Mari watched too, ignoring the housekeeper's instruction to load the dishwasher before arranging the great sheaves of fern and winter chrysanthemums delivered fresh every other day to glorify the rooms and hallways of Bedd y Cor.

Satisfied the girth was secure, Elis took hold of the reins and vaulted into the saddle. "We'll be all right. Horses have more sense than people." The smile was fleeting.

"Do they? Then why doesn't he stay in his nice warm stable?"

The housekeeper waited in the breakfast-room, menu book in one hand, engagement diary in the other. Mari brought a tray of fresh coffee, and the three women sat together, as on every other morning when Rhiannon was at home, discussing dinner parties and seating arrangements, the house and its staff, oiling the cogs of the machine Elis engineered for his wife and himself, and the boy who blighted their life. Half-listening to the chatter of woman and girl, Rhiannon thought of the secrets Arwel perhaps shared with Mari, and felt shamed and anxious about the tales told, the truths concealed, in her own machinations with authority.

"Shall I send your blue velvet dress for cleaning, ma'am?" Mari asked. "You'll want it for the dinner with the marquess."

Her eyes, Rhiannon thought, were knowing. What knowledge had been granted to a waif and a bastard but denied to herself? "No, thank you. The beaded black chiffon will be more appropriate."

"Black would be more fitting for Madam at the moment," the housekeeper observed.

"Do you know when the funeral will be, ma'am?" Mari asked, that knowledge still lighting her eyes.

"No," Rhiannon muttered. Her hand nudged the cup, sending splashes of half-cold coffee around the rim of the saucer. She looked mutely at the girl, power suddenly deserting her and lodging with her servant, and ventured to guess one of the secrets shared.


"It's the usual story," Janet told McKenna. "Nobody wants to talk to the police." She pulled cigarettes and lighter from her pocket. "I'm catching bad habits, sir. Do Dewi Prys and Inspector Tuttle nag every time you light up?"

"Respect for rank falls to their own prejudice at times."

"Dewi gets very jealous when you give anybody else attention."

"Don't gossip, Janet."

"I'm not." She smiled, a little condescendingly. "I don't think you realize why there's so much friction. Men tend to look at the end results, and ignore the antecedents."

"Then I must take your word for it. Talk to Mari again. You might find her more amenable now shock's giving way to understanding."

"She's tough, sir. She only says what she wants you to know."

"She learned her lessons early, didn't she?" Irritable with pain, uneasy with nameless sorrows, he rose. "Why people expect fostering to work is beyond me." He stood by the window, staring at the ash tree wreathed about with mist. "It's unnatural, yet people insist on trying, and look at the damage they cause. A ewe won't foster an orphan lamb unless it's wrapped in the fleece of her own dead offspring, yet we flout such rudimentary instinct."

"Fostering works sometimes. It depends on reason, not instinct."

"Mari seems a prime example of instinct proving the stronger."

Rapping at the door and walking in without invitation, Dewi smiled brightly at McKenna, and nodded to Janet. "Mr. Tuttle rang, sir. He might be a bit late, though he can't be fogbound, 'cos it's clearing. Mind you, it's too damp and still too bloody cold for it to shift altogether." He sat down, pulling his chair close to McKenna's desk. "I've been chatting to Bryn from the local radio."

"You're under strict instructions not to talk to the media."

"He's heard something about a minister, and rang to see if we knew."

"Which minister?"

"The Reverend Christmas Morgan from Capel Bedwyr."

"He hasn't been there since Easter," Janet said.

"You'd know, wouldn't you?" Dewi asked. "Where is he now, then?"

"On retreat somewhere."

"And d'you know what he's retreating from?" Dewi asked. "Bryn's heard the reverend's got too much of a liking for the sins of the flesh. Young flesh in particular."

• • •

Fidgeting with paper-clips and pens, Jack waited for McKenna to finish his telephone conversation, before apologizing for his late arrival.

"Not to worry, Jack. Dewi's trawling the silt which clogs up the streams of life around here, trying to locate a renegade minister." McKenna pulled his arm from the sling, flexing his fingers, massaging the elbow. "What kept you?"

"Children," Jack sighed. "My own."

"The twins don't often cause trouble."

"It's been brewing for days. Talk about secret lives! And parents are the last to know. Still, we know now. Em says you'll have to deal with it."

"Deal with what? Have they taken to a life of crime?"

Jack smiled wanly. "One's got a boyfriend, and the other's got her nose pushed right out of joint. They've had an almighty fight. Fists, hair-pulling, screaming, then floods of tears. We were up half the night, and of course, Em wouldn't let them go to school today." Picking at a scratch on the desk, he added, "They've been so tense the past few days I thought they'd explode. The boyfriend's just started back at school. He's been in Blodwel, because he got a bit out of hand when his dad walked out."

"You'll never approve of any boyfriend, whatever his background."

"I won't, will I?"

"What does Emma want me to do?"

"Talk to him, and the twins, if necessary. He knew Arwel, but that's all they're telling us."

"And you really think they'll tell me more?"

"Information's like currency," McKenna told Owen Griffiths. "The more you have, the richer and more powerful you become, especially if the information is potentially scandalous and damaging. I'd like a share of the wealth."

"What wealth?"

"The riches stored in the minds of our most senior officers, or written in the files shoved at the back of the safe in
the chief constable's office."

"Why?"

"I think undue influence is being brought to bear."

"That's a very serious allegation."

"I can't think of any other reason why this investigation
should be deliberately hampered. Can you?"

"Who says it is?"

Unwarranted anger surged in McKenna, running through
the pain, diluting its power. He thought distractedly of the
power of distraction. "Why not just tell me what you're being
told to do or not do?"

"I'm not being told anything."

"Is that true, or are you coasting along to retirement doing
your own imitation of Pontius Pilate? You've had your ear to
the ground well enough for years. You could point me in the
right direction, but the only help we're getting is from a hack
reporter on local radio."

Emma Tuttle placed a mug of coffee within reach of
McKenna's good arm, an ashtray beside it, and thought how
frail he looked, almost exhausted of life-energy. "You look ill."

"I'm not sleeping very well. Too much pain, I expect."

"Jack can't understand why you don't take time off."

"And what would I do? Mope about the house, bored and
still in pain?"

"You could go away. You haven't had a holiday for ages.
You know we'd look after the cat."

"Perhaps when this mess is sorted." He sipped the coffee,
watching her, wishing and despairing simultaneously. "Seen
Denise lately?" he asked, finding another occupation for his
thoughts.

"Not lately. She's otherwise occupied."

"Best of luck to her, I suppose."

"Don't you mind?"

"No." He lit a cigarette, and leaned back. "I don't, and there's a tragedy in there somewhere."

"I think she rather hoped you would, hence the rather public spectacle she wants you to notice. She doesn't know you very well, does she? Always miscalculating."

"We're walking separate roads, Emma, further and further apart. I imagine Denise is going where she wants."

"And where are you going?"

"I'm marking time." He smiled wryly. "Perhaps I'm too old to start a new journey. I've renewed the lease on the house. Dug in, as it were."

"You do need a holiday," Emma insisted. "Foreign places, foreign sunshine, and new people to take you out of yourself."

"What would I do with new people? And the terrible disappointment of finding they aren't what I hoped after all the effort of getting to know them?"

Emma stared at him, tempted almost beyond conscience. He raised his eyes, awareness ablaze. "Tell me about the twins, and the boyfriend."


"I know Gary Hughes," Dewi said. "His mam kicked her old man out about a year ago, 'cos he wouldn't keep away from other women."

"So what's new about that?" Janet commented.

"Has he been in trouble with us?" McKenna asked.

"He just gave his mam a hard time after his dad left. Boys always blame their mother, don't they?" Dewi said. "Mothers are supposed to keep things together, not let the world fall apart."

"Why can't men ever see things from a woman's perspective?" Janet demanded. "What was she supposed to do? Stay with a philandering jackal for the boy's benefit? What about her own life?"

"Oh, spare us the women's lib stuff, Constable," Dewi said. "I'm saying how it is, not making moral judgements."

"Where's the Reverend Morgan?" McKenna asked.

"A place called Hafodty on Sychnant Pass," Janet said. "I asked my father."

"You and Inspector Tuttle can visit him, then."

Janet frowned. "D'you think I should, sir? I know him."

"All the better, don't you think? He'll be pleased to see a friendly face."


"God! What a dump!" Dewi drew into the kerb, running over empty beer cans in the gutter and plastic carrier-bags brittle with frost. "The navvies who built the railway lived in this terrace, sir, and that was a very long time ago. Most of the houses still don't have a bathroom or inside lavvy." Locking the car, he added, "And most of the people in them'll be scrounging dole or income support, so they don't deserve any better, do they?"

Gary Hughes's mother, small and dark, and sharp in face and shape, stared at the two men. "What do the police want with Gary? He's never been in trouble."

"We want to ask him about Blodwel," McKenna said.

"Oh," Mrs. Hughes said. "I see."

Decorated in beige and brown, unrelieved by imagination, dominated by a large old television set, the small sitting-room smelt of mildew and rising damp. Mrs. Hughes crouched on the edge of her beige chair. "I'm not sure he should talk to you. He's worse since he came out of that place than when he went in." Distress clouded her eyes. "I never wanted him there, but the social worker said he should go for assessment, to help him and me get on better, but Gary thinks I tried to get shut of him, like he says I got rid of his dad."

"How has he been worse?" McKenna asked.

"Oh, I don't know!" Tears glimmered. "Like he hates me! God knows what people've said to him."

"It might help if he tells us," McKenna suggested. "Especially if his experience at Blodwel was unpleasant."

"Who told you about him? Social Services?"

"He knows the daughters of one of our officers. These young people seem very distressed about the death of the Blodwel boy."

"He was on the run, wasn't he? Gary says the children run away a lot. He didn't because he was scared of going to prison for it."

"Did Social Services help you with him?" Dewi asked.

Mrs. Hughes smiled grimly. "Not that I've noticed. The social worker brought him back when Blodwel finished with him, dumped him on the doorstep, and went. We haven't seen or heard from her since." She wiped her thin hands over her eyes, restoring the contours of her face. "You may as well talk to him, but you'll have to come back after school. He's going every day. I know he's not dodging because I check. Somebody's put the fear of God in him about that. It's the nastiness to me I can't cope with."


Standing knee-deep in golden bracken rimed silver-white with frost, Janet looked up the drive to an imposing stone house, double-fronted and steeply gabled. "D'you know why it's called *Hafodty*, sir? It must've been a *hafod*, a summer holding where the farmer moved his animals to fresh grazing."

"When?" Jack asked, with little interest.

"In the old days. Moving people and stock according to the time of year is called transhumance."

Jack gazed at mountain flanks bare and frost-hard, girdled with swathes of the dying bracken, hollows filled with mist drifting like gunsmoke. "And where did they live the rest of the time?"

"Lower down." Janet kicked at the bracken, sending puffs of leaf dust and frost in the air. "In a *hendre*. That's why so many houses are called *Hafod* and *Hendre*."

A string of horses clattered up the road, led by a huge black animal with a white blaze aslant its face. Janet watched, hands deep in her pockets. "There's a riding stables down the pass. Did Mr. McKenna fall off one of their horses?"

"He landed somewhere in the middle of Anglesey, and I had to go for him because he wouldn't have an ambulance, then my wife had to drive over later for me to get his car. He should've known better!"

"People fall off horses quite often. You're taught how to do it without hurting yourself when you learn to ride."

"Nobody ever taught the chief inspector, did they?" Jack marched to the wide white gate barring the driveway, un-hooked the latch, and pushed it open. "How well d'you know this minister?"

"As well as we know most of the local ministers, I sup-pose."

"What's he like?"

"Usual sort of minister."

"Oh, I see," Jack said, stamping his feet as they waited for the door to be opened. "It's usual for ministers not to be able to keep their grubby hands off the youngsters, is it?"

"I didn't mean that!" Janet snapped. "I just meant he never seemed different to anyone else."

The room was like a summer garden, Jack thought, preserved for the bitter months of winter. He sat in a deep chair, its linen cover splashed with leaves and peony roses, his feet buried in thick green carpet. A huge log fire blazed with high-summer heat, crystal wall-lights in chimney alcoves and a crystal chandelier lit gauzy flowers of pink and purple-blue and golden yellow festooning the walls.

"Who pays for all this?"

"It's run by a health and pension fund. People come here to convalesce."

"From what? The shock of having their sins found out?"

"You're very cynical," Janet commented.

"And you're still wet behind the ears."

The carved oak door slid open, bringing a faint scent of roasting lamb and the Reverend Christmas Morgan, a short thin man with wispy greying hair and china-blue eyes, crêpey skin overlapping his dog-collar. He smiled at Janet, exposing teeth stained yellow with nicotine. "How lovely to see you, my dear! How's your dear father? And who's the friend you've brought to see me?"

"And is the Reverend Christmas Morgan queer as a nine-bob note?" Eifion Roberts asked. "I blame his parents. Fancy calling a lad 'Christmas'!"

"Dewi's informant got his wires a bit crossed," McKenna said. "This reverend ran off with a young lady. His interests seem within normal limits, but he has heard there's a trade in young boys."

"What's new? Young boys've been worth their weight in gold since mankind discovered the stuff. Who's trading the commodity round here?"

"He doesn't know. He would only commit himself to saying adultery isn't necessarily always sinful because it's sometimes unavoidable, as in his case, presumably." McKenna lit a cigarette. "So he's recovering from this unavoidable moral lapse at the expense of the chapel."

"Folk always accommodate their own, don't they? I'll wager the reverend could give chapter and verse on a damned sight more than the Bible, like Owen Griffiths knows a few dirty secrets he doesn't want to sully his mouth repeating. But that's we Welsh. Peasants so used to wading neck-deep in shit we don't notice the stink any more."

"You're irredeemably irreverent, Eifion. You'll go to Hell."

"I'll be able to keep up old acquaintanceships, then. How long d'you plan on staying in limbo while other folk dictate what you can do and when you can do it?"

• • •

"Eifion Roberts finds Arwel's situation very disturbing." Mc-Kenna lit a cigarette. "He feels the boy should be swinging the earth like a bauble from his wrist, rather than lying in a mortuary drawer with his head in pieces and his body cobbled together, although he does intend to reassemble the head properly. Undertakers don't always do a very good job, apparently."

Seated behind his desk, uniform pressed and emblazoned, Owen Griffiths looked somewhere beyond McKenna's left shoulder. "I'd prefer you not to smoke. It makes the room smell unpleasant."

"Corruption generally smells most unwholesome. Worse than Eifion Roberts's mortuary, I imagine. He wonders if Arwel rebelled against more than the usual oppression to which those in authority subject children." Smoke drifted towards the ceiling. "He says rebellion can be a moral necessity."

"Eifion Roberts never did know when to shut up."

"You do, though. Don't you?" McKenna tapped ash from his cigarette. "Elis is a Beethoven enthusiast, and as I don't want to appear a cultural Neanderthal, I borrowed Beethoven's Letters from the university library yesterday, and found the most interesting comment on the state of man. He thought friendship and monarchy and empires mere fog, which any gust of wind can transform or blow away. Citing Terence, he notes that deference begets friends, but truth begets hatred, so there must be truth in what I said earlier which transformed our erstwhile friendship."

"You don't know when to shut up, either. And you play with fire."

"And I can't screech when I get burnt." He dropped the cigarette in the ashtray, grinding it to shreds. "I won't accept the unacceptable, so I make myself unacceptable. What will you do with me?"

"What I should've done already, and insist you go off sick before you do any more damage." Griffiths stared angrily at the younger man. "If you were less inclined to let other people's ideas flummox your thinking, and spent less time gossiping with Eifion Roberts, you might be able to focus. Eifion's got no faith in religion, so he has to look elsewhere. He can't do his job unless he fills his head with outlandish thoughts, and however interesting, they won't tell you how Arwel Thomas died."

McKenna lit another cigarette, his hands trembling.

"If you want the truth, I'm bloody seething!" Griffiths added. "You've no right to speak to me the way you did, whether you're in pain or not! I'm not involved in any cover-up, and nobody's telling me what to do, and for all I know, your little performance might be a diversionary tactic, so I don't notice you haven't a bloody clue what you're doing. And don't bother saying your hands are tied. If they weren't before, it'll serve you right if they are after the way you behaved towards that boy's social worker! Was there any need to be so bloody aggressive? And fancy letting Janet Evans say what she did! What sort of example are you setting her, for God's sake?" The superintendent paused for breath, then added, "You've let Elis get under your skin, and now you're chafing others. Jack was perfectly happy thinking the world revolved around his belly and the marital bed, but now he's wittering about things he'll never properly understand or appreciate, and miserable with it. You're not doing Dewi Prys any favours, either. He'd follow you to the edge of the world, so mind you don't let him fall off." He frowned. "Have you bothered to ask yourself why Social Services don't want you at Blodwel? Has it occurred to you Blodwel staff have nothing to answer for?"

"How about criminal negligence?"

"For not listening to that doctor? Maybe Social Services made the right decision, on information they don't care to share with us. Eifion can say Arwel was raped while he was on the run from Blodwel, but he can't date the other lesions with any real degree of accuracy, and no one knows how Arwel spent most of his time before his admission to Blodwel, though we know where he spent a lot of his time after."

"I hadn't by any means discounted Elis."

"You can't discount anybody. Have you formulated any proper plan? All I can see is Blodwel blocking up the end of your tunnel vision."

"You know perfectly well what we've done so far, and what enquiries are ongoing." McKenna stubbed out the half-smoked cigarette. "And whatever my present shortcomings, your messages are rather mixed, if not confused. Am I to hand over to Jack Tuttle, or will someone else be brought in? Is Blodwel out of the running or not?"

"Oh, bloody get off your high horse, Michael! You're riding for another fall!"

Flicking his lighter on and off, McKenna stared at the flame until it began to die.

"You rammed a bitter pill in my mouth," Griffiths said, his voice softer, "but Arwel's more important than your feelings or mine, so I swallowed it. Let's hope it doesn't poison me, eh? You're to interview staff and children at Blodwel between six and eight-thirty this evening. Make the most of it, because I doubt there'll be another opportunity." He smiled. "You know what Dewi Prys'll say, don't you? Something like 'About bloody time! Hogg must've finished getting shut of the evidence.'"

Dim lights behind Blodwel's windows cast fuzzy shapes on grass sparkling with frost, tinting the white mist which drifted about the walls and in and out of the bushes and trees on the lower slopes of the hill. McKenna heard train wheels screaming between the two tunnels and thought again of Arwel Thomas.

Doris Hogg opened the front door, waiting while the officers filed past into the musty hall. Three women, Dilys Roberts among them, and a weed of a man with a straggling beard, stood silently against the wall, watching her harry the police officers towards the children's quarters.

McKenna stopped. "We shouldn't all descend on the children. Perhaps you'd show my officers where the children can be interviewed, while Inspector Tuttle and myself introduce ourselves."

As she turned about heel and began pushing the others in another direction, Dilys Roberts broke from the group, and not looking at either, led the men down the rear corridor. McKenna heard no voices, no television, no sounds of life. In the stale and heavy air, he smelt fear, that age-old scent clawing at instincts. He followed the woman, remarking on her brutish silhouette, and thought she looked as mean and forbidding as her miserable habitat.

Standing by the open door, Jack breathing down his neck, he looked into a room where eight bodies inhabited a silence punctuated by heavy panting breaths, seated in armless chairs upholstered in orange plastic, and ranged against the walls. In one corner, an antiquated television set blinked snowy pictures, without sound to relieve the tedium and silliness. Bare of pictures, the walls were painted a cold pale green, the floor covered in dun matting, the whole room nude of playthings and children's litter.

Heads tucked in chests like baby birds trying to weather a storm, three little boys crouched in their seats, beside a gangling bullet-headed youth with slitted lupine eyes, who lolled on his chair, stockinged feet thrust towards the middle of the room. McKenna noticed absently that none of the children wore shoes or slippers, and heard a giggle swallowed into extinction as the slouch-shouldered wench with rat-tail hair in the next chair put a hand over her mouth. Beside her sat a crew-cut androgynous youth, clad in jeans and sweatshirt, three rings in one ear and a spider's web tattooed across neck and jaw. Legs crossed, the girl in the next seat ran her fingers through the cloud of red-gold curly hair tumbling about her shoulders. Her face was pale-skinned and vixenish. She lowered her lashes as McKenna looked, then opened a rosebud mouth in a little knowing smile, sharp teeth biting her lower lip. She glanced at the woman beside her, who patted the thin young hand, then rose, moving to the middle of the room in a swirl of pleated skit and a drift of expensive scent. Her back to the two men, she said, "The police must ask you some questions, but there's nothing to worry about. One of the staff will be with you all the time." Turning to McKenna, she added, "I am Councillor Mrs. Elis. I trust none of you will abuse the co-operation of Mr. Hogg and his staff."

"I foresee no problems, Councillor." McKenna held out his hand. "May I introduce Inspector Tuttle? He hasn't yet had the pleasure of meeting your husband."

"Never off duty in this job." Ronald Hogg smiled unctuously, crossed his legs and nipped at trouser creases with a thumb and forefinger. "I expect you know the feeling."

"Then maybe we should skip the social chit-chat," Jack said. "Can you tell us who decided to ignore an expert medical opinion about Arwel Thomas?"

"I don't recall any such opinion."

"You were told Arwel displayed the classic signs of abuse."

Hogg nodded. "By someone who'd never set eyes on him before, and had no idea how devious he was. It's not a good idea to jump to every crack of the whip."

"But Arwel was viciously and persistently abused."

"But he didn't actually say so to that doctor." Hogg shifted in his chair, realigning the trouser creases. "Our frames of reference aren't like yours, Inspector. We have to consider all the pros and cons, and assess the impact of investigation, on the child and everyone else. Is the child strong enough to cope? Might we do more harm than good? You know how much damage can be done by disclosing abuse."

"Keeping quiet does a lot more damage," Jack commented. "It got Arwel killed."

"That's your interpretation, with the benefit of hindsight, I might add. I know the doctor's suspicions have since been confirmed, but we've no idea how the injuries were acquired."

"Perhaps he sat on the top of Snowdon too long!"

"Jack, please!" McKenna intervened.

"What is this?" Hogg looked from one to the other. "The nasty-cop-nice-cop routine?" He almost laughed. "Good heavens!"

"I'm afraid we're all under considerable pressure," McKenna said. "Inspector Tuttle meant no offence."

"Aren't we all under pressure?" Hogg smiled generously. "Institutions demoralize the people in them, and the police force is no exception." He shook his head sadly. "But they can brutalize people as well, can't they? Such a pity."

"Could you discuss the decision not to refer Arwel for further examination?" McKenna asked. "And would it be possible for us to see his file?"

"Well, not really, to either." Hogg frowned. "But the decision was fully endorsed at the highest level. The file's been returned to County Hall. You'll have to apply to the director."

McKenna nodded. "We'll do that. We'll also need a formal statement from someone about the decision not to report Arwel's absconding."

Hogg smiled again. "I'll send you a copy of the memo we had after your chief constable complained to my director about the cost, manpower, and sheer trouble of chasing absconders." The smile died. "I'll regret to my dying day that we didn't find the boy, but these things happen, and a boy as devious as that won't be found. I wouldn't be surprised if his sister knew where he was. She's a bit of a hussy, isn't she? Did you know the father's been in prison for benefit fraud? What a family!"

"Arwel had some savings, I believe," McKenna said.

"County Hall's dealing with that. I daresay the benefit agency will have first call, to offset funeral costs."

Flattening his hand against the radiator in McKenna's office, Jack said, "Some idiot's turned the heating down."

"It's after nine," McKenna said. "Most people have gone

home." He rubbed at knotted muscle and stiffened sinew. "We should've gone home, as well, instead of wasting our time at Blodwel."

"That little exercise was scuppered before it started," Dewi said. "Fancy wheeling in Rhiannon. She's very matey with the Hoggs, isn't she?"

"They're all watching out for each other. How did you get on with the children?"

Dewi tossed a sheaf of statement forms on the desk. "Guess. Nobody knows nothing."

"Nobody dare say anything, you mean," Janet commented. "Doris stuck to me like a bloody leech, frowning and shaking her head every time the kids looked like saying more than 'dunno', or 'I can't say, miss.' Poor little things were frightened half to death, and they're dreadfully tense."

"They're not 'poor little things,'" Jack said irritably. "Your sympathy's overcoming your common sense. They're the next generation of villains and slags and general bad apples."

"Mr. Tuttle's right," Dewi said. "They look like God didn't quite make them right, so we'd know who to look out for. That redhead in the tight jeans was dead pretty 'til she opened her mouth. She's got the weirdest teeth, off-centre and pointy like fangs, and the biggest tongue I've ever seen outside of a cow's mouth."

"Trust you to notice." Jack's face pinched with disapproval.

"Couldn't help myself, sir. She was licking her lips and making up to me all the time."

"Pity you couldn't charm some information out of her, isn't it?"

"The staff don't look normal either," Janet said. "The women look dog-rough, and that man like he's been reared in a cupboard."

"He's only been there a few months," McKenna said. "He's a psychology graduate who now wants to help young people grow into worthwhile citizens, so he'll train as a social worker, once he's proved his mettle in the 'demanding field of residential childcare.' He's enjoying the challenges already."

"What a brown-nose!" Jack sneered.

McKenna sighed. "Eifion Roberts brands them all suspect, but there must be some decent people in social work, even though it's a thankless job." He paused, lighting a cigarette. "I can't help but feel sorry for those children. However mischievous they are, they're only children."

"They're the dregs of society," Jack said.

"Can we get back on track, sir?" Janet asked. "It's getting late."

"And what track would that be?" Dewi said.

"The one leading to the others who legged it with Arwel. Although you didn't notice, Constable, most of them have done a disappearing act."


Comforted somewhat by a hot bath, a near overdose of analgesics, and the cat, warm and purring in his lap, McKenna leafed through the first volume of Beethoven's Letters, pausing now and then to read the Teutonic syntax of the composer's French, before returning to the first letter, and the poignant statements of a sixteen-year-old boy recently bereaved of his mother.

The telephone interrupted his reading and, fearing it was Denise, who had pushed a note through the letterbox sometime during the day, he let the answering machine take the call, picking up the receiver only when he heard Jack's voice, brittle with anxiety.

"I know it's late. Jesus! We could do without this!"

"What's happened?"

"Trouble too close to home." Jack coughed. "Em's frantic. One of the twins ran away, and I've just found her by Menai Bridge, sitting in the bus shelter crying her eyes out."

"But why?"

"That Hughes boy, would you believe? He went home at dinnertime, found you'd called, and went berserk with the girls. He says he never wants to set eyes on them again, and they've ruined everything."

"What could they ruin?"

"I don't know! Em's no idea, either."

"Do the girls know?"

"I don't know!"

"Think! Getting hysterical won't help, will it?"

"I can't think! You've no children, you don't know what it's like! You can't even imagine how it feels when your child goes missing. It's like the end of the world! Indescribably dreadful, like someone's ripping out your guts!" His voice began to rise, edged with panic. "Suppose they do it again, and we can't find them?"

"Pull yourself together and talk to them. They must have some idea what's wrong."

"I've broken their trust, and they'll never tell me anything ever again," Jack said bitterly. "Because I told you, and you went to see Gary Hughes."

"They're overwrought. They're too intelligent to believe that sort of rubbish."

"Are they? You could've fooled me! Em says their emotions are running wild, and she should know."

"Emma's as distraught as you, if not more so." McKenna put down the book, reaching for his cigarettes. "Where are they now? In bed?"

"Are you trying to be funny? They're locked in their room, and Em's sitting on the floor outside, begging them to come out, or just talk to her. What if they go through the window? They could climb on the kitchen roof and be off."

"D'you want me to come? I can get a taxi."

"Please!" Jack's breath caught, almost a sob.


Dewi, voice slurred with sleep, said, "Mrs. Hughes won't fancy being knocked up in the middle of the night, sir. It isn't really her problem, is it?"

"We don't know what the problem is, or who it belongs to. Call me at Jack Tuttle's if there's anything to report."

• • •

Emma crouched at the top of the staircase, hair wild, face blotched and sodden with tears, clothing twisted and rumpled. "I'm so terribly, terribly sorry!" she whispered. "Oh, God! They didn't go to school until after lunch. Oh, God!"

McKenna put out his hand and smoothed the damp hair from her forehead, while Jack crashed around in the kitchen below, making coffee. Catching hold of his fingers, Emma squeezed so hard she hurt, holding his hand while more tears splashed down, burning his flesh. Had Rhiannon Elis, he wondered, svelte and groomed and unruffled, shed such bitter hot tears over her own child?

"Are the twins in bed?"

"I don't know. I don't know what they're doing."

McKenna stood up, weary like the old man he felt he had become. Emma held fast to his hand. "Let's see if they'll talk to me." He pulled himself gently away, and knocked on the bedroom door. The scuffling sounds ceased, as if the room and occupants held their breath. "Let me in, will you? I need to talk to you."

"Why?" demanded one of the girls, her voice sharp and hard and angry.

"Because you're caught up in something that isn't your problem."

"That's his fault! He'd no right to say anything."

"Your father had a responsibility to tell me. One boy from that place is dead, Gary's very frightened, and you're no help behaving like this."

"You grown-ups are all dishonest! You swarm around us to get what you want, then start being horrible! You don't care!"

Wondering idly which twin spoke, or if each poured out her distress in turn, he leaned against the door. Emma stood in the middle of the landing, all progress suspended, all normality evaporated.

"If we didn't care," McKenna pointed out, "I wouldn't be

here, and your parents wouldn't look like a bomb exploded in their faces. You'll be sixteen in a few months, so why not act your age?"

"That's what they say!"

"It's valid comment in the circumstances. We were all out of bed a lot earlier than you this morning, and we're very tired."

"Were you in bed when he rang?" The voice was tentative, softer.

"I'd had a bath."

"Is your arm still bad?" The voice was closer, its owner behind the door.

"It hurts. It hurts even more when I'm cold and tired."

The key turned in the lock, and the door was pulled open. A more youthful replica of Emma looked up at him, while the other sat on her bed, wrapped in a flowery quilt. Emma, lunging forward, found her way barred by McKenna. "Leave them to me for now."


"Which one of you is Gary's girlfriend?" McKenna sat on the other bed, leaning on the pillows.

"He's not a proper boyfriend."

"How long have you known him?"

"Oh, ages. Since we went to senior school."

The other girl frowned. "He disappeared one day, and nobody knew where he'd gone. We thought he was dead, then we saw him in town with the Blodwel kids, wearing that horrible uniform."

"Has he been different since he came home?"

"Yes."

"How different?" McKenna yawned.

"Strange. Quiet, but sort of angry underneath, probably because his mother made him go there."

"Like most parents in her circumstances, Mrs. Hughes trusted professional advice."

"Gary say social workers are crap, and he wouldn't put a dog in Blodwel."

"What else has he said? What did he say today?"

"It didn't make any sense, did it?" The twins looked at each other. "He shouted and sort of screamed and then started crying."

"What was he shouting about?" Downstairs, McKenna heard the telephone ring.

"He was raving about Hogg and other people, saying we'd ruined everything, and Hogg would send him to a lock-up in South Wales, but he didn't make any sense. He hasn't done anything wrong, has he?"

"Not that we know of." McKenna heard feet padding up the stairs. Emma stood in the doorway, a tray of hot drinks in her hands.

"Coffee's ready downstairs, and Dewi Prys is on the phone."


"Looks like Gary's done a bunk, sir," Dewi said. "He didn't come back from school, and his mam says there's clothes missing."

"Dear God!" McKenna said. "Why didn't she tell us earlier?"

"She thought he might've gone to his cousin in Caernarfon. He's been going regular since he left Blodwel, but she's been there, and nobody's seen him. She can't think where else he might be 'cos he lost touch with most of his mates being in Blodwel."

"Where are you now?"

"Collecting a missing person's form. You don't want to leave circulating his details, do you?" Dewi paused. "And I called Blodwel, to see if anyone's missing. Doris says not, and we're not to harass them any more."

Chastened, quietened, the twins crouched on the sofa, one each side of Emma, clinging to her arms.

"We'd tell you. Honestly, we don't know where he's gone."

"Who's he friendly with at school?"

"Only us, really. The others've been dead snotty since he came back."

"Why?"

"Because he went to Blodwel!" The girl sounded exasperated.

# •Chapter•
# 5

"People say you can catch sin as easily as the plague," Owen Griffiths said. "This running away's reaching epidemic proportions. Pity Jack's girls got near the source of infection, isn't it? D'you think there's a bit of hysteria there? Adolescent attention-seeking?"

McKenna yawned, and shivered. "Probably where the twins are concerned, but not with Gary Hughes. He seems to be in some distress."

"That can be catching, too. If you could see yourself, you'd call the doctor. What time did you get to bed? Not before the early hours, I'll bet."

"You've often told me sleep's a luxury in this job." McKenna took out cigarettes and lighter. "We must find Gary quickly. He's the only person who's admitted to being friendly with Arwel, and he could be in danger."

"You can use whatever resources you need. Who's his social worker?"

"Same as Arwel's."

Griffiths smiled wryly. "You've a cat in hell's chance of any help from her, then."

"I wouldn't ask. I don't want Social Services to know we're interested in him. The fewer the better, in case we alert the person he's cause to fear."

Doodling on his blotter, Griffiths said, "Arwel was probably friendly with the kids who've disappeared from Blodwel in the past few days, but you can't even employ subterfuge to find them, can you? We don't know their names."

"Dewi's asking around. Finding one would be enough." Lighting the cigarette he had been holding, McKenna added, "They may be red herrings. Persistent absconders need more security than Blodwel can offer. Or they were moved as part of an existing treatment plan."

"More casework decisions, you mean? When a doctor's treatment makes the patient worse, it's called an iatro-genetic syndrome. What d'you call botched social work interventions?"

"You don't. Negative outcome's ascribed to the innate incorrigibility of the client. People would say nothing can be done with the likes of the Thomases, for instance," McKenna said. "Jack took exhaustive statements about their whereabouts last week, which Caernarfon police are checking. Tom Thomas eventually admitted to spending time at the bookies and in the pubs with his mates when Peggy thought he was actively seeking work, as the saying is, and she eventually owned up to a part-time job the benefit agency doesn't know about. Neither of them wanted to admit Elis took Arwel to see them."

"You'd be afraid with all those authority structures holding power over your head like the Sword of Damocles. What about Carol?"

"She seems to have said all she wants us to know."

"Let's hope you can make her change her mind, then. Will you be seeing our local luminary again soon?"

McKenna stubbed out his cigarette. "His wife might be more use to us."

Slumped at his desk, Jack yawned jaw-wrenchingly, drained of all feeling by the firestorm of the night. He wondered if his sensation of lightness was a product of exhaustion, or true foreknowledge that the worst was over, and smiled weakly at Dewi Prys, slumped in another chair.

"Can you get sleep-bankrupt?"

"Most probably," Dewi said. "Dunno where you'd go for a loan."

"Bankrupts can't get loans."

"Then Hogg's only morally bankrupt." Dewi stood up to stretch. "I checked his credit rating. Smell of roses all round, in fact, 'til you're close enough to smell the shit he's standing in."

"What's that horrible smell in Blodwel?"

"Fear. The kids are afraid of the staff, the staff are terrified of the kids, and everybody shits themselves when Hogg shows up. Even the lovely Doris. He's a nasty vicious bastard and they're all his prisoners, all doing time."

"Social Services don't seem to think so."

"He's a con artist. I told the chief inspector, I'm telling you, and I'll tell anybody who cares to listen."

"That's slander. You could get done for it."

"Hogg'd have to prove me a liar first."

Jack yawned again, and leafed through the statements taken at Blodwel. "Either these kids are stupid, like people say, or terrified, like Janet said. Where is she?"

"Asking Mari Williamson if she knows Gary Hughes." Dewi yawned. "Let's hope she asks Mr. Posh ab Elis and his wife as well."

"D'you think there's a Menai Triangle?" Jack asked. "Like the Bermuda Triangle, only kids disappear instead? Four gone like a puff of smoke from Blodwel, one gone off the face of the earth from school. You sure he didn't get a visit or phone call at school?"

"The teachers say not. He must've taken his clothes at dinnertime, 'cos his mam was home all afternoon." Dewi flicked the slats of the venetian blind. "I reckon we panicked him. Have you noticed it's not so cold?"

Jack shivered. "I'm too bloody tired to be warm."

"What say I talk to the cousin in Caernarfon?"

"Caernarfon police already did. He's not seen Gary for weeks, despite what Mrs. Hughes thinks."

"Wouldn't tell us if he had. Kids close ranks when outsiders start asking questions."

"Fancy that," Jack said. "Just like us and Social Services."


Mari wept, copiously and noisily, rocked in Rhiannon's arms, her tears leaving muddy splotches on the costly cloth of the woman's jacket. Janet watched, wondering if the girl was her surrogate child, sound in mind and limb if not in pedigree.

"When will your husband be back?"

"Can't you ever forget your job?" Rhiannon demanded. "Have you no feelings?"

"We have very strong feelings, Mrs. Elis," Janet said. "Especially about Arwel. I'm sorry talking about him upsets Mari, but we must."

"It upsets all of us. You can't know how much."

"Mari wasn't upset the other day."

"Things take time to sink in. All we need now is the media hanging around like vultures."

"I didn't see anyone on the way in," Janet said. "Why should they bother you?"

"Because we're good copy, aren't we? And someone will drop a hint in the right direction sooner or later." Rhiannon pulled another tissue from the box by her side, and wiped Mari's face. "I appreciate your concern about this other boy, but Mari knows nothing of significance. She'd tell you if she did." She sighed, and stroked the girl's damp hair. "These children are like flotsam on the tide, orphans of savage family storms."

"They share things with each other, especially when there's no one else."

"Not always, and you must believe what Mari says. You owe her that. You mustn't harass her because you've nobody else to question." Rhiannon frowned. "And it was wrong to interview the children at Blodwel that way."

"Social Services made the arrangements."

"They should know better, and I'm surprised Mr. Hogg

hasn't complained. Would you pour the coffee, please? I can't reach."

Janet marvelled at the weight of the solid silver pot, the delicacy of the translucent china banded in blue and gold. "D'you know the Hoggs well?" She added hot milk from another silver pot, and pushed the cups within reach of Mari and her guardian.

"Mr. Hogg has tremendous professional experience, of which the council would be very shortsighted not to take full advantage. Hence his extensive responsibility for childcare services."

"How long have you held the committee chair?"

"Since the last elections."

"And what will the committee do about his unfortunate business?"

Rhiannon frowned. "What should we do? These things happen. Childcare is very risky work, and social workers are very vulnerable."

"To what?"

"Complaints. Violence." Rhiannon picked up her cup, and Mari reached forward for her own. "And to being held responsible for everything the children might do. It's an impossible job."

"Have there been complaints about Blodwel?"

"I understand a boy alleged ill-treatment before he went to juvenile custody for a string of offences."

"Who investigated the complaint?"

"The director assured the committee the complaints were malicious, and we were happy to support his decision not to investigate."

"Might that not be a little shortsighted, Mrs. Elis? Councillors hold the legal responsibility, and endorsing such a decision might appear a conspiracy to outsiders."

"The director is well able to judge a situation and its implications."

Mari coughed suddenly, slopping coffee on her hand, and began her wailing again. Rhiannon pulled a handful of tissues from the box, dabbing at the reddened skin, soothing the girl's distress.

Janet stood up. "You need cold water on that, Mari. Let's go to the kitchen." She pulled the girl to her feet, hurrying her from the room. Standing beside her at the kitchen sink, holding the trembling hand under the spurting tap, Janet felt a feverish trembling course through the girl's whole body. "If you've anything to tell me, Mari, for God's sake do it!"

Mari wrenched herself away, and fled the room.

"The elected members on most councils defer to the experts in their employment," McKenna said. "They're usually happy to believe what those experts tell them. I'm more interested in what you said that made Mari weep so bitterly."

Janet lit a cigarette. "She had nothing more to say about Arwel and his parents, so I asked about Carol, and she said Carol's a bloody slag, and burst into tears. Then Rhiannon walked in. Mari says she's never heard of Gary Hughes. Neither has Rhiannon. I thought of asking her where Hogg dumped those other kids, but she might've thrown a wobbler."

"As well you didn't." McKenna frowned. "When did Elis go away? He said nothing to me."

"He'd need to go further than Germany if he wanted to leg it properly. Rhiannon said he's buying a horse. I asked her how she got on with Arwel, but she didn't know him well. She and Elis have quite separate interests, and as horses aren't one of hers, Arwel wasn't either, though she'd noticed he was always hungry, always in the kitchen, cadging stuff off Mari and the cook. Those kids we saw last night looked half-starved, didn't they? And Dr. Roberts found Arwel's stomach virtually empty."

"About the Blodwel children, Janet."

"For some odd reason, they call the redhead with the funny teeth Mandy Minx," Janet said. "And the one with a bad perm and huge breasts is pregnant. Dilys Roberts was furious when she told me."

"Hogg has made a complaint, on behalf of the staff, claiming you and Dewi tried to make them leave you alone with the children."

"That's a lie!"

"He feels we may be subjecting Blodwel to unreasonable pressure, and refusing to accept that Arwel's death is entirely unrelated to his placement there. Dewi didn't help by ringing up Doris at midnight."

Janet flushed. "I'm sure our hierarchy can find somebody with two blind eyes and two deaf ears to take charge of the investigation. They could ask for volunteers at the next Lodge meeting."

"Have a care, Janet," McKenna warned. "Your career's just beginning. Upset the wrong people now, and you'll retire a constable."

"I'll resign rather than compromise my conscience!"

"Will you, though? I've seen many young officers strut the moral high-ground, only to accommodate their scruples and return to earth after a few enforced stumbles." Pulling a cigarette from the open packet on the desk, he added, "Protecting the institutional body always outweighs protecting the individual. Defective components have to be removed, much as a gangrenous limb is amputated."

"You don't believe that."

"I may be the exception necessary to prove the rule. I may not care to be an insider. I may be abnormal. I probably am. Robert Oppenheimer believed all men of goodwill desire the approval of their colleagues."

"He invented the nuclear bomb, didn't he?" Janet frowned. "So maybe the sort of approval he talked about ends in death and devastation."

"Where are they all?" Griffiths asked, standing at the door of McKenna's office, in the shadow of an early twilight. "The CID office is empty, and I can't find Jack Tuttle."

"I sent Jack home to get some sleep before the twins go on the rampage again. The others are traipsing round town asking questions, trying to find Gary Hughes, and whoever wasted Arwel Thomas."

"You shouldn't use Americanisms like 'wasted.' Not that it doesn't sum up what happened to Arwel." Griffiths sat down, hands on knees. "Seen Elis again yet?"

"He's done a bunk to Germany."

"I hope he hasn't. Extradition's a pain in the arse."

"We'll know when he doesn't come back."

"In my experience, absconding's an effect, not a cause. Jack knows that, doesn't he? I wish we could be more sure why children go from Blodwel with such depressing regularity."

"What's happening with Hogg's complaint?" McKenna asked.

"It's metaphorically under my bum for now." Griffiths smiled. "For as long as I can keep it there."

"If you'd like to create a diversion, you could make a complaint on our behalf," McKenna said. "Blodwel has sash windows with metal and plastic frames and perspex glazing, and the top sashes can't be opened more than a couple of inches because wood blocks have been nailed underneath on the outside. I didn't get a chance to examine the fire exits, but I wouldn't be surprised if those are locked or blocked."

"That's very serious. I'll have to inform the chief fire officer right away, won't I?"


Looking at the photograph provided by Mrs. Hughes, McKenna decided Gary was another pretty boy, wholly without Arwel's incandescent loveliness, but still pretty enough, although more of a man and less of a boy, his features already hardening into maturity. He wore a coquettish look, a heavy gold ring in one ear, his curly brown hair artfully styled to make the most of his face. Bedd y Cor and its leaf shroud reminded McKenna of one poem written in the fourteenth century. Dafydd ap Gwilym wrote too of the Gary Hughes of his day, calling him a pale-faced flirt of a boy with a lady's hair upon his head. McKenna prayed this boy flirted with nothing more than the power of his youth, but putting away the image in the newly opened file, he realized how fiercely that power invited its own extinction.

"Saw Dai Skunk," Dewi told McKenna. "Leaning against the wall by Valla's chippy at the bottom of High Street."

"Doing what?"

"Waiting for the Grim Reaper most probably."

"I daresay he won't have long to wait."

"One of Nain's friends is fed up waiting to find out what's happened to her grandson. He was shifted from Blodwel the other day without a word, and sent to South Wales. He's called Darren Pritchard."

"Where in South Wales?"

"Dunno yet. We'll find out. I had the impression we won't be shown the door by folk who've had kids in Blodwel, 'cos they reckon Hogg needs sorting. The local paper's planning a big spread about kids running away and getting killed, and some TV reporter's been talking to the locals and filming interviews." Dewi paused. "I get the feeling Blodwel's near internal collapse, so too much of the wrong sort of attention could be the last straw, couldn't it?"

"I wouldn't lay odds. Any news about Gary?"

"I waylaid a few kids outside school, but nobody wanted to talk about him."

"We'd better see his mother again." McKenna stood up. "She must be distraught. The Tuttles were beside themselves."

"She's nobody to turn to, has she?" Dewi said. "Still, you don't need to credit her with proper feelings, 'cos she lives in a shitty hole and looks like she doesn't deserve any better. D'you think social workers'd think twice about what they do to people if someone snatched their own kids and put them in Blodwel?"

"Needing social work is an admission of inadequacy, so it's a contradiction in terms to credit clients with normal feelings or perceptions." McKenna walked downstairs, Dewi in his wake. "Social workers are agents of social control, employed to keep the unruly hordes in some kind of order. Notably, the poor unruly hordes, which is why people fall over themselves to accommodate the likes of Elis." He shivered as freezing night air crept around his ankles, pulled a scarf high around his neck, and shivered again.

Dewi looked up at a sky milky with cloud, the moon a pale hazy disc. "It's full moon tonight. It could get warmer."

"It could get colder, too," McKenna said. "Always expect the worst, then you'll have such lovely surprises when it fails to arrive."

Parking in the only space available, behind a battered Ford Escort half on the pavement, Eifion Roberts puffed and panted up the hill towards McKenna's house, and saw Denise McKenna, snug in a new sheepskin coat, unlocking the door of her own brand new car. She ignored him, driving off with a flourish of tyres and plumes of exhaust fumes, her pale face and gilded hair luminous in the dashboard light.

"Your wife looks very glamorous," he said, as McKenna closed the front door. "Very cosily posh in her new coat. An early Yuletide gift from her admirer, d'you think?"

"I don't know. I didn't care to ask."

"Did you care to ask if she knows Elis?" Roberts sat on the chesterfield, drawing a protest from the cat, a louder one from the springs, holding his hands to the fire.

"He doesn't mix socially."

"Won't be much use as Lord Lieutenant then, unless Councillor Rhiannon does enough mixing for both of them. Stupid woman! Fancy letting herself be fobbed off over that Hogg and his nasty habits."

McKenna hovered over him. "D'you want anything in particular? Not to be churlish, but I'm tired. No one had much sleep last night."

"I won't keep you from your lonely bed too long." Roberts eyed the sling on McKenna's arm. "You want to get that off before the circulation seizes up, never mind the muscles."

"The hospital said a week. The ligaments were badly wrenched."

"They'll be healing." He stood up. "Let's have a look."

McKenna bit his lips to quell a screech of pain as the pathologist removed the sling, pulled the stiffened arm straight, and began a vigorous massage from wrist to shoulder and across the back of the neck.

"You're all knotted up," he commented, kneading and pummelling, digging thumbs into the hollows beneath McKenna's shoulder-blades. "I rang the lab today. Arwel's blood tests aren't ready, but a good DNA profile came from the semen traces in the body. What about the site search?"

"Hundreds of tyre tracks," McKenna said, words punctuated by the rhythms of Eifion Roberts's hands. "Enough litter and other rubbish to silt up Menai Strait." He coughed. "No sign of Arwel's clothes, or anything else useful. How long will the blood tests be?" His own blood began to course through atrophied muscle and tissue.

"A few days." Roberts held McKenna's arm at the elbow and gently rotated the shoulder. "Are you making any progress?"

"We're eating our way through the *tartine de merde*." McKenna winced. "Had another big slice today."

"What's a *tartine de merde*?"

"In polite terms, a manure pie. Voltaire said—"

"Voltaire!" Dr. Roberts squeezed McKenna's upper arm and pushed the humerus into the socket. "You've a head full of other folks' words. Have you no thoughts of your own?"

"You're hurting!"

Roberts blithely continued his manipulations. "It's all very well citing others, but Voltaire wasn't necessarily always right because he was Voltaire, even though he wasn't far wrong about the English shooting an admiral from time to time to keep the others in line." He peered down at McKenna. "You tend to upset the folk with the big guns a bit too often."

"We're in Wales."

"I don't recall the Welsh ever being slow to borrow when it suits. You should watch your back."


Hands deep in pockets, face shrouded by a thick scarf, Janet traipsed slowly along the High Street, irritable and despondent, precious off-duty hours wasted in pursuit of local youths frittering away time in bars and on street corners. She asked about Gary Hughes and Arwel Thomas and Darren Pritchard, about Blodwel and its master, and lost count of the faces staring blankly, mouths shut like traps, the backs insolently turned.

Bright lights swagged around the porch of The Black Spaniard bar promised warmth at least. Crossing the road, she was almost felled by two girls lurching on to the pavement, holding each other, giggling and snorting. The brassy-haired hussy in a tiny skirt, her legs pimply with cold, pushed past in a draught of cheap perfume and expensive liquor. Cloudy hair stippled purple and gold and pink by the lights, lipstick staining her pointed teeth; the other girl simply gaped.

"What are you doing here?" Janet demanded, catching her arm. "You shouldn't even be out, never mind pub-crawling."

The other girl pushed Janet in the chest. "Fuck off!"

"Shut *up*!" Mandy whispered. "She's a cop."

"So?" The blonde girl stared at Janet. "She can still fuck off." Shoving and pushing, she tried to pull Mandy from Janet's grasp. "She's not done nothing, so fucking mind your own fucking business, Miss Piggy!"

Janet elbowed her away. "Shut up, like Mandy says, you loud-mouthed bitch!"

Anger blazed in eyes fringed with lashes improbably thick and stickily black. "One more step," Janet warned, "and one more word, and you're done for assault."

The girl spat on the ground. Mandy whimpered. "Go away, Trace. *Please!* Go away!"

Tossing her head, her hair so sticky with spray not a wisp moved, Tracey clattered down the road, stopping after a few yards to gesture obscenely to Janet. Mandy sagged against the wall, snivelling, licking her lips with the huge purple tongue.

"Oh, be quiet!" Janet snapped. "What the hell are you up to?"

"You won't tell I was in a pub, will you?" Mandy whined.

"Are you on the run?"

"No!" Mandy stared, aggrieved.

"I'll hear the same from Blodwel staff when I take you back, will I?"

Mandy smirked and licked her lips. "Mr. Luvvyduvvy said for me to be back by half ten. I'm getting the bus."

"Who's 'Mr. Luvvyduvvy'? Who said you could be out at all?" Janet demanded. "You're not allowed out without staff."

Mandy giggled, drink rising to quench her earlier fears. "Who told you that crap?" She belched and put her fingers to her lips, giggling again. "Staff let us out so they can sit in the office jangling."

"And did they let Arwel go out?" Janet asked, her voice quiet.

Mandy slumped further down the wall, her legs beginning to buckle. "Him and Gary and him what got sent all the way to South Wales before we got up." She giggled again, nodding her head wildly like a silly ornament in the back of a car. "Sexy Gary and sexy Arwel came back with lots of fags and lots of cash, and bitchy Doris took it all. . . ." Her eyelids blinked, and she lurched towards Janet, gulping convulsively. "I feel dead sick, miss."

Averting her eyes from steaming vomit running in the gutter and swirling against kerbstones glittering with frost, Janet hauled the weeping, whining girl towards the telephone box by the railway bridge. Pushing Mandy inside, she squeezed in behind, and dialled McKenna's number. A strange voice answered, snappish and male. "Who wants him?"

"DC Evans."

"Thought it might be somebody else," Eifion Roberts grunted. "It's for you," Janet heard him say.

"I'm sorry to bother you, sir," Janet said. "I found Mandy on a pub crawl with another girl. She says she's got permission to be out. What shall I do with her? She's just been sick all over the road."

"Has she really?" McKenna said. "Does she look ill?"

Mandy stared vacantly, face waxen, bluey lips gasping, eyes sunk in shadowy sockets trimmed with navy-blue mascara, the smell of vomit on her breath making Janet heave.

"She looks ghastly, sir. She might've had more than drink."

"Indeed she might," McKenna agreed. "I'll send a car to take you to the police station. Dr. Roberts won't mind looking at her."

Doris laughed harshly. Robert Lovell, the bearded man, Mandy's "Mr. Luvvyduvvy," stood deferentially at her side, hands clasped in front of his genitals.

"What's so amusing about a drunken fifteen year old?" McKenna demanded.

"I told the social worker that girl can't be trusted, but would she listen? 'Mandy's got to learn to cope with her freedom,' she said. Stupid creature! Those social workers don't get dragged out of bed in the middle of the night to sort out the mess!"

"It's eleven o'clock," McKenna pointed out. "Hardly the middle of the night."

"Decent God-fearing people think so," Doris said sanctimoniously. "Even if you don't."

Crossing his legs, almost happy with the resurrection of his arm, McKenna lit a cigarette. "Contrary to what you and your husband led us to believe, Mandy says children often go out alone."

"You've no right to question her without us there!"

"Her interests couldn't be more compromised than they already are." McKenna blew smoke towards the ceiling, and Lovell tentatively pushed a metal waste bin towards him. "Others seem to be similarly compromised by your less-than-responsible attitude towards child care."

"Get out!" Doris shouted, so loudly, so suddenly, Lovell jumped. "I'll ring the director if you don't. I've got his home number. Get *out*!"

McKenna rose. "If that's what you want. We'll be back."

"Don't you threaten me with your snide remarks! Wait 'til Mr. Hogg finds out!"

"There are limits to what can be hidden indefinitely, Mrs. Hogg, however friendly you are with Councillor Elis."

Striding down a path slippery with frost, McKenna heard the front door slammed violently. Janet shivered, fumbling with the car door. "Bitch!" she muttered. "Bloody bitch!"


Thinking only of warmth and shelter and food in his belly to quell hunger gnawing at his innards like rats, Gary Hughes sat beneath the road deck which swooped over two massive stone lions, once guardians of the entrance to the long-vanished tubes of Britannia Bridge. Back against a concrete stanchion, knees hunched up to his chest, his whole body trembled with terrible cold. If he picked up his bag and walked the couple of miles back home, his mother would ask no questions, for since his return from Blodwel, instinct warned she might learn what no mother ever wished to know. She cared for his physical needs, letting blind hope care for the rest, while Gary despaired of the dreadful wounding words thrown in her face which built themselves into a barrier too huge for mother or son to surmount. Her plea for help brought the social workers, but instead of demolishing the barrier, they erected their own edifice around the family remnants, a prison from which no one could escape. Idly, he wondered if the moisture on his cheeks was icy mist curling up from the dark foul waters of Menai Strait, or the tears of a child wanting his mother's arms.

Rhiannon replaced the telephone receiver, disconnecting the number before it rang out. She sat in a silk-upholstered chair, silk-embroidered slippers on her thin elegant feet, and about her body, a peignoir of ice-grey silk chiffon, dyed marabou feathers frosting hem and cuffs and whispering with each breath she drew. She pulled suddenly at the neck of the fragile garment, disrupting its graceful silhouette. The slam of a door disrupted the quietness of the house. Mari, she thought, unable to sleep, restless with some misery or guilt. And what undermined her own resignation? Not the misery grown supple and familiar as the fingers which punched out the stream of numbers once more, or the guilt fostered out of duty. Again, she dropped the receiver before the number connected, contemplating the marriage she had come to view as love in altered circumstances, asking herself where that love ended and disgust began.

Mandy Minx vomited twice more during the night, crawling on all fours, from the room she shared with another girl, along scuff-scarred lino tiles to the lavatory. Her retching brought company the second time. Not the room-mate, who cowered under her quilt feigning sleep, but her own Mr. Luvvyduvvy, who stood by the cubicle door, wrinkling his nose at the stench, his eyes on the young buttocks firm beneath the thin pyjama trousers.

"You all right?" he ventured, when the retching abated. Mandy leaned over the lavatory bowl, fingers clenching the rim, sweat-dark hair brushing the porcelain, a stream of bloody spittle hanging from her chin.

"You'd best get back to bed."

He moved to take her arm, and she wrenched away, rolling into the corner, one arm raised to ward off violence, the other wrapped about her body, comforting pain. Her eyes glittered with terror.

"Hey!" He jerked upright, suddenly recalling the long minutes Mandy had spent in the Hoggs' flat after the police left, and before she reeled up to her room. "Don't make a row. You'll wake everybody up, then Mrs. Hogg'll be after you."

Mandy shivered so violently the cistern rattled. He fidgeted, despairing of his ability to deal with the girl who crouched and glared like a wild animal. How did he come to be in this place in the dead hours of a dark November night? What skills could control these alien beings with the same brash fearlessness displayed by Ronald Hogg and his wife? Neither would stand inept, as he did, but would make this crazy child return to her bed, so that sleep might erase a little more of the terrifying time in this enclosed world, where he and his colleagues contained children threatening devastation, who functioned like wolfpacks or marauding cybernauts from a time beyond nuclear holocaust.

Would he be standing thus in four hours' time, trapped by the vixenish creature crouched beside the lavatory, when Doris Hogg slip-slapped along the upstairs corridors in her bedroom slippers, dressing-gown trailing? Cook and cleaners would be at work, gossiping in hushed voices, clattering pans and banging metal buckets, swishing raggy stinking mops back and forth through rooms and corridors, leaving dirty shreds of rust-stained cotton under chair legs and doorframes and cupboards. The smell of frying eggs would seep through walls and floors, overlaying the other smell infesting every nook and cranny of the building. Fear coursed through his body like icy water when he thought of being found by Doris Hogg, of being found so wanting as she came upon them, he scratching at this thin beard, the wild-eyed girl wedged between wall and lavatory, blood spittle smeared over her face.

One hand rested now on the lavatory rim, the other slowly massaged belly and midriff, and violence contorted her face as he watched. She rolled over, body convulsing, and retched yet again, and he saw a dark stain seeping down her pyjama leg.

# •Chapter•
# 6

I don't think they're happily married," Dewi insisted. "What've they got in common? He's taken up with horses and making money, and when she's not being a big shot on the county council, she's entertaining royalty or the like."

Janet's mouth hardened with irritation. "People shouldn't live in each other's pocket just because they're married. Separate interests are healthier."

"Jack Tuttle didn't think so when his wife went on holiday without him and the girls. And Mr. McKenna left Madame Denise 'cos they've got nothing in common. That one's got more side to her than Elis and his wife put together."

"Gossiping's very unseemly in a young man." Janet sniffed. "My parents are very happy, because they trust each other, and I imagine the Elises are the same."

"Your parents are happily keeping up appearances, for the benefit of your father's flock."

"My parents have nothing to hide!" Janet snapped. "Don't judge everyone by your own nasty council-house standards!"

"Oh, get real! You live in bloody fairyland half the time." He thrust a sheet of paper in front of her. "Seen this, Miss Clever-Clogs? Elis had a lady passenger when Traffic stopped him on Port Dinorwic bypass."

"So what? It was probably his wife."

•   •   •

"We've got to be careful," Owen Griffiths said. "I don't hold with fifteen year olds on a pub crawl any more than you do, but Doris Hogg said she didn't want the girl out on her own."

"Expressing our disapproval in writing would give Mr. and Mrs. Hogg something to wave under the nose of the next social worker who suggests unsupervised jaunts," McKenna pointed out.

"You expect me to swallow that? You'd no more help those two than cut your own throat."

"Mandy told Janet most of the kids go out alone, Arwel Thomas, deceased, and Gary Hughes, whereabouts unknown, included." McKenna fidgeted with his lighter. "We should use that information to put pressure on Blodwel. What other lies have they told? We're more than entitled to stress the risk to these kids. One's already dead, after all."

"What else did Mandy say?"

"This and that. She wasn't very coherent. She and other girls clean Hogg's flat and his house near Bethesda, and the boys do gardening and general donkey work, presumably as part of the rehabilitation package. Punishment routines include cutting grass with nail scissors and scrubbing floors with a toothbrush."

"She said all this last night, when she was drunk? She could've been romancing, or exaggerating things out of all proportion to get herself off the hook, and make you feel sorry for her."

"Unless we talk to her when she's not in her cups, without Ron's storm-troopers breathing down our neck, we'll never know."


"How's the family?" McKenna asked.

Slumped in the chair opposite McKenna's desk, Jack yawned. "I thought kids of their age could be left to their own devices once in a while, so you can get on with being married." He coughed. "I suppose it's fallout of a kind. Would you believe they cried during the night, and Em rushed in, just like when they were babies? She stayed there, as well." He frowned at McKenna. "I'm bloody fed up with these youngsters. Dewi Prys and Janet Evans are squabbling again. Don't they get on your nerves?"

"Janet's too pushy and competitive for Dewi's liking, and too well educated. They're jealous of each other."

Jack smiled briefly. "He's a closet chauvinist. He likes his women seen and not heard."

"Modern woman can be rather daunting. You weren't happy when Emma started flexing her muscles."

Jack shifted in his seat. "That's water under the bridge, and maybe I over-reacted. It was only a holiday."

"Does Emma know you've repented?"

"She knows without being told, via intuition and instinct, like all women. It's a shame Janet lets reason get in the way so often. She's rowing Dewi because his instincts say things in the Bedd y Cor garden are far from rosy. According to the Traffic report on Elis's speeding jaunt, he had a woman passenger. A blonde, which Rhiannon isn't, and it was gone midnight when he was stopped."

"Elis's kind don't need to wait for night to hide their mischief."

"But they will. It's an instinct, isn't it? And there was more mischief last night. Somebody broke into a railway maintenance hut near Treborth. I sent Janet to see the Transport police, to keep her out of mischief for a bit."

"Anything missing?"

"They didn't say."

"She can go to Blodwel later to ask after Mandy."


Eifion Roberts dropped a thick buckram-bound book on McKenna's desk. "A translation of Lombroso's thesis on the inevitability of the criminal type." He dropped a thin paperbound volume on top. "And essays on the inevitability of child abuse, the even greater inevitability of the cover-up, from a European organization researching backlash, backlash being what folk upsetting the status quo can expect." He squinted at his companion. "So you know what's in store, not that you give a monkey's."

"Early retirement is the worst I could expect. I wouldn't be the first."

"You'd likely be the first stuck with your principles rather than a load of shit." Roberts grinned. "Haven't you found any ex-social workers booted out for criticizing Hogg's notions of childcare?"

"Social Services keep enemies as well as friends close by."

"Then you'll have to rely on the suffering little children, like that poor girl with the Hutchinson's teeth. They're the ruinous inheritance of congenital syphilis. Lombroso would've loved her." Dr. Roberts leaned back on the chair, lifting its front legs from the floor, rocking gently. "Why not capitalize on things?"

"What things?"

"Teenage girls and men, teenage boys and women. Seduction rather than competition is the probability. That girl wasn't half giving you the glad-eye last night."


"More fool you!" Doris said. "You'll learn."

Beyond the office window, Robert Lovell saw a crumpled sheet of newspaper, an empty crisp packet and battered polystyrene food tray encroaching on Blodwel territory, harried by a mean wind risen off the mountains and already scouring pavement and flagstones of the damp clinging like grease for days past. He stifled a yawn, feeling again the urgency in his bladder, a heaviness borne not of water but of hours of tension and fatigue.

"She was ill, Mrs. Hogg. I could hardly leave her alone."

"As I said, you'll learn. We're not nursemaids. She can get herself drunk, so she can take the consequences." She frowned. "You're no use to us if you're too tired to do your job, are you? Fancy staying up all night with the likes of her."

"I don't have your experience." He squeezed his thighs together, staunching the terror which sprang from the prospect of excusing his inadequacies to this woman's husband, who was yet to emerge from their flat. He strained his ears, like an animal to the hunter. "I really thought she was ill. She's started her period."

"That's what's wrong, then. She's always sick, drunk or not."

"I marked her file. Was that right? I haven't been shown."

"Female staff do it," Doris said. "Girls don't like telling men that sort of thing."

"And I had to give her sanitary pads."

"How many? I'll have to mark the stock book."

"How many?" His pale face flushed, his hands trembled. "I—I gave her a packet."

"You'll learn about that as well." She looked up, eyes glittery in the cold morning light. "If we let you stay on after the trial period." She reached for a large file from the shelf above the desk, breasts unbridled on the pages of the log book from which she had read of the night's events. "They get three pads a day. If they have a whole packet, they don't have to ask, and we don't know if they're on or not, so we wouldn't know if they'd got themselves in trouble." She opened the file, turning its pages slowly. "And if I don't get the packet back, the others'll try it on."

"I noticed—" He coughed, pushing his fist against his teeth to quell the noise.

"Yes?" Doris asked. "What did you notice?"

"She had a period just over a week ago." He coughed again. "Shouldn't she see the doctor? Having periods so often can't be good for her."

"It's her age. She saw the doctor when she came here." She picked up a biro and marked the stock file, snapping it shut. "The drink brought it on again. She was probably drinking gin."

"She said she had a lot of pain," he ventured. "She was sort of clutching herself."

"Oh, she's really got your sympathy, hasn't she? Has she said somebody hit her yet?" Doris sniggered. "You want to watch yourself, because she might say you touched her up, and you can't prove you didn't. Wicked lies come easy to her sort. Like I said, you've a lot to learn."

"I wasn't allowed to see Mandy Minx, sir. She's been sick all night, keeping the staff from their cosy beds, causing no end of inconvenience. My heart bleeds!" Janet stood before Jack's desk, eyes bright with anger. "And I object to doing the work of British Transport Police. The railway and everything to do with it is their business."

"Not if it might impinge on our territory, as you well know."

"Somebody else could've gone. I'm assigned to a murder investigation, not a piddling little break-in at a railway hut!"

Jack sighed. "Do stop bellyaching, Janet, and stop squabbling with Dewi Prys. You aren't doing yourself any favours."

"He's a bloody know-it-all!"

"I can't see much to choose between you in that respect."

Anger and embarrassment reddened her cheeks.

Jack yawned. "We're all on edge, with one thing and another. Mr. McKenna's already commented about personal feelings, and you're lucky he missed you and Prys this morning. Don't push your luck, because he won't stand for any nonsense, and you might find yourself doing something a lot less career-enhancing than investigating burglaries at railway huts."

"It wasn't a burglary. Someone just dossed there for the night."

"No harm done then, is there?"

"What's Mandy Minx's proper name?" McKenna asked.

"Jones, probably," Dewi said. "Look on the reports we made at Blodwel. She's named for her mam, 'cos she's known for putting it about. Can't get enough, so they say, like a minx, whatever sort of animal that is."

McKenna grinned. " 'Mink,' you idiot! Not 'minx.' "

"She looks like a rodent with those teeth, doesn't she?" Dewi shuddered delicately. "I wouldn't fancy kissing her."

McKenna hid behind a cloud of cigarette smoke, Eifion Roberts's precocious image of the girl acquiring more disturbing presence. "Where's Darren Pritchard?"

"A privately run lock-up near Abergavenny. The government's selling off child care as well as prisons and everything else. Darren's mam was favoured with a visit from Social Services yesterday," Dewi said. "Who's going to see him? You or Mr. Tuttle? You'd need a driver, wouldn't you?"

"Nobody's going unless Superintendent Griffiths agrees, and there must still be trains, despite the drawbacks of rail franchise."

"Cardiff takes nearly a day, then you'd have to get from Cardiff to Abergavenny, and from Abergavenny to wherever, and if you took all that time getting there, you might find Darren spirited elsewhere."

"So he said: 'Why can't you telephone, and save a lot of money and trouble?' " Jack reported. "Since when did a superintendent need permission to authorize a visit to South Wales?"

"He's anxious about encroaching on Social Services' territory," McKenna said. "Among other things. Hogg's already made one complaint, which he can only ignore so long."

"That was a set-up, to get us off his back."

"D'you want a trip to Abergavenny, then? That *would* warrant a complaint."

"Send Janet. She could try out her new car."

"I didn't know she had one."

"A posh French 2.0 litre in a rather fetching metallic blue. They're not cheap."

"Has Dewi seen it yet?"

"I would imagine so, from the atmosphere between them. It's parked in the yard next to that clapped-out thing he drives."

"He can't afford anything else. He's been the breadwinner since his dad was made redundant."

"Lucky Janet, then."

McKenna massaged his arm, eyeing Jack. "I hope she's not taken over first place on your hit-list."

"I don't have a hit-list, but I had to haul her over the coals earlier. She as good as said a bit of leg-work isn't good enough for her any longer."

Mari Williamson leaned against the front door of Bedd y Cor, looking over McKenna's shoulder at night clouds drifting in from the east. The vestiges of a distant winter sun cast drab gold lights on her hair and a little colour to her pale face. Her eyes were red, as if she had wept much and slept little.

"Mr. Elis isn't here."

"I'd like a word with Mrs. Elis. Is she in?"

The girl shivered, wrapping her arms around her body. "It's still so cold, isn't it? And so dark and miserable. I hate this time of year. I feel like my shadow's inside me." She lifted her head, staring hard at the man who still waited on the doorstep. "You expect horrible things to happen. Like what happened to Arwel." Her eyes were as dull as the creeping cloud. "Was he really naked? People are saying he froze to death. Is that true?"

"He was already dead, Mari. Someone put his body in the tunnel."

"Will you find out who did it?"

Rhiannon came around the side of the house, momentarily unrecognizable in dirty wellingtons and work clothes. Her dark hair sparkled with frost, and her cheeks glowed pink. "I thought I heard voices. What are you thinking of, Mari? You shouldn't keep Mr. McKenna at the door."

Breezily hospitable, she almost pushed McKenna into the

house, and stood on the mat easing off her wellingtons. "Put these in the boot room, please, and ask Cook to serve coffee." The girl took the dirty footwear from her mistress, and walked away, head bowed, feet dragging on the stone slabs. Rhiannon took her visitor through an ornate door into a large luxurious drawing-room. A gigantic log fire spat and crackled in the wide stone hearth.

"Do sit down," she said. "I was helping with evening stables. There's such a lot to do once the horses come in for winter. The grooms can't manage alone, and my husband isn't back yet." She stretched her legs toward the fire, wriggling her toes in their thick woollen socks, incongruous amid the finery in her scruffy clothing. "Mari seems to be going to pieces." She brushed a stray tendril of hair with the back of a grubby hand. "She'll be better when my husband returns. They get on very well."

"She asked me about Arwel."

"Did she?" Rhiannon asked absently. "She's not as tough as you'd think, just very good at hiding her feelings."

"That's not surprising, giving her background."

"She was sexually abused, in one of the many foster homes."

"I didn't know."

"Her social worker said she made an allegation about a foster brother, and had to be moved. I took it as a veiled warning Mari could pose a threat to my husband or the male staff." She smiled fleetingly. "But so far, so good."

"Was the allegation investigated?"

"She was only about eight or nine, and Social Services concluded she was lying. Children in care often allege abuse, out of spite, or just to get attention." She stared at the fire, flame shadows dancing on her skin and hair. "It's part of child's nature to lie, isn't it? For all sorts of reasons, apart from deception."

"If your own child said he was abused, would you believe him?"

"We pay for the best possible care."

"Can you buy that kind of guarantee?"

"I must believe I can, Mr. McKenna. I must hope only the likes of Arwel and Mari are vulnerable, otherwise I'd go out of my mind." She jumped to her feet. "Where is she? Why can't she do as she's told?"

She snatched at the door, almost flooring the woman on the other side, who put a huge silver tray on a side table, smiled briefly at McKenna, and left.

"Is your arm better?" Rhiannon asked brightly, handing coffee to her guest. "I noticed the sling's gone."

"Much better, thank you."

"That's good." She smiled, lips tight, as if she intended to permit no further betrayals. "Riding's terribly risky. My husband falls off sometimes, but so far he's been lucky. One of his friends was killed a few years ago when her horse shied at a lorry." She shuddered. "It happened so fast. No one could have saved her."

"Arguably better than a lingering death," McKenna observed. "Does your son ride? Horses are very therapeutic for the handicapped."

"I don't wish to discuss my son," Rhiannon said quietly. "You don't mince your words, do you?"

"Dissembling rarely elicits the truth."

"My husband thinks truth and delusion wear the same mask. If he's right, how can we tell the difference? Are we all condemned to spiritual and moral wilderness?" She sighed. "As for my son, he's too disabled to sit on a horse. I don't expect he can even tell the difference between a horse and himself. He's little more than a vegetable, but one must dissemble, and say he has 'profound learning disability.' So you see, he could never accuse anyone of anything, could he?"

"This cold fair gets in your bones," Owen Griffiths said. "Shouldn't you keep your sling on? That injury'll haunt you every time there's a change in the weather, like rheumatics."

"My shoulder's much better. Eifion gave it a going over."

"Folk used to say he's got the power of healing. He should've stayed with the living."

"He's an excellent pathologist," McKenna commented.

"He takes things too much to heart, and he can't bring folk back from the dead. He's rattling cages all over the place about this lad."

McKenna lit a cigarette, watching smoke drift towards the ceiling. "He's disgusted by the complacency, and the way paid professionals divest themselves of responsibility at the first sign of trouble."

"We're only the keepers of law and order. Morality's for the likes of Janet's father."

"The wretchedness of the Blodwel children is everyone's responsibility."

Griffiths sighed. "Stop feeling sorry for them. They're bound to be miserable. They're too much bloody trouble for themselves and everyone else."

"Too many children go into institutions through no real fault of their own, acquire bad habits and a worse reputation, and end up as adults with no hand in their own making, devoid of resources and derelict of hope." McKenna tapped ash from the end of his cigarette. "We can't survive without hope."

"Near the English border, there's a village called Hope and another called Caergwrle. People say if you live in Hope, you'll die in Caergwrle, so I suppose that's only another name for despair," Griffiths said. "I wonder what keeps Elis and his wife going."

"She talked about the boy today. Apparently, he's little more than a vegetable, though perhaps he still has feelings."

"Did she say what sin he's the punishment for?" Griffiths asked. "You could ask Elis, if he comes back. D'you still want to go to South Wales?"

"Jack's going. I couldn't drive that distance."

•    •    •

"Why can't we come with you?" Jack's twin daughters sat together on the sofa, threatening tears.

"It's not a pleasure trip," Emma said impatiently. "You can help me with the Christmas shopping."

"Town's horrible. Great long queues of people buying rubbish nobody in their right mind'd want."

"And people rattling begging bowls for charity."

"And beggars by the town clock."

"And a fat old fool dressed up like Santa Claus."

"Perverts could dress up like Santa, couldn't they? Santa's an anagram of Satan."

"It's also Spanish for saint!" Jack snapped. "Have you both finished?"

"Christmas gets rammed down our throats, every year, for weeks on end!"

"If you both feel you've outgrown boring tradition, your father and I will be happy to forego Christmas," Emma said silkily.

"We didn't say that."

"We said it's horrible and commercialized and tacky."

"And it'll be more so in South Wales," Emma said. "Far more people to do whatever you deplore."

"You're not coming, anyway," Jack added. "You can clear out that pigsty of a bedroom instead. Why don't you ever hang up your clothes?"

"They're not ours."

"Whose are they, then? Santa's?"

"Denise thought the girls might want them," Emma said. "They won't fit me."

"Denise? Are we reduced to having her charity?"

"Don't be ridiculous!" Emma snapped. "The clothes are far too expensive for the charity shops."

"They might be very expensive," Jack said with gritted teeth, "but as far as I'm concerned, anything off her back is far too cheap for my wife and daughters, so next time she brings her tacky nasty hand-me-downs, I hope you'll tell her what to do with them!"

• • •

"What's Elis's child called?" Dewi asked, placing a mug of tea beside McKenna.

"I don't know."

"Has Elis found Arwel's book yet?"

"Rhiannon didn't say."

"Do Social Services know Mr. Tuttle's off to the deep south tomorrow?"

"No." McKenna rubbed his shoulder, where pain had crept back under cover of darkness. "Any word about Gary? Ideas? Suggestions?"

"Only that he's a loner, and keeps his doings well and truly to himself." Dewi paused. "Is it worth talking to the gippos?"

"Don't say 'gippos,' Dewi. It's one of the unacceptable words of this day and age."

"I knew there was something!" He dragged a bundle of papers from his pocket. "I've cracked some of Arwel's clues."

McKenna scanned the creased and scrawled-upon pages, pursuing lines of thought as if deciphering an abstruse mathematical equation. The answers were underlined with three flourishes of red ballpoint. "Beastly," "pants," "beggar," "dwarf," "slow-witted," "shit-lump"—

"It's very antiquated Welsh, isn't it?" Dewi asked. "Made me wonder if Arwel didn't pinch the words from a Dafydd ap Gwilym poem, or some such."

Frowning, McKenna scribbled on his notepad. Dewi craned over the desk to read. " 'Beastly beggar, slow witted dwarf, shit-lump pants.' Not very nice, is it, sir?"

"It's not supposed to be," McKenna said. "Wales's most famous bard had a mate called Rhys Meigen, but they fell out when Rhys insulted Dafydd and his forebears in verse. Legend has it Rhys dropped dead from shame when he heard Dafydd's reply." Frowning again, he added, "Don't you wonder how Arwel Thomas knew enough medieval welsh to make crosswords from it when he hardly ever went to school?"

"Not really," Dewi said. "The teachers ram Welsh literature down your throat 'til you feel like throwing up, and a bright lad like Arwel was said to be, wouldn't find it hard to learn anything that took his fancy." He flicked the raggy papers, smiling. "If the story about Rhys Meigen's true, it proves the pen's mightier than the sword, doesn't it? Is that poem what people call a 'death verse'? Why don't we try it out on Hogg, and see what happens?"

"And what if it worked?" McKenna asked. "I don't think we should actively invoke the Celtic other-worldliness."

"It'd be one way of solving a few of our problems, wouldn't it?" Dewi said. "Have you got a copy of the poem, sir? I'd like to read all of it. Can I borrow it?"

"Only if you swear not to recite the juiciest bits to Jack Tuttle next time you have a difference of opinion."

"It wouldn't work on him. He wouldn't understand the Welsh." Dewi smiled again. "Detective Constable Clever-Clogs Evans is another matter, though."

"And where is she?"

"Wasting her time harassing Carol Thomas in Caernarfon."

"Maybe you should talk to the girl. Capitalize on the laws of nature, as Dr. Roberts suggests."

"You think?" Dewi asked. "I didn't have much luck with Dai Skunk, did I? Despite his inclinations."


Behind the counter of the hardware store, Carol dealt absently with the few customers who demanded her attention, glancing repeatedly at her wristwatch, trying to will away that dreadful gnawing pain in her belly. Perhaps, she thought, in a few days or weeks or months, she would no longer stand behind this counter as she had through all the dismal dreary months since leaving school. People walking or shuffling or barging through the narrow glass-panelled door would be faced instead with the embodiment of her pain, its end result, a monstrous object grown in the darkness of her heart, like a cancer which consumed her from the inside out. She stared at the glass shelves opposite the counter, at a jumble of clocks, each telling a different time, and begged God to turn back their hands through hundreds of revolutions, to invoke the magic of Time, and bring Arwel back to life.

Her parents wanted him buried. They whined and niggled and argued, banged from the house to the call-box over the road, and returned to vent their frustration on their other child, but Arwel remained in his mortuary bed, the embryo of a man inside a winding sheet, and Rhiannon Elis's awesome power fell to dust.

Carol pressed her fists to her eyes, staunching tears that came unbidden, day and night, in private or public, and went to lock the door. Turning the sign from *Agored* to *Wedi Cau* — *Open* to *Closed*, she watched the straggle of late shoppers, cowed by a freezing wind off the sea, and saw the police-woman, dressed in her smart country clothes, waiting to accost her, to importune her with questions to which she would never provide answers.

# •Chapter•
## 7

Jack left early for Abergavenny, long before the twins awoke. He kissed the drowsy Emma and crept downstairs, afraid that his daughters, still beloved for themselves but to be feared for what time and youth wrought in there, might be in pursuit, and insist on travelling with him. He raised the garage door quietly, wincing as the hinges squealed, shut the car door with a gentle click, and reached the end of the road, glancing more than once in the rear mirror, before he felt safe.

Patchy black ice made the Dolgellau road treacherous. He concentrated on its sudden dips and blind bends, trying not to think of the twins, of the schism to come, but as the miles disappeared under the wheels of the car, and grey dawn light brought shape to the world fleeing past him, he began to fret once again.

Waiting for the cat to return from her first foray, McKenna sat shivering by his parlour fire, looking through the window at cold grey sky and wasted rags of leaf. A wind had risen late yesterday, blowing the tatters of fog out to sea, but died in the night, killed by frost lying thick and suffocating on the ground and about the roots of trees and bushes.

The cat leapt on the windowledge and scratched the glass, and he opened the door. She rushed indoors and shot up the staircase, but he stood by the open door, freezing air about his body, listening for birdsong, trying to recall when he last heard gulls screeching and mewling about roof-tops and chimney stacks, or the clacking jays in the trees below the garden.

The hay was almost too warm, Gary thought, the heat rising about his head and warding off a bitter draught through the unglazed window high in the wall of the cow byre. He turned over sleepily, stretching his legs, stalks of dried grass tickling his ankles where his jeans rucked up during the night. He scuffed the jeans in place with the toe of his boots, and sniffed the air around him, the scent of summer still trapped in the great bales of hay. Pulling at a desiccated clover head, feeling hunger draw in his belly, he wondered if he could knock at the farmhouse door like a traveller in history, and be given sustenance, but knew himself for a fool if he ever believed hope might triumph over experience. He heard the thump of hoof upon earth as the cattle below him roused, smelt the warmth of their rising breath, and turned on his side, drifting back to sleep.

Jack's destination lay well beyond Abergavenny, along winding roads verged with muddy grass, scarred with wheel tracks and strewn with litter. Set in a shallow depression in the misty hillside, the house looked ill-kempt and rundown, the short drive naked of most of the gravel once laid there. He clattered up four stone steps and rang the bell, an old ceramic button dirtied and chipped by a thousand fingers.

A bearded man led him to a small waiting-room scented with boiled cabbage and chip-fat, grumbling. "Social Services should say when someone's coming. Darren Pritchard's enough of a problem without this sort of thing." He stood over his visitor, stroking the beard, and Jack wondered idly if he was kin to the bearded man who dithered among the children of Blodwel, both cloned from a master model for the purposes of containing derelict youngsters, neither aware of life beyond the walls of the prisons they inhabitated. "It's very disruptive," he added. "We've got all sorts here. Arsonists, rapists, murderers. We can't be too careful."

Jack yawned. "That bad, is it? I'm surprised. Even juveniles go to prison for arson and the rest."

"Social workers prefer special placements like this."

"Before or after the trial? Darren hasn't been killing or torching or raping as far as we know."

"He's got bad potential. This is a preventive placement. He caused mayhem at the Bangor home." The man stroked his beard again. "Why d'you want to see him?"

"He can help us with a current investigation."

"Maybe I should check with his social worker."

"Social workers don't normally work Saturdays," Jack pointed out. "And I haven't spent five hours on the road to be told I can't talk to the boy. Just go and get him, will you?"

"He's in the secure unit. It's your funeral if anything goes wrong."

Accessed by a heavy fire-proof door at the rear of the house, the secure unit was bright with fluorescent light, noisy with the clang of metal upon metal and the rattling of keys. Four boys, clad in pyjamas and bedroom slippers, leaned against raw brick walls, staring as the door thudded shut behind Jack. He trailed the wispy girl who exchanged escort with the bearded man, through the dayroom and into an office.

"Would you like a cup of tea?" The girl frowned. "Where are you from, did you say?"

"North Wales."

"And you drove down this morning? It must've taken you hours. You should see the taxi bills for admissions from your area. And, of course, there's no money left for the kids to have home leave, is there? Not on top of our fees." Placing a mug of weak tea in front of him, she prattled on, voice monotonous with the sing-song accent of the South. "Darren was an emergency admission a few days ago."

"Is that so?" Jack gulped the watery liquid.

"We get a lot of emergency admissions." She sat down,

legs carefully crossed so not a whisper of thigh beguiled his fancy. "I used to work in a Cardiff community home, and we always had admissions just before Easter, just after schools start back in September, and just after Christmas." She smiled knowingly. "Christmas is worst, of course, because bad families only get worse with the drink inside them. Things get so nasty when people drink too much, don't they?"

"That's our experience."

"What d'you want from Darren?" Her eyes, vague and watery as the tea, turned sharp and dark. "What's he done? Nobody said he's wanted by the police."

"He isn't 'wanted.'" Jack felt irritation rouse itself. "I need to talk to him."

"Because juveniles in care must have a friendly adult present at police interviews." She droned on as if he had not spoken. "We must protect their interests."

Jack smiled disarmingly. "I'm here protecting the interests of juveniles, Darren's included."

She rose, again modestly, and went to the door. Hand resting lightly on the handle, pose deliberate, she said, "His social worker didn't say you were coming. They always tell us."

"Perhaps they forgot. A lot's happened in the past few days."


Restless, irritable, Janet stood at the large bay window of the manse drawing-room, listening to her father rehearse his sermon. Watching a small robin peck jerkily at the lawn and twitter away with a wriggling bit of worm in its beak, she wondered if the chapel congregation would heed a word of Edwin Evans's discourse on the true meaning of Christmas when they hurried away to the superstores and clothing markets trading on Sunday tedium.

"You're not listening," her father said tetchily.

"There's nothing I haven't heard a hundred times before."

"You haven't been on the earth a hundred Christmases, Janet, so you haven't heard a hundred of my sermons."

"Oh, don't be so pedantic!"

"And don't you be so impudent!"

She leaned her forehead against glass cold and damp with condensation. At the bottom of the garden, a dark glossy laurel hedge bound the glebe and its smooth lawns, the borders colourful with variegated erica even on the most dismal day, and the empty beds, like fresh little graves, where her father's prize pansies would bloom in the spring. Fronds of pampas grass grew tall and graceful at each side of the wide gate.

"D'you know any closet perverts?" she asked. "Does the chapel shelter the wayward like the Roman Catholic church?" Turning to face him, she added, "Is there another Hafodty where the truly wicked hide from justice?"

"You're being insolent."

"I'm asking legitimate questions," she insisted. "You tried to put me off the scent by dropping Christmas Morgan under my nose, and you only did that because I'd already heard the rumours."

"Don't be ridiculous!" Her father stood up, snatching the scattered pages of his sermon. "You're becoming quite unbearable! You judge half the men in the world perverts of one kind or another, and if this is what so-called liberation does to women, I can only thank God your mother was never deluded by it!"

"It's nothing to do with women's liberation," Janet muttered, heart thudding, as always when she roused her father's anger. "One boy is dead, and God alone—truly God alone—knows how many others are abused every single day." The tears of her own anger spilled down her cheeks. "And people like you make me so sick, because you pretend everything's all right, and you'll go on pretending as long as you damned well can!" She gulped, rage rising in her gorge. "You might have to stop before long, when one of your holier-than-thou colleagues gets a cold which won't go away, and comes out in nasty black sores!" She walked to the door, legs stiff and unyielding. "Arwel Thomas was buggered by any number of men, so he was probably HIV positive. He may have developed

AIDS. You may not like what I say, and you may object to the way I say it, but none of that alters the fact."

"He won't talk to you. He says he hasn't done anything."

"Oh, for God's sake!" Jack exploded. "What did you tell him?"

The young woman bridled prettily. "I just said the police wanted to see him."

"Where is he?"

"In his room. They have separate rooms here."

"I'm not interested in the sleeping arrangements!"

She shrugged. "He's got the right to refuse. You can't just barge in. He's entitled to his privacy."

"You call this social work?" Jack demanded, his voice rising. "Letting these yobbos call the shots?"

"We're encouraging self-determination." Her cheeks flushed. "Don't be so nasty! We get enough of that from the kids!" She glanced anxiously at the door. "And stop shouting. The others can hear you."

Four faces gaped at the office door, and one boy let out a bray of near-hysterical mirth.

"Be quiet! Go away!"

The boy giggled. "Darren's shitting bricks 'cos he thinks he's off to the slammer."

"Why should he think that?" Jack asked.

"The man said, didn't he?"

Leaning against the door-frame, hands deep in his pockets and the tension of long hours behind the wheel of a car in his arms and shoulders, Jack watched Darren Pritchard stare sullenly at the floor, and thought the boy would be almost handsome without his misery. "You can't wish me away."

Darren began opening the drawers of a small chest under the barred window. "Where am I going? Which nick?" Underclothing and T-shirts were thrown on the bed, a holdall dragged from underneath, and Jack saw four massive steel brackets bolting the bed to the floor. Stuffing clothes willy-nilly in the bag, Darren added, "Hogg is a sodding liar like the rest of them. I haven't said a bloody word."

"What are you talking about? Why are you packing?"

"I'm going to prison, like Hogg said." He zipped the bag closed, the sound as harsh as his breath. "As if this dump isn't a bloody prison, anyway." He smiled bitterly. "Why did I believe him? Stupid, or what? People say I'll never learn. They must be right, mustn't they?"

Jack sat on a cube-like contraption bolted to wall and floor, a thin cushion shifting under his buttocks. "You're talking riddles, and I'm too tired and too hungry to play games."

"Ask the pretty screw for some sarnies, then."

"D'you want some?"

Darren banged on the cell door. "Mr. Policeman wants some food before he takes me away!"

"Stop shouting, Darren Pritchard!" The girl's voice was muffled, like her footsteps as she clicked away along the tiled floor.

"They always listen at the door," Darren said. "Then they write down what you didn't want them to hear. Everybody reads it, and the shrink hums and hahs, then decides if you're a headcase." His face grew bleak. "They map out your whole life, on gossip and second-hand opinion, and nobody ever asks how you feel about it."

"You're very cynical for a teenager," Jack observed.

"I'm not a teenager. I'm a problem, a burden on society."

"Did you go to school at Blodwel?"

Darren sat on the edge of the bed, hands loose between his knees. Jack saw "A.C.A.B." roughly tattooed on the knuckles of one hand, and four dots inked on the knuckles of the other. "I had the benefit of that crap-artist they call a teacher. He's a bigger bastard than Hogg."

"Why?"

"Why?" Darren laughed. "Why, Mr. Policeman, I'm not telling you! Your sarnies'll come in a minute, so why not eat them all up like a good copper then take me wherever we're going?"

Inept in the face of adolescence, too old to recall the triumphs and terrors of his own youth, Jack rose. Darren stood up, and dragged his bag off the bed, rumpling the cover.

"Sit down," Jack said. "I came to talk to you, that's all, but you've nothing to say, so I'll bugger off."

"What about?"

"About Blodwel. About the Hoggs. About Arwel Thomas."

"Arwel?" Darren smiled. "We were good mates. He's a good kid. How is he?"

"He's dead."

"Oh, Christ!" Darren slumped on to the bed, the bag on his knees. "Oh, Jesus!"

"He was found in one of the railway tunnels late on Sunday night, stark naked, with a broken neck and his head smashed in. And—" He stopped speaking as the door swung open, and the girl walked in with a plastic tray of coffee and sandwiches.

"Everything all right?" she asked.

"Yes, thank you," Jack said. "When you go out, d'you mind making sure nobody's listening at the door? Like you said, Darren's entitled to his privacy."

She stormed out of the room, slamming the door so hard the window bars rattled.

"You know how to make friends, don't you?" Darren commented.

"I've made lots more like her in the past week, especially at Blodwel." Jack offered the plate of sandwiches, and picked up one of the plastic beakers. "Arwel'd been on the run for several days before he turned up dead, so Social Services don't want to know about him."

"He went before I left."

Jack chewed the sandwich, surprised by the tasty filling. "Social Services don't want to know about us, either, so we're not making much progress towards finding out who killed him." The coffee was strong and hot. "We only found you because your Nain knows somebody else's. Social Services don't know I'm here, and there'll probably be all hell let loose when they find out." Taking another sandwich from the plate, he added, "I was hoping your statement might help point us in the right direction."

"You take statements about crimes. Blodwel's a shit-hole, but that's not a crime, is it? People don't go to gaol for running a shit-hole. You can't do anything. Nobody can."

"And what exactly makes it like that? Why do kids run away at every opportunity?"

Darren shrugged, then rubbed his eyes. Jack saw the sheen of tears on his cheeks.

"What goes on there, Darren? Is it bad enough to kill Arwel?"

"You're always hungry, always dirty, always shit-scared. Kids wet the beds out of fright, then get beaten up for doing it. Hogg gobs in your food for fun, and Doris pisses herself laughing." He looked up, eyes haunted. "They're bad enough to kill Arwel, but you'll never know if they did, 'cos nobody cares. Hogg's boss doesn't give a shit. Look what happened to me? Why d'you think I'm here?"

"You've lost me," Jack said. "Weren't you moved for legging it with Arwel? You went out at night, like him and Gary Hughes, and came back with money and cigarettes, and Hogg didn't want us to talk to you."

"I was moved because Hogg can do any bloody thing he wants. He said he'll have me locked up for good if I ever open my mouth, and he will. He reckons to know coppers all over the country who'll jump whenever he shouts. But I didn't leg it with Arwel, and I never went out at night."

"A girl from Blodwel said you and Arwel and Gary went out at night!"

"Which girl?"

"Does it matter?"

"It matters a lot to me."

"Mandy Minx said: 'Arwel and Gary and the one they sent to South Wales.' "

Darren chewed at his lower lip. "Arwel was already out on one of his jaunts when the others legged it, and I don't know if he ever went back." He stood up and walked to the window, gazing through the bars at a simpleton's jigsaw of scrubby wind-blown bushes and distant foggy hills. "I took a beating off the teacher, while Hogg stood by, laughing and egging him on. It wasn't the first time, and the other kids just watched, thanking God Almighty it was me and not them. Anyway," he went on, turning to face Jack, "when he'd finished with me, there was a lot of blood threatening to muck up the floor, so Hogg kicked me all the way down to the bogs to clean up. I legged it and hitched a ride to Caernarfon."

"Then what?"

"I told Hogg's boss everything, and fair play to him, he listened. He gave me a cup of coffee and a couple of fags and a promise, then put me in a taxi and said: "Darren, I want you to go back to Blodwel and put all this unpleasantness behind you, and I promise it won't happen again." He even patted me on the shoulder, in a fatherly kind of way."

"And?"

"The taxi stopped in front of Blodwel, and I got out, then out came Doris, screaming like a sodding banshee. She threw my bags in the taxi, pushed me in after, and screeched: "Go!," like they do in American police films, thumping on the roof. "Go! Go! *Go!*" And he went, and he didn't stop 'til we got here." Darren sat again on the bed, his eyes cloudy with memory. "But I can tell you who legged it." He recited a list of first names and nick-names, ages and potted histories.

"Out of how many?"

"Eleven."

"You sure?"

"Shut up in places like Blodwel and this dump, your world's so small you know everything. Which staff's on duty, what's going on in all the meetings they have. . . ." He flexed his fingers, and massaged his disfigured knuckles. "You wouldn't survive if you didn't." He paused, struggling to give voice to instinct. "Nobody ever tells you anything, nobody ever tells you the truth, so you're forced to live on your wits."

"There are eight children left at Blodwel," Jack said. "Who's been moved?"

"Who's still there?"

Jack read a list of names from his file.

"You want Tony. Tony Jones, from Llandudno." Darren sighed. "Not that you'll find him there. God knows where Hogg sent him. Are you going to bugger off now? It'll be dark very soon."

"We haven't talked about Gary Hughes yet, or this Tony Jones."

"You must be a glutton for punishment. They say the same about me." Darren smiled again, and Jack wondered if others ever saw the person behind the label. "Gary went out, like Arwel and Tony, in the evening, and when I boldly asked Hogg why some could go out but not others, he booted me in the guts. I'm still pissing blood." Sighing again, he added, "I don't know if Gary and Arwel and Tony liked going out, because they never talked about it, but Gary threw a wobbly one night. He'd been away all weekend, so we reckoned he'd sucked up to Hogg for home leave, and needed a talking to. We went to his room after Dilys fart-face'd gone to sleep."

"And?"

"Poor bugger!" Darren shivered, wrapping his arms around his body. "Poor sod! Somebody's painted purple varnish on his toe-nails. He was sitting on the floor trying to scrape it off with a penknife, crying so much he couldn't see, and saying he wasn't a bum boy, no matter what anybody said, or anybody did."


Stopped in his tracks south of Dinas Mawddwy by a blizzard of awesome magnitude screaming with demon force from the mountains, Jack pulled into the car-park of a roadside inn, struggled out of the car against a wind threatening to tear the door from its mounting, and ran, head down, into the bar. Lodged for the night, he telephoned Emma.

"The weather forecast was bad before you left. Why didn't you stay in South Wales?"

"Because I wanted to get away!" Jack shivered, sounds of the battering wind outside banging against his skull. "It's a dreadful place, Em. Bare as a barn, and it costs two and a half grand a week for each kid! My God, what a racket!"

"Talking of barns, a farmer near Pentir found someone in his barn this morning. Whoever it was ran away. It was on the local news."

"At least the place wasn't torched." He coughed. "How are the girls? What did they do today?"

"Cleaned out their room."

"About time, too."

"And they tried on Denise's clothes. They're only clothes, after all, and the twins look very smart."

"I'm too tired to argue, and you've made up your mind anyway. Only next time she brings her cast-off finery, say no, will you? I'd rather you all wore rags than clothes off her back. She's little better than a tart."

# •Chapter•
# 8

"Jack Tuttle ran into a blizzard in Meirionydd on the way home last night," McKenna said. "His journey was rather a waste of time, as Mandy Minx neglected to tell us Tony Jones and not Darren Pritchard is the boy we want. Dewi Prys is out round Pentir, on the assumption Gary may be the barnstormer."

Janet ground out her cigarette and immediately lit another.

"Why didn't you go to chapel this morning?" McKenna asked.

"I didn't want to. I'm not a child. I don't have to go every Sunday."

"The congregation might think something's amiss if the minister's family suddenly breaks the habit of a lifetime. Defaults on an obligation, as it were."

"They can think what they like!"

"Is this a bid for independence, or is there a problem at home?"

"There's my father, so there's a problem. He's very uncomfortable about what I'm doing."

"This isn't a pleasant job for anyone's daughter."

"I mean he's uncomfortable with himself. I asked him yesterday if he's anything to tell us, and he got rather spiteful, like he does when you hit a sore spot."

"He can be uneasy without having compromising knowledge," McKenna said. "Child abuse provokes suspicion. Some innocuous incident in the past, which seemed trivial at the time, can suddenly appear significant. Perhaps he's simply being cautious."

"Everybody's being cautious!" Janet snapped. "The social workers spout about confidentiality, the kids are terrified of everyone, the parents think we're shit, and bloody Hogg and his wife rule the world!"

McKenna sighed. "We've no evidence that Arwel's death is connected with Blodwel, despite what we know of the place and the Hoggs."

"So what's left?" Janet demanded. "Elis? Can you really see him as a paedophile?"


McKenna saw Elis as ambiguous and intrusive, a man whose organizing principles were not of his own choosing. Parking on the forecourt of Bedd y Cor, arm and shoulder strained by the drive up St. Mary's Hill and down narrow pot-holed lanes, he sat for a moment, watching dusk wash over the distant mountains. Lights within the house spilt soft wedges of colour across darkening ground and on the gleaming enamel of the beautiful car parked by the entrance to the stable yard. Kinetic art, McKenna thought, regarding the car's exquisite contours, like the music with which Elis filled his empty spaces, and the horses on which he tried to break for freedom.

Waiting by the front door, he heard the whinnying of a horse, the clatter of hoof upon cobble, and saw the prancing shape of the thoroughbred mare as she was led out to the field. The groom nodded.

"Is anyone at home?"

"Only the staff."

"I thought Mr. Elis would be back."

"So did Mrs. Elis. Reckon the weather's held him up. There's been snow, so I hear. Won't trouble us, will it? Still too bloody cold."

"Are you putting her out?" McKenna gestured towards

the fractious animal trying to shake her head from her keeper's grasp.

"Only so I can change her bedding without getting kicked to death." He stroked her neck, murmuring. "It's her first foal, and she's crabby as hell, 'cos she's not quite sure what's happening."

"When's it due?"

"No more than six weeks. She went to the stallion last January end." He stroked her again, running his hands over the swollen belly. "Should be a little beauty. Her for a mother, and sired by a Derby winner. Did you know?"

"Mr. Elis mentioned it."

The groom laughed. "I'll bet he did! The stud fee was more than this place is worth. He's on pins waiting to see what he got for his money."

The groom moved away, half-dragged by his fretful charge, while McKenna perforce wondered if Elis thought money could buy a child as easily as it bought a foal.


Dewi waited in ambush outside the office. Walking through the door he held open, McKenna felt overcome by weariness, assailed on all quarters by demands for approval, protection, forgiveness, and other, deeper things to which he could not give name.

"I sent you out."

"I've been out, sir. DC Evans has been back and forth a bit. She's looking for Mandy's mate Tracey. I came back to do some telephoning." He stood before the desk, waiting perhaps for an advance on approval.

"So?"

"So I called some of the South Wales homes off the list. I said we want to interview the Tony Jones from Llandudno who was admitted a few days ago. I didn't think you'd mind."

McKenna lit a cigarette, watching doubt begin to creep over Dewi's face, and a smoke ring drift towards the dingy ceiling. "Depends on whether the outcome is a lot of flak and bugger-all else."

"There'll be flak sooner or later, but I located him, so maybe we can get there before anybody puts the mockers on it by shifting him again."

"Where is he?"

"Denbigh Hospital. Hogg put him in a secure unit near Swansea, they sent him to Denbigh yesterday."

"Why?" McKenna snapped. "Why must I drag out every bloody detail?"

"Apparently Tony claimed he'd been abused. The home contacted our Social Services and they probably told Hogg, because a taxi turned up first thing yesterday, with two great hulking blokes and a driver, and whipped him away. I rang the hospital. He's on a locked ward, so it'll be hard to see him without a doctor backing us."

By six o'clock, when she would normally be preparing to accompany her mother to chapel, Janet was on the coastal expressway, pushing her new car to its limits and listening to a song about the Road to Hell, smoke from the cigarette in her left hand stinging her eyes. She had nowhere to go, no one to call upon and find welcome, her home frostier than the night outside the speeding car with her father's disapproval and her mother's resignation. Passing the Talybont turn off at ninety miles an hour, she glimpsed a panda car with its lights doused. Lights suddenly blinding, it drew out in pursuit, and she pushed her foot on the accelerator, losing the hunters in a blaze of speed beyond the slip road to Llandegai.

She drove hither and thither, on and off the expressway, undecided and fretful, nothing to report to McKenna except failure and opprobrium, even less to say to her parents, but more opprobrium to receive. She circled Treborth roundabout twice before turning towards Menai Bridge. A few cars passed on the other side of Treborth Road, dazzling her eyes as they took the bends. House lights twinkled behind high conifer hedging on the steep slope near the Antelope Inn, and she thought how shell-like a house seemed when lit so, insubstantial and hollow.

She crossed the floodlit bridge, its reflection shimmering in the icy waters a hundred feet below, and drove towards Llanfairpwll, stopping by the lookout point to smoke two cigarettes, then fired the engine and retraced her tracks. Turning once more on to Treborth Road, she entered another world as the houses fell behind, and was engulfed by night and huge dark trees crowding down from the hillside to her left. Remembering tales of phantom figures rushing from the trees, she lit another cigarette, pushed another CD in the player, and watched the speedometer creep up to seventy miles an hour and beyond, tapping her fingers on the steering-wheel in time to Bad Medicine, savouring the smoke in her lungs and the sense of restrained power in the car she drove. She saw the figure too late, as it leapt out in her path. The car swerved wildly, careered over the white lines then back again, coming to rest with a terrifying thud against the steep verge. Air bags exploded in her face and at her side, stunning more than the impact, then deflated, exposing her to whatever lay outside the fragile shell of the car in which she cowered.

"You lot are draining scarce economic resources." Eifion Roberts loomed over McKenna, his bulk darkening the small hospital lobby. "First you. Now her and the other one."

"David Fellows isn't down to us," McKenna said. "Janet didn't hit him."

"The silly mare smashed up thousands of quids' worth of car because a rabbit jumped out on her. Good God! What next!"

"It was a white hare, and you know the local superstition about hares and souls and witches. Why don't you go home, and annoy your wife instead?"

The pathologist sat down. "I'll have a customer if Dai Skunk snuffs it. What happened to him?"

"His mother made her monthly visit and found him collapsed in the bedroom, in a pool of blood. I'm waiting to find out if he'd been attacked."

"You pulling him for questioning over Arwel could've given folk reason to attack him."

"I know."

"Can't be helped, you've a job to do. How is Miss Evans?"

"Hysterical. Her father's with her."

"He won't be best pleased, will he? That one's more arrogant than the God he claims to serve," Dr. Roberts commented. "Toe his line, or suffer for it. He tried to stop Janet going to university, then put the mockers on her doing social work. She probably only joined up to spite him."

"He's a typical Welsh patriarch. Maybe you recognize his characteristics because you share them."

"I don't browbeat people the way he does."

"Is that fact or fiction?" McKenna demanded. "How d'you know all this stuff you spout?"

"Hush up!" Dr. Roberts warned. "Here they come."

Slumped against the tall figure of her father, Janet limped slowly down the corridor. Completely ignoring the pathologist, Pastor Evans stopped in front of McKenna, and looked down upon him, sternly and unforgivingly.

"I cannot help but blame you, Chief Inspector. Janet should have been at home, not driving all over the county when she's obviously near exhaustion." He looked then upon his daughter, who hid her face in the folds of his dark grey overcoat. "See how shaken she is? I trust you won't expect her back at work for a few days."

Watching the retreating figures of pastor and child, Roberts observed, "Put you in your place, didn't he?" He chewed his bottom lip. "Notice how he pretended I don't exist? He's never forgiven me for doubting God's mercy."

McKenna stood. "I'm going to see about David Fellows."

The pathologist rose, panting slightly with effort. "Wouldn't bother, he was already in theatre when I arrived. You eaten

yet, Michael? There's a Lob Scouse in the oven at home. Just
what a body needs on a night like this."


The mattress beneath her lumpy with the impress of other
bodies, Mandy rolled gingerly on her side, fearful of greater
pain blazing along the pathways of her nerves. Dilys Roberts
had opened the bedroom curtains before going to her own
cubicle, letting night and tendrils of freezing air invade the
room. Unblinking, Mandy listened to the porcine snuffling
and snoring of the girl in the next bed, waiting for the noise
to reach its peak. The girl gasped and grunted, then turned
over on her face, and Mandy thought of the qualities of silence, the wide singing silence she knew as a child at her
grandparents' mountain farm, and the silence she knew now,
charged with such strident tension.

Her grandfather died of cancer when Mandy was seven.
Her grandmother sold the poor living and the flock of sheep to
pay their debts, moved to a small flat where her night silence
was engulfed by traffic roaring in and out of the industrial estate, and sank into misery and depression. The grandparents
buffered Mandy from her mother's excess of wantonness, and
when Grandfather went to Heaven and Grandmother to limbo,
the child was left in the Hell on earth her mother created, until
the social workers found another hell in which to place her.

A psychiatrist reported on her deteriorating behaviour.
Where Hogg used brutality, and Doris invoked the huge resources of her spite, the psychiatrist employed trickery and
cajolery to force upon her the conformity apparently demanded by society. Hogg ranted constantly of conformity, in-
toning at meals, interrupting lessons, imposing himself on the
most innocent recreation, using words and language Mandy
could not comprehend, but the meaning of which she must
absorb and obey. Like the other children to whom she dared
voice her confusion, she understood nothing, except, as time
progressed, the folly of not obeying Hogg's dictates to the last
syllable. Deadly routine, imposed for its own sake, brought

stultifying predictability to each day, killing the smallest hope, the least initiative, the youthful dreams of jobs and boyfriends and babies. Blodwel-time existed within its own dimensions, limited to the day to come and the terrors it would bring.

Wandering, sleepy thoughts jerked chaotically, tangled up inside her head. She stared at the ceiling, eyes fixed on a patch of dampness creeping from the corner of the room like a cloud, her breath loud and panicky, terrified once more of suffocating under her own helplessness. She lifted her head from the pillow, a wreck of a child clinging to a bit of hope, and looked at the lump of humanity in the other bed, fast in righteous torpor under the thin quilt. Pulling day clothes out from the pillow, she dressed, cloth against flesh so tearingly loud she expected Dilys Roberts to come running down the corridor, feet slapping on the linoleum tiles. No one woke, no one came to fling her bodily to the bed and stand over her, mouthing viciousness. She crept to the showers, closed the door, and pushed open the one window Hogg never bothered to nail shut, a vent too narrow for any but the thinnest of bodies. She wriggled out, glass pressing her head, frame biting her ribs and snagging her clothes, and hung on the ledge for a moment before dropping to the flagstones beneath.

Eifion Roberts yawned, mouth wide as a hippo's. McKenna yawned in sympathy. "Nice supper."

"Better than anything your Denise could rustle up. Bet you lived off Marks and Sparks ready mades."

"Why can't you be quiet about her?"

"She annoys me." Dr. Roberts drained his glass. "She irritates me. She's an ever-growing thorn in my flesh. I wish she'd sail off into the sunset on her boyfriend's boat." Refilling the glass, he added, "And I'd be really made up if they foundered in the Seven Sisters tides off Holyhead."

"Anybody'd think she was your wife, not mine." McKenna yawned again. "You're drunk as a skunk. I'd better help your long-suffering spouse get you to bed."

"There's a thing, eh? Dai Skunk. I hope folk remembered the rules when they patched him up."

"I'm sure they did."

"Only that virus is over-friendly, and not in the least sexually selective." The pathologist gulped his drink. "Happy to take residence wherever folk are careless enough to offer, and given some blood or bodily fluid for transport, it'll move house before you can say 'bum boy.' "

Dewi Prys waited again in ambush, outside McKenna's front door. He climbed out of his car as McKenna parked his own, a padded envelope under his arm, and switched off the radio in the middle of a plaintive song about lost love.

"What is it, Dewi? Can't it wait?"

"I'm not really the one to decide, sir."

Unlocking the front door, stumbling over the cat, McKenna switched on lights, casting an orangy glow on the darkened little street. "You can have ten minutes. I'm tired."

Rhiannon went to the ball alone, danced and drank and chattered, and let her host escort her home, arriving as the great longcase clock in Bedd y Cor's hall chimed midnight. As she said goodnight to this Prince Charming, his hand squeezed her knee. "Will you be all right on your own?" he whispered. The chauffeur glanced in the rear mirror, a knowing little smile about his lips. "Are you sure there's nothing I could do for you?"

"The staff will be waiting. Do thank your wife for a lovely evening." She escaped the fingers pawing the back of her dress and reaching for her thighs, and almost ran for the door. The car waited, and she heard its engine purr to life only when the front door closed behind her.

Mari waited in shadow at the rear of the hall. "The police came."

"Why?"

"They didn't say. Josh spoke to them."

"I expect they'll come back if it's important," Rhiannon said.

"Cook left supper."

"I think I'll go straight to bed."

"Mr. Elias rang."

"What did he say?" Rhiannon stopped halfway up the staircase, the hem of her dress cascading over the treads, fine-boned hand resting on the banister rail, diamond rings glittering.

Mari shrugged. "Nothing much. He might not be back tomorrow."

"Where is he? Still in Germany?"

"I don't know. I didn't ask him." Mari turned towards her own flat. "It's not up to me to ask him what he does with himself, is it?"

# •C h a p t e r•
# 9

I'm not surprised you're tired," Griffiths observed, with some sympathy. "You're not getting much sleep. Any word about David Fellows?"

"He had a massive internal haemorrhage," McKenna said. "His systems appear to be collapsing generally, so nobody's rating his chances."

The superintendent shuddered. "Was he attacked? Had he crossed the wrong people once too often?"

"Like Arwel?"

"Don't make connections. People like Fellows live too close to badness. They get a kick from courting danger."

"There's no evidence of assault. We treated his flat as a crime scene, but there was just a lot of junk and filth. And some home videos, which Dewi brought round to my house last night."

Griffiths drummed his fingers on the desk. "I wish Janet'd shape up like he does. I'm very disappointed with her. What was yesterday's palaver all about?"

"Stress and frustration. She's finding it hard to adjust to this kind of investigation, and she's terrified of failing. She wants to prove something to her father."

"She's employed to prove things to a court, not her father," Griffiths commented acidly. "She'll find herself back pounding the streets if she's not careful, not flashing around dressed up to the nines and being self-important. Why does she wear her best clothes to go slumming on a murder hunt?"

"She always dresses like that." McKenna smiled. "She's a well-brought up chapel-minister's only daughter, setting a good example."

"She's repressed. Yesterday was a bit of rebellion, in my opinion. Pity she didn't get it out of her system years ago, like Jack's girls."

"Is Janet coming to work today?" Dewi asked.

"Probably not."

"Is her car badly damaged?"

"Why don't you call and ask her?"

"I just wondered, sir. Is Mr. Tuttle back?"

"He was delivered safely from the teeth of the blizzard last night."

"Will he be going to Denbigh?"

"No one's going to Denbigh yet," McKenna said. "You're watching home movies, and Inspector Tuttle's on his way to Blodwel."

"Why?"

"Mandy Minx went walkies in the night, all alone."

"Maybe she's meeting Gary."

"More likely she couldn't take any more without going completely off her head."

"Mandy's been an even bigger pest since she got drunk the other night," Jack reported. "Doris reckons she had drugs along with her drink."

"Doris would," McKenna said. "Did you see him?"

"He's not well." Jack grinned. "The chief fire officer wasn't best pleased to find the windows nailed up, so Ronnie's anticipating trouble. He doesn't respond well to added stress, because there's more than enough with the job."

"I imagine he'll be thoroughly stressed out when he knows

you talked to Darren, and God knows how he'll react when we've seen Tony Jones."

"I've been trying to work out the implications of what Darren said about Blodwel and the Hoggs," Jack said. "But I can't get my head round anything solid. It's like tussling with fog."

"Owen Griffiths is having the same experience." McKenna lit a cigarette, and gazed through the window. "I'm quite sure Arwel wasn't the only abuse victim, but we can't connect the abuse with the Hoggs. We can't even accuse them of knowing about it and doing nothing. When Mandy let the cat out of the bag about the kids' nocturnal activities, she succeeded in letting them off the hook. Doris made it very clear she doesn't approve of kids going out on the tiles, because they get up to mischief. Mandy got drunk, the boys got raped."

"And what about the brutality, the sheer bloody nastiness?"

"Darren's got axes to grind, Jack. You only heard one side of the story."

"And the balance of plausibility will rest on the other."

"How much does Hogg weigh, d'you think? He's small and weedy and the wrong side of forty. And the teacher? About the same size, isn't he, and near retirement," McKenna said. "Darren's bigger than you."

"Size is nothing to do with it. Hogg terrifies these kids. They're like rabbits caught in the headlights of a truck."

In the windowless cubicle behind the canteen where video machine and television set were housed, Dewi opened the padded envelope and took out three tapes, the unlabelled casings greasy with fingerprints and scratched with much use. Pushing one in the mouth of the machine, he sat back, legs crossed, and watched images flicker to life on the screen.

The body that housed the soul of David Fellows bled inside itself again at noon, giving way to years of abuse and brutality, its organs too frail to sustain the pressure of blood flowing through them. The left kidney ruptured, leaking blood and uric acid, the right collapsed gently in the face of increased demands, their demise unremarked for critical milliseconds before the machines to which the man was wired recorded malfunction, and began a siren wailing. Before he reached the operating theatre, his heart was long in crisis, rhythms and pulses chaotic beyond recall.

Shortly after she finished lunching, his mother learned, from a gentle voice on the telephone, that her son died without regaining consciousness. The police were told soon afterwards, as the body on the trolley, sheeted and tagged, was wheeled to the mortuary by two porters.


Stirring a spoon round and around a mug of tea, Dewi said, "Those videos are gross."

"Home movies of that kind usually are," McKenna commented. "Who's starring?"

"A bunch of very consenting adults of both sexes, having it off in every way possible, some near impossible, and not a condom in sight. I know some of them, off the estate and round town."

"Then bring them in for a chat, and point out they're contributing to the black economy."

"Janet's here. She's legged it from her father's sermonizing."

"She can help identify the film stars."

Dewi frowned. "Those videos aren't fit for any women to see, let alone a minister's daughter."

"Women star in the bloody movies, don't they? She gets no favours on account of her sex, and no protection from the nastier parts of the job. Modern lady police officers want it that way, and we wouldn't want to disappoint them."

And as he walked down the stairs from his office, McKenna wondered if the eye of the camera had ever captured Denise in wantonness, leaving her image to titillate the senses long after her body decayed to dust.

• • •

"You don't often visit me here, Michael." Eifion Roberts cleared files and textbooks from the spare chair in his small office. "To what do I owe the honour?"

"Don't ask. I might say there's nothing more interesting at hand."

Squeezing behind his desk, the pathologist nodded. "Police work must get very tedious. Same old questions to the same old faces, getting the same old answers. Maybe the lad in Denbigh'll supply some novelty."

"He's not there any longer. Can I smoke in this place?" Lighting a cigarette before Dr. Roberts responded, McKenna added, "Apparently he's not mad, just bad. He tried to torch the ward, so he's been shunted elsewhere. Jack's still trying to find him."

"Can't the hospital tell you?"

"Social Services took him away late yesterday. We're trawling all the juvenile secure units, because I doubt he's walking free. He seems rather out of control."

"So people tell you." The pathologist doodled on the cover of a file. "Hearsay, presumption; what folk want you to think. I guess he was moved from Blodwel to stop him talking, only he shot his mouth off in South Wales instead, so he's shunted to the funny farm. He might've resorted to arson to get people to listen."

"Rather extreme."

"Desperate measures become the only options. Abused kids often talk because they can't stand the strain any longer, so they have to be discredited. The pity of it is that boys like Tony don't see the consequences. Attempted arson looks like badness rather than desperation. Depends who's looking." He drummed his fingers on the desk. "I've just opened up David Fellows." McKenna stubbed out the half-smoked cigarette, and lit another. "Liver and both kidneys necrotic, guts riddled with massive tumours, Kaposi's lesions all over. A veritable invasion of life in altered circumstances."

• • • •

"You don't look well," McKenna said. "Take the rest of the day off."

Jack gestured to the files stacked on his desk and spilling on to chairs and floor, and rubbed his eyes, leaving bruise marks on the skin. "There's too much to do, apart from the huge backlog of work on other cases, and I can't make any headway. I don't know what's the matter." He paused. "And quite frankly, I'm fed up with Janet's moods."

"Her father's being difficult."

"So she says," Jack said, with some bitterness. "Aren't all fathers difficult just for the hell of it?"

McKenna leaned against the window-sill, and lit a cigarette. "You might feel less distracted if you sorted out your own patch."

"I don't know what to sort. Em says the girls are going through a teenage phase, like half the kids in Blodwel, and I'm over-reacting." Jack sighed. "What's the difference between a phase and out of control? How can you tell if one kid'll grow out of whatever makes teenagers behave like bloody lunatics, and another one won't? Then the twins stuck their oar in about Arwel and Gary. God knows where they hear this talk. I dread to think who they're mixing with in school."

"What did they say?"

"Oh, just that kids go into care for their own good, and end up more neglected, disadvantaged and abused than if they'd stayed at home. And dead or missing, of course." Jack coughed. "But where d'you draw the line with kids? And when?" He rubbed his eyes again. "All the way to South Wales, I was arguing with myself. They're my children, I've known them since they were born, and I'd never, ever wash my hands of them. Then I remembered how I felt the other night. Absolutely terrified, absolutely helpless. Just like Gary's mother probably, and maybe even the Thomases." He coughed again. "But after what we've seen, I couldn't ask for help with the twins even if I was absolutely desperate."

"I'm sure Emma's right, so you won't need to," McKenna said. "Don't tar all children's homes with the same brush."

"Why not? Hogg reckons he works with the dregs of society, like prison officers, and us, so none of us can help being tainted. And fair play to him and his thuggy women, being cooped up most of the waking day and half the night with a punch of hostile kids can't be very pleasant. What's the price of survival in a place like Blodwel?"

McKenna sat down and stubbed out his cigarette. "Hogg chose his job; I chose mine. People who expose themselves to the worst in others can expect to be exposed to the worst in themselves." He lit another cigarette. "So far, I've been able to come to terms with myself, but I doubt Hogg's even bothered to try."

"That's another thing," Jack muttered.

"What is?"

Fidgeting with a paper-clip, Jack said, "What you'd call the worst in yourself, I suppose." He fell silent, then added, "Hogg's right about being tainted."

"And?"

"And count yourself lucky you've no children. There's no need for you to face up to your own potential for child abuse." He rubbed at his eyes again, almost savagely. "I'm almost scared to be in the same room as the twins. What used to be loving and wholesome and natural just seems sick and dirty now."

"Where's DC Evans?" McKenna opened the door of the video cubicle to find Dewi alone in front of the flickering television screen, making notes.

"She's gone with uniform to bring in some of this lot."

"I've had a rocket off the Traffic inspector." McKenna sat down. "She outran a patrol car on the expressway not long before she nearly ran down a hare."

"She's having problems with her father. She told me."

"I'm not surprised. She's convinced the chapel's covering up for child abusers within the ranks of the ministry."

"He wants her to resign."

"Janet's quite capable of making her own decisions. Things would be much better if she left home."

"She wouldn't want to leave her mam."

"Her mother would probably be very relieved to see the back of her. Adult children need to fly the nest."

Dewi switched off the television, and turned to face McKenna. "You've never said that to me."

"You're different, Dewi. Your family needs you, and you'll never resent that, because you've all found your place together." He smiled and switched on the television. "You don't know how lucky you are. Don't ever make waves in your lovely calm sea, or let the storms blow up from nowhere."

"Some folk like the storms," Dewi commented. "Makes them feel something's happening."

"Like shipwreck and death?" McKenna gazed at fuzziness and poorly focused images on the screen, none the less repulsive for their amateur presentation.

"They don't seem real, do they?" Dewi followed McKenna's gaze. "If I didn't know, I wouldn't believe they were."

"Human nastiness in its real colours and all its ordinariness." Feeling sick with himself for wanting to look, McKenna thought again of Denise, cast like a pearl amid the lardy bodies with mouth and crotch agape, waiting to be pierced and pleasured.

Dewi pressed the fast-forward button, invoking a blizzard of flesh, before stopping on a close-up shot of two men, hands on each other's genitals, naked on a stained and dirty bedcover. "Dai Skunk and his mate Ted. Ted must be inclined either way, 'cos he's on another film with the wife of that man we caught pushing Ecstasy tablets in the clubs." He moved the film on once more. "Here she is again, with a woman I don't know, both performing for the men. D'you reckon it's like they say, sir?"

"What?" Distracted, beguiled, McKenna eyed the women,

one thin and ageing, fingering the other, the fresh meat on the table, whose heavy thighs melted apart as the questing fingers of the thin woman cleaved her flesh like a hot knife through butter.

"Folk reckon watching women together is a turn on." Dewi laughed quietly. "They don't do much for me. One old, one flabby, and both mucky-looking."

"Is it all more of the same?" McKenna stood up. "This garbage isn't even illegal if it only involved consenting adults, no money changes hands, and it takes place in private."

"So why are we rounding them up?"

"To find out what else is available to titillate the jaded local palate."


The cathedral clock struck eleven as McKenna unlocked his front door, expecting to find the cat waiting for him as usual, but the hall was empty, and she failed to respond to his call. With mounting horror, he feared this precious waif of an animal had run away, looking for another heart to invade, and almost wept with relief when he found her at last, fast asleep under his bed. She yawned, swiped at him with one front paw, and resumed her slumber.

He made supper, drank two mugs of tea, and lay on the sofa, the radio turned low. Arm and shoulder throbbed with a passion all their own, his ribs squeezed his lungs in suffocating embrace, his throat rasped raw with excess of lust for nicotine. He gazed about the small room, seeing not the pretty wallpaper or the pictures hung over mantel and table, but the flailing bodies and contorted faces of the men and women more real than their own reality in the fantasy performed for the cyclops eye of the camera.

He sat at the table, chain-smoking, reviewing the moral law he believed he assumed from choice, and thought of the vortex of dark excesses seething in his own heart, knowing how those who lingered in the twilit reaches of society so easily embraced the evils they were charged to eradicate.

Leaving the radio playing softly, he pulled his coat from the back of the chair and went out. Striding down the hill, past the cathedral and up Glanrafon, he crossed the road by the Safeway supermarket, where lights shone brightly in the car-park, and voices and clatter echoed in the unloading bays, and entered the darkness of Ffriddoedd Road. He walked its length meeting not a soul, past dark driveways like gaping mouths, scuffing his feet through drifts of sodden leaves, flitting like a wraith from the mist-shrouded lights of one street lamp to another, thinking how quickly his journey was done, and wondering if the earth truly shrank with the setting of the sun.

By the gateway to St. Gerrard's Convent, he stopped, looking through a thicket of trees at the darkened building, and thought perhaps tomorrow morning, or night, or the day after, some ordinary person might stumble over the cold rotting body of Gary Hughes or Mandy Minx, and become for a while an extraordinary person in the sight of the knowing world. He looked up at bluey-black sky milky with strands of fog, then went on his way, walking with Night, wondering which of her children, Sleep or Death, she might send to play with him until the sun rose once again behind the mountains in the east.

# •C h a p t e r•
## 10

Standing with her back to the shop door, Mandy shivered convulsively, ratty teeth chattering inside lips chapped and pinched with cold.

Carol wiped a duster back and forth over the glass counter top, scrubbing at a stubborn finger-mark, pale hair swinging about her pallid cheeks. "I've only got ten quid in my bag."

"That'll get me a long way, won't it?" Mandy snapped. "Can't you borrow from the till?"

"I'd get the sack." Carol ceased the futile polishing to stare at the other girl. "Don't you know running away won't do any good?" She began cleaning again, wiping the duster over display boxes crammed with can openers and potato peelers and sink plugs in dirty white rubber. "You'll end up like Arwel. So will that Gary."

"They're not interested in me."

"They will be now." Carol pushed the hair off her face, frowning. "Did you have to come here? That policewoman keeps after me with her bloody questions. What if she asks about you?"

"You say nothing, like you manage to say about Arwel."

"Shut up about Arwel!" Carol whispered viciously.

"You said his name! And if you hadn't kept your mouth shut in the first place, he might still be alive."

"I promised!" Carol rubbed at the tears sliding down her cheeks. "He made me. Nobody would've believed him."

"Somebody might," Mandy insisted. "Even if they didn't, there'd've been trouble, and he wouldn't've stayed at Blodwel."

"They'd've locked him up somewhere else." Carol sobbed openly. "I wouldn't've been able to see him. I couldn't've looked out for him."

Mandy scowled with impatience. "You're so fucking stupid, Carol Thomas! People always shit on you. Did you tell Arwel it'd be all right so long as he kept his mouth shut and his arse wide-open?" She almost spat with disgust. "He trusted you! He'd've crawled on broken glass for you. Did you say the fancy boyfriend'd sort it?" She advanced towards the counter, pushing her face so close she smelt the bile on Carol's breath, whispering savagely, "You do right to look sick, 'cos it's your fault he's dead!"


"If your average nice kid from your average nice semi on Bangor's posh side got shafted and murdered, and went on the run in the teeth of winter, we'd be buzzing round like blue-arsed flies with all the world falling over itself to help, and sod the cost." Dropping the headquarters' memorandum on McKenna's desk, Jack sat down. "As it is, we get snotty memos from the accountants in charge of the force telling us how we're wasting money chasing juvenile delinquents."

"It's a reminder to keep outlay to the absolute minimum," McKenna said. "The budget's overstretched already, without trips to South Wales and all the recent overtime. There's no extra money due in the next financial year, so the current deficit will result in poorer services, fewer officers, and more pressure on us."

"Then we'd better inform the locals we can't afford more crime until next April. Make a polite request for them to drop their shit in another force area. Merseyside Police probably wouldn't notice."

"Oh, give it a rest!" McKenna snapped. "Have you located Tony Jones yet? And did you talk to the twins again about Gary?"

"We're contacting all the secure units in Britain, as well as hospitals with facilities for juveniles, and I shudder to think of the phone bills," Jack said. "The twins aren't actually speaking to me, because I'm a willing cog in the Fascist machinery that grinds people like Arwel and Gary and Mandy into the dirt."

"Are they speaking to Emma?"

"Only when necessary, like when they want clean clothes or money. They don't need us, you see."

"I see." McKenna pulled on his cigarette, throat still sore, lungs still tight.

"You're wheezing," Jack pointed out. "You'll be down with bronchitis next."


Ice as thick as snow whitened the mountain slopes, dingy under gathering cloud moving sluggishly north-east, and wreathing around the summit of Snowdon. Sitting in the car outside the school gates, waiting for the pupils to emerge for morning break, McKenna scanned the tiny clusters of habitation straggling across the mountain foothills, wondering where, in that huge frozen wasteland, the missing youngsters might be. Hundreds of manpower hours had been wasted searching empty dwellings around Caernarfon and Bangor, scouring back yards and sheds and outhouses and boarded-up shops and farm buildings, invading squats, questioning anyone who came to hand, and in the absence of finding them alive in any of the logical places, McKenna feared they could only be found dead. He lit a cigarette, seeing in his mind's eye Gary's hair frosted with ice, eyelashes rimed with hoar, eyes dulled and dead beneath; and Mandy Minx, lips blue with cold, ratty teeth glittering white, hair like a splash of dried blood on the ice. He opened the window and tossed out the half-smoked cigarette, watching it fizzle in the greasy swill of the gutter.

High-pitched voices floated on the air, footsteps rattled on tarmac, and he climbed from the car, walking towards the spill of bodies coming around the sides of the ugly concrete building. He accosted a tall youth whose face blossomed with chill and acne.

"D'you know where I can find the Tuttle girls?"

The boy's teeth chattered gently. "Haven't seen them. The school secretary'll know where they are."

The secretary told him the twins had failed to register, and the parents had failed to contact the school. McKenna sat again in the car, trying to decide what to do for the best, how to reimpose order on the chaos underlying all life which had erupted into the Tuttle household.

The house was empty of Emma and her daughters. Walking round to the back, he peered through the kitchen window at a pristine room bereft of traces of recent occupation. He lingered, looking through other windows, finding the garage vacated of Emma's small car, and the twins' bicycles leaning against one wall, dusty and abandoned, like the unquestioning innocence of childhood. He telephoned Jack, whose voice rose with hysteria, fear adding ugly harsh sounds to his words.

From the drawing-room window, Rhiannon watched the Range Rover come slowly down the lane then pass from sight, and stayed in her place, head tilted slightly, listening for wheels biting gravel, the gentle squeal of locking brakes, the chunky thud of the closing door, the crunch of her husband's footsteps as he mounted the steps to the front door. But the front door opened before the vehicle stopped, and she heard Mari's light steps and tinkling laughter. She sighed for another missed opportunity, and returned to her chair, sitting with clasped hands, listening still but hearing nothing to bring any joy.

"I can't find Inspector Tuttle," Janet complained. "He told me to report to him when I got back."

"I've sent him home," McKenna said.

Janet stood by the desk, coat hanging loose, a cashmere scarf around her shoulders. "Is he ill?"

"Do you have anything to report?"

"Not really."

"Why not?"

"There just isn't, sir. Nobody's got any suggestions."

"For God's sake!" McKenna snapped. "This isn't London! There aren't quarter of a million people in the whole county, yet you can't find a soul who can tell you anything!"

"It's not my fault!"

"Stop being childish!" McKenna warned. "You should know better. Where's Dewi Prys?"

"I don't know." Her voice was sulky. "Probably still out."

"Then go to the parade room for instructions from the inspector in charge. Jack Tuttle's girls have gone missing, and they must be found."

Emma stood by the sitting-room window, and merely glanced in McKenna's direction as he parked the car. The front door stood wide open to the icy air, strands of gold and silver foil on the newly decorated Christmas tree shivering in the draught. He shut the door, and went into the sitting-room.

"Jack's out looking," Emma said. "He's frantic. I've got to stay here for the telephone."

"Is anyone with you?"

"You are." She reached out blindly, groping for his hand. "Don't leave me."

"They're using you." Elias ab Elis stared at his wife, the forkful of venison uneaten. "I've warned you time and again."

Rhiannon picked at her own food, prodding the meat with her fork. "What am I supposed to do? Blodwel has problems."

"Of whose making?"

"Hoggs do their best with very poor resources and very little money. They're entitled to my support at times like these."

"You're naive!" He dropped the fork on the plate. "You must apologize to Cook. I'm not very hungry."

"Where were you last night?" Rhiannon stared at her own plate. "I telephoned the hotel in Bonn. They said you'd left."

"I stayed with Anselm. We had a lot to discuss." He sipped a glass of German spa water, noting the stains of tiredness about her eyes. "You must stop evading unpleasant issues. Ronald Hogg's problems are of his own making, but while he can claim the wholehearted support and friendship of the chair of committee, no one will be inclined to ask searching questions about those children."

"I know things aren't right at Blodwel."

"Things at Blodwel are very wrong. Do you ever talk to the children, without staff breathing down your neck?"

Rhiannon shrugged. "Sometimes. They don't say much."

"They don't, do they?" Elis rose from the table, and stood before the hearth, arm resting on the mantel. "Arwel never said much to me, and I don't know what he said to Mari, but I know he was desperate and unhappy." The silence lengthened, punctuated by rapid breaths and the crackling logs.

Rhiannon abandoned her own meal. Her fork chipped the plate as it fell to the table. "I don't imagine words were necessary between you and Arwel. You loved him very much and he must have known."

"Dear God!" Jack Tuttle wept in the arms of his wife. "What are we going to do?"

"Nothing for now." Emma stared over Jack's shoulder at McKenna, who sat by the fire, gazing steadily at the flames. "They're home and safe." She pulled herself away. "Let them settle down."

Bewilderment clouded Jack's eyes. "What if they run away again? What if we can't find them?"

"I don't think they will," McKenna said.

"And how would you know?" Jack demanded.

"Because they're not as stupid as you think!" McKenna

snapped. "Or as troublesome. Lots of kids take a day off school, even those from the very best homes. It's part of growing up."

"Michael's right," Emma said. "They came home at the usual time, and if he hadn't wanted to see them, we'd never know they dodged."

Jack stared at his wife, at McKenna. "So where've they been all day? Answer me that, since you know it all!"

"Round the shops," McKenna said. "Taking afternoon tea alongside the city's venerable matrons."

"How do we know they weren't shop-lifting, or drinking in pubs, or out with men?" Jack demanded.

"We don't," Emma said tetchily. "And there'll be even more things we don't know in the future. We must trust their common sense, because if they don't know how to use it now, they never will." She walked to the door. "I'm going to make dinner, and if they prefer to sulk in their room all night, they're welcome." The door slammed behind her, its draught dislodging a Christmas card from the row on the mantel.

McKenna stooped to retrieve it. "Your cards come early. I've had none yet."

"Are you going to let them get away with it?" Jack's face, blotched with tears and misery, discoloured further with incipient fury. "For God's sake! We had a full-scale missing children alert. What about the cost?"

"Pity we didn't turn up the real runaways." McKenna put the card back in its place. "The twins won't risk this hullabaloo again to dodge school for a few hours, because they've seen the consequences, and fun stops being much fun when the chickens come home to roost."

"Would you like to spend a couple of years at Blodwel?" McKenna asked.

Emma leaned against the closed door of the twins' bedroom, watching McKenna, who towered over the girls lounging on one of the beds.

"Are you looking for alternative prospects? Are you bored

with plans for university and a career? Going into care would wreck your future very quickly." He watched Emma from the corner of his eye, waiting for her to shield her young from the onslaught of harsh reality. She remained mute.

"I hope you're both listening," McKenna added. "You can ignore your parents, but you're foolish to ignore me. You put a great many people to a great deal of wholly avoidable trouble and expense, and I'm extremely disappointed. If you want to play silly games, I'll make sure you reap the consequences."

"What d'you mean?" Both girls jerked to attention, then stared at Emma. "What does he mean, Mummy?"

"The law permits us to commit juveniles to care if we think it necessary," McKenna said. "Whether or not I decide to exercise that power is entirely up to you."

"You can't do that! You can't!"

"Try me," McKenna invited.


"You *slut*!" Peggy Thomas lunged at her daughter. "You filthy *slut*!"

"Takes one to know one," Carol jeered. "You should be glad I don't take after him. Don't you always say he's fucking useless?"

"Shut your dirty mouth!"

Her father reared from his chair and swiped at her with his fist. Carol stumbled backwards, eyes alive with the rage and grief so long dammed, the beautiful yellow hair flying about her face. Still slender, agile with youth, she dodged their hands and spat in their ugly faces. "You're *shit*! You'll rot in hell for what you did to Arwel!"

"He was bad!" The woman's voice rose to a screech. "Evil bad! Devil's spawn, both of you!"

Carol leaned against the wall, out of reach, and began to laugh. "He's no devil, is he?" She nodded towards her father. "Didn't he father us? Who made Arwel and me? Don't you know? Were there so many?" She advanced towards her mother and grabbed her shoulders, feeling bone thin beneath her fingers. "Tell me, you dirty whore! Who fathered us?" She began to shake the woman, watching the head jerk, hearing the teeth rattle. "Tell me, tell me, tell me!" she intoned, watching night press itself to the grimy window, thin reflections of herself and the man and woman silent in the darkness beyond.

"*Tell me!*" she screamed. "For Christ's sake tell me!"


Patrolling the dingy basements of Caernarfon, a young policeman found Mandy trying to breach the rear doors of the Market Hall, in search of food and shelter. She struggled once or twice as they waited for a woman officer to walk from Castle Ditch, then slumped on the steps of the building and smoked the cigarette he offered, deciding to say nothing, hoping to evade the return to Blodwel which would follow identification, knowing the police would feed and house her, at least for a while. As the trio walked into darker shadow by the castle walls, Mandy thought she might say her name was "Carol Thomas," that she was almost eighteen years old, and that she was going to have a baby, and as she giggled to herself, the policewoman jerked her arm, then hustled her up the steps and into the fuggy warmth of the police station.


Janet sat in the passenger seat of McKenna's car, her subtle perfume mingling with the scents of damp night and warm engine. Sometimes, McKenna thought he detected vestiges of the chapel scent about her person: prayer books and hymnals and the muskiness of old wood.

"You must be sick of the trouble these kids are causing, sir."

"We can stop worrying about Mandy for a while."

"I wonder why she didn't go home?" Janet asked.

"Because she knows she's not welcome."

Janet smiled. "She said she's expecting. I can't think what she hopes to gain."

"A respite from that dreadful children's home, I imagine." McKenna pushed the accelerator, wanting to bring the journey to an early end. Breasting the bypass, headlamps swinging wide arcs in the sky, the car drifted momentarily as the rear wheels hit a patch of black ice.

"Is Blodwel really as bad as we think?" Janet asked. "Aren't we perhaps getting things out of proportion?"

"Blodwel is as bad as we think, if not worse. I have nothing out of proportion."


Jeans muddied, suedette boots scuffed and stained, jacket hung awry from skinny shoulders, Mandy lounged on a bench in the detention room, sucking her thumb, staring at the police officers who crowded the doorway, her eyes flicking from one to the other.

"A social worker should be here," Janet pointed out. "She's still a minor."

"D'you want a social worker?" McKenna asked.

Mandy wrapped her lips more firmly around the thumb, gnawing at the knuckle, then shook her head.

"That's disposed of that issue." The room smelt musty, its painted walls sweating with cold. "D'you want to talk to me, to WDC Evans, or both of us?"

Shrugging, Mandy sat up straight and put her feet on the floor. "Makes no odds. You'll still send me back."

McKenna sat down beside her. "I don't know we've any choice. You're in care."

The girl smiled wryly. "Yeah, I am, aren't I?"

"Why did you run away?"

"Why not?" Mandy frowned, and began to pick at a loose thread on her sleeve.

"What happened after we took you back the other night?" She watched her fingers pluck the stitching apart.

"We called the next day, but the staff said you were ill."

"Yeah, you could say that."

"Was that because you'd been drinking?"

"Yeah, it might've been."

"Could there be another reason?"

"Maybe."

Turning attention to her bootlaces, Mandy leaned forward, cloudy brilliant hair obscuring her face, slowly untying both laces, then retying them, pulling each taut before fashioning neat little bows, each loose end meticulously matched to the other.

"Why don't you tell me what happened?" McKenna asked.

"What's the point? You won't do nothing. Nobody ever does."

"Are you pregnant?"

"Maybe."

"Since when?"

"Since I don't know! Right?" The girl looked up, eyes fiery as her hair.

"You must have some idea."

"Yeah, I must, mustn't I?" She nodded and sat back, leaning her head against the sweaty walls, closing her eyes, putting out the fire.

Janet moved, shoes squeaking on the floor, and took Mandy's limp small hands in her own. "We want to help you."

The eyes flew open, fires alight. "Help? You'll take me back, whatever I say!"

"Depends on what you have to say," McKenna said. "Why not give us a chance?"

"You can't do nothing." The girl was adamant, wrenching her hands from Janet's grasp. "I'm not talking to you, so nobody can say I said anything."

"People might think you have anyway," McKenna said. "Blame you for something you haven't done."

"Wouldn't be the first time, would it?"

"What happens when you get blamed?"

"Depends."

"On what?"

"On what it is."

"Did Tony Jones get blamed for something?"

"Why don't you ask him?"

"I would if I knew where to find him."

"He's in a lock-up in South Wales, and he's only got himself to blame."

"Who said that?"

"Who said what?"

"Have you seen Gary Hughes recently?"

"Maybe."

"I'd like to know. I'm worried about him."

"He's better off than he was."

"How's that?"

"Not in that dump, is he?" Mandy looked up, eyes dulled and lifeless. "When you taking me back?"

"When d'you want to go back?" McKenna asked.

"Up to you, isn't it?" She unfastened the laces, and began the ritual tying.

"Did someone hit you the other night?" McKenna asked. "You should tell me, because I can't take you back if you won't be safe."

"Hogg said nobody'll have me except the lock-up for girls. It's called Puddlechurch, or something."

"Why should you be locked up? You haven't committed a crime."

"Tony was, and he hadn't."

"Maybe someone thought he had."

"Yeah!" Mandy announced. "And maybe they thought he'd opened his gob, like they'll think I have."

"I can tell Blodwel staff you said nothing of any consequence."

"Are you pregnant?" Janet intervened. "You should say, so you can be looked after properly."

"Like Donna, you mean?"

"Donna?" Janet asked. "Have I met her?"

"How the fuck do I know who you've met?"

"Is Donna at Blodwel?" McKenna asked.

"The social worker got her a flat off the council."

"She'd be entitled with a baby," Janet said.

"I said she was expecting!" Mandy snapped, glaring at Janet. "I didn't say she'd had it."

"So when's it due?"

"They got rid of it, didn't they?"

"Who did?"

"Doris took her somewhere. Donna told me, 'cos she was sick with the pain. She bled all over the bed, and Dilys had to get clean sheets, and she was scared."

"Who was scared?"

"Dily, 'cos she didn't know what'd happened, did she?"

McKenna watched the girl, who plucked at the loosening threads on her other sleeve, fidgeted with her clothing, glanced at Janet, then to the floor, then at the walls, and could almost see the chaos of thought and word, of hearsay and gossip in her mind, the jumble of events and nightmarish visions, understood only in that she felt their menace. He wondered if age would give her greater understanding, and thought she might stumble through whatever life strewed in her path, anaesthetized by the stupidity which bedevilled understanding.

"If I say somebody hit me, you can't take me back, can you?" Mandy asked.

"Did they?"

"He punched me in the guts."

"Who did?"

"That bastard Hogg!" She spat the words.

"Did anyone see him do it?"

"What do you think?" Mandy sneered.

"Make a statement," McKenna said. "Then I can deal with it."

"What'll happen if I do?"

"A police officer will write down what you say, then a doctor will examine you for marks or injuries, and I'll see Mr. Hogg."

"When will you?"

"Tomorrow," McKenna said. "Perhaps the day after."

"What about me?"

"Social Services will have to find somewhere else for you."

"I've told you nobody'll have me." Her voice was toneless.

"What about foster homes?" Janet said.

"They won't have me."

"How d'you know?"

"Hogg said, over and over like a fucking broken record. 'Nobody'll have you!' " She mimicked Ronald Hogg. " 'Nobody'll put up with you!' "

McKenna looked at his watch. "It's getting late, Mandy. What d'you want to do?"

The girl shrugged. "Dunno. Whatever you want."

"I can't leave you here for the night."

"What about this statement?"

"You're sure you want to make one?"

"I suppose so."

McKenna stood, stiffness in his arm, tightness creeping around his chest once again, slightly nauseous from hunger and cold and fatigue. "DC Evans will deal with it, Mandy, while I deal with Social Services."


Gary crept around the cottage interior, lighter flickering in the draught as he moved slowly from parlour to lean-to kitchen, and thence to each of the tiny ground-floor bedrooms, where little sash windows were shrouded by half-drawn curtains, shutting out the luminous mountain night. His foot caught in the drape of a bedspread, and he stumbled against a chest of drawers, rattling ornaments and knick-knacks bestrewing the surface. Putting out his hands to save himself, he felt the grittiness of dust on his fingers.

From late morning until well beyond nightfall, he had lain watch in the lee of the mountain, waiting for people who never came, looking for the minute change at the cottage telling of occupation. As the sky above him darkened, pulling long shadows around him, he watched his hands turn blue with cold, limbs so numbed his only sensation was of cold flesh rubbing against clothing.

Crouching before the gas heat in the parlour hearth, he tried ten times to make fire before realizing it lacked a canister of propane, and crept outside to search the outbuildings, finding only junk and litter. Back indoors, he took out the last of the chocolate biscuits taken from his mother's larder, and ate them, one by one, savouring each small mouthful. He found the stop-tap under the kitchen sink, leaping backwards as water gushed over his clothes and hands, cold as shards of ice, then sat before the unlit fire, on the edge of an armchair with squeaking springs, sipping the water, before going to the room which looked out on the long snaking lane from the valley floor. He wrapped himself about with blankets, mustiness in his nostrils, and fell into exhausted sleep atop the rickety bed.

The telephone summoned McKenna from restless drowsing. Glancing at the mantel clock as he picked up the receiver, he thought vaguely of the vast aeon spent in dream-time, and the bare half-hour passed in reality while he slept.

"I'm in a quandary," Eifion Roberts announced. "Young Mandy's got the sort of skin which marks easily, and she's got a lot of marks on her torso, arms and thighs, all of which could've been caused when she squeezed through a very small window to escape Blodwel. On the other hand, there's definite tenderness in the belly, as well as internal swelling, so she might well have been thumped. I can't say yes and I can't say no, although the lady doctor with me is inclined to say yes."

"Is she pregnant?"

"Doubt it. She's menstruating."

"She said she was when they picked her up."

"She didn't. She said her name was Carol Thomas. Carol Thomas is up the spout."

"Who says?"

"Mandy says. She borrowed a tenner off her this morning. The girl's quite chatty, but she didn't like your lady cop very much. Janet rubs her up the wrong way. Bit too sharpish, if you ask me. You need patience with Mandy's sort."

"Did she make a statement?"

"Claims Hogg gave her a beating because Janet caught her on a pub crawl." Dr. Roberts paused, then asked, "You're not sending her back to that hell-hole, I trust?"

"Social Services will put her in a short-term foster placement, unless you think she should be in hospital."

"We can get her a bed. Put her out of harm's way for a couple of days at least."

"Did she say much else?"

"Not really."

"Make your mind up!" McKenna said irritably.

"She witters about this and that, but doesn't seem to understand most of what goes on, and only knows enough to be scared half to death. There's not much fire in her, just a bit of a flicker now and then, and it's soon put out, like she knows how dangerous it is. She shows all the symptoms of the Stockholm Syndrome, like a prisoner of war. Robotic responses, semi-anaesthetized levels of consciousness, and almost total loss of will. Wholly typical of someone subjected for long periods to extreme stress and fear."

"Why won't they speak to us?" Jack demanded of his wife. "What have we done to them?"

"We've done nothing, and as I don't particularly want to speak to them, it's no hardship."

"I don't understand you," Jack protested. "Don't you care?"

"Why should I care about two selfish, spoiled brats who don't know when they're well off?"

"Don't be like that, Em."

"Don't be so damned mawkish!" Spots of colour burned on Emma's cheeks. "You're too bloody soft with them! They get away with murder!"

"That not fair!"

"*Fair?* What's fairness got to do with anything in this life?"

"She doesn't understand how I feel." Jack hunched like an old man on McKenna's sofa. "She doesn't see the terrible things we see, so she doesn't understand what could happen to them."

"Emma understands perfectly," McKenna said.

"You've got little enough control over kids of that age, but once it goes!" Terror haunted Jack's eyes.

"Perhaps they don't need the control you offer. Growing up involves trying out strengths to learn about the weaknesses."

"I don't know!" Jack slumped against the cushions, shaking his head. "They're so quiet, and it's bloody eerie. When they're shouting the odds and screaming, you know what they're doing, but since you left, there's just been a horrible breathing silence. God knows what they're hatching!"

"Nothing, I would imagine."

"What did you say to them? Em won't tell me."

"Nothing much."

"Because if you said the earth was flat and the moon made out of green cheese, they'd believe you."

# •Chapter•
# 11

The west wind, so long stilled by frosts from the east, began to rise in the early hours, thumping in the tall chimney of McKenna's house. Half awake, he listened to the bare branches of the trees below his window creaking as the wind dragged them from the fastness of ice about their roots. The cat lay on his feet, curled in a ball, snoring gently, and he drifted back to sleep, to dream he floated on a raft of cloud, the moon and stars brilliant above him, shining silver gilt on the hair of the girl and boy who floated with him beyond the mountains and on to nowhere.

"You wouldn't credit it," Dewi said. "Bloody freezing for days on end, then what?"

"Structural damage, the River Ogwen full to bursting, another landslip on the A5 past Bethesda, and all in the space of a few hours." Jack's face was as grey as dawn light. "It was on the news."

"The River Adda's flooded again, after all that money was spent on culverts and drainage. Caernarfon Road's half under water."

"Britannia Bridge is no doubt closed, and the ferries won't sail. So what? It happened last year, and the year before."

"It makes you wonder, that's all," Dewi said. "We still can't do anything about the weather."

"We can, actually," Janet offered. "I read in *The Times* recently that artificial clouds are creating rainfall in drought areas. Experiments on thunderstorms and lightning are being done, too."

"I haven't read that."

"I don't expect you read *The Times*, do you?" Janet responded.

Flood water swirled about sandbagged diversion signs on Caernarfon Road as McKenna turned up Penchwintan hill, joining a queue of early-morning traffic moving at snail's pace out of the city, cars and lorries, buses and vans nose to tail. Breasting Port Dinorwic bypass after interminable delays, he saw sheets of torrential rain driven in from the sea, and flinched as water hit the windscreen so hard the wipers flattened themselves.

Carol Thomas ignored him as long as possible, busying herself about the shop, tidying shelves crammed with cups and plates, bowls and saucers, in pot and china and smoky glass. He stood by the door, raincoat unfastened, water streaming from his umbrella between the blue floor tiles. Watching her slender body in its dismal clothes, the beautifully moulded arms and fine-boned hands, the glorious yellow hair, he wondered if the man who planted his seed within her had also soiled her arms with disfiguring bruises. A High Street star, fallen from the firmament of grace.

"Are you busy, Carol?" he asked at last. "We need to talk."

"What about?"

"This and that. Could you take a break?"

"I don't know." She turned to face him, little smudges of dust on her fingertips. "What d'you want?"

"Mandy was arrested last night."

"Stupid bitch!"

"She said you lent her money."

"So?"

"You must've known she was on the run."

Carol leaned against the counter, arms folded. "Going to arrest me for aiding and abetting?"

"You know all the jargon, don't you?"

"You pick it up."

Her eyes gleamed with a bright intelligence light years distant from the murkiness through which her friend would forever wade.

"Mandy said you're pregnant."

"Did she? Is that a crime now? Has that bloody government in London outlawed babies for girls like me?"

"Not that I know," McKenna said.

"So why're you asking?"

"I wondered if it had anything to do with Arwel."

"We didn't love each other that way. Don't judge everybody by the folk round Bangor."

"I didn't mean that, Carol. You know perfectly well what I'm talking about."

"You don't know yourself, so how can I?" She smiled gently, the gesture bringing heart-stopping beauty to her face. "Anyway," she added, "having a baby could be the making of me, couldn't it?"

"Who'll look after it while you work? Your mother?"

"You being funny? She didn't do much by me and Arwel, did she?"

"We found an exercise book with Arwel's things," McKenna said. "He's been making up crosswords, but we can't work out the clues."

She flicked a speck of dust from the counter. "Arwel was clever that way. He used his imagination. Pa said he used it too much."

"How so?"

"He said Arwel made up things about folk."

"What sort of things?" Was she at last trying to communicate with someone from an alien culture she had only learned to fear? He smiled encouragingly. "About whom?"

"You'll have to ask him yourself," Carol said. "Don't smoke in here," she added, as McKenna pulled out his cigarettes. "There's weedkiller and fertilizer and all sorts. You could blow up half the town."

"Don't you smoke yourself? Arwel did, I believe."

"I don't smoke and I don't drink," Carol snapped, her voice waspish. "I just fornicate, but you already know that, don't you?"

Fighting an umbrella blown inside out, McKenna battled along High Street, chased by a whirlwind of litter. He threw the ruined umbrella in a wastebin by the pedestrian crossing, and bought a replacement at a small chain store, handing his money to a wonderful oriental girl, who gossiped with her companion in guttural dialect, then crossed the road to a menswear shop, and replaced his sodden mackintosh with a waterproof drover's coat which hung almost to his ankles. Wet coat folded neatly in a carrier-bag, he went for lunch at the restaurant opposite the bus station, and ordered chicken sandwiches and strong dark tea. He wondered absently if the ratty-faced woman at the next table, smoke from her cigarette curling around her dyed red hair and under his nose, might be Mandy's mother, taking respite from her own chaos. Mandy's statement was in his briefcase. Ronald Hogg, she claimed, had hit her, thumped her in the belly, slapped her about the face, screamed at her, called her "fucking whore" and "drunken slut," like her mother. Owen Griffiths fretted over the implications and judged his authority inadequate to empower formal interview of the alleged perpetrator, counselling McKenna to caution and prudence in the face of impending disaster.

"Procedures are necessary," Griffiths had argued.

"It's not 'procedures,' " McKenna said. "It's the Taffia."

"Don't exaggerate. We're not in America."

"If Mandy said some deadleg from a council estate bashed her, we'd be there with guns blazing."

"But Hogg's a senior social worker, so we must be sure of our ground before we drop on him."

"And how do we do that?"

"Wait and see what turns up, apart from the word of a girl who's not quite all there, and might well be romancing anyway."

McKenna lit another cigarette.

"You're biased towards these youngsters." Griffiths coughed, waving away smoke from under his nostrils. "I wish you'd cut down on the cigarettes."

"Job stress. Others take to drink. How am I biased?"

"You seem to believe every word they say, whereas it's your job to keep an open mind," Griffiths said. "And I'm not sure you'd give the same consideration to the word of adults in similar circumstances."

"Offenders aren't necessarily untruthful, except about owning for their crimes," McKenna said. "Prisoners are abused, as well. Human rights and justice must be universal, or there's nothing for anyone."

"I said nothing about justice." Griffiths chewed his lip. "Have you thought of the implications? Hogg could complain about harassment, or even slander. And what about our reputation? Complaints against the force've already reached an all-time high."

Jack pushed open the door of McKenna's office, to find the room swirling with draughts from a wide-open window, McKenna lounging in his chair, and the raincoat, still patchy with damp, draped over the radiator.

"I wasn't expecting you back yet," Jack said. "I thought you were seeing the director of social services."

"The pleasure's yet to come."

"Mandy's been discharged from hospital to a foster home in Holyhead, so at least she'll be out of Hogg's way."

"You think? Have you located Tony yet?"

"No." Jack sat down. "And Gary's definitely gone to earth. What did Carol have to say?"

"Tom Thomas apparently thought Arwel was romancing about something. Dewi can go and ask what," McKenna said. "And Carol's pregnant."

"How lovely for everybody!" Jack said. "Another deadleg."

"For all we know, the baby could be another Einstein."

"No, it won't. It'll be another cancer eating up society."

"Eifion Roberts would see even cancer as a miracle of life."

"Eifion Roberts is a bit of a crackpot, to put it kindly."

"The orthodox view isn't necessarily better."

"And the majority opinion isn't necessarily second-hand," Jack pointed out. "People do think for themselves." He stared gloomily at McKenna. "The twins do. Pity their thinking doesn't relate to any known process."

"They're expressing the orthodox view from Planet Teenager. Can't you remember being that age?" McKenna asked. "One minute up in the clouds and able to move the world with a breath, the next crashing to earth."

"I just remember people being stroppy with me, and being scared of going too far. Kids these days don't know that sort of fear. They've no sense of guilt."

"You sound almost jealous of them."

"Don't be ridiculous!"

"You're redundant in the face of the next generation, and you don't like knowing it." McKenna stood up to close the window. "It happens to us all, Jack. You should read more, broaden your understanding. The human condition never changes. We just surround ourselves with different artefacts."

"What should I study? The Scriptures?"

"I'd suggest Goethe, but you might not find much comfort there, because he thought people had a "use by date," so to speak. Mozart died young to leave music for others to write."

"Oh, bloody charming!"

"It's not a fundamental truth because Goethe thought of it."

Jack sighed. "But folk like him influence others, don't they?"

"I'm very pleased to see you, Chief Inspector. May I offer you coffee? Tea?"

"Nothing, thank you." McKenna faced the director of social services across a wide desk fashioned from smooth blond timbers. Vertical blinds, half-closed, shielded the windows of an airy spacious office.

"I want to put this Blodwel business and these unfortunate allegations in proper perspective for you." The director smiled blandly. "Allegations such as you heard are an occupational hazard for staff in children's homes. They're sitting targets when children want revenge."

"Revenge?"

"Staff represent society, and impose its expectations on the deviant child who's rejected the authority of society, and who in turn, has been rejected by that society until its authority is accepted."

"Natural enemies."

"Exactly!" The director smiled again, more warmly. "Are you sure I can't offer refreshment?"

McKenna shook his head. "How often do children in your care allege brutalitty and abuse?"

"We've no statistics, but, as I said, it's a well-recognized phenomenon. I can recommend some literature if you're interested."

"Do you investigate allegations? Darren Pritchard's, for instance?"

"I decide on what course of action should be followed."

"You're obliged to follow government regulations," McKenna said. "And request a police investigation. No other body has the necessary expertise in criminal matters."

"That's correct, but I must first decide if a criminal offence is involved."

"You aren't equipped to make that decision."

"Forgive my bluntness, Chief Inspector, but I must point out that our frames of reference are considerably broader than your own. Police have a wholly simplistic view of offending." The director smiled once more. "What you, from the outside, see in black and white terms as a crime, takes on a rainbow of new colours when viewed in its proper context."

"Your frames of reference could mislead you to see the colour of the crime in terms of the status of the perpetrator," McKenna said. "And they fail to account for events. It's entirely possible you're making accommodations with wickedness."

"Let's stop hiding beyond the jargon, shall we? I accommodate the wicked in our little society," the director said. "Whether these children are born bad, or just go bad, you and I know they'll graduate from children's homes to prisons, and only ever make their stamp on the world by violence and dishonesty." He paused. "And quite frankly, I'm sick to death of subscribing to the victim culture. People must learn to be responsible for their actions, and the consequences."

"Why is Mandy Jones in care?"

"Her mother went to prison for attacking a bunch of police officers. The child was in danger of following her example, because she had no other role model."

"So Mandy has no criminal record?"

"Not yet."

"Then bearing in mind she's deprived rather than depraved, why should we disbelieve what she tells us?"

"Because she learnt nothing but lying and cheating from her mother, and all she'll have learned since is more lying and cheating." Frowning at his visitor, the director added, "Don't bother saying her new role models are insufficiently influential. A lifetime of neglect and damage can't be undone overnight. It pervades every aspect of a child's functioning like poison. That's why Blodwel's observation and assessment processes examine the whole child. We can then identify the resources necessary to proper development."

"So Blodwel's a modern version of Jeremy Bentham's Panopticon prison?" McKenna asked. "Didn't he believe people knowingly under constant surveillance will eventually relinquish wrongdoing, because light's stronger than steel?"

"I believe so." The director nodded. "External controls applied by staff are eventually internalized."

"But do your staff understand the implications of all the theories they apply? Mr. Hogg told us about the difficulties of finding the right people for the work." McKenna smiled briefly. "There are moral and social implications in separating one group of people from the rest. Devising special systems for these children acknowledges their power, and breeds fear and mistrust on both sides. Is it any wonder some of the staff can only cope by making underdogs of their charges?"

The director leaned back in his chair and folded his arms. "In my view, which you may call jaundiced, the so-called disadvantaged of society are like fleas looking for a dog to infest, and in taking on the needs of all these people, society makes itself as weak and prone to excitability as a flea-ridden dog." He paused again. "And I'm surprised to find someone in your position still able to subscribe to such sentimental views about people."

"I subscribe to the view that most of us respond to expectations others have of us. I also believe no one is immune to the depredations of others. You should bear that in mind."

"David Fellows is having his cremation tomorrow," Dewi offered. "His germs'll be incinerated, so Mr. Tuttle can stop worrying. He keeps looking in the mirror in the bogs for black spots on his neck, and he's coughing and sneezing all over the place."

Eifion Roberts chuckled. "Go away, little boy, and hush your mischief." As Dewi shut the door, he put his mug of tea on McKenna's desk, glancing through the window. "It's blowing up a storm, isn't it? Did you know high winds make folk irresponsible and homicidal?"

"They're like that whatever the weather," McKenna said. "And don't confuse our prevailing westerlies with the Mistral or Sirocco."

"They're all wind. Hot air, like what you heard off Hogg's boss, I imagine."

"He likes you to share his points of view."

"What psychology calls a *fuehrer* personality, like Herr Grofaz at Blodwel." Roberts grinned. "Grofaz is an undercover name for Hitler, an acronym of *"grosser Feldherr aller Zeiten"*, which means "the greatest strategist of all time." I came across it in a blood and guts war book when I was a kid, and it's always stuck in my mind."

"Hogg's strategy depends on oppression of the disruptive elements, and his boss implies there's no other option."

"Human nature being what it is, he might be right. Benevolent rule and effective rule are mutually exclusive states."

Dewi pushed open the door. "Apologies, sir, but I've just taken a call from Holyhead. Mandy's legged it from the foster home, and they want us to look out for her."

"Lucky for her Wales isn't an Islamic state."

"Why's that, Dr. Roberts?"

"Don't you read the papers, Dewi? At a certain point, Islam believes in separating a body from its anti-social tendencies. Mandy would've had her feet lopped off by now."


Seated at the kitchen-table, McKenna ate fish and chips bought on the way home, reading mail accumulated in the past few days. The cat sat by his feet, waiting for the fish cooling on a plate, rubbing her head against his leg from time to time, reminding him of her presence.

"Do you know, little one, if you wrecked Bangor, no one could do anything about it?" She mewled. "And when King Hywel Dda ruled Wales, a good mouser like you was worth tuppence. See how priorities change?" She purred, and nudged his leg. He picked up her plate, and she reared against him as he bent to the floor.

The front doorbell pealed while he was still elbow deep in washing-up water. He went upstairs, weariness dragging at his legs like the cat's claws, to find Jack's twin daughters outside, clad in the padded silk jackets which had briefly graced Denise's figure last winter until their novelty frayed.

"Have you run away again?"

"Mummy said we could come out."

"She told us to get out of sight."

"And what did Daddy say?" McKenna asked, shutting the door behind them.

"He didn't say anything. Mummy did all the talking."

"She was shouting."

"I'm surprised your parents don't do a runner," McKenna said, moving the cat from the chesterfield. "If you belonged to me, I'd be long gone."

"Can we have a drink, please? We've walked all the way here."

"You know where the kitchen is. I'll have tea. You can finish the dishes while the kettle boils."

The cat followed the girls to the kitchen. He heard them petting her, cooing over her, cadences of sound like the tide rippling over sand and shingle. They moved quietly, almost as stealthy as the cat, two girls functioning as one, and he wondered if they thought the same thoughts and dreamed the same dreams, and the thought he might die childless came like a blow to the heart.

"We didn't sugar your tea because you're sweet enough!" They sat on the floor at his feet, shielding his legs from the heat of the fire. He looked down at the two faces gravely regarding his, and prayed for God to offer these girls a gentle life, whether or not they took the gift.

"What can I do for you? I must go out again soon."

"Daddy's gone out again, to get away from Mummy, he said. He's looking for Gary, 'cos he's worried about him."

"We all are," McKenna said. "This is no weather to live rough. Mandy Minx legged it from her new foster home in Holyhead. Absconding seems to be in with your age group, doesn't it?"

"Mandy'll probably be with Tracey."

"And where does Tracey hang out?"

"She lives in a council house. Dewi Prys knows where."

"Tracey left home a while back." McKenna reached for his cigarettes. "Her mam neither knows nor cares where she's gone."

"She works nights at Morfa chippy, but nobody's supposed to know because she's fiddling the dole."

McKenna drew on the cigarette. "Anything else you could've told me before?"

"We just might know where Gary could be."

"We tried to tell Daddy, but he won't listen. He won't talk about Gary. He goes up the wall if you mention his name."

"That's because one of you is carrying a torch for the lad."

"We're old enough for boyfriends. Why does Daddy think we'll do something stupid?"

"Your parents are scared of all the bad things lurking round the corners of this life." McKenna sipped the scalding tea. "In your father's eyes, no young man will ever be good enough for either of you, and if you accept that now, you'll be able to walk the tightrope between not upsetting him too much, and having the independence you've a right to expect. He'll learn, given time, but don't grab that independence before you can cope with it."

"You're OK for someone your age, aren't you?" The smiles were as heart-stoppingly sweet as Carol's.

"That's because you're not my children," McKenna said. "Now tell me about Gary."


"You want me to employ what Mr. Tuttle calls my 'common touch,' and talk to tarty Tracey at the chippy," Dewi said.

"Tell her we're very worried about Mandy." McKenna

moved the telephone receiver to his good hand. "She might persuade the child to turn herself in, only don't make any rash promises about rescuing her from Hogg's clutches. And don't take what Jack Tuttle says too much to heart. He's under a lot of strain."

Dewi laughed. "Water off a duck's back, sir. I'll start fretting the day he stops being sarky with me. He'd be under a lot less strain if he wasn't psyching himself up over this promotion."

"I might not want Owen Griffiths' job even if it's offered, so there won't be any promotions to be had."

"I said he'd be better off looking elsewhere, like Wrexham or Deeside. That's more his home territory, anyway."

"And you wonder why he's nasty with you?"

Dewi laughed again, then said, "Will you look for Gary tonight? Mountain Rescue could do a better job."

"The twins don't know he's up a mountain. They only know he was very good at navigating the wilds of Cumbria via the moon and stars, and that was on a supervised orienteering course. The Snowdon and Glyder ranges are rather different."

"Same moon and stars," Dewi pointed out. "And plenty of empty holiday cottages and shepherd's huts to sleep in. I dunno where we'd start looking, though. Why don't you ask Janet's advice, sir? She reckons to know everything else."

"I've looked at places like that, sir."

Bedecked with knick-knacks, crammed with buxom chairs and dark velvet sofas squatting on carved legs and claw feet which dug into the thick plush carpet, the manse drawing-room was stiflingly hot. A log fire blazed in the hearth, brighter than the lights of the chandelier. McKenna wondered if Pastor Evans owned the manse and its opulent fittings, or if the chapel simply thought the incumbent worthy of the best of livings.

Janet's voice was tarnished by a little whine as she droned

on in her own defence. "I got details of holiday lets from all the agents, and checked as many as I could round Bethesda, Gerlan and Mynydd Llandegai, then I did Rhiwlas, Bethel, Deiniolen, Llanberis, Cwm y Glo and Llanrug. I even went as far as Waunfawr and Rhyd Ddu."

"I don't need a guided tour, Janet. I'm sure you were most thorough."

"A lot of the properties aren't empty. The owners move to relatives or a caravan for the summer, and go back when the season finishes. There aren't many second homes since the firebombing started."

"What about farm outbuildings and shepherd's huts?"

"The farmers check their own barns, and I thought it would be rather stupid to go into the mountains in this weather."

"That McKenna's here again," Mari announced to her mistress. "Shall I say you're busy?"

"Does he know Mr. Elis is out?"

"Yes."

"And?"

Mari shrugged, standing mutely by the door. Rhiannon was struck by her expression: a mingling of disdain and weariness, and some other, more elusive, emotion.

"Ask him to come back in the morning, Mari. Tell him I'm tired."

"What time shall he call?"

"Ask him to ring Mr. Elis after nine."

"What if he argues about seeing you tonight?"

"Oh, for God's sake!" Rhiannon jumped from her seat and pushed past the waiting girl, to find McKenna by the front door, leaning against the wall with his hands in his pockets.

"I don't expect my husband back until late, Chief Inspector."

McKenna smiled. "Ask him to call me in the morning, will you?"

"Did you want anything in particular?" Rhiannon asked. "I think you already know all we can tell you."

"Loose ends, Mrs. Elis." McKenna smiled again. "I'll see him tomorrow."

You don't go within spitting distance of Hogg, his wife, or Blodwel," Owen Griffiths said. "That's an order. The director's made a formal complaint about Jack's visit to South Wales, accusing us of serious interference in a delicate case-work situation. He also said it's difficult to work constructively with us given some of the views you expressed yesterday, presumably on behalf of the force."

"I suggested his frames of reference could be misleading," McKenna said.

"That's an understatement, isn't it? We're being well and truly misled, sent off in every direction bar the right one. This complaint's another diversionary tactic." Griffiths paused. "And don't bother telling me I'm inconsistent. I needed time to decide if I was looking at a mountain you'd built out of a molehill, or a cover-up thicker than a fog off the Irish Sea."

"Everybody likes to cover up their mistakes," McKenna pointed out. "Social workers, doctors, police, lawyers, any profession where mistakes can cost money and reputations. At crunch time, the director's thinking isn't determined by professional ethics, but by what the council's insurers want and expect."

"Darren Pritchard's personal injuries could be worth a six-figure sum in the High Court, couldn't they? And Mandy's."

"Apparently, Darren wasn't even marked. Like the rest of them, he's lying." McKenna sighed. "And he may well be.

Abuse is a bandwagon any child can jump on once it starts rolling."

"Don't let people faze your thinking," Griffiths warned. "Arwel's death and Blodwel might be entirely separate issues, but I'm quite sure we should be interested in both." He fell silent, then said, "I take your point about bandwagons, but children in care have a different kind of vested interest in keeping shtum about abuse. Darren and this lad Tony are good examples of what happens if they don't. For every kid lying or exaggerating about being abused, there'll be another who isn't. Nobody can hope to keep the lid tight on things for ever. They blow up in the end."

McKenna smiled. "Before embalming came into vogue, coffins had vents to allow the gases of putrefaction to escape. The vents were closed at one funeral because of the stench, and the coffin exploded. The undertakers were successfully sued for breach of contract."

"Quite." Griffiths nodded. "Everybody comments about the stench at Blodwel, don't they?"

"Elis telephoned," Jack said. "He'll be in about eleven, because he's exercising his horse until then." Glancing at the rain squalling against the window, he added, "Wouldn't fancy being out in this, would you?"

"Horses must be exercised," McKenna said. "They get nasty otherwise, and end up with fat ankles, like Doris Hogg."

Jack yawned.

"Don't you sleep at nights any more?"

"I keep waking up in the small hours, heart pounding, brain racing, and dripping with ice-cold sweat. Everything's a bloody nightmare!"

"You've let everything get out of all proportion. The twins are a credit to you and Emma. And themselves."

"You think?" Jack frowned. "I've been reading that social work literature you dumped on us. In the chapter on family dynamics, it says the rules of social engagement in some households resemble those of battle, and I thought, tell me about it! But the writer's describing the classic dysfunctional family and its interactions."

McKenna lit a cigarette. His arm and shoulder ached bitingly. "Writers write for their audience. Young women are fed nonsense about life being a bed of roses when they find the right bloke, and social workers are fed similar nonsense about what happens when the thorns on the same roses draw a bit of blood every so often. Your family's functioned smoothly for years, so a glitch now and then doesn't necessarily presage total disintegration."

Eifion Roberts walked in, sat in the vacant chair beside Jack's, and tilted its front legs from the floor. "Found those missing children yet?"

"Weather permitting, Mountain Rescue will look for Gary, and we made contact with a friend of Mandy's, so fingers crossed we'll hear if she turns up."

Dr. Roberts grunted. "I've got contacts. I'm told things other folk haven't heard as yet." His voice, weary and wearying, began to drone. "I'm told what some'll be glad to hear, and what'll make others despair." He let the chair fall back on all four legs, and leaned forward, clasping his hands between his knees. "Don't waste any more time or money looking for Tony Jones. I know exactly where he is."

"Where?" Jack asked.

"He was taken to Manchester Royal late last night from a secure unit outside the city."

"What's wrong with him?"

"Not a thing. He solved all his problems with the help of a broken bathroom tile, but he's left a bit of a mess for others."


McKenna sat in Owen Griffiths' office, looking out on another aspect of the city, at slate roofs greasy with rain, litter dropped in bare trees by an untidy wind, and an old woman, clothing unkempt and ragged, struggling up the narrow street past the Three Crowns public house. Griffiths spoke into the telephone, his voice urgent, sharp with anger.

What happened, McKenna thought, to the life energy seeping from that old woman like water from a rusty vessel, and so violently expelled from Tony's body. Where did it go? Her weariness and decrepitude visible to the most casual eye, the old woman's life-force seemed fit only to sustain a rickety baby in the Third World. What driving urgency compelled Tony to incur his own extinction? And why did Arwel Thomas die? While McKenna knew neither boy, he could grieve for Arwel, the perceptions and memories of Elis and the ethereal Carol telling something of the boy's essential quality, a service yet to be performed for the other. Glancing at Owen Griffiths, who talked now in muted heavy tones, he thought of Goethe, who suggested Mozart died not because his destiny was fulfilled, but to leave something for others to do in the long-destined duration of the world's existence. Arwel's death gave McKenna something to do, at least for a while.

Griffiths put the telephone receiver in its cradle. "Tony's the second suicide in that secure unit in the past six months. They take kids from all over that nobody else wants, and charge the earth."

"Offenders and inadequates support a huge and very profitable industry," McKenna commented. "Manchester and South Wales police will report back to us, I hope."

Griffiths nodded, rubbing his hand over his jaw. "And HQ say we can ask Social Service to explain how Tony came by the same kind of anal injuries as Arwel."

"As Jack said about Arwel, obviously not from sitting too long on the top of Snowdon."

"Don't joke, Michael. Some things never have a funny side of any description. Dear God! Is there no joy left in the world? You switch on the TV, pick up a newspaper, and it's nothing but war and disaster, poverty and cruelty, filth and perversion."

"One aspect of mankind's natural state. The few grains of gold can still be found in the blood and dirt."

"Can they?" Griffiths asked. "Where d'you find your joy, with no children, and not even a woman to your name any longer? Jack always said the girls were his pride and joy, after his lovely wife."

"They're not at the moment, but Jack's too concerned with the temporal to find compensation elsewhere."

Mari Williamson, clad in tight black pants and rich black chenille sweater, admitted McKenna to Bedd y Cor's discreetly sumptuous hall. The garments emphasized her pallor, gauntness taking an ugly toll on her youth.

"Are you not well, Mari? You look pale."

"We're all under a strain." Her voice was curt, her eyes wary. "When—" The words stuck in her throat, and she coughed raspingly. "When will Arwel be buried?"

"I don't know. His body can't be released yet. The inquest was adjourned."

"He's dead. You've cut him up. What else is there?"

"The matter of finding out who killed him, and where."

"He was in the tunnel."

"He was dumped there. He died somewhere else."

"Everybody wants him buried. They'd feel better. It's not natural not to have a proper funeral."

McKenna sat down on an ancient settle pushed against one wall, the long-case clock ticking softly. Mari sat beside him, hands clasped between her knees, eyes huge and dark in the pallid face. "It's like he's not properly dead. You know he is, but you can't believe it." She shivered. "I'm afraid I'll see him, wandering round the house and yard, wrapped in a sheet and all bluey-white and horrible like the undead in a vampire film."

"He'd be no threat to those who loved him."

"You don't know who he'd blame!"

"He'd blame the person responsible for his death," McKenna said. "I worry that putting him in the ground will stop people caring. Grieving is a process of forgetting, but while

Arwel's in that mortuary drawer, everyone's uncomfortable, like you."

"Why don't you know who killed him? It's days and days since you found him. Haven't you got any clues? When will you know?"

"It's not a matter of when, it's not a story where clues are laid out to be picked up one after another, it's not a jigsaw puzzle with the pieces simply jumbled in a mess." He lit a cigarette, and leaned back, feeling old wood unyielding against his bones. "Something happens, but you don't know why. If you know why, you don't know who, and even if you know who, you can't prove it. Murder tears holes in the neat orderly fabric we weave about life, exposing the chaos underneath."

"Are you making excuses for doing nothing?"

"I'm being honest with you." He dropped ash in the fireplace.

"You'll never find out, will you?" She stood, smoothing the sweater over her narrow hips. "Maybe you don't really want to." Her voice was challenging.

McKenna too rose to his feet. "If people would tell me what they know, I might be able to put the pieces together, but nobody will. Not even you."


"Mari spends a great deal of time in tears these days," Elis commented. "Hard to believe there's so much emotion under that cool exterior." He sat opposite McKenna, on a grey leather sofa in the cool grey room, a tray of coffee on the table.

"I upset her." Since their last meeting, subtle changes had come over Elis's face, disturbing the contours, scoring lines and painting shadows. "Was your visit to Germany successful? Your wife said you went to look at a horse."

"I looked at a number of horses, none of which took my fancy." Elis leaned forward to offer cigarettes. "How's your shoulder?"

"Healing slowly. A friend says I'm an uncomfortable reminder of human frailty, accident and sickness prone."

"So was he." Elis nodded towards the Beethoven portrait, and rose, taking a silver casket from the shelf beside the fireplace. Unlocking the clasp, he said, "I went mainly to collect this. Rhiannon wouldn't tell you because she deplores my spending thousands of pounds on an old letter."

McKenna took the stained and yellowed paper, its fabric rough to his fingers, its edges frail and crumbly, the script fading and blotched with damp and age and careless spatters of ink. Elis sat beside him, the scent of fresh cold air and horses about his hair and clothing. "Utterly atrocious handwriting, isn't it? Almost illegible."

"A lock of Beethoven's hair was sold at auction recently."

Elis nodded. "I had first refusal. People in the right places know my interests." He retrieved his precious relic, and placed it carefully in the casket. "The hair's gone to an American university. Modern science will soon be able to tell the world if he was treated for syphilis."

"Would it matter? Even Geothe didn't escape what he called the 'phantom spawned in poisonous slime.' Rather as we regard AIDS, I suppose." McKenna watched the other man. "We don't yet know if Arwel was HIV positive, but someone perhaps thought he was, and killed him out of fear or rage. Perhaps the other boy couldn't bear waiting to know if his life would be haunted by a poisonous phantom."

"Which other boy?"

"Don't you know? Mrs. Elis has probably been told. Last night, Tony Jones had what one might call a noble Roman death in a bath of hot water. He opened the arteries behind his knees with a splinter of tile, and the staff on watch noticed nothing until they saw the water turn red."

"Oh, God!" Elis slumped forward, covering his face with his hands. "Oh, God!"

"Did you know him?"

"Arwel was pally with him."

"Did he ever come here?"

"No. Rhiannon flatly refused. She said Tony was such a blabbermouth he should be called Papageno, and made to wear a padlock on his mouth."

"And what might he blabber about?"

"I don't know! She said he was the biggest troublemaker at Blodwel."

"I'd better ask her." McKenna ground out his cigarette. "Is she in?"

"I think so."

McKenna rose. "By the way, you were stopped for speeding recently. Who was the passenger?"

"Eh?" Elis looked up, his face grey.

"Who was the young fair-haired passenger in the Range Rover?"

"Carol. I was taking her home."


Rhiannon flushed. "I didn't know!"

"Shouldn't you know when a child in the council's care commits suicide?" McKenna asked.

"Rhiannon will be told when she's needed to provide an acceptable explanation for the unacceptable," Elis said acidly. "I've told her that people use her and their associations with her."

"Why did you believe Tony Jones was a troublemaker?" McKenna asked her.

"Ronald Hogg said so, and she believes everything he says."

"I asked your wife."

"Can you call me a liar, Rhiannon?" Elis sighed. "But you won't learn until Hogg and his cronies use your trust against you like a knife."

"Why d'you dislike him so much?" Rhiannon demanded. "He does a horribly difficult and thankless job to the best of his abilities. It's not his fault when wilful stupid children come to more grief. They wouldn't be in care if they were normal."

"What's normal?" Elis asked. "My instincts revolt against Hogg, and those same instincts have always held good with horses." He lit a cigarette, then tossed the packet to McKenna. "If you'd taken the trouble to get to know Arwel properly, you'd know he was a very normal teenager, underneath all the damage inflicted by Hogg and a lifetime without love."

"You think your love and your money solve everything, don't you?" Rhiannon asked.

"They can both help."

"They didn't help Arwel very much, did they? Especially not the love."

Colour drained from Elis's face, leaving dark stains under the eyes.

"I am not here to referee your fighting," McKenna said.

"My husband wanted to adopt Arwel Thomas," Rhiannon said. "He couldn't understand my objections; my perfectly normal objections!"

"Did Arwel know?" McKenna asked. "Did the Social Services department? Did Hogg?"

"There's been no formal application," Elis said. "Rhiannon and I were still discussing the matter."

"Did you tell anyone, Mrs. Elis? Did you discuss the proposal?"

Her voice held defiance. "I did not, because I would never agree, and my husband knew that. He just wouldn't accept it."


"They're not real, are they?" Jack said. "They take on these kids like other people get a cat or a hamster."

"Money turns their brain," Dewi said. "They think they can buy folk like you or me buys a newspaper."

"It's a pity nobody bought you a grammar book," Janet commented.

"It's an even bigger pity nobody bought your pa a book on decent Christian compassion," Dewi countered.

"What's my father done to you?" Janet demanded.

"Nothing, 'cos I wouldn't give him the chance." Dewi

turned to McKenna. "I'm not causing trouble, sir, but some things stick in your craw."

"What things?" Janet's voice grated on McKenna's ears.

"You dodged chapel last Sunday morning, didn't you?" Dewi asked her. "Missed your pa handing out blessings to the new mums and their offspring, and he does a nice line in blessings when the mum flashes a wedding ring in his face. But if she can't, the sanctimonious Pastor Evans lets her walk out front with the rest, then pretends she doesn't exist. He did that to Sian from our street. Can you imagine how she felt?"

Janet flushed. "She should've thought of that before she stood up in chapel, or, better still, before she opened her legs to half Bangor!"

"Daddy wouldn't like to hear you talk like that," Dewi said.

Janet jumped up, and rushed to the door. "Daddy can go to hell! And so can you!" The door slammed, and her footsteps rattled along the corridor.

"Why d'you do it?" McKenna asked. "Why d'you wind her up?"

"She needs sorting," Jack said. "She's got ideas above herself, which isn't surprising, her being the only child of a posh minister. She's very judgmental, and very prone to moralizing, which is probably why Carol Thomas won't give her the time of day."

"Has anyone seen Thomas senior yet?" McKenna asked.

"I'll try again later, sir," Dewi said. "I missed him yesterday. Shall I ask Carol what she was doing in Elis's car at midnight?"

"No." McKenna fidgeted with his lighter. "I'll talk to her again. We're going to Blodwel later. That's more urgent."

"To hear another load of hogwash?" Jack asked. "Has anybody told us the truth about anything yet?" He coughed, rubbing his throat. "D'you think Rhiannon killed Arwel to scupper the adoption idea?"

"She doesn't need to resort to murder," Dewi commented.

"She's enough clout to scupper anything. Maybe she's the reason the Blodwel kids won't talk to us."

McKenna sighed. "We scare those kids. We're just another face to the authority making their life a misery, and not their salvation, so don't judge Janet too harshly."

"Shall I send her out with Mountain Rescue when she's cooled down?" Jack asked. "They're concentrating on the Betws Garmon area, on the assumption Gary's responsible for that garage break-in last night."


Beyond the cottage window, rain swept through the valley, lashing trees cowed by the weight of wind and water. Empty soft drinks cans littered the mantelshelf, biscuit and sandwich wrappings overflowed the waste bin, and Gary, smoking a stolen cigarette, fretted again with the problem of ridding himself of his leavings without revealing his presence. Colicky pains from too many fizzy drinks wrenched at his stomach, his gut was leaded with constipation, and, too long without a bath or clean clothes, he found his flesh and odour offensive. The cold unventilated air inside the cottage held each and every smell, accentuating the sourness of his body, the staleness of food wrappings, the acrid scent of tobacco.

Holding the cigarette behind his back, he stood by the window, looking at an unchanged scene of empty lane, tumbledown walls, and mountains ghosted with streamers of mist. Rumps turned to the wind, scores of sheep grazed the fields below, fleeces dripping.

Time, he thought, had reached a dead-end, all urgency and energy evaporated, perhaps like his own journeying, terminating in this dark little cottage at the top of this steep little lane. He leaned against the window, breath condensing on the grass, roaming an inner landscape infinitely more bleak, reflecting on the company he had kept, Arwel's ghost beside him. Their experiences were the same, yet each experienced the terror and confusion and black despair uniquely, Gary debased by the same men Arwel pitied for their miserable pleasures, dictated by pain and sin. Arwel kept some life-sustaining joy flaming in the crucible of his imagination, whispering to Gary in the long dark nights when neither could sleep that even though Fate's malign daughters savaged them now, their kinder sisters must be waiting in the shadows. The cigarette burned itself out in his fingers while he stirred these other thoughts, smouldering now in his own imagination.

He had let those malign harpies invade his mother's life, simply because his childhood journeying ran out of magic and into the real world. She wanted only the peace of knowing her son was happy, but the son became an affliction and, in despair and ignorance, she handed him over to the other woman, who sent him rocketing out of innocence and into a world where everything he believed himself to be was called into question. Dropping the burnt-out stub in the wastebin, Gary wondered about the woman who dwelt behind the sour face and plain name, and for whom even Arwel could find no pity. She took him riding in her car to places his mother would not imagine in her wildest nightmares, singing to the radio, clicking her nails on the steering-wheel in time to the music, wearing black shoes with pointed toes, the back of the thin high heels scuff-white from driving.

"Where am I going?" Gary asked, as the car bumped over a little bridge.

"To meet a friend."

The narrow lane wound upwards between tall thorny hedgerows, grey in the light of a Hunter's moon drifting over the mountain ridge. Imagining grains of silver moondust on the mountain tops, wishing he could be anywhere else on earth, Gary said, "I don't like your friends. Arwel doesn't, either. Neither does Tony." The car veered as she looked at him, and he prayed it would crash.

"My friends like you." She changed gear, making the engine whine like the night wind. "And don't waste your sympathy on those two. They're as hard-faced as those mountains you like so much."

Pushed out of the car into a night so bitter the air seared

his nostrils, he walked the dirt track to the other car, from which different music throbbed, to meet a man whose name he would never know, but who charted every inch of his body, explored every orifice, and pinpointed the nerve which seduced a pain so terrible it became a pleasure, setting his innards on fire. Remembering the man, the little presents he gave, wrapped in paper as silvery as the mountain moonlight, Gary trembled with shame. After each encounter, in the chipped mirror above the bedroom washbasin, he scoured his reflection for signs of what the woman and her friends would make of him. As she watched him enter the other car, his body fleetingly silhouetted, did she ask herself where she might be sending him? Did she wonder what might be done to him? Had she ever known the terror of conscience?

The man took him on another journey, along by-ways hidden from view even in daylight, and simply darker threads in the tapestry of night, and the car took the curves and bends and rises and sudden dips as if it knew the way all by itself. The eyes of a wandering cat glittered in the depth of a hedgerow, and a horse straddled the crest of a field, like a silver unicorn in the frosty moonlight. Gary stared at configurations of stars luminous in a cloudless sky, while the music pounded in his head, and the car plunged under a tunnel of trees, headlights bleaching trunks and tangled branches, before roaring out towards the face of the moon.

"I'll give you a lovely present," the man whispered. "Afterwards."

Staring at the luminous dashboard clock, Gary wished he could force time on to that afterwards, for there was no hope of turning anything back. The car came to rest, front bumper crushing a little thicket of straggly bramble, and greed elbowed all humanity out of the way.

"I am hunting your soul," the man whispered, and began his coursing once again, pursuing a soul which would never be run to earth, for this was no sport. It ran for its life before each encounter, twisting and turning, beyond horizons of pain, swifter than the moon-white mountain hare on moon-white mountain snow, and ever more elusive. "I like this song. It makes me think of you. Listen!"

The seconds hand of the dashboard clock seemed to jerk with each word, each relentless beat.

*"Good boys go to heaven, but the bad boys go everywhere."*

"You could go anywhere, and have anything you want," the man said, feeding his shame, while the nighthawk hovered in the sky above, waiting his turn to scavenge.

Jolted from his reverie by movement at the bottom of the lane, Gary stumbled away from the window, legs numbed and icy cold. He crouched beneath the sill, watching the old farmer stomp back and forth from his truck to the sheep troughs in the field, bales of fodder hump-like on his shoulder. The sheepdog in the back of the truck suddenly lifted its muzzle, as if scenting the malodorous presence in the cottage, then yelped as the sheep began running down the field. When the farmer drove away, Gary returned to his vigil, and wondered if the mist in his view rasped like harsh cloth on flesh as it brushed the face of the crags, if the tiny spears of grass felt its weight like one body upon another, and if the mist itself, pierced by a sharp bitter thorn, knew the same shocking pain.


In her dismal back parlour, Peggy Thomas served the evening meal, the plates landing with a dull thud between the cheap cutlery Carol brought home with her ten per-cent staff discount. Tom stubbed out his cigarette in the unwashed ashtray he carried everywhere, picked up his knife and fork, and began to eat, without thanks to wife or God for the food before him. Picking up her fork, Peggy began to stab at her plate, knocking the food this way and that. Carol regarded her own meal; oven chips burnt one side and almost raw on the other, a splodge of bilious green peas, and two chicken burgers, overcooked and stained with pea juice.

"Eat up!" Tom instructed. "We can't afford to waste food. Not like your fancy friends, eh?"

"Shut up and leave her alone." Peggy looked at her daughter. "Eat up, you're looking peaky."

"What's with you, then?" Tom swallowed noisily. "You was tearing each other to bits the other day." He looked at Carol again, wiping the back of his hand across the tomato sauce smeared on his mouth. "She don't look more washed-out than normal. Always did look like a sick rabbit."

"Shut up! Leave her be!"

"She's my kid. I'll talk how I like and when I like. While she's under my roof, I'll talk when I want!"

"Talk!" Peggy speared a chip, fork squelching. "That's all you're fit for!" She gobbled on her food. "And where's it got you? Eh?"

His cutlery clattered on the plate. "Don't start on me again! It's not my fault!"

"What's not your fault?" She stabbed another chip. "Can't get a job! Don't get enough off the social! Can't help being sodding useless!" She swallowed the chip, and speared another. "You can't get a job 'cos you've been inside."

He picked up knife and fork again, and cut one of his burgers into neat even segments. "Go down the dole office yourself. There aren't jobs for anybody." He made a mouthful of burger, chips and peas on the end of his fork, and wrapped his lips around it. "Maybe you drove me to badness with your bloody nagging."

Peggy snorted. "You were born bad!"

"So was you." He made another mouthful on the end of his fork, and turned to Carol. "Your mother paid good money for that food, and she cooked it for you. Ungrateful little bitch!"

"I said to leave her alone!"

He leaned over and nudged Carol with his elbow. "Shall I do what your mam says?" He smirked. "You'd be begging me not to if I was posh Mr. Elis and his big posh car, wouldn't you?"

Carol pushed back her chair, tearing another hole in the

threadbare carpet, and stood behind her father, mouth working convulsively, words jammed chokingly in her gullet. She swallowed hard and tasted bile, and rushed from the room.

"I told you to leave her alone," Peggy said, as sounds of retching seeped down the stairs. "Now look what you've done."


"It's after six o'clock!" Rhiannon fretted to the cook. "When will dinner be ready? I have to go out."

Meticulously polishing knives, forks and spoons fashioned from solid silver, and arranging them on a silver tray to carry to the dining-room, Mari remarked upon the signs of disturbance around her mistress, and marvelled at the humanity they brought to her. "The roast's ready, and the vegetables. And the soup, I expect." She took a sheaf of white linen napkins from the drawer, and began to make scallop shapes, puzzling about the anxiety which gnawed at Rhiannon's eyes like the teeth which gnawed her lower lip.


"We could've got the same in the canteen, sir." Dewi stood beside McKenna in the High Street chip shop, reading the menu board above the counter. "I fancy sausage and chips and gravy. What about you, sir? A nice haddock in crispy batter'd please your cat, wouldn't it?" He put his hands in his pockets, and leaned against the counter. "I know you're not supposed to mix with the rank and file, but Mam would love to give you a decent meal now and then. I'm not being personal, but you eat a lot of fish and chips and suchlike, and if you were any younger, you'd come out in spots." Pausing while McKenna gave their orders, he went on, "Mrs. Tuttle does a good spread, but I don't expect they feel much like entertaining. Don't you feel really sorry for her? She's got to put up with the twins knowing too much about being teenagers, and him forgetting everything, though God knows how he's managed!" He smiled. "I wonder if I will. Do we cross over into being grown up, and forget all the dread and loneliness? I used to watch the others, and copy them so as not to stick out like a sore thumb, 'til my Nain saw me copying Jamie Thief. You've no idea how I envied him! And that brazen cheek, pinching all the excitement! But look where it got him. Maybe the likes of Pastor Evans are right about virtue and the wages of sin. The twins are very pretty girls," he added thoughtfully. "Mr. Tuttle doesn't know the meaning of worry yet." Watching their food shovelled from the hot cupboard on to yellowy-brown polystyrene trays, and wrapped in cheap white paper, he asked, "Are we going to Blodwel after?"

McKenna nodded.

"That'll be a barrel of laughs." He took the food parcels while McKenna paid. "We should've gone to the other chippy and asked if Mandy's shown her face yet."

Pastor Evans nodded to his wife, and she pushed the cheese-board towards him. He cut a hunk from a wedge of Stilton, and set about the finishing touch to his evening meal. "Pour the coffee, please, Janet."

"Pour your own!"

Mrs. Evans flushed. "Don't speak to your father like that!" Her voice was tense, fearful of impending drama.

"Why not?"

The minister sighed, tapping the butter knife on the side of his plate, annoyed by the disruption to the calm picture he liked to hold in his mind, of room and occupants displayed under the soft lights like figures in a canvas, seated by a table draped in white and strewn with gauzy porcelain, while shadows flickered in the space beyond. He nodded to his wife again, and she took the silver coffee pot, performing the service her daughter disdained.

"Have you ever disobeyed him?" Janet asked her mother. "Ever challenged him? Ever been disgusted with yourself for letting him bully you?"

"Leave your mother out of this. Your quarrel, whatever it is, seems to be with me."

"You disgust me!" Janet snapped. She picked up the coffee her mother served, the cup rattling against her teeth. "You are unbelievably hypocritical."

"Am I?" Pastor Evans licked a smear of cream from his lip. "How have I offended your socialist sensibilities this time?"

"Don't patronize me!"

Mrs. Evans held her cup halfway to her mouth, dismayed to find a faint stain from last Sunday's lunch still disfiguring the snowy damask of her tablecloth.

"I suppose you heard about Sian from the estate." He wondered when the child he adored became this angry stranger threatening the peace of his household. "Janet, you know the congregation regards me as an arbiter of public morals and looks to me for leadership, and I must understand the nature of the leadership people want and can tolerate. I've no quarrel with that poor silly girl, and nor has the congregation." He waited for a response, but she remained mutinously silent. "If I'd offered her the blessing, it would be tantamount to condoning, if not encouraging, her behaviour, and that would be misguided. There are lines we must draw, boundaries we should try not to cross, and there's no profit for anyone in encouraging girls to bring babies into the world without a husband, or the means to care for them properly. I know some women called her a brazen hussy for attending the churching, but I believe she was simply ill-advised. Sian will understand why I ignored her when she understands the need to consider the feelings of the community in which she lives."

"So you humiliated her in front of three hundred people for her own good?" Janet demanded.

"If you like. And for the good of other girls, who might be tempted by the rubbish in silly magazines about 'love-children' and 'free love.' You know that kind of love comes with an enormous price-tag. Many of those poor children in care are the consequence of stupidity, of an arrogance thinking society's rules are there to be flouted."

Janet smiled, and her mother exhaled, sensing relief from the tension. "So is that why people treat them like rubbish, and don't have qualms about beatings and buggery?" Putting down her cup, she pushed back her chair, scraping a furrow in the dense carpet. "Those children have no right to be born, have they? Like Sian's baby, their very existence is offensive." She leaned on the table, and stared at her father. "But they have their uses, otherwise the perverts so knowingly protected by church and chapel wouldn't be able to satisfy their nasty little habits. And please don't insult me by saying I'm exaggerating, because even the Church of England has finally come clean."

Pastor Evans carefully chewed and swallowed a mouthful of cheese and biscuit before responding. Looking at Janet as one might a stranger, he thought how tense and pale she was, the bloom on her lips already withering. He sniffed, and fancied there was that sourness about her youth the old carried with them like the scent of rotting flowers around a grave. "Why, Janet?" He sensed something to pity beneath the rage that glazed her eyes.

"Why what?" she snapped.

"Why d'you hold with the nonsense I'd shield child abusers? Don't you trust me any longer?" He shook his head, smiling slightly. "What's next? A suddenly recovered memory of something terrible from your childhood that's my fault?"

"The church comes first, last and always with you. How can I trust you? People don't trust the Jews, because when it comes to the church, they're loyal to their faith, not their country."

"The Jews are loyal to their conscience, as I try to be." He laid down his knife and pushed aside the plate, glancing at his wife, who sat with head bowed, staring at her untouched food, hands balled in fists beneath the shrouding tablecloth. "I told you about Christmas Morgan, and much good it did, least of all him. What right have we to parade his weakness before the rest of the world? What harm has he done, except to himself? There's not a chapel in North Wales where he'll be able to lift his head again. He'll retire."

"He's not fit to lead a congregation," Janet snapped. "He'll be cosy in his love-nest with his pension and his bit of skirt."

"The young lady walked out on him, as I daresay the fun was over once she accomplished his fall from grace." Pastor Evans watched uncertainty chase confusion over Janet's features, both devoured by the bitterness which chewed at her mouth. "Would you like your weakness held up to public scrutiny? Would you like to be treated like a freak show because, like the rest of us, you're less than perfect?"

"My weaknesses don't harm others. I don't prey on others. I don't abuse children."

"We all prey on each other and we all harm each other, to some extent. In my way, I try to limit that capacity for harm as best I can." He rose from the chair, patience suddenly exhausted, and looked hard at the girl whose eyes still held accusation. "I think you should consider leaving home. You're too old to live with your parents. Your perspectives are too narrow, and all this tension is bad, especially for your mother."

"Damn you! You're nothing but a stereotype!"

"Look in the mirror, Janet, and tell me what you see."


Blodwel used the hillside not as shelter from the elements, Dewi thought, but to hide its shameful face from the world. Seated in the car beside McKenna, he looked at the bleak dark building, then at the sleek dark shape parked beside them, the sheen on the bonnet and wing greasy with damp. "Nice car. Shame to park it round here."

"I should've told Janet to come," McKenna said.

Dewi nodded towards the other car. "We could ask Rhiannon to sit in with us."

"You know we can't." McKenna unbuckled the seat belt, and opened the door. "God knows why she's here."

"Damage limitation." Dewi trailed McKenna up the path

towards the front door. "Fronting for Hogg and ugly Doris, the general at the head of the army. Do they know we're coming?"

"We've been expecting you since early afternoon." Ronald Hogg stamped towards his office, leaving his wife to fumble with the huge bunch of keys at the front door. Dewi remained with her, a larger shadow in the ill-lit twilight of the cold fusty hall. Following Hogg, McKenna smelt again that sour odour which twisted at his innards.

"Another of your erstwhile residents is dead," McKenna said. "I went to see his parents."

"Fair enough." Hogg sat behind his desk. "But you could've let me know. I've already said these visits are disruptive, and while I appreciate the job you're doing, I can't share your single focus. Blodwel has to keep going, along with the children's treatment plans. Callous though it may sound, Arwel Thomas is history. I've got to see to the living, and make sure they're protected from more trauma."

"And what can you tell me about Tony Jones?"

Hogg sighed. "Don't you think suicide's like spitting in the face of God? He probably killed himself out of spite, hoping he'd make those left behind wallow in guilt like flies in shit." Sighing again, he added, "Despair wouldn't come into it. Boys like him don't trade in proper feelings. They copy what television and trashy videos dish up in the name of emotion. I've no doubt the parents gave a show of pseudo-grief to make you weep."

"On the contrary, they seemed beyond more grief. I suspect the family was blown apart when Tony left, and his suicide only leaves more unfinished business, more reproaches nobody can voice or negate." McKenna lit a cigarette. "They're utterly degraded, their sensibilities completely eroded, like the little thieves on the scaffold, watching those who stole all hope go scot free." He dropped ash in a metal waste bin.

"And I don't believe they should feel guilt, because they lack the wherewithal to steal anything of value."

"Except childhood from their children." Hogg wrinkled his nose as smoke drifted towards the white net curtains behind him. "Their stupidity makes them bestial."

"I'm surprised you hold such an archaic view, Mr. Hogg, when it's over two centuries since even the insane gained a toehold on the ladder of humanity."

"You tend to be pompous at times, don't you?" Hogg commented. "I daresay a lot of policemen share my 'archaic' view, but daren't say so in these politically correct times. Interminable understanding's the order of the present day, and much good it does us all!"

McKenna smiled stiffly. "Even if you're right, theft in ignorance is a lesser crime than the wanton thievery which caused Tony and Arwel to die, yet there's an enormous absence of guilt over that particular offence."

"You never knew either boy, but you've managed to fall in the trap."

"What trap?"

"I'm glad you're not in my job, Chief Inspector. Too many people identify with these children for personal reasons, and side with them against proper authority," Hogg said. "The children latch on to any weakness, then hold people to ransom when it suits, because they're devious and corrupt and end up corrupting others. Deliberately. Those two certainly knew what they were doing." He took a thin file from the drawer, and flipped open the cover. "What's hidden in that face, behind the perfect features and beautiful eyes? Grace? Truth? Inner beauty? Maybe beauty like that is enough in itself." He tapped his index finger on the photograph, and McKenna noticed a rim of dirt beneath the fingernail. "In a million years, you wouldn't think there was wickedness in his heart. We didn't, until we saw the damage he did. He mesmerized people, then poisoned them with his own corruption. He flaunted his power, just like his sister does. They use sex as a commodity, outside any moral context, to get what they want, and Arwel Thomas was a very greedy boy." Hogg shut the folder, and put it away. "And very perverse. He couldn't bear to see innocence around him, so he dragged others in his dirt."

"Who?"

"Anybody and everybody. Tony Jones, for one, and, God help us, probably others too scared to talk. Why d'you think Tony Jones was moved? Why d'you think Arwel Thomas absconded? We found out what he was doing, and he knew we'd stop him."

"How did you find out?"

Hogg frowned. "Don't interrogate me, Chief Inspector. I was doing the rounds early on a Sunday morning, and I caught them at it."

"And does your director know?"

"Of course he does! While you've been upsetting all and sundry with your suspicions and persistent questions, we've been trying to sort out the mess and spare people's feelings." Hogg sat back in his chair, tapping his fingers on the desk. "I've no time for Arwel Thomas's parents, or his sister, but they don't need to know he was buggering other kids, and Tony Jones's parents won't thank me for saying their boy was a pervert."

"Nor will such occurrences do much for your professional reputation."

"It's on record I acted immediately." Hogg frowned again. "Don't you understand children are capable of evil? Perhaps more than adults, because they've had less exposure to socialization processes. Arwel Thomas was like a filthy sickness, and God knows who else he infected. We're having to ask little kids of eight and nine about things they should never know. And what do we do if he was HIV positive?"

"And who d'you think corrupted Arwel?"

"Elis was besotted with him, and I've wondered what the boy had that the elegant Mr. Elis, with all his money and power, couldn't find elsewhere." Hogg smiled bitterly. "But I'd be less than human not to wonder if Elis realized he

couldn't buy his way out of the scandal Arwel Thomas could
make if he had all the money in the world."


Her red-gold hair pulled in a pony-tail and bound with a
crimp of cotton festooned with exotic flowers, Mandy lounged
against the wall in the chip shop. Tracey waited for an old
man to decide on his supper, while the old man's dog, a little
mongrel with a threadbare coat, whimpered outside, huddled
in the doorway under an onslaught of wind and lashing rain.
As the old man went into the night, the little dog sniffing at
the newspaper parcel in his hands, Mandy said, "I'm starving.
Give us a bag of chips."

"Where's your money?" Tracey asked.

"Don't be a tightarse!"

"Getting ready for life on the social?" Tracey scooped hot
golden chips in a tray, and speared them with a blue plastic
fork. "The coppers are after you," she added, watching Mandy
splash vinegar on the chips. "The young one with black hair
and sexy eyes wants to know if you turn up."

"Don't grass me up," Mandy whined. "They'll put me
back in Blodwel."

"They didn't before."

"They won't foster me out again now I've legged it."

"You should've stayed then. Why didn't you?"

"Doris turned up, didn't she?" Mandy stuffed a forkful of
chips in her mouth. "She told the foster people to watch 'cos
I tell wicked lies." She gobbled her food ravenously. "She said
I lied about Sir thumping me, and I'd lie about them doing
something, so they got dead nasty."

"Tough," Tracey commented. "Nobody'll ever believe Hogg
hit you."

"The cops did, and that fat doctor."

"They don't know you, do they?" Tracey sighed. "You
can't doss at my place for long. Wouldn't your Nain give you
a bed?"

• • •

"Our lady councillor's beginning to look her age," Dewi commented. "Her make-up's cracking like paint off an old picture. Have you noticed how Doris tries to copy her?"

"Doris can try 'til she's blue in the face, but people will always see her for what she is." McKenna poured boiling water in the teapot. "Rhiannon's under a lot of strain."

Dewi sat at the kitchen-table, aligning mugs and spoons in a neat row. "Does she know about Tony and Arwel in bed together?"

"So Hogg says." McKenna took chocolate biscuits from the refrigerator. "Discussions took place at the highest level as soon as Arwel's inclinations were confirmed. The best professional expertise has since been harnessed to investigate whether Arwel or Tony assaulted other boys at Blodwel. Our clumsy flatfoot intervention served to make a desperately difficult situation virtually untenable."

"Who was butch and who was bitch?"

"I didn't bother asking."

"You don't believe a word of it, do you?"

"I can't ignore the message because I detest the messenger. It's entirely plausible."

Dewi poured tea, tearing open the packet of biscuits. "The other kids reckon Tony and Arwel were OK, but kept themselves to themselves. Nobody found it strange they went out, because Mr. Hogg said they could. Mr. Hogg is like God, *ergo* his word is like God's."

"Hogg is far more powerful than God. He exists in the flesh."

"He's a wanker." Dewi munched a biscuit.

"What did Rhiannon do while you talked to the children?"

"Be motherly, say it was OK to talk, hold mucky little paws, wipe away the tears and the odd bit of snot."

"Who was crying?"

"The one who had an abortion. She's back in Blodwel, but she's crying all the time 'cos people aren't being very nice with her on account of her sinful leanings. Pastor Evans must be giving lessons, mustn't he?"

• • •

Seated at a chipped formica table in Blodwel's dining-room, hands cupped around a plastic mug brimming with weak tea, Rhiannon watched the three little boys, their crayons and colouring books neatly stacked, eating supper of jam sandwiches, mugs of the same tea beside them, and thought how hungry they looked, how forlorn and pale and starved. Every so often, one looked up from his food, to ask a question, to tell of a little pleasure or a tiny triumph in the battle of life, and she saw them like wrinkled little plants, almost withered to death for want of light. She wondered suddenly why these children scratched themselves so often, why faint ragged nail tracks disfigured their flesh and snagged their shrunken garments, why misery painted so eagerly on their tender skin.

Doris stood in the kitchen doorway. "Hurry up with your supper. Councillor Mrs. Elis has to go soon."

Rhiannon heard the intended rebuke, the implication that her presence disrupted precious routine. "They've almost finished."

Doris pursed her lips, then returned to the kitchen. One of the boys waited until she was out of earshot, then smiled at Rhiannon. "Look what I've got, miss." A small heavy object dropped from his hand, clattering on the table.

Rhiannon stared. "Where did you get that?"

The child stared back, the smile dying on his lips, the light draining from his eyes. "I didn't pinch it!" he whispered.

"Of course you didn't!" Rhiannon snatched the remnants of the smile, forcing it to her own lips, and voice. "It's just—just rather an odd thing to have, don't you think?"

"Sir said he could have it." One of the other boys intervened.

"Sir?"

"Sir. Mr. Hogg."

"I see." Rhiannon touched the prized possession, felt the warmth of the child's hand still there, and wondered fleetingly how vulnerable these children were to offers of warmth in any guise. "Where did Mr. Hogg get it?"

"Dunno, miss. He said it's not real." The child giggled. "He chucked it at the back wall, dead hard, and jumped on it, and he said it'd gone off if it was real."

She picked up the object and saw scars on the casing where Hogg's abuse proved his bravery, and felt a sudden shift of focus, as if this room, these boys, all the preconceptions and beliefs she held and trusted were shown to be distortions.

"It's got writing on it, Miss. Tiny, tiny writing on the side."

Rhiannon nodded. "It's very tiny writing. You'd need a magnifying glass to read it."

"Have you got a glass like that, miss?"

"No, I haven't."

"Sir hasn't, either."

Doris stood in the doorway again, crept silently upon them in her carpet slippers. "Bring your plates and mugs to the kitchen."

Rhiannon gathered up the used crockery, and pushed past the woman, smelling staleness and nastiness about her. Doris watched as Rhiannon washed the plates and mugs, and stacked them to dry.

"They usually wash their own pots. It's not good for them to get waited on."

"I'm sure that doesn't happen too often." Rhiannon dried her hands on a towel slung over the oven handle, tainting her flesh with the scent of Blodwel.

"When will you be coming again?" Doris asked. "Mr. Hogg wants to know."

McKenna hovered beside his chain store hi-fi system.

"Don't turn it down," Eifion Roberts said, drumming his fingers on his knee. "I know it's Beethoven, but what?"

"The Choral Fantasia."

"Much more fun than the Choral Symphony, isn't it? Is Elis broadening your perspectives?"

"My perspectives seem to be coloured by the sort of twilight Goethe described as a child of truth and untruth, ambiguous and misleading."

"I can get tired of all this intellectualizing around other folk's ideas," Dr. Roberts said, stroking the sleeping cat. "You don't share enough with your colleagues. Owen Griffiths has a good brain, and not just for police business."

"He'll be in bed."

"Jack won't be." He jerked his hand from the cat's reaching teeth. "Feisty little thing, isn't she? Cats always sleep with one eye open and one claw ready. Jack daren't close either eye at the moment, 'cos those girls've shown him what the sleep of reason conjures up, when he thought there were monsters enough in the waking hours. And Pastor Evans's offspring can't offer the female perspective 'cos she's not at her best." He grinned. "A randy boyfriend would sort her out in no time. It's a pity Dewi Prys can't take to her. Have you tapped his irrational imagination yet? He gets places in no time the best police procedures never reach in a month of Sundays."

"Elis's fancy car was outside Blodwel. Dewi said smashing Arwel's head on the wing or bonnet wouldn't leave a scratch."

Mari heard the purr of the car's engine and the soft crunch of wheels on gravel sodden with rain. Moving the drawing-room curtain aside, she saw water dripping from the bronzed leaves outside the window, and watched the car's rear lights disappear behind the house, leaving a faint afterglow in the darkness. "Madam's back."

"She's late," Elis commented.

"Will she want supper?"

"She may have eaten at Blodwel."

"I doubt it. Madam's too particular."

Walking down the back hallway, Rhiannon heard her husband's soft laughter and the lighter notes of Mari's voice, and halted, watching shapes and shadows beyond the ornate door of traceried wood and acid-etched glass, thinking of the bare cold building she had just left, and the resonance of terror. Mari's shadow flitted hither and thither, lingered lovingly behind the larger shadow, moved away but always returned, and Rhiannon considered the reality perceived within the room, and all the other perceptions she embraced as real.

She leaned against the wall, beside a table littered with petal shards from an urn of great white and yellow winter chrysanthemums, husband and servant out of sight but their voices coming to her like whispers, and thought of the guises worn by children, imagining the little boys in Blodwel as baby birds crouched without shelter in a ruined nest, Arwel and Carol jettisoned and drifting, picked up by the rip tide and dragged further out to sea, and her own as a mighty thief who stole the peace in his mother's heart.

But what, she asked herself, tumbling petal shards between her fingers, had that peace amounted to and depended upon? If, she thought, instinct was allowed to win the long conflict with guilt, she would know peace had depended on her husband's love, a perception which was yet another distortion, a belief held because it held less pain. Elias turned his eyes elsewhere not for fear of what his love produced, but because the dead dark man, whose face and music haunted her days and filled her nights with ghosts, could be whatever Elias imagined or wanted, except the maker of demands, the harbourer of expectations. And what of the boy who came to keep him company? Head bowed, the scent of dying flowers almost nauseating, Rhiannon wondered if the boy with the face of an angel had shown his own frailty, in trust and love, and found he expected too much.

Mari stood by the hearth, clad in one of her mistress's outfits that she had coveted with the greatest poignancy. Elias lounged on the Knole settee, smiling, and asked if she had eaten. Almost with the eye of an artist, Rhiannon noticed how his shadow flicked and danced around him in the firelight, yet was not only his shadow, but darkness seeping from him and lying across them all like the shadow of death.

• • • •

"Plausible. Feasible." Eifion Roberts refilled his mug with coffee, and handed the pot to McKenna. "Even very reasonable. Why should Hogg report Arwel and Tony and their alleged goings-on? Social Services like to keep their secrets secret and their mucky linen in their own washing basket, like the rest of us, and all you've actually got against Hogg is Mandy's less than reliable testimony, a handful of rumours among the restless natives, and a failure rate with kids that's par for the course."

McKenna lit a cigarette, and tossed the empty carton in the waste bin. "I wish to God we could find Gary Hughes."

"You've smoked over ten fags since I arrived," Dr. Roberts noted. "Gary doesn't want to be found, though he could be leaving you a trail of sorts." He watched McKenna pace the room. The cat too watched her master, disturbed by his restlessness. "The problem is you labelled Hogg as the cause and extent of all the troubles at the outset, and you're clinging to that, though you may well be quite misguided. Hidden agendas don't only underwrite the ethos of abusive institutions. They're dear to us all, even the Mandys of this world."

"We know about the Elises' hidden agenda," McKenna said. "He wanted to adopt Arwel, she wanted to stop him."

Munching a digestive biscuit, Dr. Roberts said, "I think there's unfinished business there, and you should be finding out what's scribbled on the other hidden agendas tucked up their couture sleeves like posh hankies. He strikes me as a damn sight more ambiguous than Goethe's twilight. She'll be like any other woman under the fancy clothes and make-up."

"You're not very helpful, are you?"

"I can't think for you." He reached for another biscuit. "You read Lombroso's epic yet?"

"Some, in between social work and childcare literature, and learned essays on the nature of institutions."

"And Beethoven's epistles, which I daresay you find more enlightening. Would Lombroso's parameters mark Elis as a baddie? Or Rhiannon? Are their ears misaligned in profile with the nose? Are the facial proportions discordant? And what about teeth?"

"Their teeth are a credit to modern dentistry," McKenna said. "Unlike Mandy's."

"Fancy being able to see your fate by opening your mouth, eh?" Dr. Roberts sighed. "I've noticed the central upper jaw incisors are slightly out of true on a lot of these troubled and troublesome girls. Did you know Beethoven had geeky teeth? Probably 'cos his father smacked him in the mouth so often." Wiping crumbs from his lips, he added, "Caring Victorian husbands banned their wives from listening to the piano music, because of that dreadful feeling it arouses in the guts, like inflamed sexual desire. Mind you, I don't expect it makes Elis want to turn his attention to his wife. Sexually, we're all as grey as a cat in the moonlight, but he's far more shadowy than most."

"He makes me think of sex." McKenna sat in the worn armchair beside the fire, and put his coffee-mug carefully on the edge of the hearth. "And the sorrow of it."

"You think too much, and that can become a dangerous habit," Dr. Roberts commented. "Looking at those porn movies from Dai Skunk's place could make you believe something crucial's missing from your life. Pictures like that can stir and heat the coldest blood, never mind sending the imagination places it could get desperate to live in." He watched McKenna rip open a new cigarette packet. "But they're just variations on a theme, because sex palls fast after that first, short, explosive journey out of childhood."

McKenna smiled wryly. "And Nature must keep our interest going somehow?"

Dr. Roberts nodded. "Until that lady's ready to finish us off, the reproductive power of the gene will rule the world, as always, while we bow down to our infatuation with our own death, and the awesome knowledge of being held fast in the slipstream of Time."

"The best minds don't accept Time as a great comet

hurtling from infinity to infinity," McKenna said. "It's a construct of artifice." He smiled. "And even without the benefit of modern science, Goethe understood that no thing decays to nothing. One form of energy simply transforms to another."

"Bully for Goethe!" Dr. Roberts observed. "Didn't stop him being terrified of dying, did it?"

Beyond the bedroom window, a pale winter moon rode high in the sky, clouds dragging across its face, and McKenna wondered what music the clouds made in heaven as they heaved and rolled and unravelled themselves, fighting winds whose only reality was the flight of the clouds they harried. In the garden below, grey in the wan moonlight, a strange cat slept beneath one of the spindly shrubs, curled in a tight ball on the cold earth.

The other cat nuzzled his hand as he lay wakeful, stroking her soft coat. A simple theme ran through his mind, the variations of its notes and intervals following one upon the other until it was over, and he fell asleep at last, some time after the cathedral clock chimed three long notes.

# • C h a p t e r •
## 13

Oh God!" Owen Griffiths groaned. "D'you really want to question Elis under caution?"

McKenna nodded. "And I want search warrants for his vehicles and house."

The superintendent frowned. "You were gunning for Hogg."

"Hogg isn't out of the frame. Putting the finger on Elis might be a diversionary tactic." McKenna rubbed his forehead, feeling the tension of an incipient headache. "But we can't ignore Elis. Maybe he's simply another victim of this sodding awful mess, and he loved the boy as a surrogate son, or maybe he indulged his preference for the love that dare not speak its name."

"Oh, God! Don't bring Oscar Wilde into this, or that upper-class pervert he was so besotted with."

"Pervert or not, Lord Alfred Douglas wrote a rather poignant verse on the subject."

"The *Ballad of Reading Goal* is a good deal more poignant, and a sight less sentimental." Griffiths took a pen from the desk tidy, and drew a row of interlocking boxes on a sheet of official notepaper. "How many vehicles?"

"Car, Range Rover, a large horsebox, a trailer and a tractor."

"Forget the tractor. Whoever dumped the boy had him in a boot or something." Griffiths began to draw bars inside the boxes. "Or a trailer." He surveyed his doodling, then drew a figure behind the bars. "And the ground was so hard with frost, we couldn't tell if a herd of elephants'd been there. Oh, sod it!" He threw down the pen, and tossed the paper in the waste bin. "I'd better contact HQ, hadn't I?"

"Unless you want to assume that mantle of responsibility yourself."

"I wanted to retire peacefully. Fat chance, eh? Is there any point searching the house? I know the boy's clothes are still missing, and Forensics are still sifting all the rubbish dredged up by the railway, but I doubt Elis is stupid enough to leave hard evidence around, and any of Arwel's stuff you found at Bedd y Cor could quite legitimately be there. He spent enough time at the place." Griffiths sighed. "Ronald Hogg could justify anything. In one breath, he's relating his dreadful suspicions of Elis, and in the next, he's saying why he did nothing to stop the association."

"But as Eifion Roberts pointed out, it's all wonderfully plausible and reasonable. Hogg can only wait and watch, as he puts it, until Elis drops himself in it. Until then, he has to take him and his motives at face value, because otherwise he might deny a very disadvantaged child the chance of a wonderful rehabilitation."

"Can't Hogg make up his bloody mind? Was Arwel a wicked, manipulative blackmailer who got his just deserts, or a poor disadvantaged victim?"

McKenna rubbed his shoulder, wondering if phantom pain would haunt the rest of his days. "One man's truth is another's deception. Life is ambiguous."

"People are ambiguous, and people make life what it is for others, and I don't like the life Hogg makes for these children." Griffiths sighed again. "I'd better crank up the engine and get the wheels going, but don't be surprised if HQ send someone more exalted than you or me to talk to Elis."

McKenna stood up. "Eifion wants a disposal certificate. No one's ever questioned his autopsy findings, and he's got all the tissue samples he needs."

"I'll ask the coroner for a burial certificate. Let Social Services know, because the Thomases'll need help paying for the funeral. The pittance of a grant this bloody government gives would just about get the poor lad tipped in a common grave. Didn't John Donne call life a common grave? We're wrapped in our shrouds from the moment of conception."

Emma Tuttle sounded as if she had been weeping. "I've called the doctor, because Jack's really ill. He's been miserable for days, but I thought it was work and the girls getting him down." She drew a rasping breath. "It's probably 'flu. His temperature's high, and he's shivering an awful lot, but I had a dreadful struggle to make him stay at home. He's fretting about that missing boy, wondering where he could be. . . ."

"Stop worrying," McKenna said. "We'll manage."

"Why are you always so kind to me?" She paused, then said, "Don't answer that. I'll call again when the doctor's been."

"I could collect the medical certificate later."

"And you can pick up the note Denise left last night because you won't return her calls. She wants to know about Christmas."

Cigarette burning in the ashtray, McKenna looked at the wall calendar and noted, with an empty feeling in the pit of his stomach, that Christmas would be upon him and the rest of the Christian world in less than three weeks' time. Denise would warrant a gift, despite the adultery she thought only a convention for the discarded wife of this modern world. Her greetings card would arrive soon, reminding him of his responsibility to the society of men. Eifion Roberts would remind him in a different way, importuning him to gaiety and seasonal amnesia with friendship and a bottle or two of spirits, and Jack would issue invitations to Christmas lunch and tea, when the twins would tease and flatter, Jack would talk of this and that, and Emma would simply be herself. The hours between the eve and the day could be spent at mass with the other Catholic souls marooned in this puritan landscape, he thought, and realized he could do anything or nothing, as he wished, but knew the days to Christmas would nonetheless be counted out until their burden was dead and gone, and only a few more hours remained before the turn of the year, when the sap would rise and life blossom once more.

Dewi walked in and sat down. "Dr. Roberts called to say the HIV and VD tests on Arwel were negative, but we won't hear about Tony yet."

"Inspector Tuttle's off with 'flu."

"More likely the stress of thinking Dai Skunk breathed AIDS on him. It's weakened his defences, so the viruses can get at him."

"Dafydd ap Gwilym wrote a poem about a hut ruined in a storm, but I think the subject describes a woman who's lost her virtue, like one of Beethoven's 'ruined fortresses'."

"Arwel's crosswords haven't helped much, have they?"

"We don't know enough about him to understand them. Like notes in music, words have personal values and embrace personal concepts, and they can be meaningless or revelatory, depending on the thoughts and experiences behind them."

"And the imagination," Dewi added. "Who'll be asking Elis the nasty questions?"

"HQ's sending a person of rank," McKenna said. "Probably more than one. Where's Janet?"

"Interviewing the lady video stars. I doubt she'll get any more joy than we had with the blokes, but at least we won't have any claims of sexual harassment by nasty brutal male officers."

"We should set Pastor Evans on them. His nose is long enough to sniff out any souls struggling to emerge from the filth."


Driving up St. Mary's hill, the car labouring in second gear, McKenna glanced at Dewi, and wondered how the Prys family spent Christmas. He imagined simple contentment, the family conversing in the shorthand, unintelligible to outsiders, which rendered them safe from invasion, then discarded romantic nonsense about the lot of ordinary folk. Like himself, Dewi was trying to escape the toil and disappointment to which he was born.

Luminous in red and green livery, a white patrol car laboured behind, bearing men to drive away the vehicles in which Elis and his wife gracefully flaunted their wealth and their differences. He thought of the huge inconvenience to which they might be put by the execution of the warrants, then cursed himself for forgetting the pretty little car in which Mari Williamson flaunted her own difference.

"Elis'll probably go ballistic," Dewi said. "I can't see him and Rhiannon hoofing it to town for a pack of bog rolls."

"I expect Mari does the nitty-gritty bits of keeping their persons in comfort, and it doesn't help that I forgot all about impounding her car."

"We'll just take it. They'll be too up in the air to notice anything much." Dewi wiped his cuff on a patch of condensation on the side window, and watched the high banks and bare clipped hedges flying past. "I usually enjoy this kind of thing, you know. Dropping on folk with warrants and a bunch of pounding flatfoots from uniform is exciting, like the films. I'm not enjoying this at all. It doesn't feel right."

"It's necessary. We do our job without malice or favour."

"We might mean no malice, but the rest of the world won't see it like that." Dewi frowned. "Hogg's set us up, and we're dancing to his horrible little tune."

"Elis has questions to answer, and I should have asked them a damned sight earlier than today." A few drops of rain spattered the windscreen as he bumped down the lane to Bedd y Cor. He took the last bend, and almost stood on the brakes as the great grey horse reared before him like a beast from a Gericault canvas, hocks down, veins throbbing, hind legs sprung with immense power, front hooves flailing over the car bonnet. He saw Elis pull back the animal, and watched something near exhilaration on his face change as understanding arrived.

As soon as she picked up the telephone, Janet had recognized the voice, breathy with fear, gabbling an address.

"It's the other girl we want. Tracey whatever-her-name-is-will keep," Owen Griffiths said. "Take somebody from uniform if McKenna hasn't hijacked them all."

"What shall I do with Mandy, sir?" Janet asked.

"Put her in the detention cell for now. We need to stop her going off again. It's a load off my mind to know she's safe."

"We're supposed to notify Social Services."

"McKenna can do that. You organize a solicitor for the girl, and sit in with her, 'cos you never know what she might want to say."

The servants huddled in the kitchen, numbed with shock, watching men in uniform steal the beautiful car. Josh watched from the door of the grey horse's loose box, saddle slung over the bottom hatch, bridle hanging from the pommel.

Mari ran from the back door, her feet skittering on the cobbles like the horse's hooves. She made as if to chase the car, the last of the convoy moving up the drive, stopped and screamed after it, then ran back indoors.

Dewi shut the door and caught her arm. "Stop it! Calm down!"

She dragged herself away, ran to the drawing-room where McKenna waited with Elis and his wife, and began to scream at McKenna, tearing her hair and the neck of her tunic, still screaming.

Elis put his arms around her from behind and held the flailing hands. "Hush, Mari, hush. You'll be all right." He held her tight, looking at McKenna, who thought sorrow embraced the girl. "You've revived all her demons, Chief Inspector, invaded the place where she felt safe from the past."

The girl slumped against his body, breath rasping. "She thinks you're about to destroy her sanctuary."

"Examining the vehicles is part of our ongoing investigation of Arwel Thomas's death," McKenna said.

"What have we done to you?" Rhiannon asked. "D'you resent us because you think we have too much?"

"The deputy chief constable will put a number of questions to Mr. Elis," McKenna added. "We neglected to include Mari's car on the warrants, and would be obliged by your permission to remove it."

Mari pulled herself from Elis's grasp and ran from the room. Within a split second, it seemed to McKenna, who thought time must surely be awry, she returned to throw a small leather fob at his feet, and watched from her harbour within Elis's arms, as Dewi bent to retrieve the keys.

"Who'll talk to me?" Rhiannon demanded. "To Mari?"

"Other senior personnel with the deputy chief."

Rhiannon sat on the Knole settee, reaching forward to brush a wisp of straw from her husband's breeches. She folded and crumpled the straw, tossed it on the blazing logs, and said, "I want to talk to you."

"I'm not authorized to interview either you or Mr. Elis. I'm sure you appreciate the reasons."

"And when will the others arrive?"

"Soon."

"Then perhaps Constable Prys would kindly ask Cook to bring coffee while we wait."


Geared for a tussle, Janet was surprised by the meek and almost agreeable manner in which Mandy relinquished herself to the police officers who suddenly arrived at Tracey's tiny bedsit above a derelict High Street butcher's shop.

"I knew she'd grass me up," Mandy said, as Janet put a mug of canteen tea on the table in the detention cell. "She doesn't want to get done for hiding me."

"You can't blame her."

"Are you going to tell Hogg?" Mandy sipped the tea, and pulled a packet of cigarettes from her jacket pocket.

"My boss will contact Social Services later. A solicitor's coming to talk to you."

"You've got to tell Hogg. He's in charge of all the kids."

Janet saw fear glitter in Mandy's eyes, heard its note rising in her voice. "I do what my boss tells me, and he told me to get you a solicitor."

"Why?"

"He thinks you need one to protect you."

"I haven't done nothing," Mandy whined. "Honest I haven't!"

Janet sighed. "Why did you run away again? Did something happen?"

Mandy tipped ash on the floor. "Doris told the foster people I made up horrible lies, so they were nasty with me, weren't they?"

"Did you lie about Mr. Hogg?"

"Where's your boss, and the one with sexy eyes?" Mandy giggled, and picked up her mug of tea.


Wrapped in musty blankets, Gary dozed as winter twilight settled about the mountains. Rain spattered the windows, harried by a wind turning this way and that before settling to blow with increasing vigour from the north-east. He shivered in his sleep, fingers of icy air poking and prying about his person, then twitched, muscles shrinking under the skin, as alien noise intruded. Motionless, he strained to place the scratching and rustling which flickered in and out of the compass of his hearing, then tumbled from the bed and ran from the tiny room, thinking only of rats come to gnaw the flesh from his bones.

He stood by the parlour window, watching night drift in from the east, the twinkling lights of the cottage dotting the mountain foothills like tiny stars fallen to earth. Hunger gnawed at his stomach more viciously than any rat, and as soon as night grew old enough to empty the village of watchful eyes, he would venture out again, beyond the low wall where the steely-plumed raven alighted each morning to sing for him its bleak morbid song, and down the empty lane.

Searching the house would be easy, McKenna thought, for Bedd y Cor housed little more than necessity. No litter, no untidiness, nothing which did not seem to fulfil ongoing and discernible purpose, as if the Elises felt compelled to remove the evidence of each spent day, in hope the next might bring something worth keeping.

He waited in the room next to Elis's study, seated on a beautiful antique Davenport beneath a chandelier of Bohemian crystal. Flames from an artfully designed gas fire flared up the chimney, their light dancing on the ebony piano, lid closed, from which the room drew purpose.

Restless, he stood up, and leafed through the book on the piano lid, hearing the spine crackle as he flicked age-spotted pages. The endpapers showed a bear grasping a winged mace, crouched in the arbour of leaves, the title page a lute-playing cherub in rococo setting. Turning to the last few pages, he found at their end the same bear in the same arbour, guarding the mace and a small photograph. As the door opened, he slipped the photograph back in its hiding place.

"Shall we go to the drawing-room?" Rhiannon suggested. "One mustn't smoke near pianos. They're more temperamental than any horse." She led him down the hallway, past the table now bedecked with fresh white pom-pom dahlias, and through the ornate door. "My husband's in his study with the deputy chief constable, and Mari was taken away by your young man and a lady superintendent." She smiled wryly. "Thank God the media don't know."

"You seem to have taken charge, Mrs. Elis."

"I'm trained to keep the world turning even if Armageddon's on the horizon. Poor Mari really sees you as one of the Four Horsemen."

"I deeply regret upsetting her."

"You terrified her, but she's probably so devastated because she's in love with my husband. Poor child! She wants him to cool the hot blood in her veins, and why not? Lust doesn't make moral distinctions. She hates Carol because she thinks he gives her the pleasuring she wants for herself."

"And does he? Carol's pregnant."

"But not by him." Rhiannon began to pick at a tiny thread disfiguring the perfect hem of her dark wool skirt. "A young man from Caernarfon fathered the child, not that it matters. I'm sure she'll produce a robust and perfect infant. Did you find the photo of our son in the sonata scores? My husband hides them everywhere. When he's in the music-room, there'll be a sudden silence, and I imagine he's staring at one of them the way he stares at the Beethoven portrait. D'you suppose he's looking for a ghost of the same intelligence in the child's eyes?"

"What went wrong?"

"No one knows." She pulled the thread, frowning when it refused to yield. "And the pain's eaten us up from the inside out, like a cancer."

"And Arwel?" McKenna ventured.

"He seemed to break through the foot-thick misery around my husband, but such young brilliance is so fickle, isn't it?" Fiddling again with her skirt, she added, "Mari doused his light when she told us why he'd gone into care. Her grandmother said everyone in Caernarfon knew he was in moral danger, so my husband walled him up behind the misery with himself and a dead man."

"And did you ask anyone to define 'moral danger'?" McKenna asked. "Arwel's admission was prompted by persistent truancy. We assume the sexual abuse came later."

"Ordinary people usually know the truth," Rhiannon said. "His parents knew, anyway."

"I'm not sure they did until we told them." McKenna lit a cigarette. "They've been befuddled by jargon, reacting to ill-founded gossip and the huge propensity for misunderstanding at the heart of verbal reports."

"My grandfather used to tell a story from the Great War." She smiled fleetingly. "Someone passed a message down the trenches, saying: 'Send reinforcements, we're going to advance,' but by the time it reached its destination, it had become: 'Send three and fourpence, we're going to a dance.' " She paused, gazing into the fire. "I thought Arwel might've confided in Mari, but he didn't. She was only interested in weighing his potential, creating a seductive dependency." Glancing at McKenna, she said, "She's not consciously calculating, just a young woman like any other, weaving savage and erotic dreams around one man, from whom she's perfectly safe, desiring what another young man would become." She frowned. "She wouldn't be safe with Arwel, would she? They'd be a congregation of terrors, clinging together like survivors from a shipwreck. I fear for her, because her native wit won't help her to live in harmony with herself." She fell silent, hands idle in her lap. McKenna noticed her fingernails, ragged and bare of polish, and thought she threatened to fall apart at the seams, like her skirt. "What questions will my husband be asked?"

"The deputy chief constable will decide."

"On your instructions, I'm sure. Why must you be so oblique?"

"It's a habit," McKenna said. "Often a necessary one."

"Obviously. You misled and disarmed my husband very elegantly."

"No, Mrs. Elis, I did neither."

She watched him thoughtfully. "Perhaps you simply touched him. Perhaps he believes you share his darkness. I can't, but it overwhelms me, nonetheless."

"You make me very sad."

"We're sad people. Two embolisms travelling the vein of life." She began to fidget again with her skirt, lifting the hem in search of the rogue thread, exposing a length of pale slender leg to McKenna's view. "My husband was reared in institutions, where the strong preyed on the weak as they've always done." She let the skirt fall, and leaned forward, hands clasped around her knees "He's very subtle in his seductiveness, isn't he? It's the habit of his lifetime, although knowing of his past won't make the slightest difference. If he killed Arwel, there's no going back on that sequence of events, because like the sequence of notes making up a piece of music, however much it's repeated, whatever differences you discern each time, the notes and their sequence always stay the same." She paused, then added, "My husband's obsession with Beethoven isn't healthy or enlightening, you know. He imagines himself chained to a past where they share a common horror, so he plays the same few pieces of music over and over again until my nerves are so tense I want to scream, because he thinks he hears echoes of his own tragedy. His past is more important than our present or future, and it governs his life."

"And is your house so tidy because you hope psychological obliteration might follow the physical?"

"Possibly." Rhiannon let the ghost of a smile touch her eyes. "It hasn't worked. Life is never so neat."

"And is this relevant to Arwel's death?"

"My turn to be oblique, Mr. McKenna." The smile flickered again. "I've taken my responsibilities as a councillor very seriously, and read as much as possible. The dysfunctional family is nothing new. Beethoven was the product of one, his father such a drunkard people expected the liquor excise to suffer when he died." She fretted again at her skirt. "But the psychological impact of an abusive childhood extends far beyond the victim, like a dirty cloud smearing everything with its filth."

"Are you talking about behaviour patterns people learn and can't break?"

"My husband learned to seduce when he was a child, and he can't break the habit, because when he was eight years old, one of the prep schoolmasters raped him." She took hold of the end of thread, and pulled viciously. McKenna heard a tiny ripping noise, then saw the curl of fibre pinched between her thumb and forefinger, rolled in a little ball, and tossed in the ashtray. "Word travelled like wildfire through the school about fresh meat on the stodgy menu, so people fell on him, wanting a bite. It sounds like a game, some arcane public-school tradition, and I suppose it's sport of a sort, like boys throwing stones at frogs. But the frogs don't die in sport, do they? They die in earnest." She began pulling at a minute length of loose wool at the cuff of her sweater. "Then he realized by seducing what he could accommodate, he could seduce protection to hold the rest at bay. D'you understand me? Those who had him protected him from those who wanted him. It was probably his first business deal."

"And where does Arwel fit in?"

"I don't know whether he was victim or predator. Perhaps he was both, preying on my husband with his love and becoming the victim of his love." She paused, then said, "I think Carol's the only one who loved Arwel for himself. My husband loved him as a companion in misery, and they went visiting that time which pulls him with its mighty chains." Turning back the cuff to look for the root of the thread, she added, "My husband can't break the habit of returning to his childhood, you see, and I fear he took Arwel with him to share the terrible burning pleasure he tells me is like no other, and the pain with a dark beauty all its own."

Returning home from servitude for one man, Carol found another wanting more. Her father stood in the back parlour, toes encroaching on the puddle of soot which had flowed down the chimney, over the hearth, and on to the threadbare rug. Blueish flames struggled to burn soot-drenched coal in the grate.

"I told her to get the chimney swept," he whined. "I told her weeks back."

"Chimney sweeps cost," Carol pointed out. "When did it happen?"

Her father shrugged. "How the bloody hell do I know? It was like it when I got in."

"And how long ago was that?"

"I don't know."

He remained in the soot, and Carol knew his feet would leave little pointed prints on the floors, like the marks of birds' claws in snow. His mouth hung open slightly, his eyes looked as dull as the soot, and she wondered if, subconsciously, he knew himself too inadequate for the simple task of sweeping soot. She picked up shovel and hearth brush, and began to clean the dingy room, thinking him perhaps too stupid even to own a subconscious. Soot motes drifted among the dust and litter of ornaments and bits and pieces, and wiping her finger on the table and windowledge, she sighed.

"I can't clean all this and cook the tea."

"I could go for a takeaway," her father offered. "If you've got any money."

Carol massaged the dull pain at the base of her spine, a new pain supplanting the earlier pain of engorged breasts. The child and the pain were like twin parasites, gorging off her meagre resources.

"You're getting fat round the middle," her father said. "What'll we do for money when you can't work any longer?"

"Social Security, like now. Like ever since I can remember! Go and get the Hoover."

"Aren't I going for a takeaway?"

"After. You can help me clean up."

He moved away from the soot puddle, and left a trail of pointed prints behind him. Carol thought she should pity his uselessness and hopelessness, then thought not, because default caused so much damage, as Arwel knew. He stole comfort and knowledge from the words and thoughts of others, and shared them with his sister, showing her how to find other truths to counter the brutal reality of the life they knew. She remembered what he said about the unacknowledged heroism of the poor, but watching her father shamble through the door, dragging the vacuum cleaner behind him, Carol searched his dull features in vain for any such nobility.

"Where's Mam?" she asked.

"Gone out. The social worker's been."

"What did that bitch want?"

"She came to say Arwel can be buried."

"What?"

"Arwel can be buried, so Mam's gone to the social to ask about money. Don't they have to give you money to bury people?"


McKenna sat in the meeting which followed upon their trespass of Bedd y Cor, marvelling that assault upon the integrity of the beautiful car should cause such greater distress than upon its owner's.

"Who'll pay for any damage to that fancy car?" Owen Griffiths demanded. "We will! How much do they cost?"

"A lot," McKenna said. "I'm sure Forensics will be extra careful."

"They'd bloody better be! I've seem them rip a car apart like a lion stripping a carcass."

"The quest for knowledge can be like a lion's gorging. Tearing the flesh from the bones, sucking out the marrow."

"Oh, you do talk crap at times, McKenna! I'm glad you managed to keep your mouth shut for once in front of the higher-ups."

"I didn't particularly want to share my knowledge."

"You might have to, however indigestible it is. Rhiannon's put her husband well and truly in the shit, though he's been very co-operative, for somebody's having yards and yards of the poshest carpet pulled out from under him. He's giving blood for analysis first thing in the morning. Why d'you think he didn't argue?"

"It's easier not to go through the enforcement rigmarole."

"D'you think the press'll get on to him?"

"Probably, and they'll crucify him."

"They love the mighty to fall, don't they?" Griffiths commented. "Mind you, the media lost interest pretty quickly."

"The media generally share the common view." McKenna lit a cigarette. "Arwel alive was a bad lot and a drain on society's scarce resources. Arwel dead is one less parasite."

"We'd only need a tiny shift in perspective to be back where Hitler left off, wouldn't we? The government's redefining one lot after another as unworthy, and expendable's the next stop down the road. Who'd miss young Mandy, for instance?" Griffiths coughed. "The solicitor says she's a risk to herself, at risk from others, and depressed as well. Her social worker told us to take her back to Holyhead, and stop encouraging the attention-seeking."

"So why is she still occupying the detention cell?" McKenna asked. "When I looked in, she was stuffing herself with a Chinese takeaway, and between mouthfuls of bamboo shoots and God-knows-what, demanding to know why Dewi Prys, or 'him with the sexy eyes,' hadn't been to see her."

"I'm indulging in lateral thinking." Griffiths smiled. "Going to my retirement with a bang. I'm asking her Nain to take her in."

"Social Services must've tried already."

"You'd think so, wouldn't you? She's never been asked. Social Services snatched the child, and she's been crashing from pillar to post ever since."


Before he fell sick, Jack had woven strings of coloured lights around the porch and through the bare branches of the trees in the garden, and walking up the path, McKenna trod through puddles of warm colour, his figure dappled with pinks and blues and golden yellow.

The twins answered the door, smiled their beautiful smiles, and pulled him to the sitting-room, where they sat beside him on the sofa, his arms imprisoned by their own, their bodies yielding and loving.

"Daddy's in bed, drugged up with cough medicine and paracetamol."

"Asleep."

"And where's your mother?" McKenna asked.

"She's gone out with Mrs. McKenna."

"We're the nurses tonight."

"I'm sure your father's in good hands," McKenna said. "Did the doctor leave a medical certificate?"

One twin left the sofa, foraged inside an old bureau, and handed McKenna the certificate. "He'll be off at least ten days." She sat down and retrieved his arm. "Have you found Gary yet?"

"No, but we found the missing girl."

"Will she go back to Blodwel?"

"I hope not," McKenna said.

"Daddy said he wouldn't wish that place on his worst enemy."

"Can I see him?" McKenna asked. "Just for a few minutes."


In the rosy bedroom lamplight, Jack's flesh gleamed with a bluish tinge, like incipient post-mortem lividity. "Scum rises to the top, like Hogg rose to the top of his profession. Elis's been floating with the scum since he first drew breath."

"Don't be so sour," McKenna chided.

"I feel sour. If I had the energy, I'd be bloody seething." Jack struggled to sit up, breath rasping, clammy sweat on his forehead. "It looks as if Hogg hit the nail on the head, doesn't it?"

"Never mind Hogg or Elis. Concentrate on getting better."

"I don't like leaving you in the lurch. Getting caught in that blizzard caused this."

"You're being well looked after. Enjoy the rest while you can."

Jack grinned lop-sidedly. "You wouldn't credit how fast peace broke out when I took to my bed. The twins're falling over themselves to help."

"You're a focus for their energies."

"Denise called earlier. She likes sick-visiting, doesn't she?"

"I suppose it gives her a focus."

"She thinks you're avoiding her, so I said you're up to your eyes in work." Jack coughed. "She's wittering about Christmas arrangements. I thought she was angling for an invitation here, but Em says not, 'cos Denise is flying out to the Canary Islands four days before Christmas."

"Who with?"

Jack coughed again, and massaged his throat. "Maybe the man with the yacht? Em won't tell me, but she might tell you. Why not ask her?"

McKenna twisted his hands together. "I don't particularly want to know."

"Well, it lets you off the hook. You could come to us for the day. You'll be quite safe with Denise out of the way, won't you?"

McKenna took a stack of files and reports home, and found solutions and endings to all but Arwel's death and Gary's whereabouts. Mandy had gone to her grandmother, perhaps giving hope and purpose to the woman's remaining years. Darren Pritchard remained in South Wales, doing his time, while the remains of Tony Jones would eventually return home, dust and ashes. David Fellowes, dust and ashes already, drifted on the Irish Sea, according to Dewi's note.

McKenna knew he was terribly depressed, but the struggle to feel any different was futile, the darkness within densely compressed by darkness without. Carol's flickering brilliance lit the misery a little, yet raised other shadows, and Rhiannon's perceptions had shed their own light, letting some of Mc-Kenna's pieces fall in place, like the pattern of a kaleidoscope. But like that pattern, the pictures changed shape and focus each time he moved the angle of view.

As the cathedral clock struck ten, the cat ventured outside. The wind had turned, bringing scents of snow, and the distant lands in the east. Shivering, he waited by the door until she scuttled indoors and slumped before the fire, twitching when the doorbell pealed.

She had changed her clothes, McKenna thought, and dressed her hair, and clawed back from the edge of loss of control. Even her nails were filed and polished. "I'm sorry to disturb you so late. I want to talk to you, and I don't know what might happen tomorrow."

"I can't discuss your husband," McKenna said. "But I'm sorry you face such dreadful uncertainty. How's Mari?"

"She'll survive."

"I'll make coffee." He hurried to the kitchen, clattering cups and saucers and spoons while the percolator seethed. She followed, trembling like a new leaf in cold April wind, then took a deep breath and exhaled slowly.

"Forgive me, I'm not usually so *distraite*. I usually hide my feelings. They're such unseemly things, aren't they?"

"Only for other people," McKenna commented.

Rhiannon sat at the kitchen-table. "We had a visit from Carol. I've just taken her home."

"How?"

"You mean: in what?" She smiled. "We've leased new cars, of course."

"I see."

"I wanted to discuss money with you." Rhiannon took her coffee. "I'd like to pay for Arwel's funeral, but thought I should ask you first." She spooned tiny crystals of brown sugar into her cup, and stirred the mixture. "My husband won't be involved." She gulped the scalding coffee. "I've never seen Carol so upset. She hides her feelings better than me. Grief must be getting the better of her at last."

"She has to cope with her parents and their distress." McKenna lit a cigarette.

"I shouldn't think their capacity for distress extends beyond bothering about what the neighbours think of the funeral show. People like them exist in a kind of twilit world where insight and awareness are strangers, don't they?" Rhiannon sighed. "But they're spared the anguish of recognizing their hopelessness."

"The Thomases of this world understand their hopelessness only too well," McKenna said. "That's why they resort to drugs and apathy and suicide. Arwel resorted to his imagination instead, but much good it did him," McKenna said. "Tell me Mrs. Elis, on the subject of suicide, why was Tony Jones called Papageno?"

She shrugged. "He was a terrible liar. Blodwel staff said he'd lie about anything to anyone because he loved to make trouble."

"And are you sure you didn't get a message about three shillings and fourpence and a dance?"

Rhiannon tapped her spoon on the side of her cup. "Of course, I'm not sure. How can I be?"

"And d'you suspect your husband abused Tony?"

"Of course not! He hardly knew him." She frowned. "Ronald Hogg found Arwel and Tony in bed together."

"How d'you know?" McKenna persisted. "Because he told you he did?"

"Why are you doing this?"

"Because you may have been wilfully misled, by someone with their own hidden agenda," McKenna suggested. "Think about it, at least."

She drained her cup, and rose. "Let me know about paying for the funeral, won't you? Carol said the benefits agency will take Arwel's savings to offset the extra funeral grant, and I wouldn't want anyone to face that kind of greed." She went to the parlour, and picked up her coat before he could help her, the silk lining rustling as she pulled it around her body. "There's another favour you could do for me." She picked at threads torn from the sofa by the cat's assaults. "One of the little boys at Blodwel has something of ours which I'd like back, but I didn't want to upset him by asking. Could you ask Ronald Hogg? I can't visit Blodwel. I'm waiting for a decision from the chief executive about my position." Her fingers taunted the threads. "I might be forced to resign."

"What is it?"

"An artefact of my husband's past." She smiled. "A tiepin made of red and white gold and shaped like a bullet, which is no doubt why the child was so taken with it. My husband was an RAF cadet at public school. The pin's missing."

"Why a bullet?"

"A joke commemorating some horseplay with their weaponry. He was once reprimanded for the negligent discharge of a firearm." Rhiannon thrust her hands deep in her pockets. "I really must go. Thank you for your help."

"How did the child come by the tiepin?"

"Mr. Hogg gave it to him. I assume my husband gave it to Arwel."

"I'm extrapolating," Eifion Roberts announced, pouring whiskey in his glass. "Anything can be extrapolated. Interpretation is infinite."

"You're keeping me from my bed," McKenna said.

"Give over! It's not midnight yet."

"D'you ever have a hangover?"

"I don't drink much when I'm not with you." The pathologist smiled. "You don't judge me like other folk. Have some. Better than caffeine."

"Sleep would be better still. I've had a taxing day."

"Haven't we all? Last thing this afternoon, I watched a ferrety little undertaker and his sidekick tip Arwel's body in a makeshift coffin and carry him away. They'll embalm him, dress him up in his going-to-chapel-Sunday-best, and put him in another makeshift coffin with fake brass handles and a cheap nylon lining which looks like silk to the teary eye."

"Rhiannon wants to pay for a decent funeral."

"Why? What's in it for her?"

"It's her way of helping the family."

Stroking the sleepy cat, the pathologist said, "You and me'll never belong to her elite, or Hogg's, but we wouldn't want to."

"Jack says he's scum risen to the top."

"He's that as well," Dr. Roberts nodded. "Social workers and psychiatrists are an elite police force, doling out punishment in the shape of treatment when folk won't toe that very rigid line between normal and not normal. Kids in care are supposed to be grateful for the relentless persecution offered by the likes of Hogg, otherwise they're branded as mad, bad and dangerous to know."

"And some of them are."

"Hogg's brand of treatment makes them worse."

"Maybe there's no other kind," McKenna pointed out. "Damage limitation by containment might be the best we can hope for. Controlling these youngsters is a real problem."

"Control's a bloody article of faith for social workers! Who says the kids are out of control?"

"The people who look after them."

"Exactly." Dr. Roberts drained his glass. "And who decides if you're mad? The psychiatrists. Definitions dependent on the observer, not the observed. Like with young Ophelia in *Hamlet*." He reached for the bottle. "Put yourself in Ophelia's place, adopt her frames of reference, and she's not mad at all."

McKenna grinned. "Tipple much more, Eifion, and you'll have a congregation of vapours in your head."

"Oh, very witty! Is there anything you haven't read? I bet you haven't read about moral architecture, or an ethical manifesto for social workers, have you?" Dr. Roberts asked. "Ethics went down the tubes when folk twigged they interfere with our slithery progress through the gut of life."

"Can we change the subject?" McKenna asked. "You put weird notions in my head."

"What shall we talk about, then? Heads?"

"Why should I want to discuss heads?"

"The sexton at Wahring Cemetery in Vienna was offered a small fortune for Beethoven's head. How much d'you reckon Elis would put up for Arwel's skull?"

"Oh, give it a rest!"

"What's wrong with wallowing now and then in human misery?"

"It's a habit people get to enjoy. Elis loves his misery, according to Rhiannon."

"She's probably jealous of it. You know how strange women can be." Dr. Roberts frowned. "Perhaps she made a Druid sacrifice of Arwel, under the huge old oak you said grows by Bedd y Cor."

"Why should she?"

"I dunno, do I? She's a woman. Isn't that reason enough?"

# • C h a p t e r •
# 14

Owen Griffiths paced his office. "We could arrest everybody, line them up, and say 'eeny-meeny-miny-mo' over and over until there's only one left. That's roughly how the Druids chose a sacrificial victim. Good God, McKenna! Don't you know better than to listen to Eifion Roberts in his cups?"

"We shouldn't shut our minds to any possibility. He wasn't drunk, anyway."

"I reckon you were both more than three sheets to the wind." Griffiths scowled. "I hope you're not seeking comfort in the bottle. I'm not sitting in judgement, but marital break-up leaves no one unscathed. You tore up roots, parcelled up unique memories, so don't pretend you don't hurt."

"There was nothing of value to tear up or put away," McKenna said. "Denise is like someone let out of gaol."

"Nature gives women resources you wouldn't imagine, so men can go to war as cannon fodder, and they stay home and rule the world."

"Rhiannon has resources, and extraordinary depth," McKenna said. "She might've seen Arwel as an intolerable threat to Elis's fragile stability."

"But she'd have to be psychotic with jealousy to destroy someone he loved so much." He stared at McKenna, looking for signs of disintegration. "Jack Tuttle couldn't've chosen a worst time to be ill. You look worn out. If Eifion slips up with his scalpel, you don't hear a squeal of protest from his customers, but if you slip up on this case, there'll be a howling from here to the English border and back."

McKenna smiled. "What will I do when you retire, Owen?"

"Miss me, I hope."

Dewi placed two mugs of tea on McKenna's desk, and a plate of sandwiches. "I saw Elis downstairs, with a polished-looking bloke in blue pinstripes, carrying a briefcase."

"His solicitor, supervising the volunteered tissue samples."

Dewi selected a cheese and tomato sandwich, and began to eat.

"Why've you brought sandwiches at this time of the morning?" McKenna asked. "Jack Tuttle isn't here."

"I thought the weather might be making you hungry. This wind feels like it's scouring your innards." Dewi shivered. "Why's Elis here instead of kicking up an almighty fuss in court?"

"Because he knows he's nothing to fear?"

"All the more reason. It's a hellish trespass on his rights."

"I think he learned the hard way why he daren't disobey authority. Have you been to Blodwel?"

Dewi nodded. "And had the pleasure of seeing *Herr Grofaz* again. He was giving the bearded wonder a real tongue-lashing over something. I don't know how folk put up with him." He dropped the little bullet on the desk, and it rolled, coming to rest against McKenna's ashtray. "He had a tantrum with me when I asked for this, glaring and stamping and snarling: 'What a fuss about a silly little toy!' Then he stomped to the sitting-room, and I heard the kid wailing, so I reckon Hogg'd snatched it off him, like a big playground bully."

McKenna examined the scratches and peered at the tiny lettering on the case, then put the bullet in the drawer.

"Hogg asked if we'd done anything about Elis," Dewi said. "I told him to route queries to the chief constable." Selecting another sandwich, he added, "He said we must bear in mind that people are cheaper than paintings or cars or horses, and whereas the rich are vulnerable to their own vices, the poor are vulnerable to the vices of others."

"How very subtle and perceptive," McKenna commented. "I wonder how he'd know that?"

"He says he's got a degree from the 'University of Life,' which presumably justifies his general ignorance and lack of decency."

"Eifion Roberts thinks we react to Hogg and his kind the way people react to us." McKenna sipped his tea. "He's become your latest *bête noire*, Dewi, so watch yourself."

Dewi grinned. "Talking of beasts, black or otherwise, I saw Beti Gloff hopping and hobbling down the road from Salem Village, so I gave her a lift. Mary Ann's having meals on wheels and a home help 'cos of her rheumatics, so Beti was gabbing and gobbing about the wonderful social workers helping the old folk."

"Social workers might do a lot less damage giving practical help instead of indulging in pseudo-psychiatry."

"I can't imagine Hogg grafting. He's only fit for spouting crap, fancying himself, and bullying kids. He'd be unemployable elsewhere. We wouldn't even want him, would we?"


The engine of the old brown Cavalier from the police car pool fired at the fourth try, plumes of exhaust vapour snatched by the wind and torn to shreds. As Janet drove out of the village, the car heater blew cold air and petrol fumes in her face, and she cursed her own stupidity. Her own car, back at the factory, was unlikely to be returned before New Year, and only then if her father paid the bill.

The village street meandered along the valley floor, low stone houses roofed with steely-blue slate on little escarpments above the river. She overtook a green and white double-decker bus and passed a group of teenagers, sporting the shaven-headed caste mark of their type, and wondered if they came from the council estate opposite, or one of the tiny settlements straggling up the mountainside. Satisfied Gary Hughes was not among them, she drove on, fiddling with the heater, thinking of the poverty in her view and unable to imagine its reality. For her, poverty threatened if a whim could not be gratified immediately, or if, she realized with a jolt in her stomach, home comforts could not be replicated elsewhere. Her father's stance was beyond comprehension, for the continuity of her family was unthinkable with an essential element missing. Even for the Thomases, already beached on the shores of misery, Arwel's loss pushed hope further out to sea, for however tragic or ramshackle, the family formed the geography of living, her own like a sunlit island surrounded by third-world misery. Carol was a third-world girl, old before her time, trying to make the frayed and rotten ends meet as she watched them move further and further apart.

A tall young figure strode along the narrow verge, curly brown hair ruffled by the wind, hands deep in the pockets of a padded jacket. Janet slowed to a crawl, and leaned over to peer at the figure, the hair, the smooth young face with its rosy cheeks, trying to recall the contours of Gary's face. The owner looked at her, then away, and walked doggedly on. She trailed at walking speed, passenger window open, the engine knocking slightly, and the figure suddenly stopped and turned and said, "Sod off, you ugly dyke, or I'll set the coppers on you!"

Standing at the front door of Bedd y Cor, McKenna wondered if Rhiannon would have the heart to decorate her home as Jack bedecked his own. The drive was bare, its gravel raked smooth, the lawns a livid yellowy-green in the stormy light. Dark clouds heavy with snow seethed behind the mountains, spilling huge shadows down the valley, and an icy wind poked fingers in the bronzy creeper, snatching a leaf now and then to toss on the gravel.

Aping her mistress in more than dress, Mari offered him

a tight civilized smile, this control, her own article of faith, raking over the urchin heritage as well as yesterday's distraught face.

"Madam isn't in." The long-case clock in the hall struck once. "Mr. Elias doesn't want to be disturbed."

Beyond the echo of the clock, behind closed doors, McKenna heard another resonance. "Is that him?"

"He's been in the music-room since he came back from the police station. He hasn't had lunch yet."

"I won't disturb him, Mari." He took a small envelope from his pocket. "Would you give him this?"

She shook the little bullet from its hiding place, and gasped, control ebbing from her face. "Where did you get this? Mr. Elias gave it to Arwel."

"I know." McKenna squeezed her trembling hand. "That's why I've returned it."

She snatched her hand away, and shook her head, as she had the day before. "You don't understand! Where did you get it?"

"One of the boys at Blodwel had it."

"Oh, God!" Mari clutched the bullet, and wailed, all control gone. "Who had it? Where did he get it?"

"Mrs. Elis saw it the other night. She asked me to retrieve it."

"She doesn't understand either!" Mari snapped.

McKenna held her arm. "Will you stop talking in riddles?"

She pulled away. "Arwel always wore it." She examined the bullet, turning it over and over in the palm of her hand. "Who broke the pin?"

"I don't know."

"Then why don't you find out?" Her eyes glittered with rage. "I said Arwel *always* wore the pin! *Always!*" Her voice rose, obliterating the music. "Anywhere it couldn't be seen. It was his secret lucky charm." Tears began to fall, the notes of her voice broken by sobs. "He said a silver bullet keeps werewolves at bay, and nothing bad could ever happen while he wore it."

•  •  •

"It's very funny, Janet, even though I don't much feel like laughing," McKenna said.

Janet blushed again. "No one's ever called me a lesbian before."

"You shouldn't kerb-crawl after teenage girls," Dewi commented.

"I didn't know, did I?" Janet snapped. "I thought it was Gary."

"Gary's not daft enough to walk round in broad daylight," Dewi said. "He lies doggo 'til the dead of night, then creeps out like a wolf on the prowl. Want to bet he's tearing sheep apart before long?"

"Stop baiting Janet," McKenna said. "You could've made the same mistake."

Dewi grinned. "But she wouldn't've called me an ugly dyke!"

Janet looked at him. "Quite a few names for you come to mind, and none of them very flattering."


Darkness from the mountains already washed the streets of Caernarfon when McKenna parked on the quay beneath the castle walls. He climbed the steep short hill below Queen Eleanor's Gate, and walked across Castle Square to the dingy little shop where Carol Thomas plied the wares of others. Wind swirled around him, caught between the buildings, slapping litter, and he felt the sting of sleety rain on his face.

"She's not in today." The youth in Carol's place gazed blankly at shelves of clocks, all set to a different time. "She'll be in Monday, I think." He frowned. "There's a funeral, isn't there? I'm not sure when."

Retrieving his car, McKenna drove to the council estate, where children sat on walls, smoking and drinking from cans, or trailed like refugees in groups and braces up and down the ill-lit dirty streets, a whole generation displaced. Drawing into the kerb by the broken gate, behind a shiny new car which looked vaguely familiar, he thought the same internal collapse must threaten here as any inner city, and as a lone girl passed him on the pavement, eyes averted, he decided children were insufficiently valued for their impact on the world to be absorbed.

Washing snapped on the line at the side of the house, one leg of Tom Thomas's pyjama trousers screwed up inside itself like an amputee's. Dim light shone behind thin curtains drawn at the window of the front parlour. Carol opened the door, smells of stale tobacco and soot eddying in the frosty darkness.

"Mam and Dad are out." She looked over McKenna's shoulder, and lifted her eyes to the sky.

"Will they be long?"

She shivered. "I don't know."

"Can I come in? It's cold. You shouldn't stand at the door."

She took him to the back parlour, where a new layer of dirt sat upon the old, sooty dust furring the windowledge and skirting-board and furniture, and stood before the meagre fire, her hands clenched. Time had wrought swift change, McKenna thought, since he last saw her, changing the contours of her body, pulling her clothes awry. Her eyes held a strange expression, soft and dreamy.

"Arwel's come home. They brought him back this morning."

He heard what sounded like a muffled sob from the other room. Carol smiled, brilliant amid the dross of her surroundings. "Mrs. Hogg came to pay her respects." She laughed. "Isn't she kind?"

Iciness slithered up McKenna's spine. "Perhaps I should do the same." He moved slowly to the door.

Carol pounced, barring his way. "Oh, no!" Her breath rasped. "I wouldn't want you paying the same respects as Doris. You don't owe like her." She laughed again, a tinkling little sound absorbed by an atmosphere heavy with menace.

McKenna caught her arm, the poor stuff on her jumper so

different from the richness shrouding Mari Williamson. "Let me pass, Carol."

She scampered to the hall, and threw open the door of the front parlour. The icy room stank of must, of soot frothing in the hearth, of dust and flowers and death and food. Poor dismal furniture was pushed against the walls, poor bits of china busied the sooty mantelshelf, poor thin carpet trod underfoot, poor Carol stood beside the other woman, and relinquished all her status to her poor dead brother, whose embalmed and mutilated corpse lay in a coffin on the table, a vase of giant white chrysanthemums at his head, and a feast upon his breast. Carol grabbed a handful of Doris's hair and pushed her face down in the coffin, to gorge on the sins of others, and on death itself.

"No!" McKenna whispered. "Carol! Don't do this!"

"Eat! Eat! *Eat!*" Carol chanted, while Doris struggled and keened, feeble as a child, choking on the food. Still holding her by the hair, Carol dragged her upright, and presented her head to McKenna as one slain. Eyes black, mouth and face smeared red and brown, Doris gaped, and he thought her marked forever, feared and shunned like the Aghoris of India, who feast on rotting human corpses and their own excrement in the quest for redemption.

As if wading in sluggish water, he moved clumsily, and gathered up the corners of the cloth laid on Arwel's chest, making a parcel of the bits of bread and meat and vegetable. He put the cloth on the floor, then unhooked Carol's clawed fingers from the woman's hair.

"Get out!" Carol spat. She pushed her, and Doris stumbled against the table leg, snatching at the coffin to save herself. "Don't you *dare* touch my brother!" Carol screamed. *"Get out!"*

Doris staggered through the door, and down the hallway, McKenna in her wake, but she eluded him, scuttling down the path and through the rotting gate to her car, fighting like a wild animal as he tried to wrest the keys. She knocked him violently against the fence, and was gone before he recovered his balance, the car swerving and rocketing along the road, rear lights leaving a puddle of smoky colour. He telephoned Owen Griffiths, then went back to Carol and her dead brother.

Fine thin hands resting on the edge of the coffin, she smiled at Arwel, then frowned when she noticed the stain on his shirt. McKenna forced himself to look at the boy amid the folds of ivory fabric, dressed in the stained white shirt, trousers, socks and plastic shoes in black, and a black bow tight around his neck to cover the scar Eifion Roberts made when he dug in his scalpel and turned Arwel inside out. Thin child's hands with ragged nails were folded on his chest, another faint stain on the edge of one cuff.

"He can't be buried in a dirty shirt," Carol said.

"I'll make sure he isn't," McKenna said. "Don't worry."

Looking up, she offered that heart-stopping smile. "Will you? Can you do that?" She leaned over, tracing her fingers down the side of Arwel's face and neck. "His neck's dirty." She began to rub the dead flesh.

"Don't, Carol." He pulled her hand away. "It's a bruise."

"They've made his hair all stiff." She caught McKenna's hand, and made him stroke the lacquered blond hair. "Arwel had beautiful hair, all soft and silky like a baby's." She smiled again. "I helped him walk and talk. We were always together."

"Come away," McKenna persuaded. "It's so cold in here."

She nodded, then leaned over, her own beautiful hair swinging forward, and kissed Arwel's forehead and cheeks, trying to lift one of his hands to her lips. McKenna took her fingers, unclasping their hold, the cheap papery coffin dressing brushing his flesh as Arwel's dead fingers dragged over his hand and back to their resting place.

He sat with her in the other room, the touch of her hair like gossamer, and heard the grief and rage she would carry in her heart for the rest of her days, from which there would be no delivery, and felt the crushing weight of her tragedy more dreadfully than anything felt in his whole existence.

•     •     •

"Dear God!" Owen Griffiths leaned against McKenna's office window, his gaunt reflection adrift in a penumbra of darkness. "Dear God! How could we let such a terrible thing happen?"

"How could we know?" McKenna asked. "Perhaps it was necessary."

"Necessary?" Griffiths turned. "Who could possibly benefit from that barbaric practice?"

"Arwel." McKenna stubbed out his fourth cigarette.

"I can't believe all the sins visited on Arwel are now languishing in Doris's soul."

"Your opinions don't matter," McKenna said. "Carol believes in the power of sin-eating, and for all we know, so does Doris. She certainly seemed to understand what was happening."

"I suppose." Griffiths sat down wearily. "I've heard a sin-eater lived on Bangor Mountain until just before the last war. What a terrible legacy we Welsh have in our hearts, eh?" He sighed. "What was Doris eating?"

"Sausage, bread, cake, cream crackers, all cut up small, smothered in brown sauce and jam, and laid out on paper plates from Woolworths and Peggy's Sunday best tablecloth." He lit another cigarette, trying to quell the taste of death, lingering in his mouth and worming through his body in search of a resting place.

"Did you bring it back? It's evidence."

"I threw it away."

"Why in God's name did Doris go there?"

"Carol told her Rhiannon was visiting and wanted to meet her there."

"And Doris couldn't resist the siren call of the most powerful woman in her small universe," Griffiths said. "Even if Rhiannon's stripped of her power, it's served its purpose for Carol, hasn't it? But who'd think the girl capable of something like that?"

"She'd given her parents bus fare to visit relatives in Pwllheli."

"We should harness resources like that instead of letting them go to waste, or worse. Who else knows?"

"No one, probably. The Thomases came back about five, and Carol shot to the kitchen when she heard them at the door. I doubt they'll notice anything amiss, except perhaps the stains on Arwel's shirt."

"And I doubt Carol will be lost for an innocent explanation," Griffiths said. "Did you get any sense out of her?"

"She said Doris sets herself up as better than anyone's own mother, but she didn't protect Arwel, so she's guilty of his death, and she must suffer." McKenna stubbed out his cigarette, and lit another. "I had the impression Doris hasn't even begun to suffer yet."

"What should we do?"

"Charge Carol with assault, I suppose, and let the law take its course."

"You'd be happy with that?" Griffiths demanded. "She'd go down for a long time, pregnant or not." He paused, then said, "I'm taking an executive decision: we do nothing, and tell no one."

"And if Doris makes a complaint, or shoots her mouth off?"

"I'll say the girl was understandably distraught, and not herself, and ask Doris what she was doing at the house in the first place."

"You could be storing up a great deal of trouble for yourself."

"Yes, I could." Griffiths nodded. "And see if I care."


"I saw Mandy in town with her Nain, sir, buying new clothes," Janet told McKenna. "You could take them for twins, except for her Nain's wrinkles. She seems pleased to have Mandy."

"Let's hope it lasts."

"Mandy's going back to school after Christmas." Janet smiled. "Isn't it strange how the ordinary little things matter so much? School, family, a few new clothes."

"Routine, predictability and affection add up to security," McKenna said. "Mandy'll get bored to death with the routine, but she might appreciate the rest of it."

"Hogg asked where she is," Janet said. "I said Superintendent Griffiths took an executive decision about placement."

"What did he say to that?"

She smiled wryly. "Even the chief constable, apparently, doesn't have that power with children. Hogg will be 'seeing about it.' " Offering a cigarette to McKenna, she added, "I've tried not to, but I really dislike him. Dilys Roberts is another nasty piece of work. He made her sit in while I talked to the boy, and even though she didn't actually do anything, she frightened him half to death."

"And the tiepin?"

"Somebody found it, gave it to Hogg, and he chucked it round to prove how brave he is. When it didn't blow his ugly face to bits, he gave it to the kid, who showed it to Rhiannon."

"Who found it? When?"

"Hogg said: 'Oh, really! Can't you find better things to do with your time than pester me about a trivial matter like this?' And Dilys didn't know because she wasn't on duty."

"If she doesn't know when the bullet turned up, how can she know if she was on duty?"

"Because, sir, she would know if she'd been on duty. Therefore, she wasn't." Janet paused, tapped ash from her cigarette. "They've got an answer for everything. I said we'd been told Arwel always wore the pin, so if it was broken when he was killed, he must've died at Blodwel. Hogg looked down his nose at me and said: 'But who knows when it was broken?' "

Dressed in a sinuous gown of black devore velvet, a rope of crystal chunks around her neck, Rhiannon opened her own front door. Her make-up was flawless, and her hair glistened under the lights.

"I'm sorry," McKenna said. "Are you going out?"

She sighed. "I'm trying to set my house in order. Routines

are so important at times of crisis, don't you think?" She led him to the drawing-room. "We dressed for dinner, which was a most civilized meal, and my husband took coffee in the music-room. I won't see him again tonight, so your visit rescues me from splendid isolation."

"I spoke to Mari this afternoon."

"I know, and she may have misled you. Guilt impels her to do something." Rhiannon pushed a silver ashtray across the table. "I hope she hasn't put you to any trouble."

"No one seems to know who found the pin, or when."

"It was only important to my husband and Arwel." She paused, sipping her coffee. "Have you any news for us, Mr. McKenna?"

"Forensic examinations take time. It's an exacting science."

"So much depends on the outcome, doesn't it?"

"In some cases." McKenna opened a new packet of cigarettes, and tossed the wrapping on the flames roaring up the chimney. "One of my officers commented on your husband's willingness to co-operate."

"Did you tell him he knows no other response to power?"

"I also said Mr. Elis may know he's nothing to fear."

"He'll always have something to fear, like a former addict in the face of temptation. Those around him share the terror."

"Perhaps you encourage his morbid condition by accepting it."

"I tried every other ploy, but I've nothing to offer that he wants." She stared at her visitor. "You've resurrected so many demons I thought were laid to rest, so many questions I don't want to answer. My marriage is a wasteland, and always will be, because nothing has any value to my husband except his own needs, this darkness he cherishes like a lover. He sees tragedy as his consort." Picking at her cuticle, she added, "I don't. All I can see is a romantic justification for self-centredness of tragic proportions."

"He spent childhood in the company of merciless strangers," McKenna said. "He learned to fear more than most."

"We're all afraid," Rhiannon snapped. "We fear what value

others put on us, if they hate us, if they plan our destruction."
She shivered. "All that mystery ruling other hearts! We never
know when its power might be turned against us, do we?"

"Terror is part of the human condition," McKenna said.
"Is your husband ever violent?"

Her cheeks flushed. "I'm not a council-house wife!"

"Indeed no, but like sex and death, violence is a great lev-
eller." Beyond the roaring of the flames in the chimney,
McKenna heard another fire in the music-room. "And although you can buy any distraction, you're no more immune
from life than the Thomases and their ilk."

Rhiannon smiled bleakly. "You must be very good at your
job. You make people expose themselves." She emptied the
ashtray into the fire, then said, "Have you seen Carol's other
side yet? She can be violent, in her own way. Did you know
Peggy Thomas claims her husband didn't father the children?
Carol's been browbeating her mother for weeks, trying to get
at the truth, because she was afraid her baby might have been
fathered by a half-brother." She shuddered gently. "Or even
her natural father."

"Peggy'll use any stick to beat her husband. Unfortunately,
she wounds others at the same time," McKenna said. "Was
Carol's mind put at rest?"

"Not before she tried to abort herself with a bottle of gin,
like in the good old days. Doctors and hospitals are just another aspect of hostile authority as far as she's concerned."
Rhiannon sighed. "Mari took the gin from our cellar. Silly
girl! She knows my housekeeper's a strict accountant, and ac-
counting for every drop of drink and morsel of food is her ar-
- ticle of faith."

"And what did you do?"

"I told Mari to ask next time she wanted something." She
laughed. "She's taken me at my word, as you've no doubt noticed from her dress." The laughter faded. "Then I went to
see Carol, because I was horrified, and she's Arwel's sister,
and I'm rich, and she's poor and ignorant. My husband doesn't
know, and he mustn't. I offered to pay for the abortion if she

really wanted one, and said I'd give her money to buy a decent flat and bring up the child if she didn't. I suppose I showed her a way out of her own misery, so you could say I've bought the child, in an ambiguous way."


McKenna sat on his worn sofa, reading of child abuse in Europe and America and Australia, of spectacular denial, of the underlying pathology, and of the prevalence of abuse throughout recorded history. The cat sniffed at the back door, and paced around his legs, mewling. Letting her out, he found on his doorstep the same poor animal he had seen under the bare shrubs in the little garden. His own cat watched as he filled bowls with meat and water, laid them on the step, and closed the door, then she climbed on his lap. Listening to the scrape of dishes on the outside step as the other cat feasted, he said, "Do you cats talks to each other? Is word out I'm a soft touch for strays?"

He closed his eyes, imagining the other cat metamorphosed, like the little animal on his knee, who came to him as a threadbare wormy stray, and drowsed, thoughts rambling through the forest of words heard and read, music charting a more certain course. He let the music play in his head, marvelling at such complexity imprinted on memory, fretting a little because he could not bring the notes to the forefront of his mind and make them louder, and fell asleep wondering why one never could.


The telephone woke him, and the cat leapt off his knee to lie before the fire.

"Sorry to disturb you." The hard edges of Jack's voice were blunted by congestion. "You weren't in bed, were you?"

"Is anything wrong?"

"I can't get to sleep. I'm disturbing Em, so I got up."

"Have some hot milk and brandy," McKenna suggested.

"I might. Any news? Anything interesting happened?"

"Bits and pieces, odds and ends." McKenna lit a cigarette. "Hogg's giving us the runaround."

"He'll get his comeuppance one day." Jack coughed. "I hope I'm there to see it." His breath wheezed. "Any news on Gary?"

"Somebody robbed food and fags and cans and soap from a village shop last night, so Dewi's spending the night on watch with the shopkeeper."

"He pulls his weight, doesn't he? How's Miss Evans?"

McKenna stifled a yawn, then laughed. "She had a run-in this morning with a teenager she was following in the car. She thought it was Gary, and it was a girl, and the girl called her an ugly dyke and said she'd get the police on her."

"Oh, God!" Jack wheezed and chuckled. "Sod's law, isn't it?"

"Your chest sounds bad."

"Secondary infection, according to the doctor. He's given me antibiotics, and they've given me the runs and an almighty headache."

"Then you'd best stay off the drink."

"I hate being ill. It throws all your routines, I'm bored rigid, and I can't settle to anything."

"Read a book. Wrap up and watch late-night TV."

"There's nothing on except wrestling and reggae. I'll get my lovely daughters to rent some videos tomorrow. *Bambi* or *Snow White* or something. There's more than enough sex and violence at work."

"*Bambi*'s full of violence," McKenna said. "It was the first film I ever saw, and I cried so much I was sick."

"I'll bet your mother was pleased. Is that why you're a pushover for animals?"

"I'm being visited by another stray cat."

"Like that old rhyme? 'Not last night but the night before, two tom cats came knocking at my door.'" Jack laughed. "Talking of visitors, the phone keeps ringing but nobody says anything. It's happened three times in the past few days."

"To the others as well?"

"They haven't said, not that Em's saying much, anyway. She's thoroughly fed up in general, and in particular with me under her feet all day." Jack paused. "Denise's done it again, you know. She's made Em feel hard done by and resentful because she can't swan off to the Canaries for a winter holiday."

"You could all go on holiday, and avoid Christmas."

"It's an idea, isn't it? When she's in a better mood, I'll suggest a break from the ritual and routine, and the bloody awful relatives." Jack paused again. "We can't, can we? Em and the twins want you here for Christmas Day."

"We'll see, shall we? By the way, where are the calls coming from?"

"How should I know?"

"If you were less of a Luddite, you'd know how to retrieve the number. It's called technological progress."

"Oh, that. Well, there's no point trying now. Denise called Em after, to gloat about her holiday."

# •Chapter• 15

Owen Griffiths yawned. "I've been awake half the night. I can't get over what happened yesterday." He shook his head, in wonder and in awe. "Did you sleep, or was your night full of monsters?"

"I slept like the dead," McKenna said.

"I want you to interview Doris. She pushed you, and you fell, so technically, she assaulted a police officer." Griffiths yawned again. "She might tell you what she and Carol know and we don't, if you frighten her enough."

"Rhiannon's frightened, and of more than the possibility of being married to a paedophile," McKenna said. "For all her eloquence, she manages to say very little, and she never gives a straight answer. I asked her if Elis is prone to violence."

Griffiths smiled. "And did you really think she'd tell you? Her sort never give anything away, in case it bounces back and makes a hole in the posh façade."

"She still wants to pay for the funeral, and reminded me Elis will want to go."

"Funerals are open to all. I just hope Hogg can find something better to do on the day." Griffiths sighed. "Let's take up Rhiannon's offer, if only to get Arwel out of that house."


"Why don't you go home for some sleep?" McKenna asked.

"I'm not that tired," Dewi said. "Me and the shopkeeper

took turns, and nothing happened except a bloody great cockroach ran over my foot. I'll go out with Mountain Rescue if you don't want anything else done." Pulling a thick parka from the back of the chair, he asked, "Did something happen yesterday, sir? You seemed a bit odd when you came back from Caernarfon."

McKenna flicked his lighter on and off. "Let's say I saw powerful emotion rip away the thin veneer of civilized behaviour."

Dewi grinned. "Caernarfon folk wouldn't know civilized behaviour if it smacked them in the gob."

The director of social services telephoned shortly before midday, as McKenna prepared to leave for Blodwel.

"I've received a complaint, Chief Inspector."

"Have you?"

"We've spent the last couple of days running round after the Thomases, at the expense of other clients." The voice was harsh. "Getting the funeral grant from the benefits agency, filling in endless forms for extra funds, ferrying the parents here, there and everywhere. Now we find the time was completely wasted! My social worker went to the immense trouble of visiting the family this morning, and that insolent girl not only told her to go away, but had the brazen impudence to blame this department for the boy's death. Perhaps you can explain what's happening?"

"I'm sorry, I've no idea. May I suggest you discuss your complaint with Superintendent Griffiths?"

"My God, do Social Services actually work weekends?" Owen Griffiths asked. "He won't call me. I'm too high up the ladder to push around. Rhiannon called to say the service'll be at St. Mihangel's, probably Tuesday or Wednesday. The undertaker's already taken Arwel. D'you think they'll ring the church bells for him?"

"It would be a nice touch," McKenna said. "I can hear

the bells from the house when the wind's in the right direction."

Griffiths began to draw a border of crude bell shapes interspersed with crosses around the edge of a statement continuation sheet. "Manchester police released Tony's body, so he's being cremated. The soles of his feet were covered in cigarette burns, apparently, His funeral's in Manchester, 'cos it's cheaper." He stared bleakly at McKenna. "You'll have to be buried, won't you? The pope's against cremation as well as contraception."

McKenna smiled gently. "You can't be resurrected if your body's been incinerated."

"And what makes you think I'd want to be?"

On his way home to feed the cat, McKenna walked through the Bible Gardens, along paths strewn with drifts of sodden leaves that not even the scouring wind from the east could dry. The great trees threshed and shivered, abandoned by the squirrels which scaled their heights in autumn to garner winter stores, hurling nuts to the ground and often, he recalled ruefully, on the heads of passersby. At the bottom of Glanrafon, the little sapling planted to replace the ancient Reformer's Tree, felled on a hot July day after it rotted from the inside out, threshed and shivered like its ancient companions.

The votary light gleamed behind the great Gothic window of the cathedral chancel, and music, serene and beautiful, echoed within the vaulted building. Entranced, he stopped to listen, mourning the medieval schism which took this music from his own church and handed it to the Protestant heretic. He pictured the boys in the choir stalls, whom he often saw coming from evening practice, dressed in jeans and sweatshirts and trainers, kicking a football against the railings of the cathedral yard, and was suddenly overcome by thoughts of corruption within the glorification, like poisonous dregs in the Communion chalice.

He climbed the steps by the old almshouses, treading on a

mosaic of epitaphs in slate and granite, and crossed the road by Debenham's elegant frontage, opposite the great empty space occupied for three centuries past by the Castle Hotel, before it too rotted from the inside out.

The stray cat crouched outside the parlour window, scrawny fur riffled by the wind, staring at his own cat, who lounged on the inside, her tail swinging lazily. He fed both, then lunched on sandwiches and tea, while they ate peacefully side by side in the kitchen. Locking the front door, he walked down the hill, wondering in what mayhem they might indulge in his absence.

Fitful sunshine dappled thin colour on the hillside behind Blodwel and pushed shadows against walls and roof. Walking to the front door, McKenna shivered, cold with the spirit of this place, this *genius loci* almost a thing of substance. The bearded man unlocked the door, fumbling with the keys.

"Why d'you need so many keys?" McKenna asked.

"I don't know." Lovell smiled wanly. "They make holes in your pockets." The smile evaporated. "Did you want Mr. Hogg? He's off duty for the weekend."

"And Mrs. Hogg?"

"She's supposed to be off as well, but she's in the flat." He lingered, chewing the inside of his mouth like Peggy Thomas, then walked away, keys swinging and jangling.

McKenna followed. "You don't work every weekend, do you?"

"Three out of four. Dilys comes on duty as I go off."

"Who works with you?"

Lovell smiled wryly. "That famous person by the name of Nobody. There aren't enough staff to double up all the time."

"Why don't the Hoggs help out, then?" McKenna asked.

"You'll have to ask her, won't you?"

Doris seemed only annoyed. The dog snuffled at her feet, then at McKenna's, its rancid smell like an aura. "I'm busy. I've got reports to write. Everything's behind with all this coming and going and asking questions, and it's not me you should be after, anyway. It's rich folk who can buy their way in and out of everything."

"Might we go to the office?" McKenna suggested.

"I've told you, I'm busy."

"The sooner you answer my questions, the sooner you can get back to work." McKenna felt tempted to kick both woman and dog. "I don't plan to leave until you have."

She pushed past him, and unlocked the door of the little office where old metal desks and rickety chairs crowded the floor. "What d'you want?"

McKenna pushed the door shut. "I'm surprised you didn't contact me, if only to apologize for your behaviour yesterday."

"My behaviour?"

"You lashed out at me quite without provocation."

Her face mottled with rage. "How dare you!"

McKenna lit a cigarette. "I'm even more surprised you didn't complain about Carol Thomas. Should I expect another call from your director? He said nothing this morning. Doesn't he know?" He paused. "Shouldn't we discuss Carol?"

"She's mental! They should put her away!"

"What she did was extreme, but her reasons seem eminently sane. She believes you owe her brother. Why is that?"

"How should I know? She's mad!" Doris shivered. "She's disgusting! Sickening! She should die for shame over what she did to that body. She defiled him!"

"Arwel's degradation came from other hands," McKenna said. "But Carol's degraded you, hasn't she? Have you been sick yet?" He blew a smoke ring towards the ceiling, and watched its slow disintegration. "Did you know sin eating's like a family inheritance? It's often passed from mother to daughter in a very Biblical fashion."

"You're talking rubbish," Doris said, her composure returning. "Nobody believes that stuff these days."

"Carol does." He blew another smoke ring, and watched it travel towards the ceiling. "And she made you ingest all the sins visited on Arwel. They'll be more than enough to poison the stoutest spirit." He stubbed out the cigarette. "If you were Roman Catholic, you could seek help from the church, although I imagine those sins are beyond the redemptive power of any priest. If you were a mother, your own child could take them in the fullness of time. But you're neither papist nor parent, and I can't think how you might be shriven. Doesn't that put the fear of God in you?" Opening the door, he found the dog athwart the opening, barring his way. He nudged it aside with his foot, and walked away from the sounds of the woman's unholy terror.

Owen Griffiths paced his office again. "Forensics've finished with the horsebox and trailer, and I hope you've finished with Doris." He sat down, and began fiddling with his pens. "I wouldn't've credited you with nastiness of that order. It's bordering on wanton cruelty, to any God-fearing soul."

"If she was God-fearing, or had a soul worth the name, she wouldn't condone what goes on there, let alone be part of it."

"Maybe she's scared of Hogg, maybe she sees nothing wrong. Values get distorted in institutions, without people knowing."

"That's a very foolish and misguided viewpoint," McKenna snapped. "Fear and ignorance are always put forward to excuse Germany under Hitler, and all the other excesses of wickedness that besmirch history."

"There's too much likening of Hogg to Hitler," Griffiths said. "I've heard the gossip. And Doris Hogg isn't Eva Braun!"

McKenna dragged a cigarette from the packet. "Places like Blodwel are the breeding grounds of wickedness, wherever it crops up." Lighting the cigarette, he added, "Delve into your own heart with a little more brutal honesty, and you'll know exactly what I mean."

"You giving me another lecture?"

"I'm giving you the benefit of the doubt, because you haven't seen the light in their eyes, or smelt the odour they carry, like something rotting." McKenna paused. "Seeing evil as inhuman lets us exclude evil people from the human race, so we aren't forced to examine how they bring to life and act out the dark and complex fantasies of every human psyche, and don't need to accept the similar potential in us all, given the right triggers and the right climate."

"I'm fully aware of the limits of my potential," Griffiths said. "I know exactly what I could and couldn't do."

"Only in your present environment. You've no idea what you might do elsewhere, any more than I have. Our parents' generation slaughtered men, women and children because they were led to believe such destruction was necessary to survival, but I don't expect they saw themselves as murderers."

Strapped in the front passenger seat of McKenna's car, Eifion Roberts pulled at the belt cutting across his belly, muttering, "They build cars like they make clothes these days, and if you're not thin as a stick, God help you!"

"Stop bellyaching," McKenna said. "You should go on a diet. How many of your cadavers died from obesity?"

"I don't bloody know, 'cos I don't keep tally! God, McKenna, I never thought you'd join the PC lobby."

"I worry about you."

"Because I drink a bit, and eat three square meals a day? I was a fat bouncing baby and a big strapping lad, and now I'm a fat old man. So what?"

"You're hardly old."

"I feel like Methuselah some times."

McKenna grinned. "Dracula's more up your street."

"Oh, shut up!" Dr. Roberts fidgeted again with the seat belt. "Blood's got a nasty metallic taste."

"I wonder how sin tastes."

"We could ask Doris, couldn't we? Why didn't you do what Griffiths told you, and keep shtum?"

"It's left a horrible taste in my mouth."

"It's no worse than a lot of Celtic traditions."

"I'm appalled by the implications for Carol."

"She might feel a lot better."

"Doris said she defiled Arwel's body."

"Fat chance after everybody else'd had a go!"

McKenna turned towards Deiniolen and the mountain passes. "It was a truly horrible experience."

"Carol isn't guaranteed eternal damnation for taking her own bit of vengeance. For all we know, God's happy to offload some of the work. He's stuck with the same boring routines for eternity." Roberts grinned. "He can't even die to get away from the daily grind, can He?"

"Do you and God talk on a direct line?"

"We don't need the help of priest or pastor. When I strip a body to its bare bones, I see such wonder, so maybe He shows me the secrets of life as well as death. I've seen it all, except the colour of the soul." Gazing through the window at thorny trees stripped bare by the harsh breaths of winter, the pathologist added, "Don't you wonder where all those souls go?"

"Heaven or Hell, after a few thousand millennia in purgatory."

"What about the practical details? Does our construct of linear time survive after death? Has the pope visited Heaven or Hell or purgatory?"

"One has faith," McKenna said. "It's all very simple."

"So do I pity you or envy you?" Dr. Roberts asked. "I think the soul is simple energy. You can't make it, you can't destroy it."

"And is mankind going to the devil because we've exhausted the supply?" McKenna drew up in the forecourt of the shop-cum-garage on the village street.

"Don't ask me. I'm not your priest." Muttering again, he struggled from the car. "What're we doing in this Godforsaken place?"

McKenna locked the car and set the alarm. "Looking for Gary."

"Why should we fare better than your lot and Mountain

Rescue?" Looking up and down the street, squinting at the hummocks and rises of the foothills, strewn with outcrops of veined white rock Eifion Roberts added, "And don't think I'm hiking up those bloody mountains, 'cos that horrible mountain darkness'll drop on us like a bloody shroud before long." He looked into the distance, at cloud massed around the peaks overhanging Llanberis Pass, vapours trailing against escarpments of slate, a monochromatic scene of white sky beyond the grey cloud, of black mountain shapes in the foreground etched against grey mountain shapes in the distance, awesome, grandiose and terrifying. Trailing in McKenna's wake, he said, "It's no wonder folk here turn to crime. There's nowt else to do but bash the wife and kids and ogle a good-looking ewe every full moon. Talk about limited horizons!"

"Will you shut up?" McKenna snarled. "People might hear you!"

"What people? I don't see any people." Panting gently, Dr. Roberts caught up with his companion. "They're all inside those poky little hovels with the doors shut tight."

"You wanted to come, so stop moaning, and save your precious breath for walking."

"I was bored. Nobody's died needing my attention, and there's nothing worth watching on telly. I've got limited horizons of my own." He slumped down on the low stone wall bordering the road. "We won't suddenly come upon young Gary, you know. If he's here to be found, the others'll find him, sooner or later."

Sitting beside his friend, McKenna lit a cigarette. The stones ground against each other under their weight, gathering energy. Dr. Roberts coughed as smoke, pungent in the cold air, drifted past his face, and McKenna felt the slab beneath his buttocks rock.

"Forensics found a few strands of Arwel's hair in the cab of the horsebox, but nothing else of interest, nor in the trailer."

"Have they demolished that sculpture on wheels yet? They're wasting time and money on that." Dr. Roberts rubbed his hands together, then thrust them in his pockets, and a gently shivering passed through his body to the wall. "I doubt we'll match Elis's samples with Arwel's. The preliminary profile is quite different."

McKenna dropped ash to the ground, where it lay in a little grey tube, rolled gently by the wind creeping through the valley. "Tony Jones told a boy at the South Wales home he'd been sodomized and beaten and humiliated, but didn't say by whom."

"What about the other lad Jack Tuttle saw?"

"He told South Wales police to see Tony, then said he wasn't surprised Tony killed himself because most kids in his position end up dead one way or another."

"Poor little devils!" Eifion Roberts shivered again. "And what can anyone ever do to make it better?"


The two cats slept side by side before the fire. Glancing around the parlour, McKenna found nothing amiss, and went to the kitchen to heat a casserole Denise left in the freezer after his accident. His arm ached, and his collar-bone ground against other bone as stones in the roadside wall ground against each other. Sitting at the kitchen-table, watching the microwave's electronic display, he wondered what happened afterwards to the energy thawing and heating his food. Perhaps, he thought, cutting slabs of fresh bread, it went on to cook his innards, for he could not envisage such primal force owning the intelligence to distinguish between cold dead animal meat to roast, and warm living human meat to shun. Energy, he decided, was like the gene, intent only on survival, and wondered if Eifion Roberts ever puzzled over a mysteriously microwaved gut or gullet.

They had tramped lanes and sheep tracks and village streets, past shop windows where Gary's face smiled prettily under the legend HAVE YOU SEEN THIS BOY?, down the narrow muddy path beside the river, and along the main road beyond the village, stumbling over tussocky verges under a sky luminous with distant stars.

"I'm having a rest," Eifion Roberts had announced, sitting on another tumbled wall. He took out his flask and drank deeply, before handing the flask to McKenna. "Why don't we call it a day?" He pointed to the lower slopes of the mountains beyond the little village. "See those lights twinkling and bobbing? That's your lot and Mountain Rescue, doing the job properly. We're just farting around, 'cos you're worried sick and can't settle. You shouldn't feel guilty about what other folk do."

McKenna had lit a cigarette, smoke and raw cold mountain air burning his throat. "We panicked him."

"It could be pure coincidence. Gary could be living it up in the Smoke for all you know. I doubt he's still round here. You've had near saturation cover in the media, never mind posters up all over the county." Dr. Roberts coughed, and patted his chest before pulling his scarf tighter around his throat.

They had walked another mile deeper into the mountain pass, pressing against rough walls as cones of light against trees and rock preceded the occasional car, the weight of darkness and mountain pressing from both sides and above as the sky dwindled to a narrow ribbon of lighter darkness between the crags, before turning back, like empty-handed hunters in the night, Eifion Roberts pale and weary as an old man.

The cat purred around his legs while he ate, the other animal by the kitchen door, eyes large with hunger. Even in distress it was beautiful, fine-boned and elegant, eyes alive with intelligence. Part Siamese, McKenna decided, and looked down at his own, who resembled a little fur pudding. Thinking of Jack Sprat and his wife, his thoughts drifted from cats to Ronald Hogg, thin and less than elegant, stripping children's souls of the fat and the lean. Doris Hogg was another pudding, a stodgy unappetizing confection, indigestible as sin. He wiped the last of the gravy with a piece of bread, and wondered at the horizons of the strange landscape to which the loneliness he mistook for solitude had brought him.

"St. Mihangel's called, sir," Dewi said. "Arwel's funeral is on Tuesday at two-thirty in the afternoon."

"It's hardly likely to be two-thirty in the morning, is it?" McKenna snapped.

"It's not our fault we couldn't find Gary," Dewi protested. "Between us and the volunteers and Mountain Rescue, there were thirty odd people, and we walked miles. We looked everywhere there is to look."

"You'd have found him if you had."

"Perhaps we're searching the wrong area," Janet ventured. "The mountains cover hundreds of square miles. He could be anywhere."

"And he could very well be dead!" McKenna snarled.

"We weren't to know he'd leg it, sir," Dewi said. "And I've lost count of the times we've been back and forth pestering anybody who might know where he's gone."

"It may not be our fault at the moment, Constable Prys, but when Gary's body, or what's left of it, is found in the spring, stuck in a mountain gully with only a dead sheep for company, it *will* be our fault!"

Dewi jumped up. "I'll own for what I do or don't do, but I won't carry the can for the rest of the world!" He went to the door, eyes bright with anger. "It might be our job to shovel the shit the rest of the world drops, and the rest of the world thinks that's all we're good for, but I'm damned if I'll take the blame 'cos the shit's there in the first place!" The door shuddered as he wrenched it open, shuddered again as he slammed it shut.

Janet coughed. "Will St. Mihangel's minister take the service, sir? The Thomases are chapel, and St. Mihangel's is church."

"If God Himself took the service, through the person of your righteous father, it wouldn't make the slightest difference, because the Thomases are heathens, like the rest of the bloody Welsh!"

"We do understand, sir," Janet said gently. "It's horrible for all of us, but you're responsible for everything."

"You are patronizing me, Constable Evans. I am not a 'case' to be analysed, nor am I an errant member of your father's flock!"

"I wasn't!" Janet too rose from her seat, eyes awash with tears. "We're doing our best, but you change like the weather, and we don't know where we are from one minute to the next." The tears spilled down her flushed cheeks. "I can't say right for saying wrong, can I? You're just like my bloody father!"

Dewi assaulted the bastion of McKenna's displeasure with bacon sandwiches, a pot of tea, and an apology. "And Janet's gone to see Gary's mother again."

Showing him a memo faxed from headquarters, McKenna said, "The accountants have computed time and manpower expended on Gary, so we stop looking unless more concrete evidence turns up." He took a sandwich from the plate. "And they took the trouble to compute his probable safety, correlated with the number of juveniles who go missing each year, and are presumably tagged on city streets, in hostels, or detention."

"He might just be on the run, and perfectly OK." Dewi licked melted butter from his fingers. "But I reckon he ran 'cos he's scared of Hogg."

McKenna wiped his own fingers on a paper napkin. "We should discuss Hogg, Dewi, because Superintendent Griffiths raised a very legitimate objection about the extent of gossip likening Hogg to Adolf Hitler, and was particularly irritated to see you goose-stepping round the squadroom with your arm raised in the Nazi salute singing 'Ronnie rules the bloody world" to the tune of *Deutschland über alles.*'

Dewi choked on the remnants of his sandwich.

"Don't give a repeat performance, will you?"

"I'm sorry, sir." He poured tea, passing McKenna a new china mug flaunting roses and bright green leaves. "Is there anything special you want doing? All the paperwork's up to date."

McKenna lit a cigarette. "If you're not too tired, see if you can get any more sense out of the Thomases, then bring Carol back here. I want to talk to her."

"It's a waste of time talking to the parents, sir. They don't give a toss about those kids, else they'd've taken Arwel back home when he said Hogg was beating him up," Dewi said. "Arwel would still be alive if they'd believed him."

"I've told you before not to judge people too harshly. What could they do? Kidnap the boy? Social Services were calling all the shots."

"They could've done something!" Dewi insisted. "Most folks'd thank God on bended knee for children like Arwel and Carol. Look at what Elis was landed with."

"Elis might deserve his punishment; Carol and Arwel might deserve Tom and Peggy. There's always far more to see than what people lay in front of you, and in any case, we only know the Thomases after the event, when they're trying to come to terms with Arwel's degradation and death, and their own part in it." McKenna lit another cigarette. "Before all this, they muddled along, like millions of others."

"I suppose." Dewi stacked plates and mugs on the tray. "But if there's any bad in that lass and her brother, I reckon somebody else put it there, and the parents had most opportunity." He picked up the tray. "I wonder what Hogg's parents were like? D'you think he just crawled out from under a lump of slate one night?"

"I expect Mr. and Mrs. Hogg Senior were perfectly ordinary people," McKenna said. "Just like Alois and Klara."

Dewi frowned. "Alois and Klara who?"

"Guess."

•   •   •

Jack sniffed. "Fancy traipsing round those mountains. I'm surprised Eifion Roberts didn't have a heart attack."

"I rang to ask after your health," McKenna said. "I don't want another lecture."

"Who's given you a lecture?"

"Who hasn't?"

"People expect the killer handed over on a plate, like John the Baptist's head." Jack coughed. "I reckon you've done everything humanly possible in the circumstances. Arwel wouldn't be the first unsolved death, you know, and he won't be the last." He coughed again, more raspingly. "God! My chest's bad. I hope these antibiotics shift the bugs before Tuesday."

"We're expecting a lot of media interest." McKenna rubbed the nagging pain in his shoulder. "People like a good funeral even better when there's somebody posh to gawp at, though nobody seems to know about our interest in Elis yet."

"Nobody's interested in Arwel, so Elis doesn't need to use his clout and cash to get injunctions against nosy-parker journalists." Jack coughed again. "That's another way rich folk buy poor ones with no comeback. How's your shoulder, by the way?"

"Hurting like hell."

"Doris probably sat up all night making your voodoo doll, and now she's ramming pins in it," Jack said. "God, it's a miserable world, isn't it? Never mind, the longest night's on its way, then after Christmas, the days start stretching. We keep hoping, don't we?"

"Only because day follows night and spring follows winter," McKenna said. "Or so we're led to believe."

"Happiness follows despair, as well, if you don't die waiting."

"Is sickness making you appreciate the interdependency of opposites?"

"I'm stretching my intellect round that Goethe biography you lent me. Some of his ideas are really fascinating." Jack coughed again, a breathy sound rattling in his lungs and echo-ing in McKenna's ears. "I know he was just a poet, but it makes you wonder if poets can't divine the truth, long before the scientists can prove it. Mind you, if the greatest bard in Wales divined the truth about Arwel's death, we'd never prove it, would we?"

Mari answered the telephone at Bedd y Cor, and snarled at McKenna like a wounded cat.

"When will Mr. and Mrs. Elis be back?"

"I don't know!"

"I'm sure you do know, Mari."

"They've gone to see the boy. They were late leaving be-cause of the other things."

"Ask Mrs. Elis to call me tomorrow, then."

"Why? Haven't you done them enough harm yet?"

"Carol's waiting outside, sir." Dewi sat down, frowning. "I didn't manage to talk to the parents. I thought he was drunk at first, 'cos he's rambling and slurring his words and lurching round, but apparently he's had tablets off the doctor. She's like a cat on hot bricks, really agitated and all breathless, so I asked what was wrong, and he said: 'What the bloody hell d'you think's wrong?' He called me a stupid fart or some such." Two little spots of colour erupted on his cheeks. "Ig-norant sod!"

McKenna fidgeted with a pen. "And Carol?"

"She'd taken to her bed yesterday evening and not moved since. They actually seemed worried about her."

"Then why didn't you leave her there?"

"She wanted to come, sir. I didn't force her."

"Are you ill?" McKenna asked.

Dressed in faded jeans and worn grey sweater, Carol sat in

an old upholstered chair from Owen Griffiths' office. She shook her head, the luminous hair swirling about her pallid skin and starved features.

"Why were you in bed?"

"I'm tired."

"What's wrong with your parents?"

"Apart from Arwel getting murdered, me getting pregnant, and them being sodding useless?" She looked down at her hands, balled in little fists in her lap. "They know about yesterday, and think you'll put me in court, or Doris will."

"Who told them?"

"Mam guessed when she saw the stain on Arwel's shirt. She's not as stupid as she looks." She frowned. "My father's really stupid, though." The frown disappeared, leaving her face blank. "Arwel's not there any more. Mrs. Elis had him taken away, so I told the social worker to sod off."

"I know all about it," McKenna said.

"No, you don't. You'll never know about anything like this." She stared at him gravely. "Will I be charged with common assault on a bitch as common as muck?"

"Why did you do it?"

"I told you why."

"You said Doris owes for not protecting Arwel." McKenna lit a cigarette, thinking Carol's baby had already known far worse than the taint of tobacco smoke. "What was she supposed to protect him from?"

Carol's hands unfurled, like claws. "Social Services said Mam was a lousy mother for neglecting Arwel, so they took him away and gave him to that bloody bitch, and now he's dead!"

"You think little enough of your parents."

"That's between them and me!"

"Perhaps you should blame yourself instead of Doris," McKenna suggested. "I think Arwel told you everything, hoping you'd put a stop to his agony. He thought the sister he worshipped wouldn't fail him like everyone else. But you did, didn't you?"

"No!"

"I think you decided to use Arwel's suffering for your own profit." He stubbed out the half-smoked cigarette. "You've set yourself up nicely for a few years, but you got him killed."

"What are you talking about?"

"I'm talking about you and your beautiful brother." McKenna leaned back in his chair. "Arwel was irresistible, like a rare flower, but one after the other, men pulled off the petals, until there was nothing left." He lit another cigarette. "But your body's like a rich pasture, and you can grow a perfect child for people too impoverished by nature to make their own. Or are you just harvesting their guilt?"

"What are you talking about?" Carol demanded again.

"Rhiannon Elis offered you a ticket out of poverty," McKenna said. "In exchange for what? Does she get the baby? Or is she paying the first instalment on the price of your silence?"

Carol levered herself out of the chair, and pulled on her jacket. "Tell me I'm wrong," McKenna said. "If you won't, you're as good as accusing Elis of killing your brother."

"You're doing the accusing! You and them sodding social workers think you know bloody everything, don't you?" She dragged at the jacket zip, catching the jumper in its teeth. "Oh, you'll be sorry!" she breathed. "You'll wish you'd never been born!"

She plunged from the room, and by the time McKenna reached the corridor, the fire door at the head of the staircase was closing behind her. He ran downstairs and rushed outside, but the street was deserted, as if night had consumed the girl and her unquenchable light.


"You shouldn't have secrets. They ricochet, like stray bullets." Eifion Roberts sat on McKenna's sofa, nursing the black cat. "You're involved in a conspiracy of silence with Doris Hogg, and she's the last person to be involved with in anything. Look where your conspiratorial theories've led now.

Carol's got enough grief, without being told she's liable for Arwel's death."

"I'm not blaming her," McKenna said. "She didn't kill him."

"You can't actually be any more sure about that than about anything else in this world. She's capable of it." The black cat raised its head, and nuzzled the pathologist's hand. "I think you've lost your grip. There's more crap silting up your brain than there is in Menai Strait, because you let Elis and Rhiannon beguile you with their nonsense. They're unhappily married, Michael. As prosaically and tediously unhappily married as you were. There's nothing special about their misery."

"Rhiannon thinks Elis killed Arwel."

"How d'you know she's not just looking for a way to get shot of him? She's probably very bitter. You're bitter about the years wasted hoping things with Denise would turn out good. If Elis loved his wife half as much as he loves his self-pity, she'd be a very happy woman, and I expect she's realized that."

The black and white cat rubbed around McKenna's ankles, then jumped on his lap. "Child abusers frequently suffered abuse themselves," he said. "I can't ignore that fact."

Dr. Roberts stroked the black cat's ears. "D'you know, I think Elis is too lazy to bother with the subterfuge of abusing children. He spends most of life sitting on his backside. On horses, at the piano, listening to music, in his posh vehicles, at board meetings. What does he achieve with his time?"

"He's probably chronically depressed."

"Self-pity does that. We often find the person we've grown into wasn't worth waiting for, and can't cope with the disappointment of knowing nothing better's likely to show up." The cat rolled over, paws in the air. "Elis and his maundering's enough to make Beethoven turn in his grave. He wanted to write wonderful music, so he did, regardless of the poverty and disease and death snapping at his heels. Elis does bugger all except whinge, but I doubt he'll understand the waste even on his deathbed. He'll find somebody else to blame."

Rubbing the cat's belly, the pathologist added, "Somebody profited from Arwel's death, you know, and it's probably the same person who profited from him and Tony when they were alive."

"And that could well be Elis," McKenna pointed out.

"I mean profit in the prosaic sense of hard cash. These boys must've been sold like meat off a butcher's slab, but Arwel could've been mauled around too much and gone past his use-by date, so he got chucked in the swill bucket."

# •Chapter•
# 16

McKenna dreamt he was at work, but snug under a thick quilt, its cover scented with the freshness of the wind which blew it dry. He dreamt the telephone shrilled and his good arm reached out lazily, and dreamt he heard words, punctuated by static, telling him something urgent and important. He smiled to himself, and dreamt he was dreaming.

"*Sir!*" Dewi's voice pierced the dream. "Did you hear me? Blodwel's on fire!"

Stumbling down the staircase to the bathroom, down the next staircase to the parlour, he searched in the darkness for car keys and telephone, then switched on the light, and closed his eyes, the imprint of the room searing his eyelids. The cats watched, their bright gaze following his disjointed movements around the room and up the staircase. Pulling his coat from the rack, he went out into the night, and unlocking the car, fancied he smelt acrid smoke on the wind and saw the sky behind the mountain glowing red, stars eclipsed by the sparks shooting up to heaven.

There were no flames or sparks, but the air smelt of brimstone, and smoky orange and livid crimson licked and flicked through the rooms of Blodwel and around the window orifices. Smoke pulsed in great heavy draughts, driven by the force of heat, and McKenna watched the plastic windows bubble and wrinkle before suddenly exploding outwards. The chief fire officer pushed him back. "Don't go any nearer. The smoke's toxic."

The lane was strewn with fire engines and ambulances, television news crews, and people, roused by alien tensions in the night. "Is anyone still inside?" McKenna asked, jostled from both sides by people struggling to see. Firemen and uniformed police officers pushed them away from the billows of black dirty smoke rolling from the building and down the lane.

"We got them all out." The fireman gestured towards a drab figure standing over a small group of children and teenagers. McKenna recognized Dilys Roberts, and watched her cuff one of the weeping children. Even from this distance, he could see them shiver and tremble, hear their whining above the dull roar from within the building. "We had to smash the fire door with sledgehammers, 'cos it was locked, and the bloody windows'd been nailed up again. That woman was crouched behind the door with the kids, and they'd have suffocated within seconds. I'm going to make sure that bloody Hogg and his boss are done for criminal negligence."

"A vain hope," McKenna said. "Is it arson?"

"Probably one of the kids having a sly fag and dropping it. You won't stop them smoking, and it's far more dangerous when they have to do it in secret. This place could've been smouldering for hours, like that store in Caernarfon."

There was a sudden roar from behind the building, and flames erupted upwards and outwards, shooting sparks up to the sky. The hillside glowed, fire crackling around the roots of bushes and small trees, trickling along the bare branches, then taking hold and running out of control.

"What will they do with the kids?" Dewi's face was smutty with soot.

"I don't know," McKenna said. "Who reported the fire?"

"Dilys Roberts. The smoke alarms went off."

"Why didn't she get the kids out? Surely she had keys."

"She can't say. She probably panicked, and couldn't find the right key."

"Where's Janet Evans?"

"Talking to somebody from Social Services."

"Then I want you to go to Caernarfon." McKenna turned away from the blazing building, the skin on his face taut with heat, his coat collar almost burning hot. "You must ask Carol what time she arrived home, and her parents must verify whatever she says."

"It's almost two in the morning. They'll be in bed."

"Then you'll have to get them out, won't you?"

Griffiths sat beside McKenna in his car, shivering. "I'm too bloody old for this caper."

"You didn't need to come. There's nothing to be done tonight."

"Got to show willing, Michael." He nodded towards the man talking to Dilys Roberts. "If the deputy director of social services can rise from his bed, so can I. What d'you reckon, then? An Act of God? The cleansing fire? Arson? A children's revolution?"

"Civil disobedience might be the last refuge of the disaffected, but the will to resist is well subdued in those children."

"They'll carry the can, one way or another," Griffiths said. "Social Services can't afford to keep scapegoats and not use them."

"You've become too cynical," McKenna said. "The director warned me of the dangers of siding with the sub-culture."

"I've never sided with anything except fair play," Griffiths said. "What's the matter with her now?" he added, watching Janet, her face ugly with rage, confront Dewi Prys before striding away. "I don't know where she gets the energy for rowing with people at this time of the morning. She'd better pull herself together, or I'll put her on traffic duty for the next six months."

"There's still conflict with her father."

"Yes, I know, and I'm not surprised with her attitude. Her head's awash with silly ideas about men making victims of women at every turn, so she does the Annie Oakley routine, shooting at everything in trousers, and wonders why men get shirty with her. Silly madam! Pastor Evans should've tanned her hide a bit more often when she was little."

"He wants her to leave home."

"And so she should," Griffiths commented. "Festering resentments build up just as nastily when a child stays at home too long as when a marriage goes sour."

The telephone woke McKenna again, as the cathedral clock struck seven.

"It's on the national news," Jack said. "Breakfast TV. Why didn't you call me? I wasn't asleep."

"I was," McKenna said. "I went back to bed an hour ago."

"Bits of sleep are worse than none at all."

"Some of us snatch sleep when we can. We can't all lounge in bed all day with a loving wife dancing attendance."

"Em's fed up with the sight of me, and I wasn't in bed all day. I've been pottering round, doing this and that, and I'd still be asleep but for another of those damned phone calls."

"And did you check on the number?" McKenna rubbed his shoulder.

"Yes, and a female electronic voice informed me there wasn't a number available. Em says that means it's being barred."

"I know you've sent Dewi Prys and Janet up a different mountain looking for that boy, contrary to instructions, but I'll pretend I don't," Griffiths said. "Will they kiss and make up behind a handy boulder?"

"Janet's more likely to smash Dewi over the head with one." McKenna yawned, and picked up a mug of tea. "What shall we do about Blodwel?"

"Thank God it's been gutted. One less place for kids to be

abused." Griffiths yawned. "Are you sure Carol didn't torch the dump?"

"As sure as I can be, given the thoroughly disturbing streak of ruthlessness in her nature."

"She'll need it in this life. Anyway, she's not strayed yet further from the side of the angels than most folk would blame her for."

"The Thomases were all fast in righteous slumber when Dewi got there, and Peggy said Carol arrived home about an hour after she left here. Allowing for Sunday bus services, she didn't have time to go anywhere near Blodwel."

"Not even to stuff smouldering fag ends in every orifice?" Griffiths smiled a little. "Not that I'd pursue her over-zealously if I thought she had, as nobody was hurt." As McKenna yawned again, he added, "Go home for some sleep. I don't want you off sick as well."

"I'm going to see Mr. and Mrs. Hogg and their minions, and then the director."

"Why?"

"To express my sympathy for the partial fall of their empire."


Dawdling outside Woolworth's, Robert Lovell stared at his reflection in the window as the Monday-morning crowd of Christmas shoppers swarmed past, then crossed the road to the Deiniol Centre, to see his ghostly image amid the glitter of gold and chips of diamond in the window of the jeweller's shop. In the café next door, he took his coffee to a window table, where he could watch shoppers parading through the little mall, and listen to Christmas carols blaring from the loudspeakers. Sipping his drink, he marvelled that the simple act of shaving off the straggling silly beard and moustache could create such wholesome and decent feelings, and hoped divesting himself of his dangerous little secrets would complete the process begun when he picked up the razor early that morning, after hearing the news about Blodwel.

• • • •

Rapt before the huge colour television in her grandmother's tiny parlour, Mandy watched the report on the Blodwel fire for the fifth time since early morning. As soon as the lurid pictures of burning building and excited crowds disappeared, she flicked to the teletext reports, moving from channel to channel in search of more than the bare bones of the story.

"You've seen all there is to see." Her grandmother took the remote control from the girl's tense fingers, and switched off the set. "Nobody got hurt, and it's nothing to do with you now. You can't be blamed for anything, and you're not going back to Blodwel or anywhere like it."

"Hogg nailed the windows up so we couldn't run away," Mandy muttered. "Will they do anything to him?"

"Does anything ever happen to the likes of him? Now, stop fretting. We're going out to buy you something nice to wear at that poor boy's funeral tomorrow."


The director of social services whitened with anger. "You should get off your high horse, Chief Inspector, before someone pushes you!"

"Finding out what happened at Blodwel is more in your interests than ours," McKenna pointed out. "Especially as there's evidence of criminal disregard for the safety of children and staff."

"My staff live with criminal disregard day in and day out! Dilys Roberts acted in a thoroughly professional way, and probably averted a tragedy."

"She couldn't evacuate the building because the fire escapes were locked."

"Nonsense! She was about to open the door when the firemen bludgeoned it to smithereens."

"I've seen the locks on the doors and the nails in what's left of the window frames," McKenna pointed out. "And you will please instruct all your staff, including Mr. and Mrs. Hogg, to stay away from the building. I had to stop Mrs.

Hogg entering the flat this morning. She'd already tried to interfere with the forensic examination."

"Blodwel is council property. You require my permission to be there, and that permission can be withdrawn at any time!"

"Crime doesn't observe boundaries," McKenna said. "We're obliged to follow where it trespasses."

"You trespass long before a crime takes place! You've created untold disruption and anxiety at Blodwel because of that delinquent Thomas boy. Why d'you think those children rioted and set the place alight?" Frowning, he added, "It's a sorry day when professionals like us, who should be on the same side of the fence, are set against each other by the wiles of a few delinquents."


"Where was Ronnie, then?" Eifion Roberts perched on the edge of McKenna's desk.

"Distraught, according to Doris. Life's work gone up in flames etcetera," McKenna said.

"He doesn't half hide behind her fat bum. Why does he need a troubleshooter?"

"Because he causes trouble." McKenna sighed. "Go away, will you? I'm too tired for your brand of talk."

"Suit yourself." Dr. Roberts slid off the desk. "You missed your chance. You could've arrested her for tampering with evidence. By the way, someone called Robert Lovell's waiting to see you. D'you know that rhyme about Richard the Third and Robert Lovell? 'The cat, the rat and Lovell our dog, ruleth all England under a hog.' "


As the latter day Robert Lovell sat in the chair Carol Thomas occupied the day before, looking anxious, the ancient rhyme tripped back and forth in McKenna's head, and he wondered idly if the other Lovell had sported a beard.

"I barely recognize you," he said. "Are you out of a job?"

"Blodwel staff've been dispersed round the other homes," Lovell said. "I'll probably get the sack when Hogg finds out I've come here, but I've run out of choices. I'm not one for conspiracies of any sort."

"Is there a conspiracy?"

"Any number." Lovell took a packet of cigarettes from his pocket. "They probably started accidentally, but they've taken on a different colour."

McKenna pushed an ashtray across the desk. "I had you down as biddable and dutiful."

"Worms turn, don't they? I've had a strictly confidential letter from the director. I thought it was my notice at first." He took a long white envelope from his inside pocket, and handed it to McKenna. "He wants me to sign that piece of paper set out like an affidavit, and send it back to him. Dilys said everyone's had the same letter."

"And will they all sign?"

"We're supposed to stick together, because we can't do the job without each other's support and loyalty."

McKenna read the letter again. "There's nothing truly contentious here. He's asking you not to disclose confidential information about your work to outsiders, which must be a condition in your contract of employment, confirming your permanent employment, and reminding you to channel any concerns to your line manager."

"Hogg's my line manager." Lovell lit the cigarette in his fingers. "So it's a bit difficult telling him the kids say he's abusing them."

"Are they? Have they actually told you? Have you witnessed assaults?"

Lovell frowned. "You're not being very helpful."

"I'm obliged to abide by evidence. Not speculation, or even wishful thinking."

"I know that." Lovell nodded. "But there isn't a kid alive who'd dare say his face looked like a punchbag because Hogg bashed him, and not because he fell into a door. They're all terrified, and Blodwel stank of that fear, like an open grave." He stubbed out the cigarette, splattering ash and shreds of tobacco on the desk. "The weeping in the night made your flesh crawl, but if you tried to comfort them, they'd cower away, like you're a monster."

"They're children in distress," McKenna said. "Homesick, rootless, guilt-ridden, and fearful. I can understand your frustration, but you're saying nothing which isn't easily and convincingly countered."

"Oh, I know!" Lovell said. "I found bloody sheets on Tony Jones's bed once, and Doris said he must've been picking the spots on his back." He shook his head. "And I believed her! My instincts are yelling crap!, but I still believed her."

"Instincts and conscience are abstracts of personality," McKenna said. "Perhaps too abstracted in modern man. They tend to lie very low." He rubbed his shoulder, trying to dispel the gnawing ache of tiredness. "Still, yours've been roused."

"Better late than never, you mean? It's too late for Tony and Arwel and the kid Hogg beat to a pulp the other night, isn't it?" He dragged his hand over the newly naked flesh of jaw and cheek. "I've doubted myself so much I became absolutely impotent, conned by Hogg and Doris into believing my values, and not theirs, were off the wall." Dragging another cigarette from the packet, he said, "It's like water dripping on stone. You see somebody do something you never thought possible, then they keep on doing it, 'til you end up thinking it's normal."

"You're ashamed of yourself, and even bitter, but you can't blame yourself for the children's tragedies."

"I'm guilty for doing nothing."

McKenna picked up a pen. "Then give me some facts we can use as a basis for investigation."

• • • •

"Lovell-Our-Dog should feel a tad better knowing his sense of decency didn't wholly fall to Hogg's brand of seduction," Owen Griffiths observed, scanning McKenna's notes. "He hasn't given us much, has he? Fancy Hogg having the gall to plan a visit to Arwel's funeral with Blodwel kids done up in their Sunday best."

"He should be warned off," McKenna said. "We'd need a SWAT team to keep Carol off him and Doris."

"I'm inclined to let God's will prevail. It's nothing to Arwel, is it?"

"Carol's near the end of her tether, and we couldn't ignore a public brawl."

"I suppose. I'll fax Hogg's boss." He flicked the sheet of notes. "What can we do with this?"

"Lovell supports Mandy's allegation of assault, and he saw Darren Pritchard unmarked before he visited Hogg's office, then immediately afterwards, when Darren looked like he'd embraced the chassis of a Safeway's truck."

"Very picturesque. What about the little kid?" Griffiths peered at the notes. "Your writing gets worse by the day. Why don't you get a laptop computer, or something?"

"With what?"

"The money you'd save if you quit smoking." Griffiths wrinkled his nose. "According to Lovell-Our-Dog, after Janet talked to the little boy about the silver bullet, Dilys Roberts took him to Hogg's flat, and the kid was in tears five or ten minutes later when he was taken upstairs. Is that right?"

"And when Lovell next saw the child, later that night, his face was battered, and he complained of pains in his stomach and back."

"And Doris, who's not very inventive with her excuses, said he'd fallen over. These kids do an awful lot of falling over."

"Children do."

"Mine were always falling over their own feet, I must admit. What's this scribble? Looks like 'Inspector Somebody or Other.' "

"Hogg reckons to have a tame copper under his thumb, who arranges for the mouthy kids to get locked up, then throws the key out to sea."

"Bloody charming! Do we know this helpful person?"

"Lovell wasn't sure of his name, but we could always ask Darren."

"There was no need for a visit, Mrs. Elis," McKenna said, taking the box from her arms. "One of us could've collected this."

"I had to get out of the house. It's like a prison, where you meekly wait for the end of the world." Slumped in the old soft chair, Rhiannon stared at her feet in their fine kid boots. "Arwel's funeral will be the end of something, but I don't know if other beginnings are possible, and I'm frightened to death."

"Arwel's funeral will be nothing more than a small ritual, unless you want it otherwise."

"Do we ever know what we want before we have it?" She smiled gently. "My husband seems to want you to take over where Arwel left off, but that wouldn't be very good for anyone, would it? I know he's desperate to talk to you. I've seen the signs before." She sighed. "He's been abandoned by his other hero, too. Even the dead give up the ghost eventually."

Watching this sad, rich, pretty woman through a veil of cigarette smoke, McKenna asked, "Can't you ever say what you mean, Mrs. Elis?"

She shrugged. "Perhaps we can't know what we mean until someone deciphers what we've said. My husband's not the only one feeding off you, Mr. McKenna. He sees your ruthlessness as strength, I see it as salvation. Cross purposes, as always." The smile died, clouding her face. "D'you ever doubt what you see before your eyes?"

"Like most of us, I get caught between believing what's put in front of me, and not letting reason be dulled by emotion, or even simple habit. And there aren't any rules to show what to do and when."

"My husband was made irresolute, and even devious, by his childhood experiences, and he brought out the same lack of resolve in me, the same willingness to take the line of least resistance," Rhiannon said. "I dug in my heels when he warned me about the Hoggs and Blodwel because I've learned never to trust his frames of reference. He taught me to suspect all he says and does. Of course, I don't show it, because I've become as deceitful as he is." She began to pick her cuticle. "I don't like myself at all at the moment, and I'm disgusted by my own stupidity, and really, it's all your fault."

"How come?"

"Your talk of violence. I think I'm worse off than any council-house wife with a drunken vicious husband, because I thought I wasn't." McKenna watched blood swell from the torn cuticle. "Violence isn't limited to the physical or sexual, you know. My husband is incredibly destructive. He values nothing except his own needs, and he's also very greedy, because he thinks the world owes him for the past. Anyone and everyone is liable for the debt."

"You owe him nothing in that sense," McKenna said.

"Oh, I know!" Rhiannon said. "But I daren't tell him. I daren't threaten his precious image." She paused, rubbing at her bloody nail, frowning. "He seems to be kept alive only by his past, and he's terrified of letting that go because there's nothing to put in its place. That fear lashes out like a subhuman force, totally indiscriminate, intent only on survival, and I've become so afraid of him." She looked up. "I'm afraid of growing older and more frail, of being isolated and at his mercy. I'm afraid of these horrible undertones in his personality, which you only sense, like the sounds between musical notes. And most of all, I've become afraid of the feelings he engenders in me. But I can't expect you to show the quality of your mercy and tell him, can I?"

• • •

Dewi and Janet returned from the mountains as the dreary December day fell to night. Cold and dispirited, they sat in McKenna's office, relating a trail of disappointment.

"Those mountains are like the end of the world." Janet shivered. "And so cold! Will we ever find Gary?"

"I can't justify further searches." McKenna fiddled with a paper-clip. "Dilys Roberts is coming in to make a statement. Social Services seem to think the fire was caused by rioting children, unable to contain the unbearable pressure and intense anxiety we created. There may be a formal complaint, so I hope your conduct with the children and staff was exactly according to the rules."

"Sodding cheek!" Dewi exclaimed.

"It was definitely arson." McKenna lit a cigarette. "Accelerants have been found in three locations so far, and several smoke detectors were disabled, but it's impossible to say when they were tampered with. Blodwel was taken off the direct emergency link last year because of false alarms. The last notified drill was two months ago, and the fire service relied on Blodwel to do the job properly and report any problems. As all the records were burnt, no one can check."

"I reckon Hogg torched Blodwel to create a smoke-screen," Dewi said.

"Faith is the substance of things hoped for, the evidence of things not seen," Janet intoned. "According to my father. It's a pity he wouldn't know how long we keep hoping the evidence of what Ronald Hogg doesn't want us to see will eventually turn up."

McKenna glanced at his watch. "Get your tea, then start on the stuff Forensics brought from Blodwel. It's in the lock-up store outside." He picked up the box Rhiannon had delivered. "And this is what Arwel left at Bedd y Cor."

Dilys Roberts declined the seat in the interview room. "Why am I here? I told the director everything!"

"I need your statement about the fire," McKenna said.

"But the director's dealing with everything. He said."

"We must formally investigate, nonetheless."

"What d'you want to know?"

"Anything which might be relevant. You must be anxious to know what caused the fire." McKenna forced a smile. "But for you, I'm told, there would have been a tragedy."

Owen Griffiths switched off the tape recorder, and closed the blind, shutting out the night pressing its face to the window. "Doesn't she witter and ramble? Her reports on the goings on at Blodwel must be worse than useless."

"She's no worse than most," McKenna said. "She's not trained, so she's got to rely on the Hoggs for everything she knows, and permission to put it in practice."

"Get the tape transcribed, then see if you can glean any sense from it." The superintendent smiled. "She wasn't happy admitting she'd had a letter from the director, was she?"

"She's probably afraid to admit anything without Hogg's say so."

"He's like some sect leader. Why do folk get taken in so easily?"

"Because they're gullible, especially if they think they've been chosen for special confidences or privilege." McKenna put the tape in an envelope. "Dilys repeats her catechism like a good disciple, just like the children, but if you listen hard enough, you can catch the echo of the thoughts none of them dares voice."

"Your Irish fancies always take hold when you're short of sleep," Griffiths said. "You shouldn't credit everyone with imagination."

"People always know far more than they think, but can't always interpret what they know. Dilys, for instance, wouldn't dream of questioning Hogg's numerous visits to Blodwel over the weekend, because he's the great white chief and can do as he likes, but when she had to think about the visits, she realized it was odd. I almost heard the rusty gears in her head cranking themselves up."

"She didn't say so."

"She's thinking about it."

"Even if she is, she won't come running back to tell you."

"Don't be such a wet blanket. She said enough. The dog wasn't left for the staff to look after, and she overheard Doris screaming at him."

"Doris was yelling about somebody knowing something, that's all, and the dog's neither here nor there."

"It's out of character." McKenna yawned. "A sudden change in routine."

"If you say so." Griffiths yawned. "You've started me off now. We should go to bed at sundown, like the rest of the animal world. Not that we've seen the sun today, either up or down." He began drawing crescent moons around the blotter. "Rhiannon's a bit up and down, isn't she? D'you think she's a headcase? What did she really want?"

"Nobody's mind is perfectly balanced all the time. Stress makes people act strangely."

"I think she's hoping you'll do her dirty work for her, and tell Elis he's a total shit."

"I imagine he's known that for years, but never expected her to find out for herself."


"I hope you're not leaving those cats alone too long," Eifion Roberts said. "Did you put an advert in the paper like I told you?"

"I've been home to feed them, and I put ads in the paper and the vet's surgery, but no one's called to say 'Give me back my beloved pussy'."

"I doubt they will." The pathologist squeezed his bulk in the old armchair. "Stray cats, stray kids. Who cares? Your house is a cat's Blodwel."

"I don't ill-treat animals, and I'm not likely to torch the house."

"You'll never lay that or anything else on Hogg." Dr. Roberts yawned. "Too many others in line for the blame."

"Did you want something, other than to gossip?"

"Have I done something? You've hardly got two words for me today?"

McKenna smiled wearily. "I'm just exhausted. And dreadfully worried about Gary."

"He doesn't want to be found, does he?"

"I pray the choice is still his."


Janet shivered so violently her teeth rattled. "Why are we freezing out here in this damned shed?"

"I bet you don't swear in front of your father."

"I do, as a matter of fact!"

"Who's a brave girl, then?" Dewi resealed a bag crammed with charred papers from Blodwel's main office, and put it to one side.

"It's a bit of a waste of time, really," Janet commented.

"What is?"

"Trying to shock my father. He never does what you want."

"That's 'cos he won't give you the satisfaction." Watching her sift the contents of another bag, her hands in pale surgical gloves, Dewi noticed the hair curling in mist-damp tendrils around her face, soft, and almost touchable. "Fathers can be like that."

"He says I should leave home."

"Where would you go?"

Janet smiled. "Somewhere cheap. I can't afford to live in style and keep the car." She fingered a shred of dark-blue knitted fabric. "Doesn't everything stink of smoke?"

"There's a nice flat coming vacant at the bottom end of town." Dewi snipped the sealing tape on another bag. "The girl's marrying a bloke from RAF Valley, so she'll live in married quarters." He emptied the bag on the table. "The flat's part furnished."

"When's she moving?"

"They're getting wed next Saturday, then off to Malta on honeymoon. He's back on duty over New Year." He picked up a half-sheet of lined paper, its edges crumbling. "I'll give you the address if you want."

"I could look, couldn't I?" Janet fingered the filthy, sodden remnants of a rugby shirt, its once white collar a hard mass of melted fibre. "And there's enough spare in the manse to furnish half a dozen flats. Shit!" She ripped off the glove, blood oozing from a small puncture in her thumb. "Oh, God! What if it's a syringe?"

"Don't count any chickens, Dewi. The eggs are probably addled."

"You're as bad as Janet for looking on the black side, sir."

Spreading the bagged and ruined rugby shirt on the desk, he showed McKenna where the broken gold pin which wounded Janet was lodged inside the breast pocket. "It was with stuff from Hogg's flat. Forensics'll be able to match the pin to the bullet and the shirt to Arwel, won't they?"

McKenna frowned. "It's sodden, and the collar's charred beyond recognition. Any identifiable residue could well've been destroyed." He pushed the bag aside. "Have you examined the things Rhiannon brought?"

"Not yet, sir." Dewi paused. "What about Elis? And the vehicles?"

"I've put Elis on hold for now."

"I said it was a waste of time and taxpayers' money."

"And I heard you, at least twice a day." McKenna lit a cigarette. "You can give yourself a pat on the back if you're proved right."

"Can I collect Ronnie and Doris, and give myself a treat?"

"Let them finish watching *Coronation Street*."

"Do we caution them?"

"You bring them here."

"What if they won't come?" Dewi asked.

• • •

"You look very flushed, Jack," McKenna said. "Should you be out?"

"I can't settle," Jack grumbled. "I feel like a caged animal."

"Rhiannon said much the same thing earlier."

"Not only is her cage posher than mine, but she's probably got the key in her pocket." Jack coughed. "I'm sure I've got this seasonal affective disorder, you know."

"You've too much time on your hands."

"Why can't I have seasonal depression?"

"Did you have it before you read about it in the papers?"

"I suppose not," Jack admitted. "By the way, before I get an answer about the holiday, Em wants to know what you're doing for Christmas."

"Given the chance, pretend it doesn't exist."

"You'd feel different if you had someone to share it with."

McKenna took a cigarette from the packet, then replaced it. "I really don't want to do anything."

Jack smiled. "Have the twins over then. You can all ignore Christmas together, because it's an 'outmoded shibboleth,' and a 'commercialized travesty.'"

"So what you save on presents can go towards the holiday."

"Fat chance! We've no choice but to 'kowtow to convention.' " He sighed. "You can't win, and you don't even realize it's a battle with kids until it's too late."


"It's rather late," Janet said, lighting her third cigarette. "Where d'you think they are?"

"Conspiring with the director of social services over something we haven't heard about yet." Dewi looked once again at the fussy red-brick house behind its barbered privet hedge. "Hogg's slaves keep his garden very tidy, but it's still a dismal hole."

"You're unbelievably cynical!" Janet snapped. "You turn everything into dross. I'd much rather live here than in a council house."

"Why? Do the likes of Ronnie make for better neighbours?" Dewi asked. "From our place, we can see as far as Llandudno. The only view from here is boring bloody suburbia, where you can't hang out your washing of a Sunday, and daren't annoy the neighbours."

Tapping ash in the dashboard tray, Janet said, "That apology for a dog they keep must irritate people. It's been yapping off and on since we got here."

Dewi opened the window, to dispel the gathering smoke. "This car'll be as yellow as Mr. McKenna's office by the time Hogg comes back. D'you have to smoke so much?"

"Oh, stop nagging! And shut the window. It's bloody freezing!"

"The east wind's come up again. Can't you hear it in the trees?"

"All I can hear is what Saunders Lewis called a sound beyond fear and darkness," Janet said. "That's how he described the night wind in that play about the man on a train."

"Oh, yes?" Dewi asked. "Did he go 'beyond fear and darkness,' then? Even if he did, he couldn't've known at the time."

"Don't be so pedantic," Janet chided. "He used his imagination. The man didn't want to be on the train and the train wouldn't stop, so he thought he was being taken to his own destruction. Lewis got the idea from Sartre. He said we're all passengers without tickets on a train going to an unknown destination, where there won't be anyone waiting."

"Very existential. Tony Jones must've read it."

Janet frowned. "Tony Jones? Why?"

"Lewis's character can't bear the waiting, so he chucks himself off the train, doesn't he? Tony threw himself off, after a fashion." Dewi stared through the windscreen, at a black sky riven with splinters of cold silvery light. "I wish to God we could find Gary, before he jumps off, or gets pushed."

Following his gaze, she said, "The same stars are looking over him. Don't they make you think about eternity and God?"

"I don't have the benefit of your 'All things bright and beautiful' mentality," Dewi commented. "The stars don't twinkle and the moon hasn't got a face at all, never mind a friendly one. Up there's far more beyond fear and darkness than Saunders Lewis's night wind."

"Oh, shut up!" Janet opened the car door, and wind swept in. "You're more depressing than McKenna at times." Marching down the brick path, she banged hard on Hogg's front door, rattling the glass panes. Incarcerated within the house, the dog set up a frantic yelping, notes rising and falling as it scuttled from room to room.

Dewi watched her stamping her feet on the porch, and as she disappeared around the side of the house, reached behind him for the box Rhiannon brought from Bedd y Cor.

# •Chapter•
## 17

God Almighty!" Owen Griffiths' voice was heavy with sleep. "You're like bloody Blodeuwedd from the Mabinogi. D'you turn into an owl at twilight? It's after one in the morning!"

"For all I seem doomed to haunt the night, I haven't had a sex change as well," McKenna said. "I'm sorry to disturb you, but I need your consent."

"Can't it wait?"

"The Hoggs hardly ever stay out, and never as late as this, according to the neighbours. Very out of character, apparently." McKenna shook the last cigarette from the packet. "If they are out, of course."

"Where else would they be?" Griffiths demanded. "Locked in a last passionate embrace, empty bottles of sleeping pills strewn about their unlovely bodies? That *would* be out of character. Anyway, you said the car's missing."

McKenna replaced the cigarette. "It could've been stolen. They could be robbed, beaten, badly injured. Who knows?"

"And who cares? The dog wouldn't starve for a while, would it? We've got no sodding choice, have we? Tell Dewi Prys not to do more damage than necessary, and to make sure the house is secured after. And don't phone me again unless you've got really exciting news."

•   •   •

"There's no sign of the gaudy gear Doris favours, or the sharp suits he preens in, and no passports, chequebooks, bank statements or credit cards." Dewi consulted his list. "One tatty old travel bag, lots of fat furniture and fluffy carpets, scores of videos I've told uniform to confiscate in case Ronnie's version of *Brief Encounter* isn't the one we know and love, hundreds of romantic novels likewise, and a sunbed in the back bedroom big enough to fry an elephant. And the dog. That's in the kennels outside, waiting for the RSPCA, if mummy and daddy don't come back."

"Anything else?" McKenna opened the cigarettes Dewi bought at the all-night garage on Beach Road, and wondered if he would ever be allowed to sleep again.

"A really dirty kitchen." Janet shuddered. "That nasty sort of dirt the roaches love. Even the microwave was filthy."

"And the horrible smell that got up your nose at Blodwel, before the fire," Dewi said.

"It's a real sloven's kitchen," Janet added. "But I've always had Doris down as a slattern."

"Mr. and Mrs. Hogg have taken a few days' leave, according to the director," McKenna said. "To recover from their recent ordeals, particularly the one by fire."

"If they've gone away legit, why didn't they tell us?" Dewi riffled the stacks of papers on McKenna's desk. "When we faxed the director about Hogg going to the funeral, he faxed back that Hogg had his wholehearted support in any decision he chose to make. He wouldn't plan a grand arrival at the cemetery if he was going away."

"He's had time to change his mind," McKenna pointed out.

Dewi shook his head. "They've done a runner, and left the dog to starve. It was already tearing up the house, and there was a pile of shit by the back door."

McKenna sighed. "First thing in the morning, Dilys or another disciple will turn up with key, dog-food, and poopa-scoopa."

Dewi shrugged. "If she does, she does."

"And where will that leave us?" Janet asked.

Dewi shrugged again. "With egg on our faces instead of all the shit chucked at us lately." He frowned. "Why can't we accept they've legged it? Why's Hogg so good at making people doubt the obvious?"

"Maybe he's taken her to Lourdes." Owen Griffiths glanced through his office window, at a sky tumbling with cloud, rosy pink in the rising sun. "It should stay fine for the funeral, but it's bitter cold. Did you get any sleep? You look like death warmed up."

"Why should Hogg take Doris to Lourdes?"

"Well, maybe Treffynnon. But the passports are gone, aren't they?" Griffiths sat down, and cradled a mug of tea. "She probably cracked up. First the sin-eating, then the fire, and in between, what you said to her. She needs healing."

"There's no healing for them if they comb the ends of the earth."

"Your Christian charity's deserting you."

McKenna rose, joints loose with weariness, like a marionette flopping at the end of its strings. "I don't have an inexhaustible supply, so it's expended wisely."

"You don't have an inexhaustible supply of energy, either. Take tomorrow off, I can hold the fort." Griffiths sipped his tea. "Given any more thought to taking over when I retire?"

"Your job comes with too much politicking."

"It's a game. I listen a lot, but I never heed much. I've heard all the reasons for not investigating what's really gone on in the children's homes since Hogg set foot over the county border, which boil down to one bad lot bad-mouthing another bad lot, and the huge difficulty of prosecuting child abuse allegations," Griffiths said. "We'd be lucky if Crown Prosecutions took up one case in fifty, and for every paedophile or child-batterer sent down for a few years on Rule 43, another's waiting in the wings, because abuse of the helpless is part of human nature."

"That's no reason for ignoring it."

"Indeed no." Griffiths smiled. "And even those of rank blessed with the ability to see all sides of everything all the time have agreed that Hogg and his behaviour are as palatable as a rat butty."

"Somebody up there must love you," McKenna said.

"Me and my judgement are held in high regard, so I'm told. So don't fret. We'll track them down eventually, and dish out just desserts."

"I do hope so." McKenna gathered up papers and files from Griffiths' desk. "I'd hate them to feel safe in their bed. People say memory amounts to eyes staring and fingers pointing with the likes of him and Doris. D'you think they know that?"

At noon, McKenna went home to change his clothes and feed the cats. His own waited behind the front door, pirate face pressed to the reeded glass, watching for him to round the corner of the little street. She retreated as he opened the door, leaving dusty paw prints on Denise's note.

Waiting for the kettle to boil and his egg to poach, he sat in the kitchen, shivering with fatigue, and the bitter air sidling under the back door. Denise was taking a holiday, he read, unable to bear the misery of another Welsh winter. He put her note beneath a pile of unopened letters, and dragged himself upright. The cats looked up briefly from their feeding, then turned away.

"You look very pretty," Mandy's grandmother said. "The black really sets off your hair."

Preening before her reflection in the hall mirror, Mandy thought how smart she was in her new garments. She fluffed her hair and smiled, because the hair looked beautiful, with life of its own, then remembered why she looked so startlingly different today, and that dreadful churning feeling turned her innards to water yet again.

"They won't be there." Her grandmother was insistent. "Even that Hogg and his wife wouldn't have the face to go to Arwel's funeral."

"What if they are?" Mandy whispered.

"Then I'll see to them. You just keep your mouth shut tight."

Mandy nodded, staring again at her pale face and glistening red hair, while her grandmother wondered, for the thousandth time, how this child came by such terrible teeth.

"If they do go, Nain, what will you do?" Mandy persisted.

The older woman laughed. "Wait behind Carol Thomas for the left-overs. We all know what happened Saturday, don't we?"

Jack coughed, and rubbed his chest, wheezing.

"Why on earth did you go out yesterday?" Emma demanded.

"I've hardly seen daylight this week. I'm getting claustrophobic."

"There's little daylight to see at this time of year."

"All the more reason to be out in what there is." Jack hesitated over a white shirt and a grey one. "Which goes better with the suit?"

Emma sighed. "The white one, not that anyone'll care. They'll all be looking at Rhiannon, and Carol Thomas."

"I care." Jack regarded his wife, mysterious in black, and wondered how anyone could keep their hands from her, let alone their eyes. "You don't look a day older than the girls." He smiled, the skin around his eyes and mouth crêpey and lined, and Emma thought this brief sickness had stolen what little youth remained to him.

•   •   •   •

Elias ab Elis stood motionless in Rhiannon's bedroom while she checked his suit, brushing a speck of fluff from the fine dark weave.

"You're losing weight." She stared critically at the tall still figure. "The jacket used to hang perfectly, and now it's creasing across the back of the neck."

"No one will notice. I'll wear a coat."

Rhiannon sat on the windowseat, looking out on the drive. "What time is it?" She fidgeted with her watch. "The cars will arrive soon. I do hope Mari's ready."

"I wish you wouldn't lend her your clothes. She's paid more than enough to buy her own."

"She couldn't afford clothes like mine."

"Most girls of her age can't. Most girls of her age wouldn't be seen dead in clothes like yours." Elis smiled bleakly. "There's no street cred in couture. At least, not in this neck of the woods."

"I'm her role model. Who else does she have?"

He touched her hair, and let his hand linger on her cheek. "I pray she finds a better husband than you did."

Rhiannon jerked her head away. "And I pray she won't have to pay debts she didn't incur!"


On Sunday, Peggy Thomas had wedged the bundle of fifty-pound notes in a biscuit tin under the kitchen sink, and there most of the money remained. "We don't need charity, and we don't want it. Not off Rhiannon Elis, not off anyone."

"Except the social," Tom observed. "You'll take every penny you can scrounge off them. And what's the funeral, if it isn't bloody charity?"

"That's for Arwel," Peggy said.

"She gave us hundreds," Tom persisted. "You could've had a new coat. And why couldn't I have a new suit?"

"You'll wear what you've got, like me."

"No sodding choice, have I?" Tom snarled, and slammed from the room.

Standing beside Peggy before the mirror in the back parlour, Carol felt grudging admiration for her mother's bloody-mindedness. Twitching the brim of an old felt hat, Peggy said, "I wore this coat and hat for my mam's funeral, and that was a long time ago."

"You've not put on a bit of weight, have you?" Carol said, smoothing down the collar.

"It still looks quite nice." Peggy fastened the big black buttons. "It's a nice bit of cloth. Don't put that over your head." She took the scarf from Carol's hands, and tucked it around her neck. "You're too young to cover your hair." Stroking the beautiful hair, she whispered, "My God! Where did you and Arwel get it from?"

"Nobody knows that but you, Mam." She smiled briefly, then frowned. "I'll have to take my coat off at Bedd y Cor, won't I? We are going, aren't we? Mrs. Elis is doing a special meal. Will this dress look all right?"

"You look lovely." Peggy smiled through the tears in her eyes. "And if your dad asks about your new clothes, tell him you got maternity money off the social."

"Are you giving the rest of the cash back to her?" Carol asked.

"Only if she asks." Peggy took her gloves and handbag from the table. "D'you think she will?"


McKenna ate lunch, washed the few dishes, put fresh food and water out for the cats, and crawled up the two steep staircases to his bedroom. He sat on the bed, trying to decide what clothes to wear, and found the dilemma too enormous to resolve.

Hammering on the front door at ten minutes past two, Dewi woke him from the sleep of the dead.


Behind the tower of St. Mihangel's church, the last light of the westering sun coloured the sky, gilding the straggle of mourners meandering up the cemetery path, their shadows lengthening before them, McKenna in their wake. A cruel east wind reddened pallid cheeks and scoured salty tears, and set the branches of the yew trees threshing like mad women flailing their limbs around the procession behind parson and corpse, which added its own whisperings to the sigh of the wind.

Listening to the quiet chatter of two reporters and the television cameraman who dogged his footsteps, McKenna rested for a moment, then walked on, barking a shin on the great stone anchor athwart the body of Josiah Clayton, through the small necropolis of leaning obelisks and lichen-stained monuments, and towards the old granite chapel at the top of the path, and the new grave in the lee of the cemetery wall. Standing beside the dark narrow hole in the earth, next to Elias ab Elis, he wondered if this elegant man might return under the shroud of night, and with bloody fingers and desperate strength, search for the truth beyond the hope of sure and certain resurrection.

At St. Mihangel's altar, his body dignified by wealth, and the perfume of incense and flowers, Arwel received the last respects to the plaintive notes of a psalm. Looking on the boy whom he last saw in squalor, debased by Carol's grief and the odours of soot and poverty, McKenna thought of another, whose skin was also perhaps as pale as alabaster from Penmon Quarry, said to have left the world in an aura of beauty, after a brief fright, a quick pain. But, he thought, turning away to let Owen Griffiths look for the first and last time on the dead boy, Death never kept such kind company.

The light of the dying day softened faces stony with grief and bitterness, and the wind abandoned the wild trees to tease Elis's glossy hair, taunting McKenna's senses with scents of cologne and flowers, newly turned earth and damp turf.

At the head of the grave, the parson swung the silver censer, his words coming to McKenna in wind-torn snatches, like a faulty broadcast.

"I had no prescience," Elis whined, like the questing wind.

"Yet even a horse senses the presence of death. Why didn't I feel his terror? Why didn't I know when he died?"

"You wept when you knew," McKenna said.

"Bitter tears! So much weeping and anguish! So much more than I ever spared for my own."

"You mourned the lost promise." McKenna started like an animal as the muffled bells in the tower began to peal. "Knowing the difference is no betrayal." Throbbing on the air, seven bells weaved a dancing dirge and the great tenor tolled time, their clappers wrapped in leather. "What's your son's name? I've never known." He raised his voice, and wanted to put his hands over his ears.

"We called him Pryderi, but he's an accident of nature, salvaged by money and skill and shortsighted ambition. We should have let him die." A bleak smile touched Elis's lips. "In her heart, Rhiannon believes she was given the evil eye, by a crippled hag called Beti Gloff who cleaned for us. Rhiannon called her a witch."

"Beti's simply a sad old woman, Mr. Elis, but people see only her ugliness and usefulness."

The group around the grave undulated, changing its contours, as the parson reached out, censer swinging from his left arm, fingers holding down the fluttering pages of the Book of Common Prayer, his right hand clasping the hands of Peggy Thomas, whose old black clothes lent her figure an archaic dignity. He touched Tom Thomas's shaking arm, and made tears flow from the man's rheumy eyes past a nose painted red by the wind, then squeezed Carol's thin fingers with his own.

Everyone watched her, McKenna thought. Had her own kind also come to know the extravagance of her mercilessness? He caught the eye of Mandy Minx, who stood behind Carol, sheltered by her grandmother's arm. Mandy smiled at him across the wounded earth, displaying the teeth which heralded her own slow dissolution. Jack Tuttle smiled too, his feverish face swaddled by a thick scarf. Emma stared at the ground, holding her husband's arm, while her daughters clung to each other, hair tangled about their faces, looking through McKenna to a bleak landscape of their own. He watched Mari lean forwards to brush earth from the heel of her shoes, then frown with displeasure because her fine leather glove was soiled instead. She moved restlessly, and Rhiannon caught her hand, pulling her close, as Mandy's grandmother held her own kin.

"They'll shovel earth on him," Elis mourned. "They'll put out his light for ever."

*"Pridd i bridd,"* the parson intoned. *"Llwch i lwch. Lludw i ludw."*

Earth and gravel rattled down on the coffin, tossed by Peggy Thomas. Carol gathered an armful of white roses, threw them in the air, and let them fall to earth like a shower of snowflakes, melting into darkness. The contours of the group shifted again, as people moved back to let the gravediggers finish what they began in the long darkness before the winter dawn. McKenna turned as a movement caught his eye, but instead of seeing the evil spirit of Doris Hogg, come to curse the quick and the dead, he saw Eifion Roberts, a darker shadow beneath the yew trees.

The gravediggers worked like demons, spades clanging dissonantly as the bells hunted each other up and down the scale. Watched in silence by the parson, whose Book of Common Prayer still fluttered its pages in the wind, sweat froze on their backs as night dragged long heavy shapes across earth and sky. Soil began to show above the lip of the grave, tamped down with spade backs before more was heaped upon it, until only a few black crumbs littered the trampled grass, and dappled flower petals here and there amid the bank of wreaths and crosses laid out along the wall.

Coaxing Arwel's parents to her side, holding Mari close, Rhiannon walked carefully around the grave, the heels of her shoes spiking the ground, and nodded to her husband, before starting down the path, Elis stumbling in her wake with a last despairing glance at McKenna. Mandy's grandmother was the first to follow, others drifting behind, treading with care on the darkening path, pursued by the parson, who touched

Carol's hair as he went on his way, the wind pasting his cassock to his portly body. McKenna looked at the girl, luminous as the heaped blossoms in the gloaming, and wondered if this man of God also wished his shroud fashioned from that miraculous hair.

Picking up the wreath from which she had torn the white roses, Carol placed it precisely at the head of the grave, rubbing the small of her back as she stood upright. Her face was pinched with cold, her thin body disfigured by the weight of her child, and McKenna feared the browbeating wind and punishing bells might shatter her before his eyes.

She smiled gravely at him. "It's a kind place, isn't it?" She leaned against the wall, hands deep in her coat pockets. "I shan't mind leaving Arwel here. He won't mind, either."

"I'm sorry about what I said to you on Sunday." McKenna moved to the lee of the wall, and lit a cigarette. The wind whipped away the smoke, and made the tip burn bright. "And I'm sorry you were dragged out of bed later on. I had to be sure you weren't responsible for the fire."

"I've no quarrel with the kids at Blodwel."

"Ronald and Doris have gone on the run."

"They can't hide. Not from Arwel."

The cigarette burned away, consumed by wind. Carol touched his arm, smiling. "Wasn't he beautiful? He didn't need anybody's money for that." Her hand rested on his sleeve, and the fingers began to pinch the cloth. "He was the light of my life, but in my heart, I knew he'd go away." The fingers stilled, but kept their hold. "We feel things like that, don't we? Do you?"

"I feel things I can't explain or understand."

Carol nodded, and the fingers fluttered. "He wasn't like other kids, you know. When we played in the sunshine, his shadow had a light inside it. The teacher said it was a trick of the light you could see anywhere on a bright summer day, but I'd still rather believe God made him different." The fingers fretted at his sleeve, and she smiled again. "Am I going mad, d'you think? Or was I always mad?"

"Perhaps madness is like being the one-eyed man in the realm of the blind," McKenna said gently. "And you've light of your own, under this black grief."

"Oh, I'm not like Arwel." She gestured to her swollen belly. "All the world knows I'm just flesh and blood."

"When's the baby due?"

"In May. It's a lovely month, isn't it?" She pushed herself away from the wall and began to walk down the path, the last vestige of the light of day rosy on her face. "Arwel said babies are miracles, even the ones like Pryderi, and he pitied the Elises, because they're too selfish to realize." She shivered. "Mam's forgiven me for hitting her, but will God forgive me for trying to kill a miracle?"

"He'll understand." McKenna took her thin arm in his own. "Have you thought of a name yet? If it's a boy, might you call him Arwel?"

"Oh, no!" Carol stopped. "There couldn't be another Arwel for me. Dafydd would be nice, wouldn't it? And Morfudd for a girl, because Dafydd ap Gwilym loved her all his life."

"He said she was baptized by May."

"I know." She smiled, luminous still. "Have you seen that big green poetry book? I gave it to Arwel for his thirteenth birthday, because he only had that kiddie's book with the picture of the man with a harp." She grinned briefly. "He'd pinched it from school. You won't tell, will you?"

"I won't tell." Loose gravel slipped under his shoes and clattered down the path. "Mrs. Elis found the book at Bedd y Cor. Would you like to have it back?"

Carol nodded, then turned to look where her brother lay under six feet of cold earth, the white wreath glowing in velvety darkness. "I'll come here often, and I'll bring my baby." She leaned against him, taking short careful steps on the steep path. "D'you think Arwel might walk with us sometimes?" She smiled again. "On a bright sunny day, there might be another shadow beside mine and my baby's and it might have a heart of light. You can never know, can you?"

"No," McKenna said. "You can never know."

She stopped once more, but the grave was no longer in view, only the dark silhouettes of leaning obelisks and threshing yew trees in their sight. "I don't pity the Elises," Carol said. "They can buy anything, so they think everything's got a price." She walked on again, still leaning against him. "You think I've let her buy me and my baby, don't you?"

"To be honest, Carol, I don't know what to think."

"I want my baby now I know there's nothing to be ashamed of." Stopping again, she stood before him, a thin hand on each of his arms, her fingers fretting at his sleeves. "Mam says Mrs. Elis might've offered me money out of kindness, but nobody's like that, are they? I think she's trying to make up for Arwel."

"Why should she need to do that?"

"They played with him, like they play with Mari. Mr. Elis took Arwel on trips and played at horses with him like kids play with dolls and Teddy bears." Letting go of his arms, she walked towards the cemetery gates. "He didn't do any of it for Arwel, you know. It was all for himself. He doesn't deserve any pity, and she should be ashamed of herself for letting him be like that."

A small group of sightseers waited outside the cemetery, heads bowed under the wrathful noise of the bells. McKenna held the door of a long black car while Carol climbed in, to sit beside her mother and father, then hurried to his own, fearing to see the church tower blown apart by the monstrous pressure within.

"You look dead in your shoes." Owen Griffiths examined McKenna's face. "What an awful day! And those bells! Rhiannon's paid for a full peal of something called Grandsire Triples. The ringers'll still be hard at it at teatime."

"A muffled peal is a tribute."

"Is it? My scalp wanted to crawl right off my skull." Griffiths riffled through the list of telephone messages. "Rhiannon said we'd be welcome at Bedd y Cor for the funeral meal, which was very magnanimous in the circumstances. She waited ages to speak to you. What were you and that crazy girl talking about for so long?"

"Arwel mostly. Carol seems the only person able to rejoice that he lived." McKenna lit a cigarette. "What did Rhiannon want?"

"She asked about the vehicles, so I said we're investigating new material, and probably wouldn't keep them much longer."

"Is that all?"

"She's resigned."

"To what?"

"From the chair of social services committee and the council."

"She's been expecting the sack since we questioned Elis."

"She's done it off her own bat, because she noticed the stink of something very rotten in the borough, and wants to discuss her 'shift of perspective' with you, because you'll understand better. As you reckon folk know more than they think, she's probably right."

"Nice to have one big gun firing on our behalf, isn't it?"

"There's no need for sarcasm," Griffiths chided. "You'll feel more charitable after a good night's sleep. I've sent your minions home, because they were up all last night and most of the night before. Jack wanted to come back, but he's got a nastier cough than I ever heard on you, and he doesn't touch the tobacco."

"It's all the passive smoking he's forced to do."

"It's the bugs getting to him when he's down. I've never known him so miserable." Doodling mindlessly on a sheet of headed notepaper, Griffiths added, "I told him to follow Denise's example and take a holiday over Christmas."

"And I've told him the same, but I doubt he'll take the advice."

"He's fretting about those girls, isn't he? Did you notice how strained they looked at the funeral? And they didn't even know Arwel." Sighing, he tore up the paper and dropped the shreds into the waste bin. "You can't get to grips with modern youth, can you? Can't know what they're thinking, or why, can't know what they'll do next. Has it occurred to you that Carol provoked the fire at Blodwel, never mind sending Ronnie and Doris off on their travels? How do we deal with that sort of power? And don't say she won't see it that way. She might not at the moment, but I'm sure she'll be putting two and two together before long."

"She'll see this collision of random events for what it is," McKenna said. "But that's not to say the rest of the world won't invest her with the power." He smiled. "According to Eifion, all perceptions depend on the judgement of the perceiver, not the perceived."

"He's as barmy in his own way as she is." Griffiths frowned. "She alarms me, you know, because she'll only answer to herself."

"She won't cause any harm while her conscience sits firmly on her back," McKenna said. "At least, not to anyone who doesn't deserve it."

"Scratch a Celt and find an anarchist?"

"Depends on your perception of anarchy." McKenna lit a cigarette. "Call it giving God a helping hand."

"Pastor Evans'd say a mere mortal can't know when God wants one."

"And Pastor Evans can't know if God would want to judge a girl like Sian because she had a baby out of wedlock, but he takes it upon himself to condemn her in His name."

Griffiths began defacing another sheet of paper. "Scratch a papist and find some compassion, eh? There's little enough of it warming the hearts of most chapelgoers. Peggy Thomas was telling me how people've treated them since Arwel died. Not a word of condolence, and most folk crossing the road rather than pass the time of day." He sighed. "I suppose they're held to blame for Arwel dying."

"They're held to be contaminated, and people cross the road because they're afraid of catching their own death."

• • •

Arwel's funeral merited a brief mention on the local teatime news. The cameraman made these extraordinary people look banal, McKenna thought, grief painted on their faces for the occasion, the dreadful thudding bells reduced to a vibrant humming beneath the reporter's voice. The report occupied fifty-five seconds, followed by whole minutes on council over-spending, where the director of social services justified his further negligence, and the councillors expressed outrage about wasted money.

Shivering inside his padded coat, a tissue-wrapped bottle under his arm, Eifion Roberts arrived as McKenna put his empty milk bottles on the front doorstep.

"I expected you to wait after the funeral," McKenna said.

"Didn't feel like it." Hanging the coat over the back of a dining-chair, the pathologist sank on the sofa, arranging his feet around the sleeping cats. "Harrowing, wasn't it? You look more bloody awful than usual."

"I've had precious little sleep since Saturday."

"Arwel can sleep all he wants, but I don't expect you'd fancy a swop." He unwrapped the bottle and unscrewed the cap. "Get the glasses, Michael."

"I don't much feel like drinking."

"You can watch me, then." Tipping out a huge measure of whiskey, Dr. Roberts added, "And you can shut up with your nannying platitudes about drink and the other little pleasures that stop mortal man putting an end to it all every so often!"

"I'd no intention of saying anything."

"That'll make a change, won't it?" Peering over the rim of his glass at McKenna, he said, "I was watching Elis at the fu-neral. He gawps at you like you're some sort of saviour. Does he think you've mastered the art of walking on water? You should tell him even papists just wash in it, like the rest of us."

McKenna sighed. "Is this going to be one of those times when you do a verbal autopsy on anyone unlucky enough to cross your orbit?"

"I got to thinking, that's all." Dr. Roberts gulped his drink.

"Maybe it wasn't very charitable to say Elis does bugger all. Did you know some Roman bod said he never let a day pass without writing a line? It's fine when you know what you're supposed to do with all this time, but what do I do? What's my motto? 'Never a day without a carve-up?'." Emptying the glass, he said gloomily, "Not much of a purpose, is it?"

"Are you busy, sir?" Dewi stood on the doorstep, a powdering of snow on his hair and shoulders.

"I thought you'd be in the Land of Nod." McKenna retrieved milk bottles toppled by the wind, then closed the door. "Which is where I'd like to be. I'l bet Janet's tucked up at the manse."

"She wasn't half an hour ago." Standing at the foot of the stairs, Dewi gazed upon the pathologist, fast asleep on the sofa, half-empty bottle at his feet, two cats in his large lap. "Is he all right?"

"He will be. You can help get him home when you've said what you want." Sitting at the table, McKenna added, "What were you and Janet doing?"

"Fighting over words, and it's a bloody good thing she stormed off back to Daddy before I found the death verse." Opening Arwel's book of medieval poetry, Dewi pointed out the number above each title, the printed numbers at intervals beside the lines, then showed McKenna the handwritten margin annotations, the underscorings of letters and numbers. "She got very snotty about council-house kids defacing books."

Rubbing his eyes, McKenna leafed through the book. "They're not all marked. Maybe Arwel was learning some of them, or just fancied the imagery." Haltingly, he began to read the archaic language. "It's very beautiful, isn't it? Very fresh."

"Not all the poems are marvellous," Dewi said. "Still, I expect even Beethoven managed to write crappy stuff at times."

McKenna smiled. "Policing's doing wonders for your cultural development."

"Obscuring my origins, you mean?"

"Leave the bitchiness to Janet." Leafing again through the pages, McKenna said, "And never underestimate the intelligence of the uneducated. Carol sees things others miss. Her imagination's not been smothered by learning, and neither was Arwel's." He stared at one of the marked verses. "So what was he doing?"

"Not wantonly vandalizing books, but Janet got so steamed up she wouldn't even bother thinking about the combinations of letters and numbers he'd marked. If you ignore what's not marked, these read like vehicle registrations, don't they?"

Tossing and turning in bed, McKenna came to violent wakefulness again as the cathedral clock struck eleven, head and heart thudding. One heavy, one light, the cats lay on his feet, the black cat sporting a new silver collar. The other cat stirred as the owl called, winging over the sleeping city, and McKenna thought of the legendary Blodeuwedd, sprung from flowers and doomed never to know the love of mortal man. He thought too of Pryderi, the stolen child, whose name was fashioned from the word for worry, and whose legacy was vengeance.

Wrapping himself in his dressing-gown, he crept downstairs to sit by the parlour fire. Immune to his terror, the cats slept on, sure that day would pursue night and that death dogged life, wise to the tensions holding all infinity in infinite balance.

# • C h a p t e r •
# 18

The shrill note of the telephone roused McKenna from sleep, and as he groped for the receiver, he imagined again the acrid fumes of Blodwel alight. Instead of Dewi's voice, sharp with urgency, he heard the soft breathy tones of Emma Tuttle, panting with fear.

"The girls've gone!"

"Gone where?" He glanced at the bedside clock. "It's past one in the morning."

"I know what time it is!" Emma's voice rose.

The cats protested as he sat upright. "Was there another row?"

"Not really. They wanted to go to Bedd y Cor after the funeral, but we said no. It's not as if they knew the boy."

"They're young. He was one of their kind."

"I think they wanted to see inside the poshest house in the county, as a matter of fact. Oh, why are we wasting time?"

"When did they go out?"

"I don't know! They went to bed about eleven. Jack was already asleep, worn out after the funeral."

"And you?" McKenna switched on the bedlamp.

"Twelve? I did the ironing first."

"Did you check on the girls?"

"Of course I did! They were reading."

"So they've been gone less than an hour." He climbed from the bed, back and legs stiff enough to snap.

"There might've been a telephone call," Emma said. "Something woke me, but there's nothing on the answering machine."

"When?"

"I don't know! I went back to sleep."

"So what woke you again?"

"I don't *know*! Instinct, probably."

"Is there a recall number stored?"

"I couldn't think of anything except calling you." She sobbed.

"Is Jack still asleep?"

"I don't want to wake him. He's really not well."

"I know." Pulling underclothes and top clothes from drawers and wardrobe, he began to dress. "I'll get your number checked now. What about the bikes?"

"In the garage."


"It's not only council-house kids who go off the rails," Dewi said.

"I didn't mean that, and you know I didn't!" Janet snapped. "I don't see Inspector Tuttle's girls that way."

"I don't expect he does, either."

"Why should they want to run away?" Janet demanded.

"If we find them, you can ask, can't you?" McKenna said.

Dewi snatched at the telephone on McKenna's desk before the first peal rang out, scribbled numbers and notes on a sheet of paper, then dialled out. "There's no incoming number stored, but somebody rang out at midnight forty-one to—" He broke off to speak, gave instructions, and waited, the secrecy button activated. "Bettacabs. They've taken a fare some place. He's asking the driver exactly where."


"They've gone to meet Gary Hughes," Janet shivered.

"How d'you know there isn't a rave in the mountains like on Penmon cliffs during the summer?" Dewi concentrated on the dark narrow road, an unforgiving thoroughfare through the detritus of an Ice Age glacier.

"Look at all that ice. And it's snowing. You'd have to be out of your mind to go up there."

"Druggies usually are."

"You can be so stubborn."

"Mrs. Tuttle's stubborn, isn't she? No way would she stay in the house." Dewi glanced in the mirror, at the lights of McKenna's car behind. "I wouldn't like to be in the twins' shoes when we catch them."

"If." A volley of snow hit the windscreen, sheared from the mountainsides. Janet watched the car headlights swing up and down, glittering on cataracts of ice in crevices and gullies like black holes in a solid universe. "What do we do when we get to the village?"

"What we're told, like always." Dewi grinned. "Mushroom management, isn't it? Keep us in the dark and shovel shit on us every so often."

"Don't jest." Janet shivered again. "We watched one poor kid put six feet under yesterday, and Tony's already dust and ashes. Pray God there won't be any more."


A hundred yards beyond the last terrace of village houses, Mountain Rescue vehicles and police cars littered the verge, and men in Alpine gear, festooned with ropes and ice axes and survival equipment, cast huge hump-backed shadows in the light of flickering lanterns and headlamps. Maps were laid out on walls, pinioned by hands and small rocks, people spoke in low measured tones, and radios crackled with static from the high peaks.

"We'll only get in the way. That's why Mr. McKenna wants us to stay in the car." Emma's tension was palpable, Janet thought.

"They're my children!"

"They can't have gone far in less than two hours."

"And how long does it take to freeze to death in the mountains?"

"We don't know they're in the mountains. Why should they be?"

"How the hell should I know?" Emma shouted. "I don't even know why they went!"


McKenna sank to a crouch, breath rasping. "I'll catch up."

Two of the rescue team and a local police officer crunched away up the lane, leaving Dewi and McKenna to the strident mountain night and the screaming wind.

"Why not go back to the cars, sir? You're in no fit state." Dewi shouted to make himself heard, lips brittle with cold.

"I've had no less sleep than you of late."

"With respect, I'm a lot younger, and I haven't had an accident." Putting his hand under McKenna's elbow, Dewi pulled him upright, as he and McKenna had earlier manhandled Eifion Roberts into Dewi's car to be driven home. Propping McKenna against the rough wall around a mountain pasture, he added, "You can't stop moving. The wind chill's at least minus fifteen."

"All the more reason to find those girls." McKenna gazed upon a world empty save for Dewi and himself, and huddles of sheep in the lee of the wall. The wind thudded against the rock faces, screaming with the pain, and he wondered if his head would ever be free of the dreadful noises of this day and night. "Why aren't they searching that place?" He pointed up a stony track beyond the pasture, to a small dwelling at the foot of a sheer-sided crag.

"It's a holiday let. Been done already."

"There's a light inside."

"Where?" Dewi scanned the distance, and saw nothing amiss. "Your eyes are playing tricks, sir. Folk reckon you'll see hobgoblins in these mountains at night."

McKenna said stubbornly: "I saw a light."

"Probably a reflection."

McKenna staggered a little as he moved away from the wall. "We'll make sure, shall we? We've nothing to lose."

Stones on the track rolled away under their feet, turning ankles, as treacherous as the cemetery path. He leaned into the wind, feeling it an entity and enemy, strong enough to halt the most determined progress, and thinking he glimpsed the silvery-white coat of a mountain hare fleeing their advancing shadows, wondered what shapes the goblins took upon themselves. Gasping for each breath snatched from the teeth of the wind, bent double, he almost fell when the mountain flank suddenly cut off the gale and left them becalmed, overwhelmed by a massive rock face obliterating the sky.

"You were right." Dewi stopped to rest. "I can see it myself now."

The cottage was built of cob with a low felted roof, a small sash window to each side of the little front door. There was no garden, simply a cinder path between cottage and pasture wall. A broken harrow, its rusting tines like devils' teeth, blocked the end of the pathway, and the air smelt of damp sour earth, as if the sun never reached this desolate place.

Dewi crept along the path to peer through the far window, seeing nothing but deeper shadow, while McKenna leaned against the house wall, listening to his thudding heart and rasping breath, and the faint rise and fall of voices behind the other window. He looked in, and saw Jack Tuttle's twin daughters, grave-faced and dishevelled, Denise's clothes bereft of all elegance, seated at a table draped with a red gingham cloth, amid a litter of sweet wrappers and drinks cans and candles guttering in a saucer. Back to the window, the boy shuddered and twitched uncontrollably.

The candlelight brushed feverish colour on the girls' cheeks, and drew a contour of light around the shape of the boy. Shadows moved in the recesses, tense grotesque shapes forming and reforming without any apparent reference to the solid figures and the flickering light and, mesmerized, McKenna watched, wondering on their source beyond his sight. Dewi drifted to his side, whispering, and as he stirred, catching his hand against the glass, the girls leapt from their chairs.


"Thank the Lord!" Owen Griffiths exclaimed. "It's worth being roused in the dead hours for news like this." He chuckled. "I'll bet Emma Tuttle's spitting fire, isn't she? Jack'll be as mad as hell, too. They shouldn't be too hard on the girls. They've done us all a good turn."

"Emma wanted to know why the twins didn't have the sense to say Gary'd rung, instead of haring after him." McKenna yawned. "He's been trying to call them for days, but Jack kept answering the phone."

"He's probably sweet on them both, 'cos he can't tell which is which." Griffiths chuckled again. "Where is he?"

"At home. The hospital said he's none the worse." Huddled by the parlour fire, still in outdoor clothes, McKenna wondered if he would ever be warm again. "Janet's staying 'til morning. Mrs. Hughes is close to collapse."


"Em threatened to strangle them." Clad in dressing-gown and pyjamas, Jack hunched by the sitting-room fire, shivering from head to foot. Reaching for the poker to stir the coals to greater heat, he added, "I really thought she'd hurt them. She's never frightened me with her passion before."

"Are they at school?" McKenna asked.

"Are you kidding?" Jack coughed. "Mother hen's taken her chicks out shopping. Let's hope she doesn't peck them to death."

"You sound very bitter."

"So would you cooped up with three bloody women!"

"I'm sick of hearing people whinge!" McKenna snapped. "Especially when they've nothing to whinge about!"

Jack pulled himself from the chair like an old man. "Having a whinge now and then's a damned sight better than letting things fester."

"I don't let anything fester."

"Denise eats away at you like a maggot on a corpse, only you won't admit it."

"We're reconciled to our differences."

"Considering she's flogging her assets round North Wales, that's very civilized."

McKenna flushed. "D'you always poke your nails in people's wounds?"

"You want to be careful yours don't go gangrenous."

"Medicine is rediscovering its origins," McKenna said stiffly, "and using sterile maggots to clean out the nastiest wounds."

"Denise isn't that sort of maggot." Jack sighed. "I've no quarrel with you, but she makes things fester in Em as well. Discontent, misogynism, even. She wants to taint everybody with her bitterness."

"D'you really believe Emma will let her? Can't you credit her with more sense?"

"I credit her with everything a human being is capable of, and that's very frightening." Jack rubbed his hands over his face, and McKenna heard the rasp of beard. "She's changed. She started the day you walked out on Denise, and she hasn't stopped yet. God knows when she will."

"People can't stay the same. They must grow."

"Into what?" Jack demanded. "And don't say 'themselves'!"

"You're afraid for yourself." McKenna rose, and pulled on his coat. "Emma already knows you can abandon someone you expected to love for ever. She's with you because she wants to be, so mind you don't drive her away."


Gary sat beside Dewi on the dull brown sofa in his mother's dull front parlour. He looked wasted, hard-edged and brittle with tension, his youth as dead as Arwel and Tony. His mother stood behind the sofa, and a small fire sputtered in the grate, subdued by an east wind thumping in the chimney and battering at the windows.

"We've a great deal to discuss with Gary, Mrs. Hughes," McKenna said.

Her hands hovered around her son's head, then retreated. "The doctors said he should take it easy for a while. Get his strength back."

"How d'you feel?" McKenna asked the boy.

"OK." He shrugged. "Am I going the police station?"

"Why should you?"

"He's frightened about the running away," Mrs. Hughes said. "And about breaking into the cottage."

"We're more concerned with the reasons," McKenna said. "People often run when they're frightened."

"I told you before." Mrs. Hughes brushed one of the wandering hands against her cheek, wiping away a tear. "He's never been the same since he came back from that place."

"Was it really torched?" Gary asked, hope gleaming in his eyes.

"It burned down," McKenna said. "We're not sure how, yet."

"It wasn't me." A wry smile added wistfulness to the lisping seductive voice. "But I can't prove it."

"We've no reason to suspect you." McKenna smiled, despite himself. "D'you want your mother to stay?"

"I'm OK on my own," Gary said. "And don't bother getting me a social worker. They didn't do their job before, so they won't start now."

"Some of them might."

"Not the ones I know."

"A relative, then, or a solicitor," McKenna suggested.

"No!" As McKenna thought of the determination which kept Gary alive in the mountains, and perhaps out of the way of further harm, the boy turned to Dewi, and said, "And I'm not trying to con the system, so you can take that look off your face."

"What d'you mean?" Mrs. Hughes' eyes flitted from face to face. "What's he talking about?"

"I can't be charged if I'm not interviewed according to the

rules, and I can't say I don't want my rights, because I haven't got any. Hogg made sure I knew that."

"I want to discuss the Hoggs, among other things," McKenna said.

Mrs. Hughes fretted behind the sofa, pulling at her fingers. "I don't know. Maybe somebody should be with you. . . ."

Dewi jumped up. "We'll make a *panad* while Gary has a chat, shall we?" Taking her arm, he pulled her from the room.

Running long bony fingers through his curly brown hair, Gary smiled. "People say I'm very elusive, so you ought to catch me while you can." Seeing what others had wrought from the childish clay, McKenna wondered if he deplored the outcome only because those others realized its potential. "You didn't need to get the army out last night," Gary added. "The twins'd persuaded me to come and talk to you."

"Why?" McKenna asked. "Were you fed up with talking to yourself?"

"The conversations were boringly one-sided." The boy shifted in his seat. "Can you spare a fag?"

McKenna tossed over his packet. "We've searched every bloody nook and cranny in North Wales for you. We've been worried sick."

"I know." Gary blew smoke towards the ceiling. "I saw the troops. I hid in a gully behind the cottage when anyone came up the track." He fingered the heavy gold ring in his right earlobe. "I didn't think you'd bother. You didn't care when we legged it from Blodwel."

"You weren't always reported missing."

"Yeah, I know. Bad for Ronnie's image." Gary paused, listening to the sounds of clattering crockery, water gushing into a kettle, and the rise and fall of voices from the kitchen. "The twins said him and Doris've legged it. Is it true?"

"They don't seem to be around."

"They'll be to Spain, or Tenerife, 'cos they like it hot, and he's got wads of cash. Did they take that horrible dog?"

"They left it," McKenna said. "How d'you know he's got money?"

"I've seen him counting it." A shadow passed over the boy's face. "Will you take me down town when we've had a drink? Please?"


"Will this stand up in court?" Owen Griffiths gestured to Gary's statement. "Was it worse to hear than it is to read? Dear God, man's inhumanity knows no bounds, does it? God knows how that poor boy feels!"

"He seemed relieved to talk." McKenna lit a cigarette.

"I'm not surprised with this in his head. What about counselling for him? I don't want another Tony Jones on my conscience."

"His solicitor's sorting it out."

"Not with Social Services, I hope. He'll be a hostile witness if we ever get anyone in court." He drummed his fingers on the desk. "What d'you think Crown Prosecutions'll do? Gary's a sitting target, isn't he? Any jury'd sooner put away his like."

"If Dewi's right about Arwel's secret messages, there'll be such a wailing and gnashing of teeth everyone'll forget Gary's existence," McKenna said. "Any response yet?"

"What d'you think?" Griffiths asked gloomily. "How long did DVLA take last time we wanted number combinations fed through the computer?"

"What combinations? You read from top to bottom of each marked poem. They're all quite clear."

Griffiths squirmed in his chair. "It's not quite so clear as you think. First of all, we can't be sure it's not just coincidence. Secondly, we can't assume what seems to be a vehicle registration isn't just another coincidence. And thirdly, we can't presume if they are what they seem, Arwel meant us to read from top to bottom. Maybe you read from bottom up. There's any number of ways of looking at codes like that, and we wouldn't want to drop on a perfectly innocent citizen because we got hold of the wrong end of things." He sighed. "Arwel was no more rational than his sister is, and Dewi Prys only sees the markings as code because he isn't rational, either. And while the imagination's a wonderful thing, it can lead you astray like nothing else. Look at what Carol's imaginings did." Smiling, he added: "But don't fret. Look forward to our assignation with Hogg's boss instead."

McKenna found Dewi in the CID office, head down amid a welter of papers, snoring gently, the original list of registrations crumpled under his elbow. He wrote a short note, clipped it to the list, and went home to feed the cats.

The deputy chief constable sat beside McKenna in Griffiths's office, immaculately uniformed, a subtle aroma of pipe tobacco about his person. Equally immaculate in dark suit and pristine shirt, the director of social services sat opposite, beside the ramrod figure of a councillor elevated to committee prominence by Rhiannon's defection.

"Children, staff, parents, grandparents, siblings, neighbours, all tell us the same thing about Blodwel," Griffiths said. "Some might be exaggerating, some might be inclined to malice, some might be attention-seeking, but too many tell us the same tale one way or another."

"And maybe 'tale' is the right word," the director said.

"People say comparisons are odious," Griffiths added, "so I won't make any. Suffice to say a total corruption of ethical concepts and boundaries killed two young boys, and brutally damaged God knows how many other children."

The director flicked a speck of dust from his lapel. "Mr. McKenna knows that your inexperience allowed this whole issue to get completely out of perspective. We investigated these allegations, and found them groundless."

"We know nothing of any internal investigation," McKenna commented. "Nor do your staff."

"Blodwel staff exhibit a siege mentality, and they're terrified of Ronald Hogg. They're terrified of his wife, too, because she fed him whatever fact or fiction would help settle her own scores." Griffiths paused. "They describe a regime of pathological oppression. They knew children were beaten and terrorized, but because Hogg promoted the outrages, the staff convinced themselves they were somehow justified, and became utterly desensitized to normal moral concepts, like the children they were supposed to rehabilitate. D'you have any idea how many ex-Blodwel inmates grow up into psychopaths? We've been checking records. Two of Hogg's so-called successes are currently doing life for murder."

"It's par for the course, Superintendent. You know that."

"And Mrs. Hughes tells us Gary's conduct and attitudes were infinitely worse after his time in care."

"And ninety-nine out of a hundred of these mothers would tell you the same," the director said. "But if they're right, I've never been able to fathom who breeds all the thugs."

"Perhaps they're bred in places like Blodwel. Let me elaborate," McKenna offered. "Brutality was so commonplace many children feared they would not live to see another dawn. Those who mutilated themselves in desperation were treated with further violence by Hogg, or scorn by his wife." He paused. "People see Myra Hindley as the greater evil, don't they? Doris Hogg provokes the same response. She's already suffered some revenge, but will she ever pay all her dues?"

"Mr. and Mrs. Hogg aren't able to present their side of the story," the director said. "How d'you know you haven't been hoodwinked into believing a pack of wicked, stupid lies? How d'you know these children aren't perpetrating an enormous fraud, encouraged by gullible police officers?"

"If they are, Tony and Arwel won't derive any benefit from it, will they?" Griffiths said. "And Gary's in no fit state to hoodwink anyone."

"Gary Hughes made a substantial statement which will be permissible as evidence," McKenna said. "He understands the shame and desperation which drove Tony to open his arteries and bleed to death, because he too was sold for sex by

Ronald Hogg. The market was there, Hogg could satisfy its demands, and the children had no means to resist his enterprise. He doubtless carried out similar operations in other children's homes, before coming to this area."

"That's a ridiculous assertion!" the director snapped. "We do not employ criminals! Mr. Hogg's references were impeccable."

"He has no convictions, and his previous employer simply shifted the man and his nasty habits on to your patch. Par for the course, we understand." McKenna lit a cigarette. "People say he's like a sect leader, and Gary talks of religious mania, of 'strange men' giving Bible readings at Blodwel. One of these men took him away for the weekend, painted his toenails with purple varnish, and raped him until he collapsed in his own exhaustion." He dragged smoke in his lungs. "Gary's tried to tell us about the unspeakable terror the children lived with, day in and day out. He's so obsessed with the sound of feet, and even their smell, he makes you want to scream with nerves. He'd lie in bed, waiting to hear Doris's feet slithering towards his room, or her husband's heels clipping like gunshots, and his heart kept pace with the sound of them coming for him, faster and faster as they came nearer and nearer, leaving their smell on the carpet like Devil's spoor." He frowned. "Didn't someone once write about rooms of experience some people inhabit that no one else would ever want to enter?"

"Imagination is prized by the Celtic races," the director commented. "Unfortunately, too many are unable to distinguish between fantasy and fact, so it falls to others to keep a hold on reality." He brushed another speck of dust from his lapel. "My reality involves trying to balance the needs of society against those of the children whose behaviour poses a threat to that society, and it's generally an almost impossible task. Even so, I am not endlessly accountable. The line must be drawn at some point."

"I think you'll find others have a different view of the extent of your accountability," Griffiths said. "How much supervision did Hogg receive? From what we hear, he and his wife were let loose in Blodwel to do as they pleased. He built his own empire, and everyone deferred to his wishes. Even you, we hear, wouldn't gainsay the power he wielded. How did that come about? Did you never think to question the structure he built behind the walls of Blodwel?"

"I heard nothing to give me cause for concern," the director said. "And I still haven't."

"Darren Pritchard paid you a visit, did he not?" McKenna asked. "Will we find others tried to tell you they lived with terror? Some of these children have their own guilt, because they believe they colluded with Hogg. They had no choice. The abuse of others was the price of their own survival."

The deputy chief constable coughed. "Gary Hughes shared a bedroom with an eleven year old boy, who 'loved Sir like a father.' Hogg told this child that Gary was a 'bumboy.' The child said if Gary failed to do 'what Sir wanted,' he'd say Gary had raped him." He glanced at the statement. "Mr. McKenna noted here that Gary began to weep, because he fears he's become what Hogg said he was, and wonders when he'll begin to desire what so revolts him."

"You see our difficulty?" the director of social services asked. "Allegations of child abuse attach a terrible social stigma to accused and accuser alike."

"Is that an excuse for doing nothing?" Griffiths demanded.

"There's no need to be hostile, Superintendent. We're all on the same side in this battle. Unfortunately, you seem blinded by the dust of the conflict. I must keep sight of the problems and principles."

"Arwel and Gary and Tony embody a principle your professional jargon describes as the paramount interest of the child." Griffiths leaned forward, breathing heavily. "They embody a problem, too, so you jettisoned principles for the sake of convenience."

"Shall we discuss Arwel?" McKenna intervened. "Did you ever see him? We saw him only in his coffin, but he kept his rare beauty even after death. His sister's also very lovely, and despite seeming very ordinary and nondescript, his parents are forever distinguished by having had one of their children done to death. It's going against Nature to outlive your child, isn't it? Tony's mother said it's like breaking one of God's laws, and I imagine the Thomases are no less devastated, for all their bitterness and confusion."

"These boys've been too easily written off as bad kids from bad ignorant families, and a waste of space alive or dead," Griffiths added. "Beyond a passing usefulness, their living was as trivial as their dying. Gary's given us a lot of insight, you see. Arwel was Hogg's most profitable commodity because he looked so virginal. Tony was the 'bit of rough' for people who wanted that sort of thing, and Gary seems to have been all things to all men."

"Including friends of David Fellows," McKenna said. "He was known as Dai Skunk for years, because he smelt of dirty sex. When he developed AIDS, people called him Dai Death instead. He died last week. Hogg knew him, and knew he was selling these boys to Dai's sexual partners. He told Gary and Arwel they were trading poisoned love."

The councillor stared at McKenna, a frown creasing his forehead.

"Our investigation of Arwel's death was bedevilled from the outset by lies and evasions." McKenna stubbed out his cigarette, and lit another. "For instance, when we first interviewed Arwel's social worker, she neglected to tell us she'd found him hitching on the Bethel road the day after he ran away. She took him back to Blodwel."

"And she's facing criminal charges for not telling us," Griffiths added.

"Arwel absconded when Hogg arranged for him to spend a few days 'partying' with some well-paying customers," McKenna went on. "When his social worker returned him to Blodwel, Doris slung him in the showers, dressed him in his best clothes, and drove him to the rendezvous. She collected him on the Saturday afternoon and took him to her own house to report to her husband."

"This is becoming very tedious," the director said. "Is there a point? And how can you possibly know all this?"

"Gary was at the house," Griffiths said. "Waiting for Doris to drive him to another rendezvous. Arwel said where he'd been but he didn't bother saying what'd happened, because Gary knew for himself."

"Hogg was counting money in his sitting-room," McKenna said. "Pile upon pile of twenty- and fifty-pound notes. Arwel watched, commenting about 'blood money' and 'wages of sin,' with tears running down his face, but Hogg ignored him, fastened rubber bands round his bundles, and put them in a fancy biscuit tin. Doris was in the kitchen, 'clattering pots.' As he locked the tin in the sideboard, Hogg said to Arwel, as if discussing the weather: "You'd crawl over broken glass for your sister, wouldn't you? Did you know Dai Skunk's got AIDS? Men go with him, then they go with you, then they fuck your sister, 'cos she's a whore like you." He laughed, Gary reports, then said: 'And if you haven't given her AIDS yet, you will one day.' "

"Imagine, if you can, Arwel's rage and despair," Griffiths said. "Then try to understand his helplessness. He lunged at Hogg, Gary tried to pull him off, and Arwel went flying. His head hit the TV screen so hard the set crashed against the wall. Gary heard two crunching noises, then Arwel lay on the floor, quite still apart from his lower legs, which twitched and jerked forever."

"He knew Arwel was dead when urine stained his trousers and trickled on the floor. Doris apparently raged about the damage to her new carpet," McKenna added. "Hogg promised to hide the body where it would never be found if Gary agreed to keep his mouth shut 'tighter than he'd ever wanted to shut his arse.' "

Griffiths watched the councillor, who stared through the window at coming night. "But of course, he didn't keep his word. He dumped Arwel in the tunnel, and Gary ran away because he knew he'd be blamed. We all know how very convincing Hogg can be, don't we?"

"It's hearsay!" The director made a dismissive gesture. "You could ruin careers with this nonsense, and I doubt you'd say to Ronald Hogg's face what you're slandering him with behind his back." He rose angrily. The councillor rose too, lower legs twitching with tension. "And don't think you can heap all the blame on us. I've heard there's a police officer involved somewhere. Maybe more than one."

Griffiths raised his eyebrows. "But you just said you heard nothing to cause you concern. What else did you ignore, I wonder?" He began to make neat piles of the scattered documents. "Never mind, time will tell. Our investigations are under way, and of course, there's the evidence."

"What evidence?"

"What we've already found, what forensic science will unearth at Hogg's house and Blodwel, and the legacy of Arwel's imagination." Griffiths smiled bleakly. "You can never write off anybody, you know. Sometime during his miserable life, Arwel found his imagination captured by medieval Welsh poetry, so his sister bought him a book he desperately wanted. He used that book to make a coded record of the car registration numbers of the men who abused him and the other children." He picked up the list of names and addresses Dewi had extracted, on McKenna's instructions, from the DVLA computers. "God willing, we'll get lucky, and put some of them behind bars where they belong. Then we'll watch for the next lot to crawl out of the woodwork. And we *will* watch, because eternal vigilance is no price at all for a child's safety, is it?"

# •Chapter•
# 19

$O$n the day his wife made her escape from misery and winter, McKenna made his last visit to Bedd y Cor, but not to show the quality of his mercy as Rhiannon wished.

Driving down the lane, he pulled into the verge to let Mari pass with her pretty car. She nodded with steely control, more of Rhiannon's mantle filched each passing day. The boy beside her ignored him, but the woman in the rear seat waved, and McKenna wondered when Gary replaced Arwel in the schemes of Mari and her mistress.

He parked by the gate, and, as he pushed it open, saw a magpie lifting from the thorny hedgerow. He looked skywards for its mate, but saw only the faint silver shape of an aeroplane thousands of feet above, exhaust streaming behind in a clear golden line. He wondered if Denise were aboard, and if she would, as Dewi hoped, see Hogg and his ugly wife indolent and grease-rubbed on a foreign beach. McKenna hoped not, and hoped never again would they see the moon and the stars, feel the sun and the wind, or know anything beyond the horror of being alone in each other's company, putrid with sin and irredeemable. The silver shape vanished into the eye of the sun, and he thought again of the children who passed on knowledge they should never own, of those who had nothing to say, and of those who wept because the man they called "Sir," and whom they revered, abandoned them when he too flew away in the big silver aeroplane of which he so often boasted.

A crabbed old man in moleskin trousers dragged a rake back and forth over the manicured grass around the house, making neat piles of blackened leaves and crippled twigs to heft on a bonfire smouldering behind the wall and puffing dark acrid smoke skywards. A steely-plumed raven circled him, pecking for worms.

"It's a fine afternoon," the old man commented. "Nice bit of sunshine to warm your bones."

McKenna smiled. "Let's hope there's more to come." He watched the gardener's mate, teetering on a little wooden ladder propped against the trunk of the oak, trying to gouge out a huge lip of fungus that pouted from a wound in the tree.

The housekeeper answered the door, and took him to Elis's study. As he stood by the window, he thought the russet leaves outside might today frame a picture from the brush of Mr. Stubbs the Horse Painter. On the sweep of turf before the house, under a pale sky streaked with drifting smoke, Josh held the fretful chestnut mare, leaning against her shoulder. Nostrils flaring, she tossed her head and snapped her hooves restlessly, gouging little divots of mud from the grass and, but for the glass before him, McKenna knew the bitter smell of turned earth would again assail his senses. Elegant in dark garments of cloth and animal skin, Rhiannon stood nearby, gloved hands resting on the handles of the chair whose wheels had scarred the ground. She took one of the boy's palsied hands, and lifted it to the animal's shoulder. Instincts surging, the mare shied violently away, wrenching the groom from his feet.

Rhiannon pulled the chair and its cargo on to the drive, then stooped to retrieve the bright wool shawl which fell from her child's shoulders when he recoiled from the terrified mare. The housekeeper appeared in McKenna's view, spoke to her mistress, then took charge of the wheelchair and its passenger as Rhiannon walked away.

•　•　•

"Come to the drawing-room." She stood in the doorway, and as McKenna followed her down the hall, scents of smokiness and perfume drifted towards him from her clothes and hair. They passed the music-room, its door wide open, the ebony piano in gauzy shrouds.

"I wanted to see your husband," McKenna said. "Isn't he here?"

"No." Dropping her coat and gloves on the floor, she slumped in a chair, gesturing her visitor to another seat.

"I saw Mari with Mrs. Hughes and Gary."

"Did you? I've offered to cover the legal costs if Gary wants to sue the council for negligence and personal injury. He needs to act quickly, doesn't he? When people see what others made of him, they'll judge him worth nothing but contempt."

"And will you offer the same facility to others?" McKenna asked. "The Thomases, for instance?"

"Even my money doesn't flow endlessly," Rhiannon said sharply. "I think I've already underwritten any dues I might have to that family."

"Your husband might think differently. Where is he?"

"Away on business."

"What kind of business?"

"His kind of business, raiding someone's emotional assets. He's almost bankrupted mine, but I don't expect he'll have the slightest difficulty finding some other fool willing to pay any price for a glimpse of that wistful smile. He's always had an excellent nose for a deal to suit himself." She stared at McKenna. "I thought for a while you were one of his conquests, before I realized you don't belong to anyone."

"You've become very cruel."

"Perhaps I've absorbed some of your ruthlessness, Mr. McKenna. Perhaps my mercy drained away. Who knows?"

"Will he come back?"

"He usually does." She held out her hands to the fire. "But this time I might tell him to go away again. I might point out I could have mounted one of the horses if I really wanted to be taken for a ride."

"A shift of perspective might reveal just another deceiving façade," McKenna said. "Your husband isn't the fatally wounded soul you imagined for so long, or the monster you see before you now. And for all you know, he might have constructed the face he believed you wanted to see. Everyone dissembles, and even your son has his mystery."

"You know nothing!" Rhiannon snapped. "You haven't lived with this suffering of his, this inner estate he cultivates like this house and land. You haven't heard him deplore the way our son was kept alive, while he's done exactly the same with his misery, instead of letting nature take its course." She paused, eyes darkening. "And you haven't had to count the cost of his companionship, over and over again. Arwel's become the estate's most recent acquisition, my husband's latest excuse."

"For what?"

"More suffering. He killed Arwel by default, so he says, so he's appropriated the guilt and the drama and the self-pity." She rubbed her eyes, leaving a smudge of shadow on her face. "Carol asked for his help, because she thought power was as thick in his hands as money. She wanted him to vanquish Arwel's pain and terror, but he did nothing. He says he was terrified of the authority controlling Arwel, but I don't believe him. He likes pain. It makes him feel he's alive, so he never lets it go, even if it's not his to enjoy. Now, of course, he hopes Carol will never forgive him, even though he wants to be allowed to believe Arwel's better off dead, and out of the clutches of the incurable sickness they shared."

"Can't you spare your husband a little charity?" McKenna asked. "If nothing else, he was right in his assessment of the Hoggs. Their last act of malice was to tell the benefits agency Mandy's placement with her grandmother wasn't sanctioned by social services, so that poor woman's been refused any money to keep the child." Lighting a cigarette, he added, "You're not without fault yourself, and neither are your former colleagues on the council. You all happily conspired in your inactivity."

"Don't you think I'm aware of that?" She flushed. "What gives you the right to judge?"

"You feel you have the right to judge your husband, and find him wholly wanting. I'm simply apportioning some of the responsibility people are always so disinclined to accept."

"Is that your excuse for telling Mari she was keeping secrets? Was there any need to make her feel guilty too?"

"Unlike you, I think Arwel shared at least some things with her, so unlike your husband, she might learn something useful from this unhappiness."

"Another judgement?" Rhiannon's voice was bitter. "You told my husband suffering is one of life's great structural lines. Was he supposed to claw his way up and find enlightenment? Don't you know he's terrified of heights?"

Watching her through a haze of smoke, McKenna asked, "Have you come across the term *folie à deux* in your self-education, Mrs. Elis? When two people feed each other's outrageous behaviour?"

"Of course." She frowned. "Are you trying to excuse the Hoggs' behaviour?"

"As you understand the phenomenon, you should be able to see its relevance to yourself." Ignoring the outrage on her face, he added, "Isn't it quite likely you simply colluded with your husband in clothing the banal tedium of an unhappy marriage with a lot of nonsense?"

She leaned forward, eyes glittering. "So what do you suggest I do about it? Your responsibility doesn't cease when you make your judgement, Mr. McKenna, even though you might think it does!"

"You must make your own decision. Half your husband's trouble stems from decisions imposed on him when he was a child, does it not? His deviousness, his lack of resolve."

"And his failure to achieve anything beyond harming others? Have I colluded with him in that, too?"

"I don't know," McKenna said. "Only you can know that."

"You're a cruel man." Rhiannon sighed. "But you're a

man, and men are another country, aren't they? A primitive, dangerous land."

He sighed. "You're doing it again, Mrs. Elis. Please don't importune me to any folly because your husband's not here."

She rubbed her face viciously. "I should have you thrown out!"

"I'll happily leave whenever you wish. I only came to tell Mr. Elis he's no longer suspected of involvement in Arwel's death."

"Did you? How kind! I'll make sure he knows as soon as he comes back."

McKenna stood up. "I understand there's a letter on its way from the chief constable's office."

She followed him out of the room and into the hall, where damp parallel tracks on the floor betrayed the passage of her hapless child.

"Have you taken your son permanently out of residential care?" McKenna asked.

"Bringing him home is one of the good intentions my husband spawns in shoals." She smiled bitterly. "It's a pity they all end up beached. It's an even greater pity he doesn't understand they have consequences, and change other people's intentions and expectations." She paused. "Most of us see stranded hopes as lost opportunities, don't we? He sees them as stolen opportunites, the grounds for endless resentment, and their fate is always someone else's responsibility, someone else's fault."

Standing on the front doorstep, she in his shadow, McKenna watched the groom being dragged once more by the chestnut mare, as he put her out to graze. "And what hopes does he have for your thoroughbred foal?"

She shrugged. "I've no idea. I doubt if he's given a moment's thought to the reality at the end of the idea. It's the same with our son." She watched the groom tramping back towards the stables. "I might call the animal Devil's Highway. Or perhaps Harsh Reality. Which would you choose?"

"You're not obliged to net his aspirations at random,"

McKenna said. "Did you deliberately marry a weak man to have him under your control?"

"If so, I gravely overestimated my powers, didn't I?"

"Bitterness such as yours, Mrs. Elis, is very corrosive, and ultimately futile."

"But perfectly reasonable, don't you think?"

As he stepped on to the drive, and began to walk away, she said, "I don't expect we'll see you again, will we?"

McKenna turned. "No, I don't imagine you will."

"My husband's wanted to ask you to ride out with him, and now you know he didn't kill Arwel, there's no reason why you couldn't." She smiled brightly. "Shall I tell him you're looking forward to an invitation? You could dine with us afterwards."

"I'm not sure that would be a good idea," McKenna said.

"No?" She sighed. "Perhaps you're right. After all, even though you know he's not a killer, you'll never know if he abused the boy, will you?"

"And will you?" McKenna asked quietly.

She turned her back and disappeared into the shadowy hall, closing the door with a muffled thud.


The mare watched as he walked up the drive, and he lingered by the fence, calling softly to her until she pranced within reach, tossing her beautiful head. He stroked her neck and shoulder, thinking of other flesh under other hands, and violations other than those wrought by lust and corruption. He instigated more violation of Gary Hughes, by police surgeons in pursuit of knowledge, and violated Gary's loyalty to the dead boys, demanding to know the truth of Hogg's plausible allegations. Gary wept and raged, and brushed the coquette's hair from his eyes, making denial after denial in that lisping affected voice which spoke so surely of the way ahead for this boy, who would travel everywhere and nowhere in flight from himself.

Wrenching suddenly from his touch, the mare flung herself across the field, swollen belly taut and heavy, then came to a juddering stop, hind legs splayed. A torrent of yellowy liquid splashed from her body, and he thought of the dried urine staining Doris Hogg's new carpet, matched by science to the urine which flowed from Arwel's body; the other stains beneath the television set, matched to the fluids which seeped from his crushed brain and out through his ears. Other samples, other fluids, abstracted from the men betrayed by their cars, yielded other truths, but justice, McKenna feared, like honour, would fall prey to expediency and the self-interest of the powerful, as was the nature of such things. Brushing a coarse golden hair from the sleeve of his coat, he thought of the fine golden hair torn from Arwel's scalp and caught in the control panel of Hogg's television, and the savage depression in the wall behind, where the energy of Arwel's death wrenched the set from its mountings.

Sighing, he walked to his car, closing the gate to Bedd y Cor behind him. Alighting on the gate post with a flurry of plumage, a magpie watched, and he wondered if it might be the mate of the one he saw before, or simply the same bird, in pursuit of itself.

# Guide to Welsh pronunciation

Welsh is a phonetic language i.e. pronounced as written, following certain rules.

A, E, I, O, U, Y are vowels. W may be a vowel or consonant, depending on the word. There is no J, K or Z in Welsh, and no equivalent soft consonant such as C in "advice."

DD: as in breaTHe rather than breaTH.

F: as in oF (sounds like V in English).

FF: as in oFF.

LL: the nearest equivalent sound is an aspirated L.

Rh: an aspirated R not occurring in English. The distinction between Rh and R is similar to the distinction between WH and W in WHen and Went.

# Welsh patronymic

The term "ab" or "ap" means "son of": "ab" is used before a vowel, as in "ab Elis"; "ap" before a consonant, as in "ap Gwilym."

# About the Author

Born into an Anglo-Welsh family, and brought up in rural Cheshire and Derbyshire, Alison Taylor studied architecture before commencing a career in social work and probation. She has been instrumental in exposing the abuse of children in care, and has written a number of papers on childcare and ethics. She has a son and daughter, and has been resident in North Wales for many years. Her interests include classical and Baroque music, art and horse-riding. She is currently working on a third novel and researching a biographical study of Beethoven.

# BANTAM MYSTERY COLLECTION

____57204-0 **KILLER PANCAKE** Davidson • • • • • • • • • • • • • • **$6.50**

____56860-4 **THE GRASS WIDOW** Peitso • • • • • • • • • • • • • • **$5.50**

____57235-0 **MURDER AT MONTICELLO** Brown • • • • • • • • • • • **$6.50**

____57300-4 **STUD RITES** Conant • • • • • • • • • • • • • • • • • **$5.99**

____29684-1 **FEMMES FATAL** Cannell • • • • • • • • • • • • • • • **$5.50**

____56448-X **AND ONE TO DIE ON** Haddam • • • • • • • • • • • **$5.99**

____57192-3 **BREAKHEART HILL** Cook • • • • • • • • • • • • • • • **$5.99**

____56020-4 **THE LESSON OF HER DEATH** Deaver • • • • • • • • **$5.99**

____56239-8 **REST IN PIECES** Brown • • • • • • • • • • • • • • • • **$5.99**

____57456-6 **MONSTROUS REGIMENT OF WOMEN** King • • • • • **$5.99**

____57458-2 **WITH CHILD** King • • • • • • • • • • • • • • • • • • • **$5.99**

____57251-2 **PLAYING FOR THE ASHES** George • • • • • • • • • • **$6.99**

____57173-7 **UNDER THE BEETLE'S CELLAR** Walker • • • • • • • **$5.99**

____56793-4 **THE LAST HOUSEWIFE** Katz • • • • • • • • • • • • • **$5.99**

____57205-9 **THE MUSIC OF WHAT HAPPENS** Straley • • • • • • **$5.99**

____57477-9 **DEATH AT SANDRINGHAM HOUSE** Benison • • • • • **$5.50**

____56969-4 **THE KILLING OF MONDAY BROWN** Prowell • • • • • **$5.99**

____57191-5 **HANGING TIME** Glass • • • • • • • • • • • • • • • • • **$5.99**

___57579-1 **SIMEON'S BRIDE** Taylor • • • • • • • • • • • • • • • **$5.50**

---

Ask for these books at your local bookstore or use this page to order.

Please send me the books I have checked above. I am enclosing $____ (add $2.50 to cover postage and handling). Send check or money order, no cash or C.O.D.'s, please.

Name _____

Address _____

City/State/Zip _____

Send order to: Bantam Books, Dept. MC, 2451 S. Wolf Rd., Des Plaines, IL 60018
Allow four to six weeks for delivery.
Prices and availability subject to change without notice.                    MC 6/98